Benjamin Franklin

The Autobiography and Essays of Dr. Benjamin Franklin

Benjamin Franklin

The Autobiography and Essays of Dr. Benjamin Franklin

ISBN/EAN: 9783337030186

Printed in Europe, USA, Canada, Australia, Japan

Cover: Foto ©Raphael Reischuk / pixelio.de

More available books at **www.hansebooks.com**

THE

AUTOBIOGRAPHY AND ESSAYS

OF

DR. BENJAMIN FRANKLIN.

COMPLETE IN ONE VOLUME.

PHILADELPHIA:
J. B. LIPPINCOTT & CO.
1864.

PREFACE.

EVERY civilized nation on the globe, has, at one period or other, produced distinguished individuals, whose actions have excited the admiration of their contemporaries, and rendered them worthy of being handed down as examples to posterity. The Memoirs of Dr. Franklin are interesting in a high degree, and worthy the perusal of every friend to science or humanity.

Mr. Jefferson, the President of the United States of America, in his 'Notes on Virginia,' thus speaks in answer to the assertion of the Abbé Raynal, that 'America has not yet produced one good poet, one able mathematician, one man of genius, in a single art, or a single science.'—'When we shall have existed as a nation,' says Mr. J. 'as long as the Greeks did before they produced a Homer, the Romans a Virgil, the French a Racine and Voltaire, the English a Shakspeare and Milton, should this reproach be still true, we will inquire from what unfriendly causes it has proceeded, that the other countries of Europe and quarters of the earth shall not have inscribed any name in the roll of poets. In war we have produced a Washington, whose memory will be adored while liberty shall have votaries; whose name will triumph over time, and will in future ages assume its just station among the most celebrated worthies of the world, when that wretched philosophy shall be forgotten which would arrange him among the degeneracies of nature. In physics we have a FRANKLIN, than whom no one of the present age has made more important discoveries, nor has enriched philosophy with more, or more ingenious solutions of the phenomena of nature. We have supposed Mr. Rittenhouse second to no astronomer living; that in genius he must be the first, because he is self-taught,' &c.

In Philosophy England can boast of a Bacon, whose Essays is one of the best proofs we can adduce of his transcendant abilities; and America claims the enlightened FRANKLIN, whose Life and Writings are the subject of the following sheets.

It will only be necessary to add, that due attention has been paid in the selection of such of his productions as may be adapted to general perusal. The following letter from the celebrated Dr. Price to a gentleman in Philadelphia, respecting Dr. Franklin will not, it is presumed, be deemed inapplicable:

'DEAR SIR, *Hackney, June*, 19, 1790.

'I AM hardly able to tell you how kindly I take the letters with which you favor me. Your last, containing an account of the death of our excellent friend, Dr. Franklin, and the circumstances attending it, deserves my peculiar gratitude. The account which he has left of his life will show, in a striking example, how a man, by talents, industry, and integrity, may rise from obscurity to the first eminence and consequence in the world; but it brings his history no lower than the year 1757, and I understand that since he sent over the copy, which I have read, he has been able to make no additions to it. It is with a melancholy regret that I think of his death; but to death we are all bound by the irrevocable order of nature, and in looking forward to it, there is comfort in being able to reflect—that we have not lived in vain, and that all the useful and virtuous shall meet in a better country beyond the grave.

'Dr. Franklin, in the last letter I received from him, after mentioning his age and infirmities, observes, that it has been kindly ordered by the Author of Nature, that, as we draw nearer the conclusion of life we are furnished with more helps to wean us from it, amongst which one of the strongest is the loss of dear friends. I was delighted with the account you gave in your letter of the honor shown to his memory at Philadelphia, and by Congress: and yesterday I received a high additional pleasure by being informed that the National Assembly of France had determined to go into mourning for him.—What a glorious scene is opened there? The annals of the world furnish no parallel to it. One of the honors of our departed friend is, that he has contributed much to it.

'I am, with great respect,

'Your obliged and very humble servant,

'RICHARD PRICE.'

THE LIFE AND ESSAYS

OF

DR. BENJAMIN FRANKLIN

My Dear Son,

I have amused myself with collecting some little anecdotes of my family. You may remember the inquiries I made, when you were with me in England, among such of my relations as were then living; and the journey I undertook for that purpose. To be acquainted with the particulars of my parentage and life, many of which are unknown to you, I flatter myself will afford the same pleasure to you as to me. I shall relate them upon paper: it will be an agreeable employment of a week's uninterrupted leisure, which I promise myself during my present retirement in the country. There are also other motives which induce me to the undertaking. From the bosom of poverty and obscurity, in which I drew my first breath, and spent my earliest years, I have raised myself to a state of opulence and to some degree of celebrity in the world. A constant good fortune has attended me through every period of life to my present advanced age; and my descendants may be desirous of learning what were the means of which I made use, and which, thanks to the assisting hand of Providence, have proved so eminently successful. They may, also, should they ever be placed in a similar situation, derive some advantage from my narrative.

When I reflect, as I frequently do, upon the felicity I have enjoyed, I sometimes say to myself, that, were the offer made true, I would engage to run again, from beginning to end, the same career of life. All I would ask, should be the privilege of an author, to correct, in a second edition, certain errors of the first. I could wish, likewise, if it were in my power, to change some trivial incidents and events for others more favorable. Were this, however, denied me, still would I not decline the offer. But since a repetition of life cannot take place, there is nothing which, in my opinion, so nearly resembles it, as to call to mind all its circumstances, and, to render their remembrance more durable, commit them to writing. By thus employing myself, I shall yield to the inclination, so natural in old men, to talk of themselves and their exploits, and may freely follow my bent, without being tiresome to those who, from respect to my age, might think themselves obliged to listen to me; as they will be at liberty to read me or not as they please. In fine—and I may as well avow it, since nobody would believe me were I to deny it—I shall, perhaps, by this employment, gratify my vanity. Scarcely, indeed, have I ever heard or read the introductory phrase, '*I may say without vanity*,' but some striking and characteristic instance of vanity has immediately followed. The generality of men hate vanity in others, however strongly they may be tinctured with it themselves; for myself, I pay obeisance to it wherever I meet with it, persuaded that it is advantageous, as well to the individual whom it governs, as to those who are within the sphere of its influence. Of consequence, it would, in many cases, not be wholly absurd, that a man should count his vanity among the other sweets of life, and give thanks to Providence for the blessing.

And here let me with all humility acknowledge, that to Divine Providence I am indebted for the felicity I have hitherto enjoyed. It is that power alone which has furnished me with the means I have employed, and that has crowned them with success. My faith in this respect, leads me to hope, though I cannot count upon it, that the Divine goodness will still be exercised towards me, either by prolonging the duration of my happiness to the close of life, or by giving me fortitude to support any melancholy reverse, which may happen to me, as to so many others. My future fortune is unknown but to Him in whose hand is our destiny, and who can make our very afflictions subservient to our benefit.

One of my uncles, desirous, like myself, of collecting anecdotes of our family, gave me some notes, from which I have derived many particulars respecting our ancestors. From these I learn, that they had lived in the same village (Eaton in Northamptonshire), upon a freebold of about thirty acres, for the space at least of three hundred years. How long they had resided there, prior to that period, my uncle had been unable to discover; probably ever since the institution of surnames, when they took the appellation of Franklin, which had formerly been the name of a particular order of individuals.*

This petty estate would not have sufficed for their subsistence, had they not added the trade of blacksmith, which was perpetuated in the family down to my uncle's time, the eldest son having been uniformly brought up to this employment: a custom which both he and my father observed with respect to their eldest sons.

In the researches I made at Eaton, I found no account of their births, marriages, and deaths, earlier than the year 1555; the parish register not extending farther back than that period. This register informed me, that I was the youngest son of the youngest branch of the family, counting five generations. My grandfather, Thomas, was born in 1598, lived at Eaton till he was too old to continue his trade, when he retired to Banbury, in Oxfordshire, where his son John, who

---

* As a proof that Franklin was anciently the common name of an order or rank in England, see Judge Fortesque, *De laudibus legum Angliæ*, written about the year 1412, in which is the following passage, to show that good juries might easily be formed in any part of England.

'Regio etiam illa, ita respersa refertaque est *possessoribus terrarum* et agrorum, quod in ea, villula tam parva reperiri non poterit, in qua non est *miles*, *armiger*, vel pater-familias, qualis ibidem *franklin* vulgariter nuncupater, magnis ditatus possessionibus, nec non libere tenentes et alii *valecti* plurimi, suis patrimoniis sufficientes, ad faciendum juratam, in forma prænotata.'

'Moreover the same country is so filled and replenished with landed menne, that therein so small a thorpe cannot be found wherein dwelleth not a knight, an esquire, or such a householder as is there commonly called a *franklin*, enriched with great possessions; and also other freeholders and many yeomen, able for their livelihood to make a jury in form aforementioned.'

Old Translation.

Chaucer too, calls his country-gentleman a *franklin*; and after describing his good house-keeping, thus characterizes him

This worthy frankélin bore a purse of silk
Fix'd to his girdle, white as morning milk,
Knight of the shire, first justice at th' assize,
To help the poor, the doubtful to advise.
In all employments, generous, just he prov'd,
Renown'd for courtesy, by all belov'd.

was a dyer, resided, and with whom my father was apprenticed. He died, and was buried there: he saw his monument in 1758. His eldest son lived in the family house at Eaton, which he bequeathed, with the land belonging to it, to his only daughter; who, in concert with her husband, Mr. Fisher, of Wellingborough, afterward sold it to Mr. Estead, the present proprietor.

My grandfather had four surviving sons, Thomas, John, Benjamin, and Josias. I shall give you such particulars of them as my memory will furnish, not having my papers here, in which you will find a more minute account, if they are not lost during my absence.

Thomas had learned the trade of a blacksmith under his father; but, possessing a good natural understanding, he improved it by study, at the solicitation of a gentleman of the name of Palmer, who was at that time the principal inhabitant of the village, and who encouraged, in like manner, all my uncles to cultivate their minds. Thomas thus rendered himself competent to the functions of a country attorney; soon became an essential personage in the affairs of the village; and was one of the chief movers of every public enterprise, as well relative to the county as the town of Northampton. A variety of remarkable incidents were told us of him at Eaton. After enjoying the esteem and patronage of Lord Halifax, he died January 6, 1702, precisely four years before I was born. The recital that was made us of his life and character, by some aged persons of the village, struck you, I remember, as extraordinary, from its analogy to what you knew of myself. 'Had he died,' said you, 'just four years later, one might have supposed a transmigration of souls.'

John, to the best of my belief, was brought up to the trade of a wool-dyer.

Benjamin served his apprenticeship in London to a silk-dyer. He was an industrious man: I remember him well; for, while I was a child, he joined my father at Boston, and lived for some years in the house with us. A particular affection had always subsisted between my father and him; and I was his godson. He arrived to a great age. He left behind him two quarto volumes of poems in manuscript, consisting of little fugitive pieces addressed to his friends. He had invented a short-hand, which he taught me, but, having never made use of it, I have now forgotten it. He was a man of piety, and a constant attendant on the best preachers, whose sermons he took a pleasure in writing down according to the expeditory method he had devised. Many volumes were thus collected by him. He was also extremely fond of politics; too much so, perhaps, for his situation. I lately found in London a collection which he had made of all the principal pamphlets relative to public affairs, from the year 1641 to 1717. Many volumes are wanting, as appears by the series of numbers; but there still remain eight in folio, and twenty-four in quarto and octavo. The collection had fallen into the hands of a second-hand bookseller, who knowing me by having sold me some books, brought it to me. My uncle, it seems, had left it behind him on his departure for America, about fifty years ago. I found various notes of his writing in the margins. His grandson, Samuel, is now living at Boston.

Our humble family had early embraced the Reformation. They remained faithfully attached during the reign of Queen Mary, when they were in danger of being molested on account of their zeal against popery. They nad an English Bible, and, to conceal it the more securely, they conceived the project of fastening it, open, with pack-threads across the leaves, on the inside of the lid of the close-stool. When my great-grandfather wished to read to his family, he reversed the lid of the close-stool upon his knees, and passed the leaves from one side to the other, which were held down on each by the pack-thread. One of the children was stationed at the door, to give notice if he saw the proctor (an officer of the spiritual court) make his appearance: in that case, the lid was restored to its place, with the Bible concealed under it as before. I had this anecdote from my uncle Benjamin.

The whole family preserved its attachment to the Church of England till towards the close of the reign of Charles II. when certain ministers, who had been rejected as nonconformists, having held conventicles in Northamptonshire, they were joined by Benjamin and Josias, who adhered to them ever after. The rest of the family continued in the episcopal church.

My father, Josias, married early in life. He went, with his wife and three children, to New England, about the year 1682. Conventicles being at that time prohibited by law, and frequently disturbed, some considerable persons of his acquaintance determined to go to America, where they hoped to enjoy the free exercise of their religion, and my father was prevailed on to accompany them.

My father had also, by the same wife, four children born in America, and ten others by a second wife, making in all seventeen. I remember to have seen thirteen seated together at his table, who all arrived at years of maturity, and were married. I was the last of the sons, and the youngest child, excepting two daughters. I was born at Boston, in New England. My mother, the second wife, was Abiah Folger, daughter of Peter Folger, one of the first colonists of New England, of whom Cotton Mather makes honorable mention, in his Ecclesiastical History of that province, as '*a pious and learned Englishman*,' if I rightly recollect his expressions. I have been told of his having written a variety of little pieces; but there appears to be only one in print, which I met with many years ago. It was published in the year 1675, and is in familiar verse, agreeably to the taste of the times and the country. The author addresses himself to the governors for the time being, speaks for liberty of conscience, and in favor of the anabaptists, quakers, and other sectaries, who had suffered persecution. To this persecution he attributes the wars with the natives, and other calamities which afflicted the country, regarding them as the judgments of God in punishment of so odious an offence, and he exhorts the government to the repeal of laws so contrary to charity. The poem appeared to be written with a manly freedom and a pleasing simplicity. I recollect the six concluding lines, though I have forgotten the order of words of the two first; the sense of which was, that his censures were dictated by benevolence, and that, of consequence, he wished to be known as the author; because, said he, I hate from my very soul dissimulation.

From Sherburn,* where I dwell,
I therefore put my name,
Your friend, who means you well,
Peter Folger.

My brothers were all put apprentices to different trades. With respect to myself, I was sent, at the age of eight years, to a grammar-school. My father destined me for the church, and already regarded me as the chaplain of my family. The promptitude with which from my infancy I had learned to read, for I do not remember to have been ever without this acquirement, and the encouragement of his friends, who assured him that I should one day certainly become a man of

* Town in the Island of Nantucket.

letters, confirmed him in this design. My uncle Benjamin approved also of the scheme, and promised to give me all his volumes of sermons, written, as I have said, in the short-hand of his invention, if I would take the pains to learn it.

I remained, however, scarcely a year at the grammar-school, although, in this short interval, I had risen from the middle to the head of my class, from thence to the class immediately above, and was to pass, at the end of the year, to the one next in order. But my father, burdened with a numerous family, found that he was incapable, without subjecting himself to difficulties, of providing for the expenses of a collegiate education; and considering, besides, as I heard him say to his friends, that persons so educated were often poorly provided for, he renounced his first intentions, took me from the grammar-school, and sent me to a school for writing and arithmetic, kept by a Mr. George Brownwell, who was a skilful master, and succeeded very well in his profession by employing gentle means only, and such as were calculated to encourage his scholars. Under him I soon acquired an excellent hand; but I failed in arithmetic, and made therein no sort of progress.

At the age of ten years, I was called home to assist my father in his occupation, which was that of a soap-boiler and tallow-chandler; a business to which he had served no apprenticeship, but which he embraced on his arrival in New England, because he found his own, that of dyer, in too little request to enable him to maintain his family. I was accordingly employed in cutting the wicks, filling the moulds, taking care of the shop, carrying messages, &c.

This business displeased me, and I felt a strong inclination for a sea life; but my father set his face against it. The vicinity of the water, however, gave me frequent opportunities of venturing myself both upon and within it, and I soon acquired the art of swimming, and of managing a boat. When embarked with other children, the helm was commonly deputed to me, particularly on difficult occasions; and, in every other project, I was almost always the leader of the troop, whom I sometimes involved in embarrassments. I shall give an instance of this, which demonstrates an early disposition of mind for public enterprises, though the one in question was not conducted by justice.

The mill-pond was terminated on one side by a marsh, upon the borders of which we were accustomed to take our stand, at high water, to angle for small fish. By dint of walking, we had converted the place into a perfect quagmire.

My proposal was to erect a wharf that should afford us firm footing, and I pointed out to my companions a large heap of stones, intended for the building a new house near the marsh, and which were well adapted for our purpose. Accordingly, when the workmen retired in the evening, I assembled a number of my play-fellows, and by laboring diligently, like ants, sometimes four of us uniting our strength to carry a single stone, we removed them all, and constructed our little quay. The workmen were surprised the next morning at not finding their stones; which had been conveyed to our wharf. Inquiries were made respecting the authors of this conveyance; we were discovered: complaints were exhibited against us; and many of us underwent correction on the part of our parents; and though I strenuously defended the utility of the work, my father at length convinced me, that nothing which was not strictly honest could be useful.

It will not, perhaps, be uninteresting to you to know what sort of a man my father was. He had an excellent constitution, was of a middle size, but well made and strong, and extremely active in whatever he undertook. He designed with a degree of neatness, and knew a little of music. His voice was sonorous and agreeable, so that when he sung a psalm or hymn, with the accompaniment of his violin, as was his frequent practice in an evening, when the labors of the day were finished, it was truly delightful to hear him. He was versed also in mechanics, and could, upon occasion, use the tools of a variety of trades. But his greatest excellence was a sound understanding and solid judgment in matters of prudence, both in public and private life. In the former indeed he never engaged, because his numerous family, and the mediocrity of his fortune, kept him unremittingly employed in the duties of his profession. But I well remember that the leading men of the place used frequently to come and ask his advice respecting the affairs of the town, or of the church to which he belonged, and that they paid much deference to his opinion. Individuals were also in the habit of consulting him in their private affairs, and he was often chosen arbiter between contending parties.

He was fond of having at his table, as often as possible, some friends or well-informed neighbors, capable of rational conversation, and he was always careful to introduce useful or ingenious topics of discourse, which might tend to form the minds of his children. By this means he early attracted our attention to what was just, prudent, and beneficial in the conduct of life. He never talked of the meats which appeared upon the table, never discussed whether they were well or ill-dressed, of a good or bad flavor, high-seasoned, or otherwise, preferable or inferior to this or that dish of a similar kind. Thus accustomed, from my infancy, to the utmost inattention as to these objects, I have been perfectly regardless of what kind of food was before me; and I pay so little attention to it even now, that it would be a hard matter for me to recollect, a few hours after I had dined, of what my dinner had consisted. When travelling, I have particularly experienced the advantage of this habit; for it has often happened to me to be in company with persons, who, having a more delicate, because a more exercised taste, have suffered in many cases considerable inconvenience; while, as to myself, I have had nothing to desire.

My mother was likewise possessed of an excellent constitution. She suckled all her ten children, and I never heard either her or my father complain of any other disorder than that of which they died: my father at the age of eighty-seven, and my mother at eighty-five. They are buried together at Boston, where, a few years ago, I placed a marble stone over their grave, with this inscription:

"Here lie

"JOSIAS FRANKLIN and ABIAH his wife: They lived together with reciprocal affection for fifty-nine years; and without private fortune, without lucrative employment, by assiduous labor and honest industry, decently supported a numerous family, and educated with success, thirteen children, and seven grandchildren. Let this example, reader, encourage thee diligently to discharge the duties of thy calling, and to rely on the support of Divine Providence.

"He was pious and prudent,
"She discreet and virtuous.
"Their youngest son, from a sentiment of filial
"duty, consecrates this stone
"to their memory."

I perceive, by my rambling digressions, that I am growing old. But we do not dress for a private company as for a formal ball. This deserves, perhaps, the name of negligence.

To return. I thus continued employed in my father's trade for the space of two years; that is to say, till I arrived at twelve years of age. About this time my brother John, who had served his apprenticeship in London, having quitted my father, and being married and settled in business on his own account at Rhode Island, I was destined, to all appearance, to supply his place, and be a candle-maker all my life: but my dislike of this occupation continuing, my father was apprehensive, that, if a more agreeable one were not offered me, I might play the truant and escape to sea; as, to his extreme mortification, my brother Josias had done. He therefore took me sometimes to see masons, coopers, braziers, joiners, and other mechanics, employed at their work; in order to discover the bent of my inclination, and to fix it if he could upon some occupation that might retain me on shore. I have since, in consequence of these visits, derived no small pleasure from seeing skilful workmen handle their tools; and it has proved of considerable benefit, to have acquired thereby sufficient knowledge to be able to make little things for myself, when I have had no mechanic at hand, and to construct small machines for my experiments, while the idea I have conceived has been fresh and strongly impressed on my imagination.

My father at length decided that I should be a cutler, and I was placed for some days upon trial with my cousin Samuel, son of my uncle Benjamin, who had learned this trade in London, and had established himself at Boston. But the premium he required for my apprenticeship displeasing my father, I was recalled home.

From my earliest years I had been passionately fond of reading, and I had laid out in books all the money I could procure. I was particularly pleased with accounts of voyages. My first acquisition was Bunyan's collection in small separate volumes. These I afterward sold, in order to buy an historical collection by R. Burton, which consisted of small cheap volumes, amounting in all to about forty or fifty. My father's little library was principally made up of books of practical and polemical theology. I read the greatest part of them. I have since often regretted that at a time when I had so great a thirst for knowledge, more eligible books had not fallen into my hands, as it was then a point decided that I should not be educated for the church. There was also among my father's books Plutarch's Lives, in which I read continually, and I still regard as advantageously employed the time I devoted to them. I found besides a work of De Foe's, entitled an Essay on Projects, from which, perhaps, I derived impressions that have since influenced some of the principal events of my life.

FRANKLIN READING BY HIS BEDSIDE

My inclination for books at last determined my father to make me a printer, though he had already a son in that profession. My brother had returned from England in 1717, with a press and types, in order to establish a printing-house at Boston. This business pleased me much better than that of my father, though I had still a predilection for the sea. To prevent the effects which might result from this inclination, my father was impatient to see me engaged with my brother. I held back for some time; at length, however, I suffered myself to be persuaded, and signed my indentures, being then only twelve years of age. It was agreed that I should serve as apprentice to the age of twenty-one, and should receive journeyman's wages only during the last year.

In a very short time I made great proficiency in this business, and became very serviceable to my brother. I had now an opportunity of procuring better books. The acquaintance I necessarily formed with booksellers' apprentices, enabled me to borrow a volume now and then, which I never failed to return punctually and without injury. How often has it happened to me to pass the greater part of the night in reading by my bed-side, when the book had been lent me in the evening, and was to be returned the next morning, lest it might be missed or wanted.

At length Mr. Matthew Adams, an ingenious tradesman, who had a handsome collection of books, and who frequented our printing-house, took notice of me. He invited me to see his library, and had the goodness to lend me any books I was desirous of reading. I then took a strange fancy for poetry, and composed several little pieces. My brother, thinking he might find his account in it, encouraged me, and engaged me to write two ballads. One, called the Lighthouse Tragedy, contained an account of the shipwreck of Captain Worthilake and his two daughters; the other was a sailor's song on the capture of the noted pirate called *Teach*, or *Black-beard*. They were wretched verses in point of style, mere blindmen's ditties. When printed, he dispatched me about the town to sell them. The first had a prodigious run, because the event was recent, and had made a great noise.

My vanity was flattered by this success; but my father checked my exultation, by ridiculing my productions, and telling me that versifiers were always poor. I thus escaped the misfortune of being a very wretched poet. But as the faculty of writing prose has been of great service to me in the course of my life, and principally contributed to my advancement, I shall relate by what means, situated as I was, I acquired the small skill I may possess in that way.

There was in the town another young man, a great lover of books, of the name of John Collins, with whom I was intimately connected. We frequently engaged in dispute, and were indeed so fond of argumentation, that nothing was so agreeable to us as a war of words. This contentious temper, I would observe by-the-bye, is in danger of becoming a very bad habit, and frequently renders a man's company insupportable, as being no otherwise capable of indulgence than by an indiscriminate contradiction. Independently of the acrimony and discord it introduces into conversation, it is often productive of dislike, and even hatred, between persons to whom friendship is indispensably necessary. I acquired it by reading, while I lived with my father, books of religious controversy. I have since remarked, that men of sense seldom fall into this error; lawyers, fellows of universities, and persons of every profession educated at Edinburgh, excepted.

Collins and I fell one day into an argument, relative to the education of women; namely, whether it was proper to instruct them in the sciences, and whether they were competent to the study. Collins supported the negative, and affirmed that the task was beyond their capacity. I maintained the opposite opinion, a little perhaps for the pleasure of disputing. He was naturally more eloquent than I; words flowed copiously from his lips; and frequently I thought myself vanquished, more by his volubility than by the force of his argument. We separated without coming to an agreement upon this point, and as we were not to see each other again for some time, I committed my thoughts to paper, made a fair copy, and sent it to him. He answered, and I replied. Three or four letters had been written by each, when my father chanced to light upon my papers and read them. Without entering into the merits of the cause, he embraced the opportunity of speaking to me upon my manner of writing. He observed, that though I had the advantage of my adversary in correct spelling and pointing, which I owed to my occupation, I was greatly his inferior in elegance of expression, in arrangement, and perspicuity. Of this he convinced me by several examples. I felt the justice of his remarks, became more attentive to language, and resolved to make every effort to improve my style.

Amidst these resolves an odd volume of the spectator fell into my hands. This was a publication I had never seen. I bought the volume, and read it again and again. I was enchanted with it, thought the style excellent, and wished it were in my power to imitate it. With this view I selected some of the papers, made short summaries of the sense of each period, and put them for a few days aside. I then, without looking at the book, endeavored to restore the essays to their due form, and to express each thought at length, as it was in the original, employing the most appropriate words that occurred to my mind. I afterward compared my Spectator with the original; I perceived some faults, which I corrected: but I found that I wanted a fund of words, if I may so express myself, and a facility of recollecting and employing them, which I thought I should by that time have acquired, had I continued to make verses. The continual need of words of the same meaning, but of different lengths for the measure, or of different sounds for the rhyme, would have obliged me to seek for a variety of synonymes, and have rendered me master of them. From this belief, I took some of the tales of the Spectator and turned them into verse; and, after a time, when I had sufficiently forgotten them, I again converted them into prose.

Sometimes, also, I mingled all my summaries together; and, a few weeks after endeavored to arrange them in the best order, before I attempted to form the periods and complete the essays. This I did with the view of acquiring method in the arrangement of my thoughts. On comparing afterward my performance with the original, many faults were apparent, which I corrected; but I had sometimes the satisfaction to think, that, in certain particulars of little importance, I had been fortunate enough to improve the order of thought or the style; and this encouraged me to hope that I should succeed, in time, in writing decently in the English language, which was one of the great objects of my ambition.

The time which I devoted to these exercises, and to reading, was the evening after my day's labor was finished, the morning before it began, and Sundays when I could escape attending Divine service. While I lived with my father, he had insisted on my punctual attendance on public worship, and I still indeed considered it as a duty, but a duty which I thought I had no time to practise.

When about sixteen years of age, a work of Tyron fell into my hands, in which he recommends vegetable diet. I determined to observe it. My brother being a bachelor, did not keep house, but boarded with his apprentices in a neighboring family. My refusing to eat animal food was found inconvenient, and I was often scolded for my singularity. I attended to the mode in which Tyron prepared some of his dishes, particularly how to boil potatoes and rice, and make hasty puddings. I then said to my brother, that if he would allow me per week half what he paid for my board, I would undertake to maintain myself. The offer was instantly embraced, and I soon found that of what he gave me I was able to save half. This was a new fund for the purchase of books and other advantages resulted to me from the plan. When my brother and his workmen left the printing-house to go to dinner, I remained behind; and dispatching my frugal meal, which frequently consisted of a biscuit only, or a slice of bread and a bunch of raisins, or a bun from the pastry-cook's, with a glass of water, I had the rest of the time, till their return, for study; and my progress therein was proportioned to that clearness of ideas, and quickness of conception, which are the fruit of temperance in eating and drinking.

It was about this period that, having one day been put to the blush for my ignorance in the art of calculation, which I had twice failed to learn while at school, I took Cocker's Treatise of Arithmetic, and went through it myself with the utmost ease. I also read a book of Navigation by Seller and Sturmy, and made myself master of the little geometry it contains, but I never proceeded far in this science. Nearly at the same time I read Locke on the Human Understanding, and the Art of Thinking, by Messrs. du Port Royal.

While laboring to form and improve my style, I met with an English Grammar, which I believe was Greenwood's, having at the end of it two little essays on rhetoric and logic. In the latter I found a model of disputation after the manner of Socrates. Shortly after I procured Xenophon's work, entitled, Memorable Things of Socrates, in which are various examples of the same method. Charmed to a degree of enthusiasm with this mode of disputing, I adopted it, and renouncing blunt contradiction, and direct and positive argument, I assumed the character of an humble questioner. The perusal of Shaftsbury and Collins had made me a sceptic; and being previously so as to many doctrines of Christianity, I found Socrates' method to be both the safest for myself, as well as the most embarrassing to those against whom I employed it. It soon afforded me singular pleasure; I incessantly practised it; and became very adroit in obtaining, even from persons of superior understanding, concessions of which they did not foresee the consequence. Thus I involved them in difficulties from which they were unable to extricate themselves, and sometimes obtained victories, which neither my cause nor my arguments merited.

This method I continued to employ for some years; but I afterwards abandoned it by degrees, retaining only the habit of expressing myself with modest diffidence, and never making use, when I advanced any proposition which might be controverted, of the words *certainly*, *undoubtedly*, or any others that might give the appearance of being obstinately attached to my opinion. I rather said, I imagine, I suppose, or it appears to me, that such a thing is so or so, for such and such reasons; or it is so, if I am not mistaken This habit has, I think, been of considerable advantage t i. e, when I have had occasion to impress my opinion on the minds of others, and persuade them to the adoption of the measures I have suggested. And since the chief ends of conversation are, to inform or to be informed, to please or to persuade, I could wish that intelligent and well meaning men would not themselves diminish the power they possess of being useful, by a positive and presumptuous manner of expressing themselves, which scarcely ever fails to disgust the hearer, and is only calculated to excite opposition, and defeat every purpose for which the faculty of speech has been bestowed on man. In short, if you wish to inform, a positive and dogmatical manner of advancing your opinion may provoke contradiction, and prevent your being heard with attention. On the other hand, if, with a desire of being informed, and of benefitting by the knowledge of others, you express yourself as being strongly attached to your own opinions, modest and sensible men, who do not love disputation, will leave you in tranquil possession of your errors. By following such a method, you can rarely hope to please your auditors, conciliate their good-will, or work conviction on those whom you may be desirous of gaining over to your views. Pope judiciously observes,

> Men must be taught as if you taught them not,
> And things unknown propos'd as things forgot.

And in the same poem he afterward advises us,

> To speak, though sure, with seeming diffidence.

He might have added to these lines, one that he has coupled elsewhere, in my opinion, with less propriety. It is this:

> For want of modesty is want of sense.

If you ask why I say with *less propriety*, I must give you the two lines together:

> Immodest words admit of *no defence*,
> For want of decency is want of sense.

Now want of sense, when a man has the misfortune to be so circumstanced, is it not an excuse for want of modesty? And would not the verses have been more accurate, if they had been constructed thus:

> Immodest words admit *but this defence*,
> The want of decency is want of sense.

But I leave the decision of this to better judges than myself.

In 1720, or 1721, my brother began to print a new public paper. It was the second that made its appearance in America, and was entitled the 'New England Courant.' The only one that existed before was the 'Boston News Letter.' Some of his friends, I remember, would have dissuaded him from his undertaking, as a thing that was not likely to succeed; a single newspaper being, in their opinion, sufficient for all America. At present, however, in 1771, there are no less than twenty-five. But he carried his project into execution, and I was employed in distributing the copies to his customers, after having assisted in composing and working them off.

Among his friends he had a number of literary characters, who, as an amusement, wrote short essays for the paper, which gave it reputation and increased the sale. These gentlemen frequently came to our house. I heard the conversation that passed, and the accounts they gave of the favorable reception of their writings with the public. I was tempted to try my hand among them; but being still a child as it were, I was fearful that my brother might be unwilling to print in his paper any performance of which he should know me to be the author. I therefore contrived to disguise my hand, and having written an anonymous piece, I placed it at night under the door of the printing-house, where it was found the next morning. My brother communicated it to his friends when they came as usual to see him, who read it, commented upon it within my hearing, and I had the exquisite pleasure to find that it met with their approbation, and that in their various conjectures they made respecting the author, no one was mentioned who did not enjoy a high reputation in the country for talents and genius. I now supposed myself fortunate in my judges, and began to suspect that they were not such excellent writers as I had hitherto supposed them. Be this as it may, encouraged by this little adventure, I wrote and sent to press, in the same way, many other pieces, which were equally approved: keeping the secret till my slender stock of information and knowledge for such performances was pretty completely exhausted, when I made myself known.

My brother, upon this discovery. began to entertain a little more respect for me; but he still regarded himself as my master, and treated me as an apprentice. He thought himself entitled to the same services from me as from any other person. On the contrary, I conceived that, in many instances, he was too rigorous, and that on the part of a brother, I had a right to expect greater indulgence. Our disputes were frequently brought before my father; and either my brother was generally in the wrong, or I was the better pleader of the two, for judgment was commonly given in my favor. But my brother was passionate, and often had recourse to blows; a circumstance which I took in very ill part. This severe and tyrannical treatment contributed, I believe, to imprint on my mind that aversion to arbitrary power, which, during my whole life, I have ever preserved. My apprenticeship became insupportable to me, and I continually sighed for an opportunity of shortening it, which at length unexpectedly offered.

An article inserted in our paper, upon some political subject which I have now forgotten, gave offence to the Assembly. My brother was taken into custody, censured, and ordered into confinement for a month, because as I presume, he would not discover the author. I was also taken up, and examined before the council; but, though I gave them no satisfaction, they contented themselves with reprimanding, and then dismissed me; considering me probably as bound, in quality of an apprentice, to keep my master's secrets.

The imprisonment of my brother kindled my resentment, notwithstanding our private quarrels. During its continuance the management of the paper was intrusted to me, and I was bold enough to insert some pasquinades against the governors which highly pleased my brother, while others began to look upon me in an unfavorable point of view, considering me as a young wit inclined to satire and lampoon.

My brother's enlargement was accompanied with an arbitrary order from the House of the Assembly, 'That James Franklin should no longer print the newspaper entitled the "New England Courant."' In this conjuncture, we held a consultation of our friends at the printing-house, in order to determine what was to be done. Some proposed to evade the order by changing the title of the paper: but my brother foreseeing inconveniences that would result from this step, thought it better that it should in future be printed in the name of Benjamin Franklin; and, to avoid the censure of the Assembly, who might charge him with still printing the paper himself, under the name of his apprentice, it was resolved that my old indentures should be given up to me with a full and entire discharge written on the back, in order to be produced upon an emergency: but that, to secure to my brother the benefit of my service, I should sign a new contract, which should be kept secret during the remainder of the term. This was a very shallow arrangement. It was, however, carried into immediate execution, and the paper continued, in consequence, to make its appearance for some months in my name. At length a new difference arising between my brother and me, I ventured to take advantage of my liberty, presuming that he would not dare to produce the new contract. It was undoubtedly dishonorable to avail myself of this circumstance, and I reckon this action as one of the first errors of my life; but I was little capable of estimating it at its true value, imbittered as my mind had been by the recollection of the blows I had received. Exclusively of his passionate treatment of me, my brother was by no means a man of an ill temper, and perhaps my manners had too much impertinence not to afford it a very natural pretext.

When he knew that it was my determination to quit him, he wished to prevent my finding employment elsewhere. He went to all the printing-houses in the town, and prejudiced the masters against me; who accordingly refused to employ me. The idea then suggested itself to me of going to New-York, the nearest town in which there was a printing-office. Farther reflection confirmed me in the design of leaving Boston, where I had already rendered myself an object of suspicion to the governing party. It was probable from the arbitrary proceedings of the Assembly in the affair of my brother, that, by remaining, I should soon have been exposed to difficulties, which I had the greatest reason to apprehend, as, from my indiscreet disputes upon the subject of religion, I began to be regarded by pious souls with horror, either as an apostate or an atheist. I came therefore to a resolution: but my father, siding with my brother, I presumed that if I attempted to depart openly, measures would be taken to prevent me. My friend Collins undertook to favor my flight. He agreed for my passage with the captain of a New-York sloop, to whom he represented me as a young man of his acquaintance, who had an affair with a girl of bad character, whose parents wished to compel me to marry her, and of consequence I could neither make my appearance, nor go off publicly. I sold part of my books to procure a small sum of money, and went privately on board the sloop. By favor of a good wind, I found myself in three days at New-York nearly three hundred miles from my home, at the age only of seventeen years, without knowing an individual in the place and with very little money in my pocket.

The inclination I had felt for a sea-faring life was entirely subsided, or I should now have been able to gratify it; but having another trade, and believing myself to be a tolerable workman, I hesitated not to offer my services to the old Mr. William Bradford, who had been the first printer in Pennsylvania, but had quitted the province on account of a quarrel with George Keith, the governor. He could not give me employment himself, having little to do, and already as many persons as he wanted; but he told me that his son, printer at Philadelphia, had lately lost his principal workman, Aquila Rose, who was dead, and that if I would go thither, he believed that he would engage me. Philadelphia was a hundred miles farther. I hesitated not to embark in a boat in order to repair, by the shortest cut of the sea, to Amboy, leaving my trunk and effects to come after me by the usual and more tedious conveyance. In crossing the bay we met with a squall, which shattered to pieces our rotten sails, prevented us from entering the Kill, and threw us upon Long Island.

During the squall, a drunken Dutchman, who, like myself, was a passenger in the boat, fell into the sea. At the moment that he was sinking, I seized him by the fore-top, saved him, and drew him on board. This immersion sobered him a little, so that he fell asleep, after having taken from his pocket a volume which he requested me to dry. This volume I found to be my old favorite work, Bunyan's Pilgrim, in Dutch, a beautiful impression on fine paper, with copper-plate engravings; a dress in which I had never seen it in its original language. I have since learned that it has been translated into almost all the languages of Europe, and next to the Bible, I am persuaded it is one of the books that has had the greatest spread. Honest John is the first, that I know of, who has mixed narrative and dialogue together; a mode of writing very engaging to the reader, who in the most interesting passages, finds himself admitted as it were into the company, and present at the conversation. Defoe has imitated it with success in his Robinson Crusoe, his Moll Flanders, and other works; as also Richardson in his Pamela, &c.

In approaching the island, we found that we had made a part of the coast where it was not possible to land, on account of the strong breakers produced by the rocky shore. We cast anchor and veered the cable towards the shore. Some men, who stood upon the brink, hallooed to us, while we did the same on our part; but the wind was so high, and the waves so noisy, that we could neither of us hear each other. There were some canoes upon the bank, and we called out to them, and made signs to prevail on them to come and take us up; but either they did not understand us, or they deemed our request impracticable, and withdrew. Night came on, and nothing remained for us but to wait quietly the subsiding of the wind: till then, we determined, that is, the pilot and I, to sleep if possible. For that purpose we went below the hatches along with the Dutchman, who was drenched with water. The sea broke over the boat, and reached us in our retreat, so that we were presently as completely drenched as he.

We had very little repose during the whole night; but the wind abating the next day, we succeeded in reaching Amboy before it was dark, after having passed thirty hours without provision, and with no other drink than a bottle of bad rum, the water upon which we rowed being salt. In the evening I went to bed with a very violent fever. I had somewhere read that cold water, drank plentifully, was a remedy in such cases. I followed the prescription, was in a profuse sweat for the greater part of the night, and the fever left me. The next day I crossed the river in a ferry-boat, and continued my journey on foot. I had fifty miles to walk, in order to reach Burlington, where I was told I should find passage-boats that would convey me to Philadelphia. It rained hard the whole day, so that I was wet to the skin. Finding myself fatigued about noon, I stopped at a paltry inn, where I passed the rest of the day and the whole night, beginning to regret that I had quitted my home. I made besides so wretched a figure, that I was suspected to be some runaway servant. This I discovered by the questions that were asked me; and I felt that I was every moment in danger of being taken up as such. The next day, however, I continued my journey, and arrived in the evening at an inn, eight or ten miles from Burlington, that was kept by one Dr. Brown.

This man entered into conversation with me while I took some refreshment, and perceiving that I had read a little, he expressed towards me considerable interest and friendship. Our acquaintance continued during the remainder of his life

I believe him to have been what is called an itinerant doctor; for there was no town in England, or indeed in Europe, of which he could not give a particular account. He was neither deficient in understanding or literature, but he was a sad infidel: and, some years after, wickedly undertook to travesty the Bible, in burlesque verse, as Cotton had travestied Virgil. He exhibited, by this means, many facts in a very ludicrous point of view, which would have given umbrage to weak minds, had his work been published, which it never was.

I spent the night at his house, and reached Burlington the next morning. On my arrival, I had the mortification to learn that the ordinary passage-boats had sailed a little before. This was on a Saturday, and there would be no other boat till the Tuesday following. I returned to the house of an old woman in the town who had sold me some ginger bread to eat on my passage, and I asked her advice. She invited me to take up my abode with her till an opportunity offered for me to embark. Fatigued with having travelled so far on foot, I accepted her invitation. When she understood that I was a printer, she would have persuaded me to stay at Burlington, and set up my trade: but she was little aware of the capital that would be necessary for such a purpose! I was treated while at her house with true hospitality. She gave me, with the utmost good-will, a dinner of beef-steaks, and would accept of nothing in return but a pint of ale.

Here I imagined myself to be fixed till the Tuesday in the ensuing week; but, walking out in the evening by the river side, I saw a boat with a number of persons in it approach. It was going to Philadelphia, and the company took me in. As there was no wind, we could only make way with our oars. About midnight, not perceiving the town, some of the company were of opinion that we must have passed it, and were unwilling to row any farther; the rest not knowing where we were, it was resolved that we should stop. We drew towards the shore, entered a creek, and landed near some old palisades, which served us for fire-wood, it being a cold night in October. Here we stayed till day, when one of the company found the place in which we were to be Cooper's Creek, a little above Philadelphia; which, in reality, we perceived the moment we were out of the creek. We arrived on Sunday about eight or nine o'clock in the morning, and landed on Market-street wharf.

I have entered into the particulars of my voyage, and shall, in like manner, describe my first entrance into this city, that you may be able to compare beginnings so little auspicious, with the figure I have since made.

On my arrival at Philadelphia I was in my working dress, my best clothes being to come by sea. I was covered with dirt; my pockets were filled with shirts and stockings; I was unacquainted with a single soul in the place, and knew not where to seek for a lodging. Fatigued with walking, rowing, and having passed the night without sleep, I was extremely hungry, and all my money consisted of a Dutch dollar, and about a shilling's-worth of coppers, which I gave to the boatmen for my passage. As I had assisted them in rowing, they refused it at first; but I insisted on their taking it. A man is sometimes more generous when he has little, than when he has much money; probably because, in the first case, he is desirous of concealing his poverty.

I walked towards the top of the street, looking eagerly on both sides, till I came to Market-street, where I met with a child with a loaf of bread. Often had I made my dinner on dry bread. I inquired where he had bought it, and went straight to the baker's shop which he pointed out to me. I asked for some biscuits, expecting to find such as we had at Boston; but they made, it seems, none of that sort at Philadelphia. I then asked for a three-penny loaf. They made no loaves of that price. Finding myself ignorant of the prices, as well as of the different kinds of bread, I desired him to let me have three-pennyworth of bread of some kind or other. He gave me three large rolls. I was surprised at receiving so much: I took them, however, and having no room in my pockets, I walked on with a roll under each arm, eating the third. In this way I went through Market-street to Fourth-street, and passed the house of Mr. Read, the father of my future wife. She was standing at the door, observed me, and thought with reason, that I made a very singular and grotesque appearance.

I then turned the corner, and went through Chesnut-street, eating my roll all the way; and having made this round, I found myself again in Market-street wharf, near the boat in which I arrived. I stept into it to take a draught of the river water; and, finding myself satisfied with my first roll, I gave the other two to a woman and her child, who had come down the river with us in the boat, and was waiting to continue her journey. Thus refreshed, I regained the street, which was now full of well-dressed people, all going the same way. I joined them, and was thus led to a large Quaker's meeting-house near the market-place. I sat down with the rest, and,

FRANKLIN ENTERING PHILADELPHIA.

after looking round for some time, hearing nothing said, and, being drowsy from my last night's labor and want of rest, I fell into a sound sleep. In this state I continued till the assembly dispersed, when one of the congregation had the goodness to wake me. This was consequently the first house I entered, or in which I slept, at Philadelphia.

I began again to walk along the street by the river-side: and, looking attentively in the face of every one I met with, I at length perceived a young quaker whose countenance pleased me. I accosted him, and begged him to inform me where a stranger might find a lodging. We were then near the sign of the Three Mariners. They receive travellers here, said he, but it is not a house that bears a good character; if you will go with me, I will show you a better one. He conducted me to the Crooked Billet, in Water-street. There I ordered something for dinner, and, during my meal, a number of curious questions were put to me; my youth and appearance exciting the suspicion of my being a runaway. After dinner my drowsiness returned, and I threw myself upon a bed, without taking off my clothes, and slept till six o'clock in the evening, when I was called to supper. I afterward went to bed at a very early hour, and did not awake till the next morning.

As soon as I got up I put myself in as decent a trim as I could, and went to the house of Andrew Bradford, the printer. I found his father in the shop, whom I had seen at New-York. Having travelled on horseback, he had arrived at Philadelphia before me. He introduced me to his son, who received me with civility, and gave me some breakfast; but told me he had no occasion at present for a journeyman, having lately procured one. He added, that there was another printer newly settled in the town, of the name of Keimer, who might perhaps employ me; and that in case of refusal, I should be welcome to lodge at his house, and he would give me a little work now and then, till something better should offer.

The old man offered to introduce me to the new printer. When we were at his house, 'Neighbor,' said he, 'I bring you a young man in the printing business; perhaps you may have need of his services.'

Keimer asked me some questions, put a composing-stick in my hand to see how I could work, and then said, that at present he had nothing for me to do, but that he should soon be able to employ me. At the same time taking old Bradford for an inhabitant of the town well-disposed towards him, he communicated his project to him, and the prospect he had of success. Bradford was careful not to discover that he was the father of the other printer; and from what Keimer had said, that he hoped shortly to be in possession of the greater part of the business of the town, led him, by artful questions, and by starting some difficulties, to disclose all his views, what his hopes were founded upon, and how he intended to proceed. I was present, and heard it all. I instantly saw that one of the two was a cunning old fox, and the other a perfect novice. Bradford left me with Keimer, who was strangely surprised when I informed him who the old man was.

I found Keimer's printing materials to consist of an old damaged press, and a small font of worn out English letters, with which he himself was at work upon an elegy on Aquila Rose, whom I have mentioned above, an ingenious young man, and of an excellent character, highly esteemed in the town, secretary to the Assembly, and a very tolerable poet. Keimer also made verses, but they were indifferent ones. He could not be said to write in verse, for his method was to set the lines as they flowed from his muse; and as he worked without copy, had but one set of letter-cases, and the elegy would probably occupy all his types, it was impossible for any one to assist him. I endeavored to put his press in order, which he had not yet used, and of which indeed he understood nothing: and, having promised to come and work off his elegy as soon as it should be ready, I returned to the house of Bradford, who gave me some trifle to do for the present, for which I had my board and lodging.

In a few days Keimer sent for me to print off his elegy. He had now procured another set of letter-cases, and had a pamphlet to re-print, upon which he set me to work.

The two Philadelphia printers appeared destitute of every qualification necessary in their profession. Bradford had not been brought up to it, and was very illiterate. Keimer, though he understood a little of the business, was merely a compositor, and wholly incapable of working at press. He had been one of the French prophets, and knew how to imitate their supernatural agitations. At the time of our first acquaintance he professed no particular religion, but a little of all upon occasion. He was totally ignorant of the world, and a great knave at heart, as I had afterward an opportunity of experiencing.

Keimer could not endure that, working with him, I should lodge at Bradford's. He had indeed a house, but it was unfurnished; so that he could not take me in. He procured me a lodging at Mr. Read's, his landlord, whom I have already mentioned. My trunk and effects being now arrived, I thought of making, in the eyes of Miss Read, a more respectable appearance than when chance exhibited me to her view, eating my roll, and wandering in the streets.

From this period I began to contract acquaintance with such young people as were fond of reading, and spent my evenings with them agreeably, while at the same time I gained money by my industry, and, thanks to my frugality, lived contented. I thus forgot Boston as much as possible, and wished every one to be ignorant of the place of my residence, except my friend Collins, to whom I wrote, and who kept my secret.

An incident however arrived, which sent me home much sooner than I had proposed. I had a brother-in-law, of the name of Robert Holmes, master of a trading sloop from Boston to Delaware. Being at Newcastle, forty miles below Philadelphia, he heard of me, and wrote to inform me of the chagrin which my sudden departure from Boston had occasioned my parents, and of the affection which they still entertained for me, assuring me that, if I would return, every thing should be adjusted to my satisfaction; and he was very pressing in his entreaties. I answered his letter, thanked him for his advice, and explained the reasons which had induced me to quit Boston, with such force and clearness, that he was convinced I had been less to blame than he had imagined.

Sir William Keith, governor of the province, was at Newcastle at the time. Captain Holmes, being by chance in his company when he received my letter, took occasion to speak of me, and showed it him. The Governor read it, and appeared surprised when he learned my age. He thought me, he said, a young man of very promising talents, and that, of consequence, I ought to be encouraged; and here there were at Philadelphia none but very ignorant printers, and that if I were to set up for myself, he had no doubt of my success; that, for his own part, he would procure me all the public business, and would render me every other service in his power. My brother-in-law related all this to me afterward at Boston but I knew nothing of it at that time; when one day Keimer and I, being at work together near the window, we saw the Governor and another gentleman, Colonel French, of Newcastle, handsomely dressed, cross the street, and make directly for our house. We heard them at the door, and Keimer, believing it to be a visit to himself, went immediately down: but the Governor inqnired for me, came up stairs, and with a condescension and politeness to which I had not at all been accustomed, paid me many compliments, desired to be acquainted with me, obligingly reproached me for not having made myself known to him on my arrival in the town, and wished me to accompany him to a tavern, where he and Colonel French were going to taste some excellent Madeira wine.

I was, I confess, somewhat surprised, and Keimer appeared thunderstruck. I went, however, with the Governor and Colonel to a tavern at the corner of Third-street, where, while we were drinking the Madeira, he proposed to me to establish a printing-house. He set forth the probabilities of success, and himself and Colonel French assured me that I should have their protection and influence in obtaining the printing of the public papers of both governments; and as I appeared to doubt whether my father would assist me in this enterprise, Sir William said that he would give me a letter to him, in which he would represent the advantages of the scheme, in a light which he had no doubt would determine him. It was thus concluded that I should return to Boston by the first vessel, with the letter of recommendation, from the Governor to my father. Meanwhile the project was to be kept secret, and I continued to work for Keimer as before.

The Governor sent every now and then to invite me to dine with him. I considered this as a very great honor; and I was the more sensible of it, as he conversed with me in the most affable, familiar, and friendly manner imaginable.

Towards the end of April, 1724, a small vessel was ready to sail for Boston. I took leave of Keimer, upon the pretext of going to see my parents. The Governor gave me a long letter, in which he said many flattering things of me to my father; and strongly recommended the project of my settling at Philadelphia, as a thing which could not fail to make my fortune.

Going down the bay we struck on a flat, and sprung a leak. The weather was very tempestuous, and we were obliged to pump without intermission; I took my turn. We arrived, however, safe and sound, at Boston, after about a fortnight's passage.

I had been absent seven complete months, and my relations, during that interval, had received no intelligence of me; for my brother-in-law, Holmes, was not yet returned, and had not written about me. My unexpected appearance suprised the family; but they were all delighted at seeing me again, and, except my brother, welcomed me home. I went to him at the printing-house. I was better dressed than I had ever been while in his service: I had a complete suit of clothes, new and neat, a watch in my pocket, and my purse was furnished with nearly five pounds sterling in money. He gave me no very civil reception; and, having eyed me from head to foot, resumed his work.

The workmen asked me with eagerness where I had been, what sort of a country it was, and how I liked it. I spoke in the highest terms of Philadelphia, the happy life we led there, and expressed my intention of going back again. One of them asking what sort of money we had, I displayed before them a handful of silver, which I drew from my pocket. This was a curiosity to which they were not accustomed, paper being the current money at Boston. I failed not after this to let them see my watch; and, at last, my brother continuing sullen and out of humor, I gave them a shilling to drink, and took my leave. This visit stung my brother to the soul: for when, shortly after, my mother spoke to him of a reconciliation, and a desire to see us upon good terms, he told her that I had so insulted him before his men, that he would never forget or forgive it: in this, however, he was mistaken.

The Governor's letter appeared to excite in my father some surprise; but he said little. After some days, Captain Holmes being returned, he showed it him, asking him if he knew Keith, and what sort of a man he was: adding, that, in his opinion, it proved very little discernment to think of setting up a boy in business, who, for three years to come, would not be of an age to be ranked in the class of men. Holmes said every thing he could in favor of the scheme: but my father firmly maintained its absurdity, and at last gave a positive refusal. He wrote, however, a civil letter to Sir William, thanking him for the protection he had so obligingly offered me, but refusing to assist me for the present, because he thought me too young to be entrusted with the conduct of so important an enterprise, and which would require so considerable a sum of money.

My old comrade, Collins, who was a clerk in the post-office, charmed with the account I gave of my new residence, expressed a desire of going thither; and, while I waited my father's determination, he set off before me by land for Rhode Island, leaving his books, which formed a handsome collection in mathematics and natural philosophy, to be conveyed with mine to New-York, where he proposed to wait for me.

My father, though he could not approve Sir William's proposal, was yet pleased that I had obtained so advantageous a recommendation as that of a person of his rank, and that my industry and economy had enabled me to equip myself so handsomely in so short a period. Seeing no appearance of accommodating matters between my brother and me, he consented to my return to Philadelphia, advised me to be civil to every body, to endeavor to obtain general esteem, and avoid satire and sarcasm, to which he thought I was too much inclined; adding, that with perseverance and prudent economy, I might, by the time I became of age, save enough to establish myself in business; and that if a small sum should then be wanting, he would undertake to supply it.

This was all I could obtain from him, except some trifling presents, in token of friendship from him and my mother. I embarked once more for New-York, furnished at this time with their approbation and blessing. The sloop having touched at Newport, in Rhode Island, I paid a visit to my brother John, who had for some years been settled there, and was married. He had always been attached to me, and he received me with great affection. One of his friends, whose name was Vernon, having a debt of about thirty-six pounds due to him in Pennsylvania, begged me to receive it for him, and to keep the money till I should hear from him: accordingly he gave me an order for that purpose. This affair occasioned me, in the sequel, much uneasiness.

At Newport we took on board a number of passengers; among whom were two young women, and a grave and sensible quaker lady with her servants. I had shown an obliging forwardness in rendering the quaker some trifling services, which led her, probably, to feel an interest in my welfare; for when she saw a familiarity take place, and every day increase, between the two young women and me, she took me aside, and said, 'Young man, I am in pain for thee. Thou hast no parent to watch over thy conduct, and thou seemest to be ignorant of the world, and the snares to which youth is exposed. Rely upon what I tell thee: those are women of bad characters; I perceive it in all their actions. If thou dost not take care, they will lead thee into danger. They are strangers to thee, and I advise thee, by the friendly interest I take in thy preservation, to form no connexion with them.' As I appeared at first not to think quite so ill of them as she did, she related many things she had seen and heard, which had escaped my attention, but which convinced me that she was in the right. I thanked her for her obliging advice, and promised to follow it.

GOVERNOR BURNET SHOWING FRANKLIN HIS LIBRARY.

When we arrived at New-York, they informed me where they lodged, and invited me to come and see them. I did not however go, and it was well I did not; for the next day, the captain, missing a silver spoon and some other things which had been taken from the cabin, and knowing these women to be prostitutes, procured a search-warrant, found the stolen goods upon them, and had them punished. And thus, after having been saved from one rock concealed under water, upon which the vessel struck during our passage, I escaped another of a still more dangerous nature.

At New-York I found my friend Collins, who had arrived some time before. We had been intimate from our infancy, and had read the same books together; but he had the advantage of being able to devote more time to reading and study, and an astonishing disposition for mathematics, in which he left me far behind him. When at Boston, I had been accustomed to pass with him almost all my leisure hours. He was then a sober and industrious lad; his knowledge had gained him a very general esteem, and he seemed to promise to make an advantageous figure in society. But during my absence, he had unfortunately addicted himself to brandy, and I learned, as well from himself as from the report of others, that every day since his arrival at New-York he had been intoxicated, and had acted in a very extravagant manner. He had also played and lost all his money; so that I was obliged to pay his expenses at the inn, and to maintain him during the rest of his journey: a burden that was very inconvenient to me.

The Governor of New-York, whose name was Bernet, hearing the Captain say, that a young man who was a passenger in his ship had a great number of books, begged him to bring me to his house. I accordingly went, and should have taken Collins with me, had he been sober. The Governor treated me with great civility, showed me his library, which was a very considerable one, and we talked for some time upon books and authors. This was the second governor who had honored me with his attention; and, to a poor boy, as I was then, these little adventures did not fail to be pleasing.

We arrived at Philadelphia. On the way I received Vernon's money, without which we should have been unable to have finished our journey.

Collins wished to get employment as a merchant's clerk but either his breath or his countenance betrayed his bad habit: for, though he had recommendations, he met with no success, and continued to lodge and eat with me, and at my expense. Knowing that I had Vernon's money, he was continually asking me to lend him some of it; promising to repay me as soon as he should get employment. At last he had drawn so much of this money, that I was extremely alarmed at what might become of me, should he fail to make good the deficiency. His habit of drinking did not at all diminish, and was a frequent source of discord between us; for when he had drank a little too much, he was very headstrong.

Being one day in a boat together, on the Delaware, with some other young persons, he refused to take his turn in rowing. 'You shall row for me,' said he, 'till we get home.'—'No,' I replied, 'we will not row for you.'—'You shall,' said he, 'or remain upon the water all night.'—'As you please.'—'Let us row,' said the rest of the company; 'what signifies whether he assists or not?' But, already angry with him for his conduct in other respects, I persisted in my refusal. He then swore that he would make me row, or would throw me out of the boat; and he made up to me. As soon as he was within my reach, I took him up by the collar, gave him a violent thrust, and threw him head foremost into the river. I knew that he was a good swimmer, and was therefore under no apprehensions for his life. Before he could turn himself, we were able, by a few strokes of our oars, to place ourselves out of his reach; and, whenever he touched the boat, we asked him if he would row, striking his hands at the same time with the oars to make him let go his hold. He was nearly suffocated with rage, but obstinately refused making any promise to row. Perceiving, at length, that his strength began to be exhausted, we took him into the boat, and conveyed him home in the evening completely drenched. The utmost coldness subsisted between us after this adventure. At last the captain of a West India ship, who was commissioned to procure a tutor for the children of a gentleman at Barbadoes, meeting with Collins, offered him the place. He accepted it, and took his leave of me, promising to discharge the debt he owed me with the first money he should receive; but I have heard nothing of him since.

The violation of the trust reposed in me by Vernon, was one of the first great errors of my life; and it proves that my father was not mistaken when he supposed me too young to be entrusted with the management of important affairs. But Sir William, upon reading his letter, thought him too prudent. There was a difference, he said, between individuals: years of maturity were not always accompanied with discretion, neither was youth in every instance devoid of it. 'Since your father,' added he, 'will not set you up in business, I will do it myself. Make out a list of what will be wanted from England, and I will send for the articles. You shall repay me when you can. I am determined to have a good printer here, and I am sure you will succeed.' This was said with so much seeming cordiality, that I suspected not for an instant the sincerity of the offer. I had hitherto kept the project, with which Sir William had inspired me, of settling in business, a secret at Philadelphia, and I still continued to do so. Had my reliance on the governor been known, some friend, better acquainted with his character than myself, would doubtless have advised me not to trust him; for I afterward learned that he was universally known to be liberal of promises, when he had no intention to perform. But having never solicited him, how could I suppose his offers to be deceitful? On the contrary, I believed him to be the best man in the world.

I gave him an inventory of a small printing-office; the expense of which I had calculated at about a hundred pounds sterling. He expressed his approbation; but asked, if my presence in England, that I might choose the characters myself, and see that every article was good in its kind, would not be an advantage? 'You will also be able,' said he, 'to form some acquaintance there, and establish a correspondence with stationers and booksellers.' This I acknowledged was desirable. 'That being the case,' added he, 'hold yourself in readiness to go with the Annis.' This was the annual vessel, and the only one at that time which made regular voyages between the ports of London and Philadelphia. But the Annis was not to sail for some months. I therefore continued to work with Keimer, unhappy respecting the sum which Collins had drawn from me, and almost in continual agony at the thoughts of Vernon, who fortunately made no demand of his money till several years after.

In the account of my first voyage from Boston to Philadelphia, I omitted, I believe, a trifling circumstance, which will not, perhaps, be out of place here. During a calm, which stopped us above Block Island, the crew employed themselves in fishing for cod, of which they caught a great number. I had hitherto adhered to my resolution of not eating any thing that had possessed life; and I considered, on this occasion, agreeably to the maxims of my master Tyron, the capture of every fish as a sort of murder, committed without provocation, since these animals had neither done, nor were capable of doing, the smallest injury to any one that should justify the measure. This mode of reasoning I conceived to be unanswerable. Meanwhile, I had formerly been extremely fond of fish; and, when one of these cod was taken out of the frying-pan, I thought its flavor delicious. I hesitated some time between principle and inclination, till at last recollecting, that when the cod had been opened some small fish were found in its belly, I said to myself, if you eat one another, I see no reason why we may not eat you. I accordingly dined on the cod with no small degree of pleasure, and have since continued to eat like the rest of mankind, returning only occasionally to my vegetable plan. How convenient does it prove to be a *rational animal*, that knows how to find or invent a plausible pretext for whatever it has an inclination to do.

I contrived to live upon good terms with Keimer, who had not the smallest suspicion of my projected establishment. He still retained a portion of his former enthusiasm; and, being fond of argument, we frequently disputed together. I was so much in the habit of using my Socratic method, and had so frequently puzzled him by my questions, which appeared at first very distant from the point in debate, yet, nevertheless, led to it by degrees, involving him in difficulties and contradictions from which he was unable to extricate himself, that he became at last ridiculously cautious, and would scarcely answer the most plain and familiar question without previously asking me—What would you infer from that? Hence he formed so high an opinion of my talents for refutation, that he seriously proposed to me to become his colleague in the establishment of a new religious sect. He was to propagate the doctrine by preaching, and I to refute every opponent.

When he explained to me his tenets, I found my absurdities, which I refused to admit, unless he would agree in turn to adopt some of my opinions. Keimer wore his beard long, because Moses had somewhere said, 'Thou shalt not mar the corners of thy beard.' He likewise observed the Sabbath; and these were with him two very essential points. I disliked them both; but I consented to adopt them, provided he would agree to abstain from animal food. 'I doubt,' said he, 'whether my constitution will be able to support it.' I assured him, on the contrary, that he would find himself the better for it. He was naturally a glutton, and I wished to amuse myself by starving him. He consented to make trial of this regimen, if I would bear him company; and, in reality, we continued it for three months. A woman in the neighborhood prepared and brought us our victuals, to whom I gave a list of forty dishes; in the composition of which there entered neither flesh nor fish. This fancy was the more agreeable to me, as it turned to good account; for the whole expense of our living did not exceed for each eighteen pence a week

I have since that period observed several Lents with the greatest strictness, and have suddenly returned again to my ordinary diet, without experiencing the smallest inconvenience; which has led me to regard as of no importance the advice commonly given, of introducing gradually such alterations of regimen.

I continued it cheerfully; but poor Keimer suffered terribly. Tired of the project, he sighed for the flesh pots of Egypt. At length he ordered a roast pig, and invited me and two of our female acquaintances to dine with him; but the pig being ready a little too soon he could not resist the temptation, and eat it all up before we arrived.

During the circumstances I have related, I had paid some attention to Miss Read. I entertained for her the utmost esteem and affection; and I had reason to believe that these sentiments were mutual. But we were both young, scarcely more than eighteen years of age; and, as I was on the point of undertaking a long voyage, her mother thought it prudent to prevent matters been carried too far for the present, judging that, if marriage was our object, there would be more propriety in it after my return, when, as at least I expected, I should be established in my business. Perhaps also she thought that my expectations were not so well founded as I imagined.

My most intimate acquaintance at this time were Charles Osborne, Joseph Watson, and James Ralph; young men who were all fond of reading. The two first were clerks to Mr. Charles Brockdon, one of the principal attorneys in the town, and the other clerk to a merchant. Watson was an upright, pious, and sensible young man: the others were somewhat more loose in their principles of religion, particularly Ralph, whose faith, as well as that of Collins, I had contributed to shake: each of whom made me suffer a very adequate punishment. Osborne was sensible, and sincere and affectionate in his friendships, but too much inclined to the critic in matters of literature. Ralph was ingenuous and hrewd, genteel in his address, and extremely eloquent. I not remember to have met with a more agreeable speaker,

They were both enamoured of the muses, and had already evinced their passion by some small poetical productions.

It was a custom with us to take a charming walk on Sundays, in the woods that border the Skuylkil. Here we read together, and afterward conversed on what we read. Ralph was disposed to give himself up entirely to poetry. He flattered himself that he should arrive at great eminence in the art, and even acquire a fortune. The sublimest poets, he pretended, when they first began to write, committed as many faults as himself. Osborne endeavored to dissuade him, by assuring him that he had no genius for poetry, and advised him to stick to the trade in which he had been brought up. 'In the road of commerce,' said he, 'you will be sure, by diligence and assiduity, though you have no capital, of so far succeeding as to be employed as a factor; and may thus, in time acquire the means of setting up for yourself.' I concurred in these sentiments, but at the same time expressed my approbation of amusing ourselves sometimes with poetry, with a view to improve our style. In consequence of this it was proposed, that, at our next meeting, each of us should bring a copy of verses of his own composition. Our object in this competition was to benefit each other by our mutual remarks, criticisms, and corrections; and as style and expression were all we had in view, we excluded every idea of invention, by agreeing that our task should be a verse of the eighteenth psalm, in which is described the descent of the Deity.

The time of our meeting drew near, when Ralph called upon me, and told me that his performance was ready. I informed him that I had been idle, and, not much liking the task, had done nothing. He showed me his piece, and asked me what I thought of it. I expressed myself in terms of warm approbation; because it really appeared to have considerable merit. He then said, 'Osborne will never acknowledge the smallest degree of excellence in any production of mine. Envy alone dictates to him a thousand animadversions. Of you he is not so jealous: I wish, therefore, you would take the verses, and produce them as your own. I will pretend not to have had leisure to write any thing. We shall then see in what manner he will speak of them.' I agreed to this little artifice, and immediately transcribed the verses to prevent all suspicion.

We met. Watson's performance was the first that was read. It had some beauties, but many faults. We next read Osborne's, which was much better. Ralph did it justice, remarking a few imperfections, and applauding such parts as were excellent. He had himself nothing to show. It was now my turn. I made some difficulty; seemed as if I wished to be excused; pretended that I had no time to make corrections, &c. No excuse, however, was admissible, and the piece must be produced. It was read and re-read. Watson and Osborne immediately resigned the palm, and united in applauding it. Ralph alone made a few remarks, and proposed some alterations; but I defended my text. Osborne agreed with me, and told Ralph that he was no more able to criticise than he was able to write.

When Osborne was alone with me, he expressed himself still more strongly in favor of what he considered as my performance. He pretended that he had put some restraint on himself before, apprehensive of my construing his commendations into flattery. 'But who would have supposed,' said he, 'Franklin to be capable of such a composition? What painting, what energy, what fire! He has surpassed the original. In his common conversation he appears not to have a choice of words; he hesitates, and is at a loss: and yet, good God, how he writes!"

At our next meeting Ralph discovered the trick we had played Osborne, who was rallied without mercy.

By this adventure Ralph was fixed in his resolution of becoming a poet. I left nothing unattempted to divert him from his purpose: but he persevered, till at last the reading of Pope* effected his cure: he became, however, a very tolerable prose writer. I shall speak more of him hereafter; but as I shall probably have no farther occasion to mention the other two, I ought to observe here, that Watson died a few years after in my arms. He was greatly regretted; for he was the best of our society. Osborne went to the islands, where he gained considerable reputation as a barrister, and was getting money; but he died young. We had seriously engaged, that whoever died first should return, if possible, and pay a friendly visit to the survivor, to give him an account of the other world; but he has never fulfilled his engagement.

The Governor appeared to be fond of my company, and frequently invited me to his house. He always spoke of

---

* Probably the Dunciad, where we find him thus immortalized by the author:

Silence, ye wolves, while Ralph to Cynthia howls,
And makes night hideous · answer him, ye owls!

his intention of settling me in business as a point that was decided. I was to take with me letters of recommendation to a number of his friends; and particularly a letter of credit, in order to obtain the necessary sum for the purchase of my press, types, and paper. He appointed various times for me to come for these letters, which would certainly be ready; and, when I came, always put me off to another day.

These successive delays continued till the vessel, whose departure had been several times deferred, was on the point of setting sail; when I again went to Sir William's house, to receive my letters and take leave of him. I saw his secretary, Dr. Bard, who told me, that the Governor was extremely busy writing, but that he would be down at Newcastle before the vessel, and that the letters would be delivered to me there.

Ralph, though he was married and had a child, determined to accompany me in this voyage. His object was supposed to be the establishing a correspondence with some mercantile houses, in order to sell goods by commission; but I afterward learned that, having reason to be dissatisfied with the parents of his wife, he proposed to himself to leave her on their hands, and never return to America again.

Having taken leave of my friends, and interchanged promises of fidelity with Miss Read, I quitted Philadelphia. At Newcastle the vessel came to anchor. The Governor was arrived, and I went to his lodgings. His secretary received me with great civility, told me, on the part of the Governor, that he could not see me then, as he was engaged in affairs of the utmost importance, but that he would send the letters on board, and that he wished me, with all his heart, a good voyage and speedy return. I returned, somewhat astonished, to the ship, but still without entertaining the slightest suspicion.

Mr. Hamilton, a celebrated barrister of Philadelphia, had taken a passage to England for himself and his son, and in conjunction with Mr. Denham, a quaker, and Messrs. Oniam and Russel, proprietors of a forge in Maryland, had agreed for the whole cabin, so that Ralph and I were obliged to take up our lodging with the crew. Being unknown to every body in the ship, we were looked upon as of the common order of people: but Mr. Hamilton and his son (it was James, who was afterward governor) left us at Newcastle, and returned to Philadelphia, where he was recalled at a very great expense, to plead the cause of a vessel that had been seized; and just as we were about to sail, Colonel French came on board, and shewed me many civilities. The passengers upon this paid me more attention, and I was invited, together with my friend Ralph, to occupy the place in the cabin which the return of the Mr. Hamiltons had made vacant; an offer which we very readily accepted.

Having learned that the despatches of the Governor had been brought on board by Colonel French, I asked the captain for the letters that were to be entrusted to my care. He told me that they were all put together in the bag, which he could not open at present; but before we reached England, he would give me an opportunity of taking them out. I was satisfied with this answer, and we pursued our voyage.

The company in the cabin were all very sociable, and we were perfectly well off as to provisions, as we had the advantage of the whole of Mr. Hamilton's, who had laid in a very plentiful stock. During the passage, Mr. Denham contracted a friendship for me, which ended only with his life: in other respects the voyage was by no means an agreeable one, as we had much bad weather.

When we arrived in the river, the captain was as good as his word, and allowed me to search in the bag for the Governor's letters. I could not find a single one with my name written on it, as committed to my care; but I selected six or seven, which I judged from the direction to be those that were intended for me; particularly one to Mr. Basket, the king's printer, and another to a stationer, who was the first person I called upon. I delivered him the letter as coming from Governor Keith. 'I have no acquaintance,' said he, 'with any such person;' and opening the letter 'Oh it is from Riddlesden!' he exclaimed. 'I have lately discovered him to be a very arrant knave, and wish to have nothing to do either with him or his letters.' He instantly put the letter into my hand, turned upon his heel, and left me to serve some customers.

I was astonished at finding these letters were not from the Governor. Reflecting, and putting circumstances together I then began to doubt his sincerity. I rejoined my friend Denham, and related the whole affair to him. He let me at once into Keith's character, told me there was not the least probability of his having written a single letter; that no one who knew him ever placed any reliance on him, and laughed at my credulity in supposing that the Governor would give me a letter of credit, when he had no credit for himself. As I showed some uneasiness respecting what step I should take, he advised me to try to get employment in the house of some printer. 'You may there,' said he, 'improve yourself in business, and you will be able to settle yourself the more advantageously when you return to America.'

We knew already, as well as the stationer, attorney Riddlesden to be a knave. He had nearly ruined the father of Miss Read, by drawing him in to be his security. We learned from his letter, that he was secretly carrying on an intrigue, in concert with the Governor, to the prejudice of Mr. Hamilton, who, it was supposed, would, by this time, be in Europe. Denham, who was Hamilton's friend, was of opinion that he ought to be made acquainted with it, and, in reality, the instant he arrived in England, which was very soon after, I waited on him, and, as much from good-will to him, as from resentment against the Governor, put the letter into his hands. He thanked me very sincerely, the information it contained being of consequence to him; and from that moment bestowed on me his friendship, which afterward proved, on many occasions serviceable to me.

But what are we to think of a governor who could play so scurvy a trick, and thus grossly deceive a poor young lad, wholly destitute of experience? It was a practice with him. Wishing to please every body, and having little to bestow, he was lavish of promises. He was, in other respects, sensible and judicious, a very tolerable writer, and a good governor for the people; though not so for the proprietaries, whose instructions he frequently disregarded. Many of our best laws were his work, and established during his administration.

Ralph and I were inseparable companions. We took a lodging together at three and sixpence a-week, which was as much as we could afford. He met with some relations in London, but they were poor, and not able to assist him. He now, for the first time, informed me of his intention to remain in England, and that he had no thoughts of ever returning to Philadelphia. He was totally without money; the little he had been able raise having barely sufficed for his passage. I had still fifteen pistoles remaining; and to me he had from time to time recourse, while he tried to get employment.

At first believing himself possessed of talents for the stage, he thought of turning actor; but Wilkes, to whom he applied, frankly advised him to renounce the idea, as it was impossible he should succeed. He next proposed to Roberts, a bookseller in Paternoster-row, to write a weekly paper in the manner of the Spectator, upon terms to which Roberts would not listen. Lastly, he endeavored to procure employment as a copyist, and applied to the lawyers and stationers about the Temple, but he could find no vacancy.

As to myself, I immediately got engaged at Palmer's, at that time a noted printer in Bartholomew-close, with whom I continued nearly a year. I applied very assiduously to my work, but I expended with Ralph almost all that I earned. Plays, and other places of amusement which we frequented together, having exhausted my pistoles, we lived after this from hand to mouth. He appeared to have entirely forgotten his wife and child, as I also, by degrees, forgot my engagements with Miss Read, to whom I never wrote more than one letter, and that merely to inform her that I was not likely to return soon. This was another grand error of my life, which I should be desirous of correcting were I to begin my career again.

I was emloyed at Palmer's on the second edition of Woolaston's Religion of Nature. Some of his arguments appearing to me not to be well-founded, I wrote a small metaphysical treatise, in which I animadverted on those passages. It was entitled a 'Dissertation on Liberty and Necessity, Pleasure and Pain.' I dedicated it to my friend Ralph, and printed a small number of copies. Palmer upon this treated me with more consideration, and regarded me as a young man of talents; though he seriously took me to task for the principles of my pamphlet, which he looked upon as abominable. The printing of this work was another error of my life.

While I lodged in Little Britain I formed an acquaintance with a bookseller of the name of Wilcox, whose shop was next door to me. Circulating libraries were not then in use. He had an immense collection of books of all sorts. We agreed that, for a reasonable retribution, of which I have now forgotten the price, I should have free access to his library, and take what books I pleased, which I was to return when I had read them. I considered this agreement as a very great advantage; and I derived from it as much benefit as was in my power.

My pamphlet falling into the hands of a surgeon, of the name of Lyons, author of a book entitled, 'Infallibility of Human Judgment,' was the occasion of a considerable intimacy between us. He expressed great esteem for me, came frequently to see me, in order to converse upon metaphysical subjects, and introduced me to Dr. Mandeville, author of the Fable of the Bees, who had instituted a club at a tavern in

Cheapside. of which he was the soul: he was a facetious and very amusing character. He also introduced me, at Batson's coffee-house, to Dr. Pemberton, who promised to give me an opportunity of seeing Sir Isaac Newton, which I very ardently desired; but he never kept his word.

I had brought some curiosities with me from America; the principal of which was a purse made of the asbestos, which fire only purifies. Sir Hans Sloane hearing of it, called upon me, and invited me to his house in Bloomsbury-square, where, after showing me every thing that was curious, he prevailed on me to add this piece to his collection; for which he paid me very handsomely.

There lodged in the same house with us a young woman, a milliner, who had a shop by the side of the Exchange. Lively and sensible, and having received an education somewhat above her rank, her conversation was very agreeable. Ralph read plays to her every evening. They became intimate. She took another lodging, and he followed her. They lived for some time together; but Ralph being without employment, she having a child, and the profits of her business not sufficing for the maintenance of three, he resolved to quit London, and try a country-school. This was a plan in which he thought himself likely to succeed; as he wrote a fine hand, and was versed in arithmetic and accounts. But considering the office as beneath him, and expecting some day to make a better figure in the world, when he should be ashamed of its being known that he had exercised a profession so little honorable, he changed his name, and did me the honor of assuming mine. He wrote to me soon after his departure, informing me that he was settled at a small village in Berkshire. In his letter he recommended Mrs. T. the milliner, to my care, and requested an answer, directed to Mr. Franklin, schoolmaster, at N***.

He continued to write to me frequently, sending me large ragments of an Epic poem he was composing, and which e requested me to criticise and correct. I did so, but not without endeavoring to prevail on him to renounce this pursuit. Young had just published one of his Satires. I copied and sent him a great part of it; in which the author demonstrates the folly of cultivating the Muses, from the hope, by their instrumentality, of rising in the world. It was ail to no purpose; paper after paper of his poem continued to arrive every post.

Meanwhile Mrs. T*** having lost, on his account, both her friends and business, was frequently in distress. In this

FRANKLIN IN HIS PRINTING OFFICE

dilemma she had recourse to me, and to extricate her from her difficulties, I lent her all the money I could spare. I felt a little too much fondness for her. Having at that time no ties of religion, and, taking advantage of her necessitous situation, I attempted liberties (another error of my life), which she repelled with becoming indignation. She informed Ralph of my conduct; and the affair occasioned a breach between us. When he returned to London, he gave me to understand that he considered all the obligations he owed me as annihilated by this proceeding; whence I concluded that I was never to expect the payment of what money I had lent him, or advanced on his account. I was the less afflicted at this, as he was wholly unable to pay me; and as, by losing his friendship, I was relieved at the same time from a very heavy burden.

I now began to think of laying by some money. The printing-house of Watts, near Lincoln's-inn-fields, being a still more considerable one than that in which I worked, it was probable I might find it more advantageous to be employed there. I offered myself, and was accepted; and in this house I continued during the remainder of my stay in London.

On my entrance I worked first as a pressman, conceiving I had need of bodily exercise, to which I had been accustomed in America, where the printers work alternately as compositors and at the press. I drank nothing but water. The other workmen, to the number of about fifty, were great drinkers of beer. I carried occasionally a large form of letters in each hand, up and down stairs, while the rest employed both hands to carry one. They were surprised to see, by this and many other examples, that the *American Aquatic*, as they used to call me, was stronger than those who drank porter. The beer-boy had sufficient employment during the whole day in serving that house alone. My fellow-pressman drank every day a pint of beer before breakfast, a pint with bread and cheese, for breakfast, one between breakfast and dinner, one at dinner, one again about six o'clock in the afternoon, and another after he had finished his day's work. This custom appeared to me abominable; but he had need, he said, of all this beer in order to acquire strength to work.

I endeavored to convince him that the bodily strength furnished by the beer, could only be in proportion to the solid part of the barley dissolved in the water of which the beer was composed; that there was a larger portion of flour in a penny loaf, and that consequently if he ate this loaf, and drank a pint of water with it, he would derive more strength from it than from a pint of beer. This reasoning, however, did not prevent him from drinking his accustomed quantity of beer, and paying every Saturday night a score of four or five shillings a-week for this cursed beverage; an expense from which I was wholly exempt. Thus do these poor devils continue all their lives in a state of voluntary wretchedness and poverty.

At the end of a few weeks, Watts having occasion for me above stairs as a compositor, I quitted the press. The compositors demanded of me garnish-money afresh. This I considered as an imposition, having already paid below. The master was of the same opinion and desired me not to comply. I thus remained two or three weeks out of the fraternity, I was consequently looked upon as excommunicated; and whenever I was absent, no little trick that malice could suggest was left unpractised upon me. I found my letters mixed, my pages transposed, my matter broken, &c. &c. all of which was attributed to the spirit that haunted the chapel,* and tormented those that were not regularly admitted. I was at last obliged to submit to pay, notwithstanding the protection of the master; convinced of the folly of not keeping up a good understanding with those among whom we are destined to live.

After this I lived in the utmost harmony with my fellow-laborers, and soon acquired considerable influence among them. I proposed some alteration in the laws of the chapel, which I carried without opposition. My example prevailed with several of them to renounce their abominable practice of bread and cheese with beer; and they procured, like me, from a neighboring house, a good basin of warm gruel, in which was a small slice of butter, with toasted bread and nutmeg. This was a much better breakfast, which did not cost more than a pint of beer, namely, three-halfpence, and at the same time preserved the head clearer. Those who continued to gorge themselves with beer, often lost their credit with the publican, from neglecting to pay their score. They had then recourse to me, to become security for them; *their light*, as they used to call it, *being out*. I attended at the pay-table every Saturday evening, to take up the little sum which I made myself answerable for; and which sometimes amounted to nearly thirty shillings a week.

---

* Printing-houses in general are thus denominated by the workmen; the *spirit* they call by the name of *Ralph*.

This circumstance, added to my reputation of being a tolerable good *gabber*, or, in other words, skilful in the art of burlesque, kept up my importance in the chapel. I had beside recommended myself to the esteem of my master by my assiduous application to business, never observing Saint Monday. My extraordinary quickness in composing always procured me such work as was most urgent, and which is commonly best paid; and thus my time passed away in a very pleasant manner.

My lodging in Little Britain being too far from the printing-house, I took another in Duke-street, opposite the Roman Catholic Chapel. It was at the back of an Italian warehouse. The house was kept by a widow, who had a daughter, a servant, and a shop-boy; but the latter slept out of the house. After sending to the people with whom I lodged in Little Britain, to inquire into my character, she agreed to take me in at the same price, three and sixpence a week; contenting herself, she said, with so little, because of the security she should derive, as they were all women, from having a man lodger in the house.

She was a woman rather advanced in life, the daughter of a clergyman. She had been educated a Protestant; but her husband, whose memory she highly revered, had converted her to the Catholic religion. She had lived in habits of intimacy with persons of distinction, of whom she knew various anecdotes as far back as the time of Charles II. Being subject to fits of the gout, which often confined her to her room, she was sometimes disposed to see company. Hers was so amusing to me, that I was glad to pass the evening with her as often as she desired it. Our supper consisted only of half an anchovy apiece, upon a slice of bread and butter, with half a pint of ale between us. But the entertainment was in her conversation.

The early hours I kept, and the little trouble I occasioned in the family, made her loath to part with me, and when I mentioned another lodging I had found, nearer the printing-house, at two shillings a week, which fell in with my plan of saving, she persuaded me to give it up, making herself an abatement of two shillings: and thus I continued to lodge with her, during the remainder of my abode in London, at eighteen pence a week.

In a garret of the house, there lived, in a most retired, manner, a lady seventy years of age, of whom I received the following account from my landlady. She was a Roman Catholic. In her early years she had been sent to the continent, and entered a convent with the design of becoming a nun: but the climate not agreeing with her constitution, she was obliged to return to England, where, as there were no monasteries, she made a vow to lead a monastic life, in as rigid a manner as circumstances would permit. She accordingly disposed of all her property to be applied to charitable uses, reserving to herself only twelve pounds a year; and of this small pittance she gave a part to the poor, living on water-gruel, and never making use of fire but to boil it. She had lived in this garret a great many years, without paying rent to the successive Catholic inhabitants that had kept the house; who indeed considered her abode with them as a blessing. A priest came every day to confess her. 'I have asked her,' said my landlady, 'how, living as she did, she could find so much employment for a confessor?' To which she answered, 'that it was impossible to avoid vain thoughts.'

I was once permitted to visit her. She was cheerful and polite, and her conversation agreeable. Her apartment was neat; but the whole furniture consisted of a mattress, a table on which was a crucifix and a book, and a chair, which she gave me to sit on, and over the mantelpiece a picture of St. Veronica displaying her handkerchief, on which was seen the miraculous impression of the face of Chrst, which she explained to me with great gravity. Her countenance was pale, but she had never experienced sickness; and I may adduce her as another proof how little is sufficient to maintain life and health.

At the printing-house I contracted an intimacy with a sensible young man of the name of Wygate, who, as his parents were in good circumstances, had received a better education than is common among printers. He was a tolerable Latin scholar, spoke French fluently, and was fond of reading. I taught him, as well as a friend of his, to swim, by taking them twice only into the river; after which they stood in need of no farther assistance. We one day made a party to go by water to Chelsea, in order to see the college, and Don Saltero's curiosities. On our return, at the request of the company whose curiosity Wygate had excited, I undressed myself, and leaped into the river. I swam from near Chelsea the whole way to Blackfriars-bridge, exhibiting, during my course, a variety of feats of activity and address, both upon the surface of the water as well as under it. This sight occasioned much astonishment and pleasure to those to whom it was new. In my youth I took great delight in this exercise. I knew and could execute, all the evolutions and positions of Thevenot; and I added to them some of my own invention, in which I endeavored to unite gracefulness and utility. I took a pleasure in displaying them all on this occasion, and was highly flattered with the admiration they excited.

Wygate, besides his being desirous of perfecting himself in this art, was the more attached to me from there being, in other respects, a conformity in our tastes and studies. He at length proposed to me to make the tour of Europe with him, maintaining ourselves at the same time by working at our profession. I was on the point of consenting, when I mentioned it to my friend, Mr. Denham, with whom I was glad to pass an hour whenever I had leisure. He dissuaded me from the project, and advised me to think of returning to Philadelphia, which he was about to do himself. I must relate in this place a trait of this worthy man's character.

He had formerly been in business at Bristol, but failing, he compounded with his creditors, and departed for America, where, by assiduous application as a merchant, he acquired in a few years a very considerable fortune. Returning to England in the same vessel with myself, as I have related above, he invited all his old creditors to a feast. When assembled, he thanked them for the readiness with which they had received his small composition; and, while they expected nothing more than a simple entertainment, each found under his plate, when it came to be removed, a draft upon a banker for the residue of his debt, with interest.

He told me that it was his intention to carry back with him to Philadelphia a great quantity of goods in order to open a store; and he offered to take me with him in the capacity of clerk, to keep his books, in which he would instruct me, copy letters, and superintend the store. He added, that as soon as I had acquired a knowledge of mercantile transactions, he would improve my situation, by sending me with a cargo of corn and flour to the American islands, and by procuring me other lucrative commissions; so that, with good management and economy, I might in time begin business with advantage for myself.

I relished these proposals. London began to tire me; the agreeable hours I had passed at Philadelphia presented themselves to my mind, and I wished to see them revive. I consequently engaged myself to Mr. Denham, at a salary of fifty pounds a year. This was indeed less than I earned as a compositor, but then I had a much fairer prospect. I took leave, therefore, as I believed for ever, of printing, and gave myself up to my new occupation, spending all my time either in going from house to house with Mr. Denham to purchase goods, or in packing them up, or in expediting the workmen, &c. &c. When every thing, however, was on board, I had at last a few days' leisure.

During this interval, I was one day sent for by a gentleman, whom I knew only by name. It was Sir William Wyndham. I went to his house. He had by some means heard of my performances between Chelsea and Blackfriars, and that I had taught the art of swimming to Wygate and another young man in the course of a few hours. His two sons were on the point of setting out on their travels; he was desirous that they should previously learn to swim, and offered me a very liberal reward if I would undertake to instruct them. They were not yet arrived in town, and the stay I should make was uncertain; I could not therefore accept his proposal. I was led, however, to suppose from this incident, that if I had wished to remain in London, and open a swimming school, I should perhaps have gained a great deal of money. The idea struck me so forcibly, that, had the offer been made sooner, I should have dismissed the thought of returning as yet to America. Some years after, you and I had a more important business to settle with one of the sons of Sir William Wyndham, then Lord Egremont. But let us not anticipate events.

I thus passed about eighteen months in London, working almost without intermission at my trade, avoiding all expense on my own account, except going now and then to the play, and purchasing a few books. But my friend Ralph kept me poor. He owed me about twenty-seven pounds, which was so much money lost; and when considered as taken from my little savings, was a very great sum. I had, notwithstanding this, a regard for him, as he possessed many amiable qualities. But though I had done nothing for myself in point of fortune, I had increased my stock of knowledge, either by the many excellent books I had read, or the conversation of learned and literary persons with whom I was acquainted.

We sailed from Gravesend on the 23d of July, 1726. For the incidents of my voyage I refer you to my Journal, where you will find all its circumstances minutely related. We landed at Philadelphia on the 11th of the following October.

Keith had been deprived of his office of governor, and was succeeded by Major Gordon. I met him walking in the streets as a private individual. He appeared a little ashamed at seeing me, but passed on without saying any thing.

I should have been equally ashamed myself at meeting

Miss Read, had not her family, justly despairing of my return after reading my letter, advised her to give me up, and marry a potter, of the name of Rogers; to which she consented: but he never made her happy, and she soon separated from him, refusing to cohabit with him, or even bear his name, on account of a report which prevailed, of his having another wife. His skill in his profession had seduced Miss Read's parents; but he was as bad a subject as he was excellent as a workman. He involved himself in debt, and fled, in the year 1727 or 1728, to the West Indies, where he died.

During my absence, Keimer had taken a more considerable house, in which he kept a shop, that was well supplied with paper and various other articles. He had procured some new types, and a number of workmen; among whom, however, there was not one who was good for any thing; and he appeared not to want business.

Mr. Denham took a warehouse in Water-street, where we exhibited our commodities. I applied myself closely, studied accounts, and became in a short time very expert in trade. We lodged and ate together. He was sincerely attached to me, and acted towards me as if he had been my father. On my side, I respected and loved him. My situation was happy, but it was a happiness of no long duration.

Early in February, 1727, when I entered into my twenty-second year, we were both taken ill. I was attacked with a pleurisy, which had nearly carried me off; I suffered terribly, and considered it as all over with me. I felt indeed a sort of disappointment when I found myself likely to recover, and regretted that I had still to experience, sooner or later, the same disagreeable scene again.

I have forgotten what was Mr. Denham's disorder; but it was a tedious one, and he at last sunk under it. He left me a small legacy in his will, as a testimony of his friendship; and I was once more abandoned to myself in the wide world, the warehouse being confided to the care of his testamentary executor, who dismissed me.

My brother-in-law, Holmes, who happened to be at Philadelphia, advised me to return to my former profession; and Keimer offered me a very considerable salary if I would undertake the management of his printing-office, that he might devote himself entirely to the superintendence of his shop. His wife and relations in London had given me a bad character of him; and I was loath, for the present, to have any concern with him. I endeavored to get employment, as a clerk to a merchant; but not readily finding a situation, I was induced to accept Keimer's proposal.

The following were the persons I found in his printing-house.

Hugh Meredith, a Pennsylvanian, about thirty-five years of age. He had been brought up to husbandry, was honest, sensible, had some experience, and was fond of reading; but too much addicted to drinking.

Stephen Potts, a young rustic, just broke from school, and of rustic education, with endowments rather above the common order, and a competent portion of understanding and gayety; but a little idle. Keimer had engaged these two at very low wages, which he had promised to raise every three months a shilling a week, provided their improvement in the typographic art should merit it. This future increase of wages was the bait he had made use of to ensnare them. Meredith was to work at the press, and Potts to bind books, which he had engaged to teach them, though he understood neither himself.

John Savage, an Irishman, who had been brought up to no trade, and whose service, for a period of four years, Keimer had purchased of the captain of a ship. He was also to be a pressman.

George Webb, an Oxford scholar, whose time he had in like manner bought for four years, intending him for a compositor. I shall speak more of him presently.

Lastly, David Harry, a country lad, who was apprenticed to him.

I soon perceived that Keimer's intention, in engaging me at a price so much above what he was accustomed to give, was, that I might form all these raw journeymen and apprentices, who scarcely cost him any thing, and who, being indentured, would, as soon as they should be sufficiently instructed enable him to do without me. I nevertheless adhered to my agreement. I put the office in order, which was in the utmost confusion, and brought his people, by degrees, to pay attention to their work, and to execute it in a more masterly style.

It was singular to see an Oxford scholar in the condition of a purchased servant. He was not more than eighteen years of age: and the following are the particulars he gave me of himself. Born at Gloucester, he had been educated at a grammar-school, and had distinguished himself among the scholars by his superior style of acting, when they represented dramatic performances. He was a member of a literary club in the town; and some pieces of his composition, in prose as well as in verse, had been inserted in the Gloucester papers. From hence he was sent to Oxford, where he remained about a year: but he was not contented, and wished above all things to see London, and become an actor. At length, having received fifteen guineas to pay his quarter's board, he decamped with the money from Oxford, hid his gown in a hedge, and travelled to London. There, having no friend to direct him, he fell into bad company, soon squandered his fifteen guineas, could find no way of being introduced to the actors, became contemptible, pawned his clothes, and was in want of bread. As he was walking along the streets, almost famished with hunger, and not knowing what to do, a recruiting bill was put into his hands, which offered an immediate treat and bounty-money to whoever was disposed to serve in America. He instantly repaired to the house of rendezvous, enlisted himself, was put on board a ship, and conveyed to America, without ever writing a line to inform his parents what was become of him. His mental vivacity, and good natural disposition, made him an excellent companion; but he was indolent, thoughtless, and to the last degree imprudent.

John, the Irishman, soon ran away. I began to live very agreeably with the rest. They respected me, and the more so as they found Keimer incapable of instructing them, and as they learned something from me every day. We never worked on a Saturday, it being Keimer's sabbath: so that I had two days a week for reading.

I increased my acquaintance with persons of knowledge and information in the town. Keimer himself treated me with great civility and apparent esteem; and I had nothing to give me uneasiness but my debt to Vernon, which I was unable to pay, my savings as yet being very little. He had the goodness, however, not to ask me for the money.

Our press was frequently in want of the necessary quantity of letter; and there was no such trade as that of letter-founder in America. I had seen the practice of this art at the house of James, in London; but had at the time paid very little attention. I, however, contrived to fabricate a mould. I made use of such letters as we had for punches, founded new letters of lead in matrices of clay, and thus supplied, in a tolerable manner, the wants that were most pressing.

I also, upon occasion, engraved various ornaments, made ink, gave an eye to the shop; in short, I was in every respect the *factotum*. But useful as I made myself, I perceived that my services became every day of less importance, in proportion as the other men improved; and when Keimer paid me my second quarter's wages, he gave me to understand that they were too heavy, and that he thought I ought to make an abatement. He became by degrees less civil, and assumed more the tone of master. He frequently found fault, was difficult to please, and seemed always on the point of coming to an open quarrel with me.

I continued, however, to bear it patiently, conceiving that his ill-humor was partly occasioned by the derangement and embarrassment of his affairs. At last a slight incident broke our connexion. Hearing a noise in the neighborhood, I put my head out at the window to see what was the matter. Keimer being in the street, observed me, and, in a loud and angry tone, told me to mind my work; adding some reproachful words, which piqued me the more, as they were uttered in the street: and the neighbors, whom the same noise had attracted to the windows, were witnesses of the manner in which I was treated. He immediately came up to the printing room, and continued to exclaim against me. The quarrel became warm on both sides, and he gave me notice to quit him at the expiration of three months, as had been agreed upon between us: regretting that he was obliged to give me so long a term. I told him that his regret was superfluous, as I was ready to quit him instantly; and I took my hat and came out of the house, begging Meredith to take care of some things which I left, and bring them to my lodgings.

Meredith came to me in the evening. We talked for some time upon the quarrel that had taken place. He had conceived a great veneration for me, and was sorry I should quit the house while he remained in it. He dissuaded me from returning to my native country, as I began to think of doing. He reminded me that Keimer owed me more than he possessed: that his creditors began to be alarmed; that he kept his shop in a wretched state, often selling things at prime cost for the sake of ready money, and continually giving credit without keeping any accounts; that of consequence he must very soon fail, which would occasion a vacancy from which I might derive advantage. I objected my want of money. Upon which he informed me that his father had a very high opinion of me, and, from a conversation that had passed between them, he was sure that he would advance whatever might be necessary to establish us, if I was willing to enter into partnership with him. 'My time with Keimer,' added he, 'will be at an end next spring. In the meantime we may send to London for our press and types. I know that I am no workman: but if you agree to the proposal, your skill in the business will be balanced by the capital I shall furnish, and we will share the profits equally.' His proposal was seasonable, and I fell in with it. His father, who was then in the town, approved of it. He knew that I had some ascendancy over his son, as I had been able to prevail on him to abstain a long time from drinking brandy: and he hoped that, when more closely connected with him, I should cure him entirely of this unfortunate habit.

I gave the father a list of what it would be necessary to import from London. He took it to a merchant, and the order was given. We agreed to keep the secret till the arrival of the materials, and I was in the meantime to procure work, if possible, in another printing-house; but there was no place vacant, and I remained idle. After some days, Keimer having the expectation of being employed to print some New-Jersey money-bills, that would require types and engravings which I only could furnish, and fearful that Bradford, by engaging me, might deprive him of this undertaking, sent me a very civil message, telling me that old friends ought not to be disunited on account of a few words, which were the effect only of a momentary passion, and inviting me to return to him. Meredith persuaded me to comply with the invitation, particularly as it would afford him more opportunities of improving himself in the business by means of my instructions. I did so; and we lived upon better terms than before our separation.

He obtained the New-Jersey business; and, in order to execute it, I constructed a copper-plate printing-press, the first that had been seen in the country. I engraved various ornaments and vignettes for the bills; and we repaired to Burlington together, where I executed the whole to general satisfaction; and he received a sum of money for this work, which enabled him to keep his head above water for a considerable time longer.

At Burlington I formed an acquaintance with the principal personages of the province; many of whom were commissioned by the Assembly to superintend the press, and to see that no more bills were printed than the law had prescribed. Accordingly they were constantly with us, each in his turn; and he that came, commonly brought with him a friend or two to bear him company. My mind was more cultivated by reading than Keimer's; and it was for this reason, probably, that they set more value on my conversation. They took me to their houses, introduced me to their friends, and treated me with the greatest civility; while Keimer, though master, saw himself a little neglected. He was, in fact, a strange animal, ignorant of the common modes of life, apt to oppose with rudeness generally received opinions, an enthusiast in certain points of religion, disgustingly unclean in his person, and a little knavish withal.

We remained there nearly three months; and at the expiration of this period I could include in the list of my friends, Judge Allen, Samuel Bustil, secretary of the province, Isaac Pearson, Joseph Cooper, several of the Smiths, all members of the Assembly, and Isaac Decon, inspector-general. The last was a shrewd and subtle old man. He told me, that when a boy, his first employment had been that of carrying clay to brick-makers; that he did not learn to write till he was somewhat advanced in life: that he was afterward employed as an underling to a surveyor, who taught him his trade, and that by industry he had at last acquired a competent fortune. 'I foresee,' said he to me one day, 'that you will soon supplant this man, (speaking of Keimer,) and get a fortune in the business at Philadelphia.' He was totally ignorant, at the time, of my intention of establishing myself there, or any where else. These friends were very serviceable to me in the end, as was I also, upon occasion, to some of them; and they have continued ever since their esteem for me.

Before I relate the particulars of my entrance into business, it may be proper to inform you what was at that time the state of my mind as to moral principles, that you may see the degree of influence they had upon the subsequent events of my life.

My parents had given me betimes religious impressions, and I received from my infancy a pious education in the principles of Calvinism. But scarcely was I arrived at fifteen years of age, when, after having doubted in turn of different tenets, according as I found them combated in the different books that I read, I began to doubt of revelation itself. Some volumes against deism fell into my hands. They were said to be the substance of sermons preached at Boyle's Lecture. It happened that they produced on me an effect precisely the reverse of what was intended by the writers; for the arguments of the deists, which were cited in order to be refuted, appeared to me much more forcible than the refutation itself. In a word, I soon became a perfect deist. My arguments perverted some other young persons, particularly Collins and

Ralph. But in the sequel, when I recollected that they had both used me extremely ill, without the smallest remorse; when I considered the behavior of Keith, another freethinker, and my own conduct towards Vernon and Miss Read, which at times gave me great uneasiness, I was led to suspect that this doctrine, though it might be true, was not very useful. I began to entertain a less favorable opinion of my London pamphlet, to which I had prefixed, as a motto, the following lines of Dryden:

> Whatever is is right; though purblind man
> Sees but part of the chain, the nearest link.
> His eyes not carrying to the equal beam
> That poises all above.

And of which the object was to prove, from the attributes of God, his goodness, wisdom, and power, that there could be no such thing as evil in the world; that vice and virtue did not in reality exist, and were nothing more than vain distinctions. I no longer regarded it as so blameless a work as I had formerly imagined; and I suspected that some error must have imperceptibly glided into my argument, by which all the inferences I had drawn from it had been affected, as frequently happens in metaphysical reasonings. In a word, I was at last convinced that truth, probity, and sincerity, in transactions between man and man, were of the utmost importance to the happiness of life; and I resolved from that moment, and wrote the resolution in my Journal, to practice them as long as I lived.

Revelation, indeed, as such, had no influence on my mind; but I was of opinion that, though certain actions could not be bad merely because revelation had prohibited them, or good because it enjoined them, yet it was probable that those actions were prohibited because they were bad for us, or enjoined because advantageous in their nature, all things considered. This persuasion, Divine Providence or some guardian angel, and perhaps a concurrence of favorable circumstances co-operating, preserved me from all immorality, or gross and *voluntary* injustice, to which my want of religion was calculated to expose me, in the dangerous period of youth, and in the hazardous situations in which I sometimes found myself, among strangers, and at a distance from the eye and admonitions of my father. I may say *voluntary*, because the errors into which I had fallen, had been in a manner the forced result either of my own inexperience, or the dishonesty of others. Thus, before I entered on my own new career, I had imbibed solid principles, and a character of probity. I knew their value; and I made a solemn engagement with myself never to depart from them.

I had not long returned from Burlington before our printing materials arrived from London. I settled my accounts with Keimer, and quitted him, with his own consent, before he had any knowledge of our plan. We found a house to let near the market. We took it; and to render the rent less burdensome, (it was then twenty-four pounds a year, but I have since known it to let for seventy,) we admitted Thomas Godfrey, a glazier, with his family, who eased us of a considerable part of it; and with him we agreed to board.

We had no sooner unpacked our letters, and put our press in order, than a person of my acquaintance, George House, brought us a countryman whom he had met in the streets inquiring for a printer. Our money was almost exhausted by the number of things we had been obliged to procure. The five shillings we received from this countryman, the first fruit of our earnings, coming so seasonably, gave me more pleasure than any sum I have since gained; and the recollection of the gratitude I felt on this occasion to George House, has rendered me often more disposed, than perhaps I should otherwise have been, to encourage young beginners in trade.

There are in every country morose beings, who are always prognosticating ruin. There was one of this stamp at Philadelphia. He was a man of fortune, declined in years, had an air of wisdom, and a very grave manner of speaking. His name was Samuel Mickle. I knew him not; but he stopped one day at my door, and asked me if I was the young man who had lately opened a new printing-house. Upon my answering in the affirmative, he said, that he was very sorry for me, as it was an expensive undertaking, and the money that had been laid out upon it would be lost, Philadelphia being a place falling into decay; its inhabitants having all, or nearly all of them, been obliged to call together their creditors. That he knew, from undoubted fact, the circumstances which might lead us to suppose the contrary, such as new buildings, and the advanced price of rent, to be deceitful appearances, which in reality contributed to hasten the general ruin: and he gave me so long a detail of misfortunes, actually existing, or which were soon to take place, that he left me almost in a state of despair. Had I known this man before I entered into trade, I should doubtless never have ventured. He continued, however, to live in this place of decay, and to declaim in the same style, refusing for many years to buy a house because all was going to wreck; and in the end I had the satisfaction to see him pay five times as much for one as it would have cost him had he purchased it when he first began his lamentations.

I ought to have related that during the autumn of the preceding year, I had united the majority of well-informed persons of my acquaintance into a club, which we called by the name of the *Junto*, and the object of which was to improve our understandings. We met every Friday evening. The regulations I drew up, obliged every member to propose in his turn, one or more questions upon some point of morality, politics, or philosophy, which were to be discussed by the society; and to read, once in three months, an essay of his own composition, on whatever subject he pleased. Our debates were under the direction of a president, and were to be dictated only by a sincere desire of truth; the pleasure of disputing, and the vanity of triumph having no share in the business; and in order to prevent undue warmth, every expression which implied obstinate adherence to an opinion, and all direct contradiction, were prohibited, under small pecuniary penalties.

The first members of our club were, Joseph Brientnal, whose occupation was that of a scrivener. He was a middle-aged man, of a good natural disposition, strongly attached to his friends, a great lover of poetry, reading every thing that came in his way, and writing tolerably well, ingenious in many little trifles, and of an agreeable conversation.

Thomas Godfrey, a skilful, though self-taught mathematician, and who was afterward the inventor of what now goes by the name of Hadley's dial; but he had little knowledge out of his own line, and was insupportable in company, always requiring, like the majority of mathematicians that have fallen in my way, an unusual precision in every thing that is said, continually contradicting, or making trifling distinctions; a sure way of defeating all the ends of conversation. He very soon left us.

Nicholas Scull, a surveyor, and who became, afterward, surveyor-general. He was fond of books, and wrote verses.

William Parsons, brought up to the trade of a shoemaker but who, having a taste for reading, had acquired a profound knowledge of mathematics. He first studied them with a view to astrology, and was afterward the first to laugh at his folly. He also became surveyor-general.

William Mawgride, a joiner, and very excellent mechanic, and in other respects a man of solid understanding.

Hugh Meredith, Stephen Potts, and George Webb, of whom I have already spoken.

Robert Grace, a young man of fortune; generous, animated, and witty; fond of epigrams, but more fond of his friends.

And, lastly, William Coleman, at that time a merchant's clerk, and nearly of my own age. He had a cooler and clearer head, a better heart, and more scrupulous morals, than almost any other person I have ever met with. He became a very respectable merchant, and one of our provincial judges. Our friendship subsisted, without interruption, for more than forty years, till the period of his death: and the club continued to exist almost as long.

This was the best school for politics and philosophy that then existed in the province; for our questions, which were read once a week previous to their discussion, induced us to peruse attentively such books as were written upon the subjects proposed, that we might be able to speak upon them more pertinently. We thus acquired the habit of conversing more agreeably; every subject being discussed conformably to our regulations, and in a manner to prevent mutual disgust. To this circumstance may be attributed the long duration of the club; which I shall have frequent occasion to mention as I proceed.

I have introduced it here, as being one of the means on which I had to count for success in my business, every member exerting himself to procure work for us. Breintnal, among others, obtained for us on the part of the quakers, the printing of forty sheets of their history; of which the rest was to be done by Keimer. Our execution of this work was by no means masterly; as the price was very low. It was in folio, upon *pro patria* paper, and in the *pica* letter, with heavy notes in the smallest type. I composed a sheet a day, and Meredith put it to the press. It was frequently eleven o'clock at night, sometimes later, before I had finished my distribution for the next day's task; for the little things which our friends occasionally sent us, kept us back in this work: but I was so determined to compose a sheet a day, that one evening, when my form was imposed, and my day's work, as I thought, to an end, an accident having broken this form, and deranged two complete folio pages, I immediately distributed, and composed them anew before I went to bed.

This unwearied industry, which was perceived by our neighbors, began to acquire us reputation and credit. I learned, among other things, that our new printing-house being the subject of conversation at a club of merchants, who met every evening, it was the general opinion that it would fail; there being already two printing-houses in the town, Keimer's and Bradford's. But Dr. Bard, whom you and I had occasion to see, many years after, at his native town of St. Andrews, in Scotland, was of a different opinion. 'The industry of this Franklin (says he) is superior to any thing of the kind I have ever witnessed. I see him still at work when I return from the club at night, and he is at it again in the morning before his neighbors are out of bed.' This account struck the rest of the assembly, and, shortly after, one of its members came to our house, and offered to supply us with articles of stationery; but we wished not as yet to embarrass ourselves with keeping a shop. It is not for the sake of applause that I enter so freely into the particulars of my industry, but that such of my descendants as shall read these memoirs may know the use of this virtue, by seeing in the recital of my life the effects it operated in my favor.

George Webb, having found a friend who lent him the necessary sum to buy out his time of Keimer, came one day to offer himself to us as a journeyman. We could not employ him immediately; but I foolishly told him, under the rose, that I intended shortly to publish a new periodical paper, and that we should then have work for him. My hopes of success, which I imparted to him, were founded on the circumstance, that the only paper we had in Philadelphia at that time, and which Bradford printed, was a paltry thing, miserably conducted, in no respect amusing, and which yet was profitable. I consequently supposed that a good work of this kind could not fail of success. Webb betrayed my secret to Keimer, who, to prevent me, immediately published the *prospectus* of a paper that he intended to institute himself, and in which Webb was to be engaged.

I was exasperated at this proceeding, and, with a view to counteract them, not being able at present to institute my own paper, I wrote some humorous pieces in Bradford's, under the title of the Busy Body:* and which was continued for several months by Breintnal. I hereby fixed the attention of the public upon Bradford's paper; and the *prospectus* of Keimer, which we turned into ridicule, was treated with contempt. He began, notwithstanding, his paper; and, after continuing it for nine months, having at most not more than ninety subscribers,

* A manuscript note in the file of the American Mercury, preserved in the Philadelphia library, says, that Franklin wrote the first five numbers, and part of the eighth.

he offered it me for a mere trifle. I had for some time been ready for such an engagement; I therefore instantly took it upon myself, and in a few years it proved extremely profitable to me.

I perceive that I am apt to speak in the first person, though our partnership still continued. It is, perhaps, because, in fact, the whole business devolved upon me. Meredith was no compositor, and but an indifferent pressman; and it was rarely that he abstained from hard drinking. My friends were sorry to see me connected with him: but I contrived to derive from it the utmost advantage the case admitted.

Our first number produced no other effect than any other aper which had appeared in the province, as to type and printing; but some remarks, in my peculiar style of writing, upon the dispute which then prevailed between governor Burnet and the Massachusetts assembly, struck some persons as above mediocrity, caused the paper and its editors to be talked of, and in a few weeks induced them to become our subscribers. Many others followed their example; and our subscription continued to increase. This was one of the first good effects of the pains I had taken to learn to put my ideas on paper. I derived this farther advantage from it, that the leading men of the place, seeing in the author of this publication a man so well able to use his pen, thought it right to patronize and encourage me.

The votes, laws, and other public pieces, were printed by Bradford. An address of the House of Assembly to the Governor had been executed by him in a very coarse and incorrect manner. We reprinted it with accuracy and neatness, and sent a copy to every member. They perceived the difference; and it so strengthened the influence of our friends in the Assembly, that we were nominated its printer for the following year.

Among these friends I ought not to forget one member in particular, Mr. Hamilton, whom I have mentioned in a former part of my narrative, and who was now returned from England. He warmly interested himself for me on this occasion, as he did likewise on many others afterward; having continued his kindness to me till his death.

About this period, Mr. Vernon reminded me of the debt I owed him, but without pressing me for payment. I wrote a handsome letter on the occasion, begging him to wait a little longer, to which he consented; and as soon as I was able I paid him principal and interest, with many expressions of gratitude; so that this error of my life was in a manner atoned for.

But another trouble now happened to me, which I had not the smallest reason to expect. Meredith's father, who, according to our agreement, was to defray the whole expense of our printing materials, had only paid a hundred pounds. Another hundred was still due, and the merchant being tired of waiting, commenced a suit against us. We bailed the action, but with the melancholy prospect, that, if the money was not forthcoming at the time fixed, the affair would come to issue, judgment be put in execution, our delightful hopes be annihilated, and ourselves entirely ruined; as the type and press must be sold, perhaps at half their value, to pay the debt.

In this distress, two real friends, whose generous conduct I have never forgotten, and never shall forget while I retain the remembrance of any thing, came to me separately, without the knowledge of each other, and without my having applied to either of them. Each offered whatever money might be necessary to take the business into my own hands, if the thing was practicable, as they did not like I should continue in partnership with Meredith, who, they said, was frequently seen drunk in the streets, and gambling at ale-houses, which very much injured our credit. These friends were William Coleman and Robert Grace. I told them, that while there remained any probability that the Merediths would fulfil their part of the compact, I could not propose a separation, as I conceived myself to be under obligations to them for what they had done already, and were still disposed to do, if they had the power; but, in the end, should they fail in their engagement, and our partnership be dissolved, I should then think myself at liberty to accept the kindness of my friends.

Things remained for some time in this state. At last, I said one day to my partner, 'Your father is, perhaps, dissatisfied with your having a share only in the business, and is unwilling to do for two, what he would do for you alone. Tell me frankly if that be the case, and I will resign the whole to you, and do for myself as well as I can.'—'No, (said he,) my father has really been disappointed in his hopes; he is not able to pay, and I wish to put him to no further inconvenience. I see that I am not at all calculated for a printer; I was educated as a farmer, and it was absurd in me to come here, at thirty years of age, and bind myself apprentice to a new trade. Many of my countrymen are going to settle in North Carolina, where the soil is exceedingly favorable. I am tempted to go with them, and to resume my former occupation. You will doubtless find friends who will assist you. If you will take upon yourself the debts of the partnership, return my father the hundred pounds he has advanced, pay my little personal debts, and give me thirty pounds and a new saddle, I will renounce the partnership, and consign over the whole stock to you.'

I accepted the proposal without hesitation. It was committed to paper, and signed and sealed without delay. I gave him what he demanded, and he departed soon after for Carolina, from whence he sent me, in the following year, two long letters, containing the best accounts that had yet been given of that country, as to climate, soil, agriculture, &c., for he was well versed in these matters. I published them in my newspaper, and they were received with great satisfaction.

As soon as he was gone, I applied to my two friends, and not wishing to give a disobliging preference to either of them, I accepted from each half what he had offered me, and which it was necessary I should have. I paid the partnership debts, and continued the business on my own account, taking care to inform the public, by advertisement, of the partnership being dissolved. This was, I think, in the year 1729, or thereabout.

Nearly at the same period, the people demanded a new emission of paper money; the existing and only one that had taken place in the province, and which amounted to fifteen thousand pounds, being soon to expire. The wealthy inhabitants, prejudiced against every sort of paper currency, from the fear of its depreciation, of which there had been an instance in the province of New-England, to the injury of its holders, strongly opposed this measure. We had discussed this affair in our Junto, in which I was on the side of the new emission; convinced that the first small sum, fabricated in 1723, had done much good in the province, by favoring commerce, industry, and population, since all the houses were now inhabited, and many others building; whereas I remembered to have seen, when I first paraded the streets of Philadelphia, eating my roll, the majority of those in Walnut-street, Second-street, Fourth-street, as well as a great number in Chesnut and other streets, with papers on them signifying that they were to be let; which made me think at that time that the inhabitants of the town were deserting it one after another.

Our debates made me so fully master of the subject, that I wrote and published an anonymous pamphlet, entitled, 'An Inquiry into the Nature and Necessity of Paper Currency.'

it was very well received by the lower and middling classes of people; but it displeased the opulent, as it increased the clamor in favor of the new emission. Having, however, no writer among them capable of answering it, their opposition became less violent; and there being in the House of Assembly a majority for the measure, it passed. The friends I had acquired in the House, persuaded that I had done the country essential service on this occasion, rewarded me by giving me the printing of the bills. It was a lucrative employment, and proved a very seasonable help to me; another advantage which I derived from having habituated myself to write.

Time and experience so fully demonstrated the utility of paper currency, that it never after experienced any considerable opposition; so that it soon amounted to 55,000*l.* and in the year 1739 to 80,000*l.* It has since risen, during the last war, to 350,000*l.*, trade, buildings, and population, having in the interval continually increased: but I am now convinced that there are limits beyond which paper money would be prejudicial.

I soon after obtained, by the influence of my friend Hamilton, the printing of the Newcastle paper money, another profitable work, as I then thought it, little things appearing great to persons of moderate fortune; and they were really great to me, as proving great encouragements. He also procured me the printing of the laws and votes o' that great government, which I retained as long as I continued in the business.

I now opened a small stationer's shop. I kept bonds and agreements of all kinds, drawn up in a more accurate form than had yet been seen in that part of the world; a work in which I was assisted by my friend Breintnal. I had also paper, parchment, pasteboard, books, &c. One Whitemash, an excellent compositor, whom I had known in London, came to offer himself: I engaged him; and he continued constantly and diligently to work with me. I also took an apprentice, the son of Aquilla Rose.

I began to pay, by degrees, the debt I had contracted; and, in order to insure my credit and character as a tradesman, I took care not only to be *really* industrious and frugal, but also to avoid every appearance of the contrary. I was plainly dressed, and never seen in any place of public amusement. I never went a fishing or hunting. A book indeed enticed me sometimes from my work, but it was seldom, by stealth, and occasioned no scandal; and, to show that I did not think myself above my profession, I conveyed home sometimes in a wheelbarrow, the paper I had purchased at the warehouses.

I thus obtained the reputation of being an industrious young man, and very punctual in my payments. The merchants who imported articles of stationery solicited my custom; others offered to furnish me with books, and my little trade went on prosperously.

Meanwhile the credit and business of Keimer diminishing every day, he was at last forced to sell his stock to satisfy his creditors; and he betook himself to Barbadoes, where he lived for some time in a very impoverished state. His apprentice, David Harry, whom I had instructed while I worked with Keimer, having bought his materials, succeeded in the business. I was apprehensive, at first, of finding in Harry a powerful competitor, as he was allied to an opulent and respectable family; I therefore proposed a partnership, which, happily for me, he rejected with disdain. He was extremely proud, thought himself a fine gentleman, lived extravagantly, and pursued amusements which suffered him to be scarcely ever at home; of consequence he became in debt, neglected his business, and business neglected him. Finding in a short time nothing to do in the country, he followed Keimer to Barbadoes, carrying his printing materials with him. There the apprentice employed his old master as a journeyman. They were continually quarrelling; and Harry, still getting in debt, was obliged at last to sell his press and types, and to return to his old occupation of husbandry in Pennsylvania. The person who purchased them, employed Keimer to manage the business; but he died a few years after.

I had now at Philadelphia no competitor but Bradford, who, being in easy circumstances, did not engage in the printing of books, except now and then as workmen chanced to offer themselves; and was not anxious to extend his trade. He had, however, one advantage over me, as he had the direction of the post-office, and was of consequence supposed to have better opportunities of obtaining news. His paper was also supposed to be more advantageous to advertising customers: and in consequence of that supposition, his advertisements were much more numerous than mine: this was a source of great profit to him, and disadvantageous to me. It was to no purpose that I really procured other papers and distributed my own, by means of the post; and the public took for granted my inability in this respect; and I was indeed unable to conquer it in any other mode than by bribing the postboys, who served me only by stealth, Bradford being so illiberal as to forbid them. This treatment of his excited my resentment; and my disgust was so rooted, that when I afterward succeeded him in the post-office, I took care to avoid copying his example.

I had hitherto continued to board with Godfrey, who, with his wife and children, occupied part of my house, and half of the shop for his business; at which, indeed, he worked very little, being always absorbed by mathematics. Mrs. Godfrey formed a wish of marrying me to the daughter of one of her relations. She contrived various opportunities of bringing us together, till she saw that I was captivated; which was not difficult; the lady in question possessing great personal merit. The parents encouraged my addresses, by inviting me continually to supper, and leaving us together, till at last it was time to come to an explanation. Mrs. Godfrey undertook to negotiate our little treaty. I gave her to understand, that I expected to receive with the young lady a sum of money that would enable me at least to discharge the remainder of the debt for my printing materials. It was then, I believe, not more than a hundred pounds. She brought me for answer, that they had no such sum at their disposal. I observed that it might easily be obtained by a mortgage on their house. The reply to this, was, after a few days' interval, that they did not approve of the match; that they had consulted Bradford, and found that the business of a printer was not lucrative; that my letters would soon be worn out, and must be supplied by new ones; that Keimer and Harry had failed, and that, probably, I should do so too. Accordingly they forbade me the house, and the young lady was confined. I know not if they had really changed their minds, or if it was merely an artifice, supposing our affections to be too far engaged for us to desist, and that we should contrive to marry secretly, which would leave them at liberty to give or not as they pleased. But, suspecting this motive, I never went again to their house.

Sometime after, Mrs. Godfrey informed me that they were favorably disposed towards me, and wished me to renew the acquaintance; but I declared a firm resolution never to have any thing more to do with the family. The Godfreys expressed some resentment at this; and as we could no longer agree, they changed their residence, leaving me in possession of the whole house. I then resolved to take no more lodgers

This affair having turned my thoughts to marriage, I looked

around me, and made overtures of alliance in other quarters; but I soon found that the profession of a printer, being generally looked upon as a poor trade, I could expect no money with a wife, at least, if I wished her to possess any other charm. Meanwhile, that passion of youth, so difficult to govern, had often drawn me into intrigues with despicable women who fell in my way; which were not unaccompanied with expense and inconvenience, besides the perpetual risk of injuring my health, and catching a disease which I dreaded above all things. But I was fortunate enough to escape this danger.

As a neighbor and old acquaintance, I had kept up a friendly intimacy with the family of Miss Read. Her parents had retained an affection for me from the time of my lodging in their house. I was often invited thither; they consulted me about their affairs, and I had been sometimes serviceable to them. I was touched with the unhappy situation of their daughter, who was almost always melancholy, and continually seeking solitude. I regarded my forgetfulness and inconstancy, during my abode in London, as the principal part of her misfortune, though her mother had the candor to attribute the fault to herself, rather than to me, because, after having prevented our marriage previously to my departure, she had induced her to marry another in my absence.

Our mutual affection revived; but there existed great obstacles to our union. Her marriage was considered, indeed, as not being valid, the man having, it was said, a former wife still living in England; but of this it was difficult to obtain a proof at so great a distance; and though a report prevailed of his being dead, yet we had no certainty of it; and supposing it to be true, he had left many debts, for the payment of which his successor might be sued. We ventured, nevertheless, in spite of all these difficulties; and I married her on the 1st of September, 1730. None of the inconveniences we had feared, happened to us. She proved to me a good and faithful companion, and contributed essentially to the success of my shop. We prospered together, and it was our mutual study to render each other happy. Thus I corrected, as well as I could, this great error of my youth.

Our club was not at that time established at a tavern. We held our meetings at the house of Mr. Grace, who appropriated a room to the purpose. Some member observed one day that as our books were frequently quoted in the course of our discussions, it would be convenient to have them collected in the room in which we assembled, in order to be consulted upon occasion; and that, by thus forming a common library of

FRANKLIN PLANNING THE PHILADELPHIA LIBRARY.

our individual collections, each would have the advantage of using the books of all the other members, which would nearly be the same as if he possessed them all himself. The idea was approved, and we accordingly brought such books as we thought we could spare, which were placed at the end of the club-room. They amounted not to so many as we expected; and though we made considerable use of them, yet some inconveniences resulting from want of care, it was agreed, after about a year, to discontinue the collection; and each took away such books as belonged to him.

It was now that I first started the idea of establishing, by subscription, a public library. I drew up the proposals, had them engrossed in form by Brockden, the attorney, and my project succeeded, as will be seen in the sequel. * *
* * * * * * * * * *

[The life of Dr. Franklin, as written by himself, so far as it has yet been communicated to the world, breaks off in this place. We understand that it was continued by him somewhat farther, and we hope that the remainder will, at some future period, be communicated to the public. We have no hesitation in supposing, that every reader will find himself greatly interested by the frank simplicity and the philosophical discernment by which these pages are so eminently characterized. We have therefore thought proper, in order as much as possible to relieve his regret, to subjoin the following continuation, by one of the Doctor's intimate friends. It is extracted from an American periodical publication, and was written by the late Dr. Stuber* of Philadelphia.]

* Dr. Stuber was born in Philadelphia, of German parents. He was sent, at an early age, to the university, where his genius, diligence, and amiable temper, soon acquired him the particular notice and favor of those under whose immediate direction he was placed. After passing through the common course of study, in a much shorter time than usual, he left the university, at the age of sixteen, with great reputation. Not long after, he entered on the study of physic; and the zeal with which he pursued it, and the advances he made, gave his friends reason to form the most flattering prospects of his future eminence and usefulness in his profession. As Dr. Stuber's circumstances were very moderate, he did not think this pursuit well calculated to answer them. He therefore relinquished it, after he had obtained a degree in the profession, and qualified himself to practice with credit and success: and immediately entered on the study of the law. While in pursuit of the last-mentioned object, he was prevented, by a premature death, from reaping the fruit of those talents with which he was endowed, and of a youth spent in the ardent and successful pursuit of useful and elegant literature

The promotion of literature had been little attended to in Pennsylvania. Most of the inhabitants were too much immersed in business to think of scientific pursuits; and those few, whose inclinations led them to study, found it difficult to gratify them, from the want of libraries sufficiently large. In such circumstances, the establishment of a public library was an important event. This was first set on foot by Franklin, about the year 1731. Fifty persons subscribed forty shillings each, and agreed to pay ten shillings annually. The number increased; and, in 1742, the company was incorporated by the name of 'The Library Company of Philadelphia.' Several other companies were formed in this city in imitation of it. These were all at length united with the Library Company of Philadelphia, which thus received a considerable accession of books and property. It now contains about eight thousand volumes on all subjects, a philosophical apparatus, and a well chosen collection of natural and artificial curiosities. For its support the Company now possess landed property of considerable value. They have lately built an elegant house in Fifth-street, in the front of which will be erected a marble statue of their founder, Benjamin Franklin.

This institution was greatly encouraged by the friends of literature in America and in Great Britain. The Penn family distinguished themselves by their donations. Amongst the earliest friends of this institution must be mentioned the late Peter Collinson, the friend and companion of Dr. Franklin. He not only made considerable presents himself, and obtained others from his friends, but voluntarily undertook to manage the business of the Company in London, recommending books, purchasing and shipping them. His extensive knowledge, and zeal for the promotion of science, enabled him to execute this important trust with the greatest advantage. He continued to perform these services for more than thirty years, and uniformly refused to accept of any compensation. During this time, he communicated to the directors every information relative to improvements and discoveries in the arts, agriculture, and philosophy.

The beneficial influence of this institution was soon evident. The terms of subscription to it were so moderate, that it was accessible to every one. Its advantages were not confined to the opulent. The citizens in the middle and lower walks of life were equally partakers of them. Hence a degree of information was extended amongst all classes of people. The example was soon followed. Libraries were established in various places, and they are now become very numerous in the United States, and particularly in Pennsylvania. It is to be hoped that they will be still more widely extended, and that information will be everywhere increased. This will be the best security for maintaining our liberties. A nation of well-informed men, who have been taught to know and prize the rights which God has given them, cannot be enslaved. It is in the regions of ignorance that tyranny reigns. It flies before the light of science. Let the citizens of America, then, encourage institutions calculated to diffuse knowledge amongst people; and amongst these, public libraries are not the least important.

In 1732, Franklin began to publish Poor Richard's Almanack. This was remarkable for the numerous and valuable concise maxims which it contained, all tending to exhort to industry and frugality. It was continued for many years. In the almanack for the last year, all the maxims were collected in an address to the reader, entitled, 'The Way to Wealth.' This has been translated into various languages, and inserted in different publications. It has also been printed on a large sheet, and may be seen framed in many houses in this city. This address contains, perhaps, the best practical system of economy that has ever appeared. It is written in a manner intelligible to every one, and which cannot fail of convincing every reader of the justice and propriety of the remarks and advice which it contains. The demand for this almanack was so great, that ten thousand have been sold in one year; which must be considered as a very large number, especially when we reflect, that this country was, at that time, but thinly peopled. It cannot be doubted that the salutary maxims contained in these almanacks, must have made a favorable impression upon many of the readers of them.

It was not long before Franklin entered upon his political career. In the year 1736, he was appointed clerk to the general assembly of Pennsylvania; and was re-elected by succeeding assemblies for several years, until he was chosen a representative for the city of Philadelphia.

Bradford was possessed of some advantages over Franklin, by being postmaster, thereby having an opportunity of circulating his paper more extensively, and thus rendering it a better vehicle for advertisements, &c. Franklin, in his turn, enjoyed these advantages, by being appointed postmaster of Philadelphia in 1737. Bradford, while in office, had acted ungenerously towards Franklin, preventing as much as possible the circulation of his paper. He had now an opportunity of retaliating; but his nobleness of soul prevented him from making use of it.

The police of Philadelphia had early appointed watchmen, whose duty it was to guard the citizens against the midnight robber, and to give an immediate alarm in case of fire. This duty is, perhaps, one of the most important that can be committed to any set of men. The regulations, however, were not sufficiently strict. Franklin saw the dangers arising from this cause, and suggested an alteration, so as to oblige the guardians of the night to be more watchful over the lives and property of the citizens. The propriety of this was immediately perceived, and a reform was effected.

There is nothing more dangerous to growing cities than fires. Other causes operate slowly, and almost imperceptibly: but these in a moment render abortive the labors of ages. On this account there should be, in all cities, ample provisions to prevent fires from spreading. Franklin early saw the necessity of these; and, about the year 1738, formed the first fire company in this city. This example was soon followed by others; and there are now numerous fire companies in the city and liberties. To these may be attributed in a great degree the activity in extinguishing fires, for which the citizens of Philadelphia are distinguished, and the inconsiderable damage which this city has sustained from this cause. Sometime after, Franklin suggested the plan of an association for insuring houses from losses by fire, which was adopted; and the association continues to this day. The advantages experienced from it have been great.

From the first establishment of Pennsylvania, a spirit of dispute appears to have prevailed amongst its inhabitants. During the li etime of William Penn, the constitution had been three times altered. After this period, the history of Pennsylvania is little else than a recital of the quarrels between the proprietaries, or their governors, and the Assembly. The proprietaries contended for the right of exempting their lands from taxes; to which the Assembly would by no means consent. This subject of dispute interfered in almost every question, and prevented the most salutary laws from being enacted. This at times subjected the people to great inconveniences. In the year 1744, during a war between France and Great Britain, some French and Indians had made inroads upon the frontier inhabitants of the province, who were unprovided for such an attack. It became necessary that the citizens should arm for their defence. Governor Thomas recommended to the Assembly, who were then sitting, to pass a militia law. To this they would agree only upon condition that he should give his assent to certain laws, which appeared to them calculated to promote the interests of the people. As he thought these laws would be injurious to the proprietaries, he refused his assent to them; and the Assembly broke up without passing a militia law. The situation of the province was at this time truly alarming; exposed to the continued inroad of an enemy, and destitute of every means of defence. At this crisis Franklin stepped forth, and proposed to a meeting of the citizens of Philadelphia, a plan of a voluntary association for the defence of the province. This was approved of, and signed by twelve hundred persons immediately. Copies were instantly circulated throughout the province; and in a short time the number of signers amounted to ten thousand. Franklin was chosen colonel of the Philadelphia regiment; but he did not think proper to accept of the honor.

Pursuits of a different nature now occupied the greatest part of his attention for some years. He engaged in a course of electrical experiments, with all the ardor and thirst for discovery which characterized the philosophers of that day. Of all the branches of experimental philosophy, electricity had been least explored. The attractive power of amber is mentioned by Theophrastus and Pliny, and from them by later naturalists. In the year 1600, Gilbert, an English physician, enlarged considerably the catalogue of substances which have the property of attracting light bodies. Boyle, Otto Guericke, a burgomaster of Magdeburg, celebrated as the inventor of the air-pump, Dr. Wall, and Sir Isaac Newton, added some facts. Guericke first observed the repulsive power of electricity, and the light and noise produced by it. In 1709, Hawkesbee communicated some important observations and experiments to the world. For several years electricity was entirely neglected, until Mr. Grey applied himself to it, in 1728, with great assiduity. He and his friend Mr. Wheeler, made a great variety of experiments, in which they demonstrated, that electricity may be communicated from one body to another, even without being in contact, and in this way may be conducted to a great distance. Mr. Grey afterward found that, by suspending rods of iron by silk or hair lines, and bringing an excited tube under them, sparks might be drawn, and a light perceived at the extremities in the dark. M. du Faye, intendant of the French king's gardens, made a number of experiments, which added not a little to the science. He made the discovery of two kinas of electricity, which he called *vitreous* and *resinous*; the former produced by rubbing glass, the latter from excited sulphur, sealing-wax, &c. But this idea he afterward gave up as erroneous. Between the years 1739 and 1742, Desauguliers made a number of experiments, but added little of importance. He first used the terms *conductors* and *electrics per se*. In 1742, several ingenious Germans engaged in this subject; of these the principal were, professor Boze, of Wittemburg, professor Winkler of Leipsic, Gordon, a Scotch Benedictine monk, professor of philosophy at Erfurt, and Dr. Ludolf, of Berlin. The result of their researches astonished the philosophers of Europe. Their apparatus was large, and by means of it they were enabled to collect large quantities of the electric fluid, and thus to produce phenomena which had been hitherto unobserved. They killed small birds, and set spirits on fire. Their experiments excited the curiosity of other philosophers. Collinson, about the year 1745, sent to the Library Company of Philadelphia an account of these experiments, together with a tube, and directions how to use it. Franklin, with some of his friends, immediately engaged in a course of experiments; the result of which is well known. He was enabled to make a number of important discoveries, and to propose theories to account for various phenomena; which have been universally adopted, and which bid fair to endure for ages. His observations he communicated, in a series of letters, to his friend Collinson; the first of which is dated March 28, 1747. In these he shows the power of points in drawing and throwing off the electrical matter, which had hitherto escaped the notice of electricians. He also made the grand discovery of a *plus* and *minus*, or of a *positive* and *negative* state of electricity. We give him the honor of this, without hesitation; although the English have claimed it for their countryman Dr. Watson. Watson's paper is dated January 21, 1748 Franklin's July 11, 1747, several months prior. Shortly after Franklin, from his principles of the plus and minus state, explained, in a satisfactory manner, the phenomena of the Leyden phial, first observed by Mr. Cuneus, or by professor Muschenbroeck, of Leyden, which had much perplexed philosophers. He showed clearly, that the bottle, when charged, cantained no more electricity than before, but that as much was taken from one side as was thrown on the other; and that, to discharge it, nothing was necessary but to produce a communication between the two sides, by which the equilibrium might be restored, and that then no signs of electricity would remain. He afterward demonstrated, by experiments, that the electricity did not reside in the coating as had been supposed, but in the pores of the glass itself. After a phial was charged, he removed the coating, and found that upon applying a new coating the shock might still be received. In the year 1749, he first suggested his idea of explaining the phenomena of thundergusts, and of the aurora borealis, upon electrical principles. He points out many particulars in which lightning and electricity agree; and he adduces many facts, and reasonings from facts, in support of his positions. In the same year he conceived the astonishingly bold and grand idea of ascertaining the truth of his doctrine, by actually drawing down the lightning, by means of sharp-pointed iron rods raised into the region of the clouds. Even in this uncertain state, his passion to be useful to mankind displays itself in a powerful manner. Admitting the identity of electricity and lightning, and knowing the power of points in repelling bodies charged with electricity, and in conducting their fire silently and imperceptibly, he suggested the idea of securing houses, ships, &c. from being damaged by lightning, by erecting pointed rods, that should rise some feet above the most elevated part, and descend some feet into the ground or the water. The effect of these, he concluded, would be either to prevent a stroke by repelling the cloud beyond the striking distance, or by drawing off the electrical fire which it contained; or, if they could not effect this, they would at least conduct the electric matter to the earth, without any injury to the building.

It was not until the summer of 1752, that he was enabled to complete his grand and unparalleled discovery by experiment. The plan which he had originally proposed, was, to erect on some high tower, or other elevated place, a sentry-box, from which should rise a pointed iron rod, insulated by being fixed in a cake of resin. Electrified clouds passing over this, would, he conceived, impart to it a portion of their electricity, which would be rendered evident to the senses by sparks being emitted, when a key, the knuckle, or other conductor, was presented to it. Philadelphia at this time afforded no opportunity of trying an experiment of this kind. While Franklin was waiting for the erection of a spire, it occurred to him that he might have more ready access to the region of clouds by means of a common kite. He prepared one by fastening two cross sticks to a silk handkerchief, which would not suffer so much from the rain as paper. To the upright stick was affixed an iron point. The string was, as usual, of hemp, except the lower end, which was silk. Where the hempen string terminated, a key was fastened. With this apparatus, on the appearance of a thundergust approaching, he went out into the commons, accompanied by his son, to whom alone he communicated his intentions, well knowing the ridicule which, too generally for the interest of science, awaits unsuccessful experiments in philosophy. He placed himself under a shade, to avoid the rain—his kite was raised —a thunder-cloud passed over it—no sign of electricity appeared. He almost despaired of success, when, suddenly, he observed the loose fibres of his string to move towards an erect position. He now presented his knuckle to the key, and received a strong spark. How exquisite must his sensations have been at this moment! On this experiment depended the fate of his theory. If he succeeded, his name would rank high among those who had improved science; if he failed, he must inevitably be subjected to the derision of mankind, or, what is worse, their pity, as a well-meaning man, but a weak, silly projector. The anxiety with which he looked for the result of his experiment, may be easily conceived. Doubts and despair had begun to prevail, when the fact was ascertained in so clear a manner, that even the most incredulous could no longer withhold their assent. Repeated sparks were drawn from the key, a phial was charged, a shock given, and all the experiments made which are usually performed with electricity.

About a month before this period, some ingenious Frenchman had completed the discovery in the manner originally proposed by Dr. Franklin. The letters which he sent to Mr. Collinson, it is said, were refused a place in the Transactions of the Royal Society of London. However this may be, Collinson published them in a separate volume, under the title of 'New Experiments and Observations on Electricity, made at Philadelphia, in America.' They were read with avidity, and soon translated into different languages. A very incorrect French translation fell into the hands of the celebrated Buffon, who, notwithstanding the disadvantages under which the work labored, was much pleased with it, and repeated the experiments with success. He prevailed on his friend, M. D'Alibard, to give his countrymen a more correct translation of the American electrician. This contributed much towards spreading a knowledge of Franklin's principles in France. The king, Louis XV. hearing of these experiments, expressed a wish to be a spectator of them. A course of experiments was given at the seat of the Duc D'Ayen, at St. Germain, by M. de Lor. The applauses which the king bestowed upon

FRANKLIN'S ELECTRICAL EXPERIMENTS.

Franklin, excited in Buffon, D'Alibard, and De Lor, an earnest desire of ascertaining the truth of this theory of thundergust. Buffon erected his apparatus on the tower of Montbar, M. D'Alibard at Mary-la-ville, and De Lor at his house in the *Estrapade* at Paris, some of the highest ground in that capital. D'Alibard's machine first showed signs of electricity. On the 10th of May, 1752, a thunder-cloud passed over it, in the absence of M. D'Alibard, and a number of sparks were drawn from it by Coiffier, a joiner, with whom D'Alibard had left directions how to proceed, and by M. Raulet, the prior of Mary-la-ville. An account of this experiment was given to the Royal Academy of Sciences, by M. D'Alibard, in a Memoir, dated May 13th, 1752. On the 18th of May, M. de Lor proved equally successful with the apparatus erected at his own house. These philosophers soon excited those of other parts of Europe to repeat the experiment, amongst whom none signalized themselves more than Father Beccaria, of Turin, to whose observations science is much indebted. Even the cold regions of Russia were penetrated by the ardor for discovery. Professor Richman bade fair to add much to the stock of knowledge on this subject, when an unfortunate flash from his conductor put a period to his existence. The friends of science will long remember with regret, the amiable martyr to electricity.

By these experiments, Franklin's theory was established in the most convincing manner. When the truth of it could no longer be doubted, envy and vanity endeavored to detract from its merit. That an American, an inhabitant of the obscure city of Philadelphia, the name of which was hardly known, should be able to make discoveries, and to frame theories, which had escaped the notice of the enlightened philosophers of Europe, was too mortifying to be admitted. He must certainly have taken the idea from some one else. An American, a being of an inferior order, make discoveries! —Impossible. It was said that the Abbé Nollet, 1748, had suggested the idea of the similarity of lightning and electricity in his *Leçons de Physique*. It is true that the Abbé mentions the idea, but he throws it out as a bare conjecture, and proposes no mode of ascertaining the truth of it. He himself acknowledges, that Franklin first entertained the bold thought of bringing lightning from the heavens, by means of pointed rods fixed in the air. The similarity of lightning and electricity is so strong, that we need not be surprised at notice being taken of it, as soon as electrical phenomena became familiar. We find it mentioned by Dr.

Wall and Mr. Grey, while the science was in its infancy. But the honor of forming a regular theory of thundergusts, of suggesting a mode of determining the truth of it by experiments, and of putting these experiments in practice, and thus establishing the theory upon a firm and solid basis, is incontestably due to Franklin.—D'Alibard, who made the first experiments in France, says, that he only followed the track which Franklin had pointed out.

It has been of late asserted, that the honor of completing the experiment with the electrical kite, does not belong to Franklin. Some late English paragraphs have attributed it to some Frenchman, whose name they do not mention; and the Abbé Bertholon gives it to M. de Romas, assessor to the presidal of Nerac: the English paragraphs probably refer to the same person. But a very slight attention will convince us of the injustice of this procedure: Dr. Franklin's experiment was made in June, 1752: and his letter, giving an account of it, is dated October 19, 1752. M. de Romas made his first attempt on the 14th of May, 1753, but was not successful until the 7th of June; a year after Franklin had completed the discovery, and when it was known to all the philosophers in Europe.

Besides these great principles, Franklin's letters on electricity contain a number of facts and hints, which have contributed greatly towards reducing this branch of knowledge to a science. His friend, Mr. Kinnersley, communicated to him a discovery of the different kinds of electricity, excited by rubbing glass and sulphur. This, we have said, was first observed by M. du Faye; but it was for many years neglected. The philosophers were disposed to account for the phenomena, rather from a difference in the quantity of electricity collected, and even du Faye himself, seems at last to have adopted this doctrine. Franklin at first entertained the same idea; but, upon repeating the experiments, he perceived that Mr. Kinnersley was right; and that the *vitreous* and *resinous* electricity of du Faye were nothing more than the *positive* and *negative* states which he had before observed; and that the glass globe charged *positively*, or increased the quantity of electricity on the prime conductor, while the globe of sulphur diminished its natural quantity, or charged *negatively*. These experiments and observations opened a new field for investigation, upon which electricians entered with avidity; and their labors have added much to the stock of our knowledge.

In September, 1752, Franklin entered upon a course of

experiments, to determine the state of electricity in the clouds. From a number of experiments he formed this conclusion :— 'That the clouds of a thundergust are most commonly in a negative state of electricity, but sometimes in a positive state;' and from this it follows, as a necessary consequence, 'that, for the most part, in thunderstrokes, it is the earth that strikes into the clouds, and not the clouds that strike into the earth.' The letter containing these observations is dated in September, 1753; and yet the discovery of ascending thunder has been said to be of a modern date, and has been attributed to the Abbé Bertholon, who published his memoir on the subject in 1776.

Franklin's letters have been translated into most of the European languages, and into Latin. In proportion as they have become known, his principles have been adopted. Some opposition was made to his theories, particularly by the Abbé Nollet, who was, however, but feebly supported, while the first philosophers in Europe stepped forth in defence of Franklin's principles, amongst whom D'Alibard and Beccaria were the most distinguished. The opposition has gradually ceased, and the Franklinian system is now universally adopted, where science flourishes.

The important practical use which Franklin made of his discoveries, the securing of houses from injury by lightning, has been already mentioned. Pointed conductors are now very common in America; but prejudice has hitherto prevented their general introduction into Europe, notwithstanding the most undoubted proofs of their utility have been given. But mankind can with difficulty be brought to lay aside established practices, or to adopt new ones. And perhaps we have more reason to be surprised that a practice, however rational, which was proposed about forty years ago, should in that time have been adopted in so many places, than that it has not universally prevailed. It is only by degrees that the great body of mankind can be led into new practices, however salutary their tendency. It is now nearly eighty years since inoculation was introduced into Europe and America; and it is so far from being general at present, that it will require one or two centuries to render it so.

In the year 1745, Franklin published an account of his new invented Pennsylvania fireplaces, in which he minutely and accurately states the advantages of different kinds of fireplaces; and endeavors to show, that the one which he describes is to be preferred to any other. This contrivance has given rise to the open stoves now in general use, which, however, differ from it in construction. particularly in no having an air-box at the back, through which a constant supply of air, warmed in its passage, is thrown into the room. The advantages of this are, that as a stream of warm air is continually flowing into the room, less fuel is necessary to preserve a proper temperature, and the room may be so tightened as that no air may enter through cracks—the consequences of which are colds, toothaches, &c.

Although philosophy was a principal object of Franklin's pursuit for several years, he confined himself not to this. In the year 1747, he became a member of the general assembly of Pennsylvania, as a burgess for the city of Philadelphia. Warm disputes subsisted at this time between the Assembly and the proprietaries; each contending for what they conceived to be their just rights. Franklin, a friend to the rights of man from his infancy, soon distinguished himself as a steady opponent of the unjust schemes of the proprietaries. He was soon looked up to as the head of the opposition; and to him have been attributed many of the spirited replies of the Assembly to the messages of the governors. His influence in the body was very great. This arose not from any superior powers of eloquence; he spoke but seldom, and he never was known to make any thing like an elaborate harangue. His speeches often consisted of a single sentence, of a well-told story, the moral of which was obviously to the point. He never attempted the flowry fields of oratory. His manner was plain and mild. His style in speaking was, like that of his writings, simple, unadorned, and remarkably concise. With this plain manner, and his penetrating and solid judgment, he was able to confound the most eloquent and subtle of his adversaries, to confirm the opinions of his friends, and to make converts of the unprejudiced who had opposed him. With a single observation, he has rendered of no avail an elegant and lengthy discourse, and determined the fate of a question of importance.

But he was not contented with thus supporting the rights of the people. He wished to render them permanently secure, which can only be done by making their value properly known; and this must depend upon increasing and extending information to every class of men. We have already seen that he was the founder of the public library, which contributed greatly towards improving the minds of the citizens. But this was not sufficient. The schools then subsisting were in general of little utility. The teachers were men ill qualified for the important duty which they had undertaken; and, after all, nothing more could be obtained than the rudiments of a common English education. Franklin drew up a plan of an academy, to be erected in the city of Philadelphia, suited to 'the state of an infant country;' but in this, as in all his plans, he confined not his views to the present time only. He looked forward to the period when an institution on an enlarged plan would become necessary. With this view, he considered his academy as 'a foundation for posterity to erect a seminary of learning more extensive, and suitable to future circumstances.' In pursuance of this plan, the constitutions were drawn up and signed on the 13th of November, 1749. In these, twenty-four of the most respectable citizens of Philadelphia were named as trustees. In the choice of these, and in the formation of his plan, Franklin is said to have consulted chiefly with Thomas Hopkinson, Esq. the Rev. Richard Peters, then secretary of the province, Tench Francis, Esq. attorney-general, and Dr. Phineas Bond.

The following article shows a spirit of benevolence worthy of imitation; and for the honor of our city, we hope that it continues to be in force.

'In case of the disability of the *rector*, or any master (established on the foundation by receiving a certain salary) through sickness, or any other natural infirmity, whereby he may be reduced to poverty, the trustees shall have power to contribute to his support, in proportion to his distress and merit, and the stock in their hands.'

The last clause of the fundamental rule is expressed in language so tender and benevolent, so truly parental, that it will do everlasting honor to the hearts and heads of the founders.

'It is hoped and expected that the trustees will make it their pleasure, and in some degree their business, to visit the academy often: to encourage and countenance the youth, to countenance and assist the masters, and by all means in their power, advance the usefulness and reputation of the design; that they will look on the students as, in some measure, their own children, treat them with familiarity and affection; and, when they have behaved well, gone through their studies, and are to enter the world, they shall zealously unite, and make all the interest that can be made to promote and establish them, whether in business, offices, marriages, or any other thing for their advantage, in preference to all other persons whatsoever, even of equal merit.'

The constitution being signed and made public, with the names of the gentlemen proposing themselves as trustees and founders, the design was so well approved of by the public spirited citizens of Philadelphia, that the sum of eight hundred pounds per annum, for five years, was in the course of five weeks subscribed for carrying it into execution; and in the beginning of January following (viz. 1750) three of the schools were opened, namely, the Latin and Greek schools, the mathematical school, and the English school. In pursuance of an article in the original plan, a school for educating sixty boys and thirty girls (in the charter since called the Charitable School) was opened; and, amidst all the difficulties with which the trustees have struggled, in respect to their funds, has still been continued full for the space of forty years; so that, allowing three years' education for each boy and girl admitted into it, which is the general rule, at least twelve hundred children have received in it the chief part of their education, who might otherwise, in a great measure, have been left without the means of instruction. And many of those who have been thus educated, are now to be found among the most useful and reputable citizens of this state.

This institution, thus successfully begun, continued daily to flourish, to the great satisfaction of Dr. Franklin; who, notwithstanding the multiplicity of his other engagements and pursuits, at that busy stage of his life, was a constant attendant at the monthly visitations and examinations of the schools, and made it his particular study, by means of his extensive correspondence abroad, to advance the reputation of the seminary, and to draw students and scholars to it from different parts of America and the West Indies. Through the interposition of his benevolent and learned friend, Peter Collinson, of London, upon the application of the trustees, a charter of incorporation, dated July 13, 1753, was obtained from the honorable proprietors of Pennsylvania, Thomas Penn and Richard Penn, Esqrs. accompanied with a liberal benefaction of five hundred pounds sterling: and Dr. Franklin now began in good earnest to please himself with the hopes of a speedy accomplishment of his original design, viz. the establishment of a perfect institution, upon the plan of the European colleges and universities; for which his academy was intended as a nursery or foundation. To elucidate this fact, is a matter of considerable importance in respect to the memory and character of Dr. Franklin, as a philosopher, and as the friend and patron of learning and science; for, notwithstanding what is expressly declared by him in the preamble to the constitutions, viz. that the academy was begun for 'teaching the Latin and Greek languages, with all useful branches of the arts and sciences suitable to the state of an infant country, and laying a foundation for posterity to erect a seminary of learning more extensive, and suitable to their future circumstances;' yet it has been suggested of late, as upon Dr. Franklin's authority, that the Latin and Greek, or the dead languages, are an incumbrance upon a scheme of liberal education, and that the engrafting or founding a college, or more extensive seminary upon his academy, was without his approbation or agency, and gave him discontent. If the reverse of this does not already appear from what has been quoted above, the following letters will put the matter beyond dispute. They were written by him to a gentleman, who had at that time published the idea of a college, suited to the circumstances of a young country (meaning New-York;) a copy of which having been sent to Dr. Franklin for his opinion, gave rise to that correspondence which terminated about a year afterward, in erecting the college upon the foundation of the academy, and establishing that gentleman at the head of both, where he still continues, after a period of thirty-six years, to preside with distinguished reputation.

From these letters also, the state of the academy, at that time, will be seen.

'SIR, '*Philad. April* 19, 1753.

'I received your favor of the 11th instant, with your new piece of *Education*, which I shall carefully peruse, and give you my sentiments of it, as you desire, by next post.

'I believe the young gentlemen, your pupils, may be entertained and instructed here, in mathematics and philosophy, to satisfaction. Mr. Alison* (who was educated at Glasgow) has been long accustomed to teach the latter, and Mr. Grew† the former: and I think their pupils made great progress. Mr. Alison has the care of the Latin and Greek school, but as he has now three good assistants,‡ he can very well afford some hours every day for the instruction of those who are engaged in higher studies. The mathematical school is pretty well furnished with instruments. The English library is a good one; and we have belonging to it a middling apparatus

* The Rev. and learned Mr. Francis Alison, afterward D. D. and vice-provost of the college.

† Mr. Theophilus Grew, afterward professor of mathematics in the college.

‡ Those assistants were at that time, Mr. Charles Thompson, late secretary of Congress, Mr. Paul Jackson, and Mr. Jacob Duche.

for experimental philosophy, and propose speedily to complete it. The Loganian library, one of the best collections in America, will shortly be opened; so that neither books nor instruments will be wanting; and as we are determined always to give good salaries, we have reason to believe we may have always an opportunity of choosing good masters; upon which, indeed, the success of the whole depends. We are obliged to you for your kind offers in this respect, and when you are settled in England, we may occasionally make use of your friendship and judgment.

'If it suits your convenience to visit Philadelphia before you return to Europe, I shall be extremely glad to see and converse with you here, as well as to correspond with you after your settlement in England; for an acquaintance and communication with men of learning, virtue, and public spirit, is one of my greatest enjoyments.

'I do not know whether you ever happened to see the first proposals I made for erecting this academy. I send them enclosed. They had (however imperfect) the desired success, being followed by a subscription of four thousand pounds, towards carrying them into execution. And as we are fond of receiving advice, and are daily improving by experience, I am in hopes we shall, in a few years, see a *perfect institution.*

'I am very respectfully, &c.

Mr. Smith.' 'B. Franklin.'

'Sir, '*Philad. May* 3, 1753.

'Mr. Peters has just now been with me, and we have compared notes on your new piece. We find nothing in the scheme of education, however excellent, but what is, in our opinion, very practicable. The great difficulty will be to find the Aratus,§ and other suitable persons, to carry it into execution; but such may be had if proper encouragement be given. We have both received great pleasure in the perusal of it. For my part, I know not when I have read a piece that has more affected me—so noble and just are the sentiments, so warm and animated the language; yet as censure from your friends may be of more use as well as more agreeable to you than praise, I ought to mention, that I wish you

§ The name given to the principal or head of the ideal college, the system of education in which hath nevertheless been nearly realized, or followed as a model, in the college and academy of Philadelphia, and some other American seminaries, for many years past had omitted not only the quotation from the Review,‖ which you are now justly dissatisfied with, but those expressions of resentment against your adversaries, in pages 65 and 79. In such cases, the noblest victory is obtained by neglect, and by shining on.

'Mr. Allen has been out of town these ten days; but before he went he directed me to procure him six copies of your piece. Mr. Peters has taken ten. He proposed to have written to you; but omits it, as he expects soon to have the pleasure of seeing you here. He desires me to present his affectionate compliments to you, and to assure you, that you will be very welcome to him. I shall only say that you may depend on my doing all in my power to make your visit to Philadelphia agreeable to you.

'I am, &c.

'*Mr. Smith.*' 'B. FRANKLIN.'

'DEAR SIR 'Philad. Nov. 27, 1753.

Having written you fully, *via* Bristol, I have now little to add. Matters relating to the academy remain in *statu quo*. The trustees would be glad to see a rector established there, but they dread entering into new engagements till they are got out of debt; and I have not yet got them wholly over to my opinion, that a good professor, or teacher of the higher branches of learning, would draw so many scholars as to pay great part, if not the whole of his salary. Thus, unless the proprietors (of the province) shall think fit to put the finishing hand to our institution, it must, I fear, wait some few years longer before it can arrive at that state of perfection, which to me it seems now capable of; and all the pleasure I promised myself in seeing you settled among us, vanishes into smoke.

'But good Mr. Collinson writes me word, that no endeavors of his shall be wanting; and he hopes, with the archbishop's assistance, to be able to prevail with our proprietors.¶ I pray God grant them success.

'My son presents his affectionate regards, with

'Dear Sir, yours, &c.

'B. FRANKLIN.'

‖ The quotation alluded to (from the London Monthly Review for 1749) was judged to reflect too severely on the discipline and government of the English Universities of Oxford and Cambridge, and was expunged from the following editions of this work.

¶ Upon the application of Archbishop Herring and P. Collin

'P. S. I have not been favored with a line from you since your arrival in England.'

'DEAR SIR, 'Philad. April 18, 1754.

'I have had but one letter from you since your arrival in England, which was but a short one, *via* Boston, dated October 18th, acquainting me that you had written largely by Captain Davis.—Davis was lost, and with him your letters, to my great disappointment.—Mesnard and Gibbon have since arrived here, and I hear nothing from you. My comfort is, an imagination that you only omit writing because you are coming, and propose to tell me every thing *viva voce*. So not knowing whether this letter will reach you, and hoping either to see or hear from you by the Myrtilla, Captain Budden's ship, which is daily expected, I only add, that I am with great esteem and affection,

'Yours, &c.

'*Mr. Smith*.' 'B. FRANKLIN.

About a month after the date of this last letter, the gentleman to whom it was addressed arrived in Philadelphia, and was immediately placed at the head of the seminary; whereby Dr. Franklin and the other trustees were enabled to prosecute their plan, for perfecting the institution, and opening the college upon the large and liberal foundation on which it now stands: for which purpose, they obtained their additional charter, dated May 27th, 1755.

Thus far we thought it proper to exhibit in one view Dr. Franklin's services in the foundation and establishment of this seminary. He soon afterward embarked for England in the public service of his country; and having been generally employed abroad, in the like service, for the greatest part of the remainder of his life, (as will appear in our subsequent account of the same,) he had but few opportunities of taking any farther active part in the affairs of the seminary, until his final return in the year 1785, when he found its charters violated, and his ancient colleagues, the original founders, deprived of their trust, by an act of the legislature; and although his own name had been inserted amongst the new trustees, yet he declined to take his seat among them, or any

---

son, Esq. at Dr. Franklin's request (aided by the letters of Mr. Allen and Mr. Peters,) the Hon. Thomas Penn, Esq. subscribed an annual sum, and afterward gave at least 5000*l*. to the founding or engrafting the college upon the academy.

concern in the management of their affairs, till the institution was restored by law to its original owners. He then assembled his old colleagues at his own house, and being chosen their president, all their future meetings were, at his request, held there, till within a few months of his death, when with reluctance, and at their desire, lest he might be too much injured by his attention to their business, he suffered them to meet at the college.

Franklin not only gave birth to many useful institutions himself, but he was also instrumental in promoting those which had originated with other men. About the year 1752, an eminent physician of this city, Dr. Bond, considering the deplorable state of the poor, when visited with disease, conceived the idea of establishing a hospital. Notwithstanding very great exertions on his part, he was able to interest few people so far in his benevolent plan, as to obtain subscriptions from them. Unwilling that his scheme should prove abortive, he sought the aid of Franklin, who readily engaged in the business, both by using his influence with his friends, and by stating the advantageous influence of the proposed institution in his paper. These efforts were attended with success. Considerable sums were subscribed; but they were still short of what was necessary. Franklin now made another exertion. He applied to the Assembly; and, after some opposition, obtained leave to bring in a bill, specifying, that as soon as two thousand pounds were subscribed, the same sum should be drawn from the treasury, by the speaker's warrant, to be applied to the purposes of the institution. The opposition, as the sum was granted upon a contingency, which they supposed would never take place, were silent, and the bill passed. The friends of the plan now redoubled their efforts to obtain subscriptions to the amount stated in the bill, and were soon successful. This was the foundation of the Pennsylvanian Hospital, which, with the Bettering House and Dispensary, bears ample testimony of the humanity of the citizens of Philadelphia.

Dr. Franklin had conducted himself so well in the office of postmaster, and had shown himself to be so well acquainted with the business of that department, that it was thought expedient to raise him to a more dignified station. In 1753 he was appointed deputy postmaster-general for the British colonies. The profits arising from the postage of letters formed no inconsiderable part of the revenue, which the crown of Great Britain derived from these colonies. In the hands of

Franklin, it is said, that the post-office in America yielded annually thrice as much as that of Ireland.

The American colonies were much exposed to depredations on their frontiers by the Indians; and, more particularly, whenever a war took place between France and England. The colonies, individually, were hitherto too weak to take efficient measures for their own defence, or they were unwilling to take upon themselves the whole burden of erecting forts and maintaining garrisons, whilst their neighbors, who partook equally with themselves of the advantages, contributed nothing to the expense. Sometimes also the disputes, which subsisted between the governors and assemblies, prevented the adoption of means of defence: as we have seen was the case in Pennsylvania in 1745. To devise a plan of union between the colonies, to regulate this and other matters, appeared a desirable object. To accomplish this, in the year 1754, commissioners from New-Hampshire, Massachusetts, Rhode Island, New-Jersey, Pennsylvania, and Maryland, met at Albany. Dr. Franklin attended here as a commissioner from Pennsylvania, and produced a plan, which, from the place of meeting, has been usually termed, 'The Albany Plan of Union.' This proposed that application should be made for an act of parliament, to establish in the colonies a general government, to be administered by a president-general, appointed by the crown, and by a grand council, consisting of members, chosen by the representatives of the different colonies; their number being in direct proportion to the sums paid by each colony into the general treasury, with this restriction, that no colony should have more than seven, nor less than two representatives. The whole executive authority was committed to the president-general. The power of legislation was lodged in the grand council and president-general jointly; his consent being made necessary to passing a bill into a law. The power vested in the president and council was to declare war and peace, and to conclude treaties with the Indian nations; to regulate trade with, and to make purchases of vacant lands from them, either in the name of the crown, or of the union; to settle new colonies, to make laws for governing these, until they should be erected into separate governments; and to raise troops, build forts, and fit out armed vessels, and to use other means for the general defence; and, to effect these things, a power was given to make laws, laying such duties, imposts, or taxes, as they should find necessary, and as would be least burdensome to the people. All laws were to be sent to England for the king's approbation; and, unless disapproved of within three years, were to remain in force. All officers of the land or sea service were to be nominated by the president-general, and approved of by the general council; civil officers were to be nominated by the council, and approved of by the president. Such are the outlines of the plan proposed, for the consideration of the congress, by Dr. Franklin. After several days' discussion, it was unanimously agreed to by the commissioners, a copy transmitted to each assembly, and one to the king's council. The fate of it was singular. It was disapproved of by the ministry of Great Britain, because it gave too much power to the representatives of the people; and it was rejected by every assembly, as giving to the president-general, the representative of the crown, an influence greater than appeared to them proper, in a plan of government intended for freemen. Perhaps this rejection, on both sides, is the strongest proof that could be adduced of the excellence of it, as suited to the situation of America and Great Britain at that time. It appears to have steered exactly in the middle between the opposite interests of both.

Whether the adoption of this plan would have prevented the separation of America from Great Britain, is a question which might afford much room for speculation. It may be said, that, by enabling the colonies to defend themselves, it would have removed the pretext upon which the stamp-act, tea-act, and other acts of the British parliament, were passed; which excited a spirit of opposition, and laid the foundation for the separation of the two countries. But, on the other hand, it must be admitted, that the restriction laid by Great Britain upon our commerce, obliging us to sell our produce to her citizens only, and to take from them various articles, of which, as our manufacturers were discouraged, we stood in need, at a price greater than that for which they could have been obtained from other nations, must inevitably produce dissatisfaction, even though no duties were imposed by the parliament; a circumstance which might still have taken place. Besides as the president-general was to be appointed by the crown, he must, of necessity, be devoted to its views, and would, therefore, refuse to assent to any laws, however salutary to the community, which had the most remote tendency to injure the interests of his sovereign. Even should they receive his assent, the approbation of the king was to be necessary; who would indubitably, in every instance, prefer the advantage of his own dominions to that of his colonies. Hence would ensue perpetual disagreemen between the council and the president-general, and thus between the people of America and the crown of Great Britain:—while the colonies continued weak, they would be obliged to submit, and as soon as they acquired strength, they would become more urgent in their demands, until, at length, they would shake off the yoke, and declare themselves independent.

Whilst the French were in possession of Canada, their trade with the natives extended very far: even to the back of the British settlements. They were disposed, from time to time, to establish posts within the territory, which the English claimed as their own. Independent of the injury to the fur trade, which was considerable, the colony suffered this farther inconvenience, that the Indians were frequently instigated to commit depredations on their frontiers. In the year 1753, encroachments were made upon the boundaries of Virginia. Remonstrances had no effect. In the ensuing year, a body of men was sent out under the command of Mr. Washington, who, though a very young man, had, by his conduct in the preceding year, shown himself worthy of such an important trust. Whilst marching to take possession of the post at the juncture of the Allegany and Monongahela, he was informed that the French had already erected a fort there. A detachment of their men marched against him. He fortified himself as strongly as time and circumstances would admit. A superiority of numbers soon obliged him to surrender *Fort Necessity*. He obtained honorable terms for himself and men, and returned to Virginia. The government of Great Britain now thought it necessary to interfere. In the year, 1755, General Braddock, with some regiments of regular troops and provincial levies, was sent to dispossess the French of the posts upon which they had seized. After the men were all ready, a difficulty occurred, which had nearly prevented the expedition. This was the want of wagons. Franklin now stepped forward, and with the assistance of his son, in a little time procured a hundred and fifty. Braddock unfortunately fell into an ambuscade, and perished, with a number of his men. Washington, who had accompanied him as an aid-de-camp, and had warned him, in vain, of his danger, now displayed great military talents in effecting a retreat of the remains of the army, and in forming a junction with the rear, under Colonel Dunbar, upon whom the chief command now devolved. With some difficulty they brought their little body to a place of safety, but they found it necessary to destroy their wagons and baggage, to prevent them from falling into the hands of the enemy. For the wagons, which he had furnished, Franklin had given bonds to a large amount. The owners declared their intention of obliging him to make a restitution of their property. Had they put their threats into execution, ruin must inevitably have been the consequence. Governor Shirley, finding that he had incurred those debts for the service of the government, made arrangements to have them discharged, and released Franklin from his disagreeable situation.

The alarm spread through the colonies, after the defeat of Braddock, was very great. Preparations to arms were everywhere made. In Pennsylvania, the prevalence of the quaker interest prevented the adoption of any system of defence which would compel the citizens to bear arms. Franklin introduced into the Assembly a bill for organizing a militia, by which every man was allowed to take arms or not, as to him should appear fit. The quakers, being thus left at liberty, suffered the bill to pass; for, although their principles would not suffer them to fight, they had no objection to their neighbors fighting for them. In consequence of this act, a very respectable militia was formed. The sense of impending danger infused a military spirit in all, whose religious tenets were not opposed to war. Franklin was appointed colonel of a regiment in Philadelphia, which consisted of 1200 men.

The north-western frontier being invaded by the enemy, it became necessary to adopt measures for its defence. Franklin was directed by the governor to take charge of this. A power of raising men, and of appointing officers to command them, was vested in him. He soon levied a body of troops, with which he repaired to the place at which their presence was necessary. Here he built a fort, and placed the garrison in such a posture of defence, as would enable them to withstand the inroads to which the inhabitants had been previously exposed. He remained here for some time, in order the more completely to discharge the trust committed to him. Some business of importance at length rendered his presence necessary in the Assembly, and he returned to Philadelphia.

The defence of her colonies was a great expense to Great Britain. The most effectual mode of lessening this was, to put arms into the hands of the inhabitants, and to teach them their use. But England wished not that the Americans should become acquainted with their own strength. Sh was apprehensive, that, as soon as this period arrived, they would no longer submit to that monopoly of their trade, which to them was highly injurious, but extremely advantageous to the mother country. In comparison with the profits of this, the expense of maintaining armies and fleets to defend them was trifling. She fought to keep them dependent upon her for protection; the best plan which could be devised for retaining them in peaceable subjection. The least appearance of a military spirit was therefore to be guarded against; and, although a war then raged, the act of organizing a militia was disapproved of by the ministry. The regiments which had been formed under it were disbanded, and the defence of the province intrusted to regular troops.

The disputes between the proprietaries and the people continued in full force, although a war was raging on the frontiers. Not even the sense of danger was sufficient to reconcile, for ever so short a time, their jarring interests. The Assembly still insisted upon the justice of taxing the proprietary estates, but the governors constantly refused their assent to this measure, without which no bill could pass into a law. Enraged at the obstinacy, and what they conceived to be unjust proceedings of their opponents, the Assembly at length determined to apply to the mother country for relief. A petition was addressed to the king, in council, stating the inconveniences under which the inhabitants labored, from the attention of the proprietaries to their private interests, to the neglect of the general welfare of the community, and praying for redress. Franklin was appointed to present this address, as agent for the province of Pennsylvania, and departed from America in June, 1757. In conformity to the instructions which he had received from the legislature, he held a conference with the proprietaries who then resided in England, and endeavored to prevail upon them to give up the long-contested point. Finding that they would hearken to no terms of accommodation, he laid his petition before the council. During this time, Governor Denny assented to a law imposing a tax, in which no discrimination was made in favor of the estates of the Penn family. They, alarmed at this intelligence, and Franklin's exertions, used their utmost endeavors to prevent the royal sanction being given to this law, which they represented as highly iniquitous, designed to throw the burden of supporting government upon them, and calculated to produce the most ruinous consequences to them and their posterity.—

The cause was amply discussed before the privy council. The Penns found here some strenuous advocates; nor were there wanting some who warmly espoused the side of the people. After some time spent in debate, a proposal was made, that Franklin should solemnly engage, that the assessment of the tax should be so made, as that the proprietary estates should pay no more than a due proportion. This he agreed to perform, the Penn family withdrew their opposition, and tranquillity was thus once more restored to the province.

The mode in which this dispute was terminated, is a striking proof of the high opinion entertained of Franklin's integrity and honor, even by those who considered him as inimical to their views. Nor was their confidence ill-founded. The assessment was made upon the strictest principle of equity; and the proprietary estates bore only a proportionable share of the expenses of supporting government.

After the completion of this important business, Franklin remained at the court of Great Britain, as agent for the province of Pennsylvania. The extensive knowledge which he possessed of the situation of the colonies, and the regard which he always manifested for their interests, occasioned his appointment to the same office by the colonies of Massachusetts, Maryland, and Georgia. His conduct in this situation, was such as rendered him still more dear to his countrymen.

He had now an opportunity of indulging in the society of those friends, whom his merits had procured him while at a distance. The regard which they had entertained for him was rather increased by a personal acquaintance. The opposition which had been made to his discoveries in philosophy gradually ceased, and the rewards of literary merit were abundantly conferred upon him. The Royal Society of London, which had at first refused his performances admission into its transactions, now thought it an honor to rank him among its fellows. Other societies of Europe were equally ambitious of calling him a member. The university of St. Andrew's, in Scotland, conferred upon him the degree of Doctor of Laws. Its example was followed by the universities of Edinburgh and Oxford. His correspondence was sought for by the most eminent philosophers of Europe. His letters to these abound with true science, delivered in the most simple unadorned manner.

The province of Canada was at this time in the possession of the French, who had originally settled it. The trade with the Indians, for which its situation was very convenient, was exceedingly lucrative. The French traders here found a market for their commodities, and received in return large quantities of rich furs, which they disposed of at a high price in Europe. Whilst the possession of this country was highly advantageous to France, it was a grievous inconvenience to the inhabitants of the British colonies. The Indians were almost generally desirous to cultivate the friendship of the French, by whom they were abundantly supplied with arms and ammunition. Whenever a war happened, the Indians were ready to fall upon the frontiers: and this they frequently did, even when Great Britain and France were at peace. From these considerations it appeared to be the interest of Great Britain to gain possession of Canada. But the importance of such an acquisition was not well understood in England. Franklin about this time published his Canada pamphlet, in which he, in a very forcible manner, pointed out the advantages which would result from the conquest of this province.

An expedition against it was planned, and the command given to General Wolfe. His success is well known. At the treaty in 1762, France ceded Canada to Great Britain, and by her cession of Louisiana, at the same time relinquished all her possessions on the continent of America.

Although Dr. Franklin was now principally occupied with political pursuits, he found time for philosophical studies. He extended his electrical researches, and made a variety of experiments, particularly on the tourmalin. The singular properties which this stone possesses, of being electrified on one side positively, and on the other negatively, by heat alone without friction, had been but lately observed.

Some experiments on the cold produced by evaporation, made by Dr. Cullen, had been communicated to Dr. Franklin, by Professor Simpson, of Glasgow. These he repeated, and found, that, by the evaporation of ether in the exhausted receiver of an air-pump, so great a degree of cold was produced in a summer's day, that water was converted into ice. This discovery he applied to the solution of a number of phenomena, particularly a singular fact, which philosophers had endeavored in vain to account for, viz. that the temperature of the human body, when in health, never exceeds 96 degrees of Fahrenheit's thermometer, although the atmosphere which surrounds it may be heated to a much greater degree. This he attributed to the increased perspiration, and consequent evaporation, produced by the heat.

In a letter to Mr. Small, of London, dated in May, 1760, Dr. Franklin makes a number of observations, tending to show that, in North America, northeast storms begin in the southwest parts. It appears, from actual observation, that a northeast storm, which extended a considerable distance, commenced at Philadelphia nearly four hours before it was felt at Boston. He endeavored to account for this, by supposing that, from heat, some rarefaction takes place about the gulf of Mexico, that the air farther north being cooler rushes in, and is succeeded by the cooler and denser air still farther north, and that thus a continued current is at length produced.

The tone produced by rubbing the brim of a drinking glass with a wet finger had been generally known. A Mr. Puckeridge, an Irishman, by placing on a table a number of glasses of different sizes, and tuning them by partly filling them with water, endeavored to form an instrument capable of playing tunes. He was prevented, by an untimely end, from bringing his invention to any degree of perfection. After his death, some improvements were made upon his plan. The sweetness of the tones induced Dr. Franklin to make a variety of experiments; and he at length formed that elegant instrument, which he has called the Armonica.

In the summer of 1762, he returned to America. On his passage he observed the singular effect produced by the agitation of a vessel, containing oil floating on water. The surface of the oil remains smooth and undisturbed, whilst the water is agitated with the utmost commotion. No satisfactory explanation of this appearance has, we believe, ever been given.

Dr. Franklin received the thanks of the Assembly of Pennylvania, 'as well for the faithful discharge of his duty to that province in particular, as for the many and important services done to America in general, during his residence in Great Britain.' A compensation of 5000*l*. Pennsylvania currency, was also decreed him for his services during six years.

During his absence he had been annually elected member of the Assembly. On his return to Pennsylvania he again took his seat in this body, and continued a steady defender of the liberties of the people.

In December, 1762, a circumstance which caused great alarm in the province took place. A number of Indians had resided in the county of Lancaster, and conducted themselves uniformly as friends to the white inhabitants. Repeated depredations on the frontiers had exasperated the inhabitants to such a degree, that they determined on revenge upon ever Indian. A number of persons, to the amount of about 120 principally inhabitants of Donegal and Peckstang or Paxton townships, in the county of York, assembled; and, mounted on horseback, proceeded to the settlement of these harmless and defenceless Indians, whose number had now been reduced to about twenty. The Indians received intelligence of the attack which was intended against them; but disbelieved it Considering the white people as their friends, they apprehended no danger from them. When the party arrived at the Indian settlement. they found only some women and children, and a few old men, the rest being absent at work. They murdered all whom they found, and amongst others the chief Shaheas, who had always been distinguished for his friendship to the whites. This bloody deed excited much indignation in the well-disposed part of the community.

The remainder of these unfortunate Indians, who, by absence, had escaped this massacre, were conducted to Lancaster, and lodged in the jail as a place of security. The Governor issued a proclamation, expressing the strongest disapprobation of the action, offering a reward for the discovery of the perpetrators of the deed, and prohibiting all injuries to the peaceable Indians in future. But notwithstanding this, a party of the same men shortly after marched to Lancaster, broke open the jail, and inhumanly butchered the innocent Indians who had been placed there for security. Another proclamation was issued, but it had no effect. A detachment marched down to Philadelphia, for the express purpose of murdering some friendly Indians, who had been removed to the city for safety. A number of the citizens armed in their defence. The quakers, whose principles are opposed to fighting, even in their own defence, were most active upon this occasion. The rioters came to Germantown. The Governor fled for safety to the house of Dr. Franklin, who, with some others, advanced to meet the Paxton boys as they were called, and had influence enough to prevail upon them to relinquish their undertaking, and return to their homes.

The disputes between the proprietaries and the Assembly, which, for a time had subsided, were again revived. The proprietaries were dissatisfied with the concessions made in favor of the people, and made great struggles to recover the privilege of exempting their estates from taxation, which they had been induced to give up.

In 1763, the Assembly passed a militia bill, to which the Governor refused to give his assent, unless the Assembly would agree to certain amendments which he proposed. These consisted in increasing the fines; and, in some cases, substituting death for fines. He wished, too, that the officers should be appointed altogether by himself, and not be nominated by the people, as the bill had proposed. These amendment the Assembly considered as inconsistent with the spirit of liberty. They would not adopt them; the Governor was obstinate, and the bill was lost.

These and various other circumstances increased the uneasiness which subsisted between the proprietaries and the Assembly to such a degree, that, in 1764, a petition to the King was agreed to by the house, praying an alteration from a *proprietary* to a *regal* government. Great opposition was made to this measure, not only in the house, but in the public prints. A speech of Mr. Dickenson, on the subject, was published, with a preface by Dr. Smith, in which great pains were taken to show the impropriety and impolicy of this proceeding. A speech of Mr. Galloway, in reply to Mr. Dickenson, was published, accompanied with a preface by Dr. Franklin; in which he ably opposed the principles laid down in the preface to Mr. Dickenson's speech. This application to the throne produced no effect. The proprietary government was still continued.

At the election for a new Assembly, in the fall of 1764, the friends of the proprietaries made great exertions to exclude those of the adverse party; and they obtained a small majority in the city of Philadelphia. Franklin now lost his seat in the house, which he had held for fourteen years. On the meeting of the Assembly, it appeared that there was still a decided majority of Franklin's friends. He was immediately appointed provincial agent, to the great chagrin of his enemies, who made a solemn protest against his appointment; which was refused admission upon the minutes, as being unprecedented. It was, however, published in the papers, and produced a spirited reply from him, just before his departure for England.

The disturbances produced in America by Mr. Grenville's stampt act, and the opposition made to it, are well known. Under the Marquis of Rockingham's administration, it appeared expedient to endeavor to calm the minds of the colonists; and the repeal of the odious tax was contemplated. Amongst other means of collecting information on the disposition of the people to submit to it, Dr. Franklin was called to the bar of the House of Commons. The examination which he here underwent was published, and contains a striking proof of the extent and accuracy of his information, and the facility with which he communicated his sentiments. He represented facts in so strong a point of view, that the inexpediency of the act must have appeared clear to every unprejudiced mind. The act, after some opposition, was repealed, about a year after it was enacted, and before it had ever been carried into execution.

In the year 1766, he made a visit to Holland and Germany, and received the greatest marks of attention from men of science. In his passage through Holland, he learned from the watermen the effect which a diminution of the quantity of water in canals has, in impeding the progress of boats. Upon his return to England, he was led to make a number of experiments, all of which tended to confirm the observation. These, with an explanation of the phenomena, he communicated in a letter to his friend, Sir John Pringle, which is among his philosophical pieces.

In the following year he travelled into France, where he met with a no less favorable reception than he had experienced in Germany. He was introduced to a number of literary characters, and to the king, Louis XV.

Several letters written by Hutchinson, Oliver, and others, to persons in eminent stations in Great Britain, came into the hands of Dr. Franklin. These contained the most violent invectives against the leading characters of the state of Massachusetts, and strenuously advised the prosecution of vigorous measures, to compel the people to obedience to the measures of the ministry. These he transmitted to the legistature, by whom they were published. Attested copies of them were sent to Great Britain, with an address, praying the King to discharge from office persons who had rendered themselves so obnoxious to the people, and who had shown themselves so unfriendly to their interests. The publication of these letters produced a duel between Mr. Whately and Mr. Temple; each of whom was suspected of having been instrumental in procuring them. To prevent any farther disputes on this subject, Dr. Franklin, in one of the public papers, declared that he had sent them to America, but would give no information concerning the manner in which he had obtained them: nor was this ever discovered.

Shortly after, the petition of the Massachusetts Assembly was taken up for examination, before the privy council. Dr. Franklin attended as agent for the Assembly; and here a torrent of the most violent and unwarranted abuse was poured upon him by the solicitor-general, Wedderburne, who was engaged as council for Oliver and Hutchinson. The petition was declared to be scandalous and vexatious, and the prayer of it refused.

Although the parliament of Great Britain had repealed the stamp-act, it was only upon the principle of expediency. They still insisted upon their right to tax the colonies; and, at the same time that the stamp-act was repealed, an act was passed declaring the right of parliament to bind the colonies in all cases whatsoever. This language was used even by the most strenuous opposers of the stamp-act: and, amongst others, by Mr. Pitt. This right was never recognized by the colonists; but, as they flattered themselves that it would not be exercised, they were not very active in remonstrating against it. Had this pretended right been suffered to remain dormant, the colonists would cheerfully have furnished their quota with supplies, in the mode to which they have been accustomed; that is, by acts of their own assemblies, in consequence of requisitions from the Secretary of State. If this practice had been pursued, such was the disposition of the colonies towards their mother country, that notwithstanding the disadvantages under which they labored from restraints upon their trade, calculated solely for the benefit of the commercial and manufacturing interests of Great Britain, a separation of the two countries might have been a far distant event. The Americans, from their earliest infancy, were taught to venerate a people from whom they were descended; whose language, laws, and manners, were the same as their own. They looked up to them as models of perfection; and, in their prejudiced minds, the most enlightened nations of Europe were considered as almost barbarians, in comparison with Englishmen. The name of an Englishman conveyed to an American the idea of every thing good and great. Such sentiments instilled into them in early life, what but a repetition of unjust treatment could have induced them to entertain the most distant thought of separation! The duties on glass, paper, leather, painters' colors, tea, &c. the disfranchisement of some of the colonies; the obstruction to the measures of the legislature in others, by the King's governors; the contemptuous treatment of their humble remonstrances, stating their grievances, and praying a redress of them, and other violent and oppressive measures, at length excited an ardent spirit of opposition. Instead of endeavoring to allay this by a more lenient conduct, the ministry seemed resolutely bent upon reducing the colonies to the most slavish obedience to their decrees. But this only tended to aggravate. Vain were the efforts made use of to prevail upon them to lay aside their designs, to convince them of the impossibility of carrying them into effect, and of the mischievous consequences which must ensue from a continuance of the attempt. They persevered with a degree of inflexibility scarcely paralleled.

The advantages which Great Britain derived from her colonies were so great, that nothing but a degree of infatuation, little short of madness, could have produced a continuance of measures calculated to keep up a spirit of uneasiness, which might occasion the slightest wish for a separation. When we consider the great improvements in the science of government, the general diffusion of the principles of liberty amongst the people of Europe, the effects which these have already produced in France, and the probable consequences which will result from them elsewhere, all of which are the offspring of the American Revolution, it cannot but appear strange, that events of so great moment to the happiness of mankind, should have been ultimately occasioned by the wickedness or ignorance of a British ministry.

Dr. Franklin left nothing untried to prevail upon the ministry to consent to a change of measures. In private conversations, and in letters to persons of government, he continually expatiated upon the impolicy and injustice of their conduct towards America; and stated, that, notwithstanding the attachment of the colonists to the mother country, a repetition of ill-treatment must ultimately alienate their affections. They listened not to his advice. They blindly persevered in their own schemes, and left to the colonists no alternative, but opposition, or unconditional submission. The latter accorded not with the principles of freedom, which they had been taught to revere. To the former they were compelled, though reluctantly, to have recourse.

Dr. Franklin, finding all efforts to restore harmony between Great Britain and her colonies useless, returned to America, in the year 1775; just after the commencement of hostilities. The day after his return he was elected by the legislature of Pennsylvania a delegate to Congress. Not long after his election a committee was appointed, consisting of Mr. Lynch, Mr. Harrison, and himself, to visit the camp at Cambridge, and, in conjunction with the commander-in-chief, to endeavor to convince the troops, whose term of enlistment was about to expire, of the necessity of their continuing in the field, and persevering in the cause of their country.

In the fall of the same year he visited Canada, to endeavor

to unite them in the common cause of liberty; but they could not be prevailed upon to oppose the measures of the British government. M. le Roy, in a letter annexed to Abbé Fauchet's eulogium of Dr. Franklin, states, that the ill-success of this negotiation was occasioned, in a great degree, by religious animosities, which subsisted between the Canadians and their neighbors, some of whom had, at different times, burnt their chapels.

When Lord Howe came to America, in 1776, vested with power to treat with the colonists, a correspondence took place between him and Dr. Franklin on the subject of a reconciliation. Dr. Franklin was afterward appointed, together with John Adams and Edward Rutledge, to wait upon the commissioners, in order to learn the extent of their powers. These were found to be only to grant pardons upon submission. These were terms which would not be accepted; and the object of the commissioners could not be obtained.

The momentous question of independence was shortly after brought into view, at a time when the fleets and armies, which were sent to enforce obedience, were truly formidable. With an army, numerous indeed, but ignorant of discipline, and entirely unskilled in the art of war, without money, without a fleet, without allies, and with nothing but the love of liberty to support them, the colonists determined to separate from a country, from which they had experienced a repetition of injury and insult. In this question, Dr. Franklin was decidedly in favor of the measure proposed, and had great influence in bringing others over to his sentiments.

The public mind had been already prepared for the event, by Mr. Paine's celebrated pamphlet, *Common Sense*. There is good reason to believe that Dr. Franklin had no inconsiderable share, at least, in furnishing materials for this work.

In the convention which assembled at Philadelphia in 1776, for the purpose of establishing a new form of government for the state of Pennsylvania, Dr. Franklin was chosen president. The late constitution of this state, which was the result of their deliberations, may be considered as a digest of his principles of government. The single legislature, and the plural executive, seemed to have been his favorite tenets.

In the latter end of 1776, Dr. Franklin was appointed to assist at the negotiation which had been set on foot by Silas Deane, at the court of France. A conviction of the advantages of a commercial intercourse with America, and a desire of weakening the British empire by dismembering it, first induced the French court to listen to proposals of an alliance

But they showed rather a reluctance to the measure, which by Dr. Franklin's address, and particularly by the success of the American arms against General Burgoyne, was at length overcome; and in February, 1778, a treaty of alliance, offensive and defensive, was concluded; in consequence of which, France became involved in the war with Great Britain.

Perhaps no person could have been found more capable of rendering essential services to the United States at the court of France than Dr. Franklin. He was well known as a philosopher, and his character was held in the highest estimation. He was received with the greatest marks of respect by all the literary characters; and his respect was extended amongst all classes of men. His personal influence was hence very considerable. To the effects of this was added those of various performances which he published, tending to establish the credit and character of the United States. To his exertions in this way may, in no small degree, be ascribed the success of the loans negotiated in Holland and France, which greatly contributed to bring the war to a happy conclusion.

The repeated ill-success of their arms, and more particularly the capture of Cornwallis and his army, at length convinced the British nation of the impossibility of reducing the Americans to subjection. The trading interest particularly became clamorous for peace. The ministry were unable longer to oppose their wishes. Provisional articles of peace were agreed to, and signed at Paris, on the 30th of November, 1782, by Dr. Franklin, Mr. Adams, Mr. Jay, and Mr. Laurens, on the part of the United States; and by Mr. Oswald on the part of Great Britain. These formed the basis of the definitive treaty, which was concluded the 3d of September, 1783, and signed by Dr. Franklin, Mr. Adams, and Mr. Jay, on the one part, and by Mr. David Hartley on the other.

On the 3d of April, 1783, a treaty of amity and commerce, between the United States and Sweden, was concluded at Paris by Dr. Franklin and the Count Von Krutz.

A similar treaty with Prussia was concluded in 1785, not long before Dr. Franklin's departure from Europe.

Dr. Franklin did not suffer his political pursuits to engross his whole attention. Some of his performances made their appearance in Paris. The object of these was generally the promotion of industry and economy.

In the year 1784, when animal magnetism made great noise in the world, particularly at Paris, it was thought a matter of

CONCLUSION OF THE ARMISTICE.

such importance, that the King appointed commissioners to examine into the foundation of this pretended science. Dr. Franklin was one of the number. After a fair and diligent examination, in the course of which Mesmer repeated a number of experiments in the presence of the commissioners, some of which were tried upon themselves, they determined it was a mere trick, intended to impose upon the ignorant and credulous.—Mesmer was thus interrupted in his career to wealth and fame, and a most insolent attempt to impose upon the human understanding baffled.

The important ends of Dr. Franklin's mission being completed by the establishment of American independence, and the infirmities of age and disease coming upon him, he became desirous of returning to his native country. Upon application to Congress to be recalled, Mr. Jefferson was appointed to succeed him, in 1785. Sometime in September of the same year, Dr. Franklin arrived in Philadelphia. He was shortly after chosen a member of the supreme executive council for the city, and soon after was elected president of the same.

When a convention was called to meet in Philadelphia in 1787, for the purpose of giving more energy to the government of the Union, by revising and amending the articles of confederation, Dr. Franklin was appointed a delegate from the State of Pennsylvania. He signed the constitution which they proposed for the union, and gave it the most unequivocal marks of his approbation.

A society for political inquiries, of which Dr. Franklin was president, was established about this period. The meetings were held at his house. Two or three essays read in this society were published. It did not long continue.

In the year 1787, two societies were established in Philadelphia, founded on the principles of the most liberal and refined humanity.—*The Philadelphia Society for alleviating the miseries of public persons; and the Pennsylvanian Society, for promoting the abolition of Slavery, the relief of free negroes unlawfully held in bondage, and the improvement of the condition of the African race.* Of each of these Dr. Franklin was president. The labors of these bodies have been crowned with great success; and they continue to prosecute, with unwearied diligence, the laudable designs for which they were established.

Dr. Franklin's increasing infirmities prevented his regular attendance at the council-chamber; and, in 1788, he retired wholly from public life.

His constitution had been a remarkable good one. He had been little subject to disease, except an attack of the gout occasionally, until about the year 1781, when he was first attacked with symptoms of the calculous complaint, which continued during his life. During the intervals of pain from this grievous disease, he spent many cheerful hours, conversing in the most agreeable and instructive manner. His faculties were entirely unimpaired, even to the hour of his death.

His name as president of the abolition society, was signed to the memorial presented to the house of representatives of the United States, on the 12th of February, 1789, praying them to exert the full extent of power vested in them by the constitution, in discouraging the traffic of the human species. This was his last public act.—In the debates to which this memorial gave rise, several attempts were made to justify the trade. In the Federal Gazette of March 25th, there appeared an essay signed Historicus, written by Dr. Franklin, in which he communicated a speech, said to have been delivered in the Divan of Algiers, in 1687, in opposition to the prayer of the petition of a sect called *Erika*, or purists, for the abolition of piracy and slavery. This pretended African speech was an excellent parody of one delivered by Mr. Jackson of Georgia. All the arguments urged in favor of negro slavery, are applied with equal force to justify the plundering and enslaving of Europeans. It affords, at the same time, a demonstration of the futility of the arguments in defence of the slave-trade, and of the strength of mind and ingenuity of the author, at his advanced period of life. It furnished, too, a no less convincing proof of his power of imitating the style of other times and nations than his celebrated parable against persecution. And as the latter led many persons to search the Scriptures with a view to find it, so the former caused many persons to search the book-stores and libraries for the work from which it was said to be extracted.*

In the beginning of April following, he was attacked with a fever and complaint of his breast, which terminated his existence. The following account of his illness was written by his friend and physician, Dr. Jones.

'The stone, with which he had been afflicted for several years, had for the last twelve months confined him chiefly to his bed; and, during the extreme painful paroxisms, he was obliged to take large doses of laudanum to mitigate his tor-

* This speech will be found among his Essays

tures—still, in the intervals of pain, he not only amused himself with reading and conversing cheerfully with his family, and a few friends who visited him, but was often employed in doing business of a public as well as private nature, with various persons who waited on him for that purpose; and in every instance displayed, not only that readiness and disposition of doing good, which was the distinguishing characteristic of his life, but the fullest and clearest possession of his uncommon mental abilities; and not unfrequently indulged himself in those *jeux d'esprit* and entertaining anecdotes, which were the delight of all who heard him.

'About sixteen days before his death, he was seized with a feverish indisposition, without any particular symptoms attending it, till the third or fourth day, when he complained of a pain in the left breast, which increased till it became extremely acute, attended with a cough and laborious breathing. During this state, when the severity of his pains sometimes drew forth a groan of complaint, he would observe—that he was afraid he did not bear them as he ought—acknowledged his grateful sense of the many blessings he had received from that Supreme Being, who had raised him from small and low beginnings to such high rank and consideration among men—and made no doubt but his present afflictions were kindly intended to wean him from a world, in which he was no longer fit to act the part assigned him. In this frame of body and mind he continued till five days before his death, when his pain and difficulty of breathing entirely left him, and his family were flattering themselves with the hopes of his recovery, when an imposthumation, which had formed itself in his lungs, suddenly burst, and discharged a great quantity of matter, which he continued to throw up while he had sufficient strength to do it; but, as that failed, the organs of respiration became gradually oppressed—a calm lethargic state succeeded—and, on the 17th of April, 1790, about eleven o'clock at night, he quietly expired, closing a long and useful life of eighty-four years and three months.'

It may not be amiss to add to the above account, that Dr. Franklin, in the year 1735, had a severe pleurisy, which terminated in an abcess of the left lobe of his lungs, and he was then almost suffocated with the quantity and suddenness of the discharge. A second attack, of a similar nature, happened some years after this, from which he soon recovered, and did not appear to suffer any inconvenience in his respiration from these diseases.

The following epitaph on himself, was written by him many years previous to his death—

THE BODY
OF
BENJAMIN FRANKLIN
Printer,
(like the cover of an old book,
its contents torn out,
and stript of its lettering and gilding,)
lies here food for worms;
yet the work itself shall not be lost,
for it will (as he believed) appear once more
in a new
and more beautiful edition,
corrected and amended
by
THE AUTHOR.

EXTRACTS

FROM THE LAST WILL AND TESTAMENT OF

DR. FRANKLIN.

WITH regard to my books, those I had in France, and those I left in Philadelphia, being now assembled together nere, and a catalogue made of them, it is my intention to dispose of the same as follows:

My 'History of the Academy of Sciences,' in sixty or seventy volumes quarto, I give to the philosophical society of Philadelphia, of which I have the honor to be president. My collection in folio of 'Les Arts et les Metiers,' I give to the American philosophical society, established in New-England, of which I am a member. My quarto edition of the same, 'Arts et les Metiers,' I give to the library company of Philadelphia. Such and so many of my books as I shall mark, in the said catalogue, with the name of my grandson, Benjamin Franklin Bache, I do hereby give to him; and such and so many of my books as I shall mark in the said catalogue with the name of my grandson, William Bache, I do hereby give to him; and such as shall be marked with the name of Jonathan Williams, I hereby give to my cousin of that name. The residue and remainder of all my books, manuscripts, and papers, I do give to my grandson William Temple Franklin. My share in the library company of Philadelphia, I give to my grandson Benjamin Franklin Bache, confiding that he will permit his brothers and sisters to share in the use of it.

I was born in Boston, New-England, and owe my first instructions in literature to the free grammar-schools established there. I therefore give one hundred pounds sterling to my executors, to be by them, the survivors or survivor of them, paid over to the managers or directors of the free-schools in my native town of Boston, to be by them, or the person or persons who shall have the superintendence and management of the said schools, put out to interest, and so continued at interest for ever; which interest annually shall be laid out in silver medals, and given as honorary rewards annually by the directors of the said free schools, for the encouragement of scholarship in the said schools, belonging to the said town, in such a manner as to the discretion of the select men of the said town shall seem meet.

Out of the salary that may remain due to me, as president of the State, I give the sum of two thousand pounds to my executors, to be by them, the survivors or survivor of them, paid over to such person or persons as the legislature of this State, by an act of assembly, shall appoint to receive the same, in trust to be employed in making the Schuylkil navigable.

During the number of years I was in business as a stationer, printer, and postmaster, a great many small sums became due to me, for books, advertisements, postage of letters, and other matters, which were not collected, when, in 1757, I was sent by the Assembly to England as their agent—and by subsequent appointments continued there till 1775—when, on my return, I was immediately engaged in the affairs of congress, and sent to France in 1776, where I remained nine years, not returning till 1785; and the said debts not being demanded in such a length of time, have become in a manner obsolete, yet are nevertheless justly due.—These as they are stated in my great folio ledger, E, I bequeath to the contributors of the Pennsylvania hospital, hoping that those debtors, and the descendants of such as are deceased, who now, as I find, make some difficulty of satisfying such antiquated demands as just debts, may, however, be induced to pay or give them as charity to that excellent institution. I am sensible that much must be inevitably lost; but I hope something considerable may be recovered. It is possible, too, that some of the parties charged may have existing old unsettled accounts against me: in which case the managers of the said hospital, will allow and deduct the amount, or pay the balance, if they find it against me.

I request my friends, Henry Hill, Esq. John Jay, Esq. Francis Hopkinson, and Mr. Edward Duffield, of Bonfield, in Philadelphia county, to be the executors of this my last will and testament, and I hereby nominate and appoint them for that purpose.

I would have my body buried with as little expense or ceremony as can be.

PHILADELPHIA, *July* 17, 1788.

CODICIL.

I, BENJAMIN FRANKLIN, in the foregoing or annexed last will and testament, having farther considered the same, do think proper to make and publish the following codicil, or addition thereto:

It having long been a fixed and political opinion of mine, that in a democratical state there ought to be no offices of profit, for the reasons I have given in an article of my drawing in our constitution, it was my intention, when I accepted the office of president, to devote the appointed salary to some public use: accordingly I had already, before I made my last will, in July last, given large sums of it to colleges, schools, building of churches, &c., and in that will I bequeathed two thousand pounds more to the state, for the purpose of making the Schuylkil navigable; but understanding since, that such a sum would do but little towards accomplishing such a work, and that the project is not likely to be undertaken for many years to come—and having entertained another idea, which I hope may be more extensively useful, I do hereby revoke and annul the bequest, and direct that the certificates I have for what remains due to me of that salary, be sold towards raising the sum of two thousand pounds sterling, to be disposed of as I am now about to order.

It has been an opinion, that he who receives an estate from his ancestors, is under some obligation to transmit the same to posterity. This obligation lies not on me, who never inherited a shilling from any ancestor or relation. I shall, however, if it is not diminished by some accident before my death, leave a considerable estate among my descendants and relations. The above observation is made merely as some apology to my family, for making bequests that do not appear to have any immediate relation to their advantage.

I was born in Boston, in New-England, and owe my first instructions in literature to the free grammar-schools established there. I have therefore considered those schools in my will.

But I am also under obligations to the state of Massachusetts, for having, unasked, appointed me formerly their agent, with a handsome salary, which continued some years; and, although I accidentally lost in their service, by transmitting Governor Hutchinson's letters, much more than the amount of what they gave me, I do not think that ought in the least to diminish my gratitude. I have considered, that, among artizans, good apprentices are most likely to make good citizens; and having myself been bred to a manual art, printing, in my native town, and afterward assisted to set up my business in Philadelphia by kind loans of money from two friends there, which was the foundation of my fortune, and of all the utility in life that may be ascribed to me—I wish to be useful even after my death, if possible, in forming and advancing other young men, that may be serviceable to their country in both these towns.

To this end I devote two thousand pounds sterling, which I give, one thousand thereof to the inhabitants of the town of Boston, in Massachusetts, and the other thousand to the inhabitants of the city of Philadelphia, in trust, to and for the uses, intents, and purposes, hereinafter mentioned and declared.

The said sum of one thousand pounds sterling, if accepted by the inhabitants of the town of Boston, shall be managed under the direction of the select men, united with the ministers of the oldest episcopalian, congregational, and presbyterian churches of that town, who are to let out the same upon interest, at five per cent. per annum, to such young married artificers, under the age of twenty-five years, as have served an apprenticeship in the said town, and faithfully fulfilled the duties required in their indentures, so as to obtain a good moral character from at least two respectable citizens, who are willing to become sureties in a bond, with the applicants, for the repayment of the money so lent, with interest, according to the terms herein after prescribed; all which bonds are to be taken for Spanish milled dollars, or the value thereof in current gold coin: and the manager shall keep a bound book or books, wherein shall be entered the names of those who shall apply for, and receive the benefit of this institution, and of their sureties, together with the sums lent, the dates, and other necessary and proper records, respecting the business and concerns of this institution; and as these loans are intended to assist young married artificers in setting up their business, they are to be proportioned by the discretion of the managers, so as not to exceed sixty pounds sterling to one person, nor to be less than fifteen pounds.

And if the number of appliers so entitled should be so large as that the sum will not suffice to afford to every one some assistance, these aids may therefore be small at first, but as the capital increases by the accumulated interest, they will be more ample. And in order to serve as many as possible in their turn, as well as to make the repayment of the principal borrowed more easy, each borrower shall be obliged to pay with the yearly interest one-tenth part of the principal; which sums of principal and interest so paid in, shall be again let out to fresh borrowers. And it is presumed, that there will always be found in Boston, virtuous and benevolent citizens, willing to bestow a part of their time in doing good to the rising generation, by superintending and managing this institution gratis; it is hoped, that no part of the money will at any time lie dead, or be diverted to other purposes, but be continually augmenting by the interest, in which case there may in time be more than the occasion in Boston may require; and then some may be spared to the neighboring or other towns in the said State of Massachusetts, which may desire to have it, such towns engaging to pay punctually the interest, and the proportions of the principal, annually to the inhabitants of the town of Boston. If this plan is executed, and succeeds, as projected, without interruption for one hundred years, the sum will then be one hundred and thirty-one thousand pounds; of which I would have the managers of the donation to the town of Boston then lay out, at their discretion, one hundred thousand pounds in public works, which may be judged of most general utility to the inhabitants: such as fortifications, bridges, aqueducts, public buildings, baths, pavements, or whatever may make living in the town more convenient to its people, and render it more agreeable to strangers resorting thither for health, or a temporary residence. The remaining thirty-one thousand pounds I would have continued to be let out to interest, in the manner above directed, for one hundred years; as I hope it will have been found, that the institution has had a good effect on the conduct of youth, and been of service to many worthy characters and useful citizens. At the end of this second term, if no unfortunate accident has prevented the operation, the sum will be four million and sixty-one thousand pounds sterling, of which I leave one million and sixty-one thousand pounds to the disposition and management of the inhabitants of the town of Boston, and three millions to the disposition of the government of the state; not presuming to carry my views farther.

All the directions herein given respecting the disposition and management of the donation to the inhabitants of Boston, I would have observed respecting that to the inhabitants of Philadelphia; only as Philadelphia is incorporated, I request the corporation of that city to undertake the management, agreeable to the said directions; and I do hereby vest them with full and ample powers for that purpose. And having considered that the covering its ground-plat with buildings and pavement, which carry off most rain, and prevent its soaking into the earth, and renewing and purifying the springs, whence the water of the wells must gradually grow worse, and in time be unfit for use, as I find has happened in all old cities; I recommend, that, at the end of the first hundred years, if not done before, the corporation of the city employ a part of the hundred thousand pounds in bringing by pipes the water of Wissahickon creek into the town, so as to supply the inhabitants, which I apprehend may be done without great difficulty, the level of that creek being much above that of the city, and may be made higher by a dam. I also recommend making the Schuylkill completely navigable. At the end of the second hundred years, I would have the disposition of the four million and sixty-one thousand pounds divided between the inhabitants of the city of Philadelphia and the government of Pennsylvania, in the same manner as herein directed with respect to that of the inhabitants of Boston and the government of Massachusetts. It is my desire that this institution should take place, and begin to operate within one year after my decease; for which purpose due notice should be publicly given, previous to the expiration of that year, that those for whose benefit this establishment is intended may make their respective applications: and I hereby direct my executors, the survivors and survivor of them, within six months after my decease, to pay over the said sum of two thousand pounds sterling to such persons as shall be appointed by the selectmen of Boston, and the corporation of Philadelphia, and to receive and take charge of their respective sums of one thousand pounds each for the purposes aforesaid. Considering the accidents to which all human affairs and projects are subject in such a length of time, I have perhaps too much flattered myself with a vain fancy, that these dispositions, if carried into execution, will be continued without interruption, and have the effects proposed; I hope, however, that if the inhabitants of the two cities should not think fit to undertake the execution, they will at least accept the offer of these donations as a mark of my good-will, token of my gratitude, and testimony of my desire to be useful to them even after my departure. I wish, indeed, that they may both undertake to endeavor the execution of my project, because, I think, that, though unforeseen difficulties may arise, expedients will be found to remove them, and the scheme be found practicable. If one of them accepts the money with the conditions, and the other refuses, my will then is, that both sums be given to the inhabitants of the city accepting; the whole to be applied to the same purposes, and under the same regulations directed for the separate parts; and if both refuse, the money remains of course in the mass of my estate, and it is to be disposed of therewith, according to my will made the seventeenth day of July, 1788.

My fine crab-tree walking-stick, with a gold head curiously wrought in the form of the Cap of Liberty, I give to my friend, and the friend of mankind, General Washington. If it were a sceptre, he has merited it, and would become it.

ESSAYS,

HUMOROUS, MORAL, AND LITERARY.

ON EARLY MARRIAGES.

To John Alleyn, Esq.

Dear Jack,

You desire, you say, my impartial thoughts on the subject of an early marriage, by way of answer to the numberless objections that have been made by numerous persons to your own. You may remember, when you consulted me on the occasion, that I thought youth on both sides to be no objection. Indeed, from the marriages that have fallen under my observation, I am rather inclined to think, that early ones stand the best chance of happiness. The temper and habits of the young are not yet become so stiff and uncomplying, as when more advanced in life; they form more easily to each other, and hence, many occasions of disgust are removed. And if youth has less of that prudence which is necessary to manage a family, yet the parents and elder friends of young married persons are generally at hand to afford their advice, which amply supplies that defect; and, by early marriage, youth is sooner formed to regular and useful life; and possibly some of those accidents, or connexions, that might have injured the constitution, or reputation, or both, are thereby happily prevented. Particular circumstances of particular persons, may possibly sometimes make it prudent to delay entering into that state; but, in general, when nature has rendered our bodies fit for it, the presumption is in nature's favor, that she has not judged amiss in making us desire it. Late marriages are often attended, too, with this farther inconvenience, that there is not the same chance that the parents should live to see their offspring educated. 'Late children,' says the Spanish proverb, 'are early orphans.' A melancholy reflection to those whose case it may be! With us in America, marriages are generally in the morning of life: our children are therefore educated and settled in the world by noon: and thus our business being done, we have an afternoon and evening of cheerful leisure to ourselves, such as our friend at present enjoys. By these early marriages we are blessed with more children; and from the mode among us, founded by nature, of every mother suckling and nursing her own child, more of them are raised. Thence the swift progress of population among us, unparalleled in Europe. In fine, I am glad you are married, and congratulate you most cordially upon it. You are now in the way of becoming a useful citizen; and you have escaped the unnatural state of celibacy for life —the fate of many here who never intended it, but who having too long postponed the change of their conditions, find, at length, that is too late to think of it, and so live all their lives in a situation that greatly lessens a man's value. An odd volume of a set of books, bears not the value of its proportion to the set; what think you of the odd half of a pair of scissors; it can't well cut any thing; it may possibly serve to scrape a trencher.

Pray make my compliments and best wishes acceptable to your bride. I am old and heavy, or I should ere this have presented them in person. I shall make but small use of the old man's privilege, that of giving advice to younger friends. Treat your wife always with respect, it will procure respect to you, not only from her but from all that observe it. Never use any slighting expression to her, even in jest; for slights in jest, after frequent bandyings, are apt to end in angry earnest. Be studious in your profession, and you will be learned. Be industrious and frugal, and you will be rich. Be sober and temperate, and you will be healthy. Be in general virtuous, and you will be happy. At least, you will, by such conduct, stand the best chance for such consequences. I pray God to bless you both! being ever your affectionate friend,

B. Franklin.

ON THE DEATH OF HIS BROTHER, MR. JOHN FRANKLIN

To Miss Hubbard.

I CONDOLE with you. We have lost a most dear and valuable relation. But it is the will of God, and nature, that these mortal bodies be laid aside, when the soul is to enter into real life. This is rather an embryo state, a preparation for living. A man is not completely born until he be dead. Why then should we grieve that a new child is born among the immortals, a new member added to their happy society? We are spirits. That bodies should be lent us, while they can afford us pleasure, assist us in acquiring knowledge, or doing good to our fellow-creatures, is a kind and benevolent act of God. When they become unfit for these purposes, and afford us pain instead of pleasure, instead of an aid become an incumbrance, and answer none of the intentions for which they were given, it is equally kind and benevolent that a way is provided by which we may get rid of them. Death is that way. We ourselves, in some cases, prudently choose a partial death. A mangled painful limb, which cannot be restored, we willingly cut off. He who plucks out a tooth, parts with it freely, since the pain goes with it: and he who quits the whole body, parts at once with all pains, and possibilities of pains and diseases, it was liable to, or capable of making him suffer.

Our friend and we were invited abroad on a party of pleasure which is to last for ever. His chair was ready first; and he is gone before us. We could not all conveniently start together; and why should you and I be grieved at this, since we are soon to follow and know where to find him?—Adieu.

B. FRANKLIN.

TO THE LATE DR. MATHER, OF BOSTON.

REV. SIR,

I RECEIVED your kind letter with your excellent advice to the people of the United States, which I read with great pleasure, and hope it will be duly regarded. Such writings, though they may be lightly passed over by many readers, yet if they make a deep impression on one active mind in a hundred, the effects may be considerable.

Permit me to mention one little instance, which, though it relates to myself, will not be quite uninteresting to you. When I was a boy, I met with a book entitled 'Essays to do good,' which I think was written by your father. It had been so little regarded by a former possessor, that several leaves of it were torn out; but the remainder gave me such a turn of thinking, as to have an influence on my conduct through life; for I have always set a greater value on the character of a doer of good, than any other kind of reputation; and if I have been, as you seem to think, a useful citizen, the public owes the advantage of it to that book.

You mention your being in your seventy-eighth year. I am in my seventy-ninth. We are grown old together. It is now more than sixty years since I left Boston; but I remember well both your father and grandfather, having heard them both in the pulpit, and seen them in their houses. The last time I saw your father was the beginning of 1724, when I visited him after my first trip to Pennsylvania. He received me in his library; and, on my taking leave, showed me a shorter way out of the house, through a narrow passage, which was crossed by a beam over head. We were still talking as I withdrew, he accompanying me behind, and I turning partly towards him, when he said hastily, 'Stoop! stoop!' I did not understand him till I felt my head hit against the beam. He was a man who never missed any occasion of giving instruction; and upon this he said to me: 'You are young, and have the world before you: stoop as you go through it, and you will miss many hard thumps.' This advice, thus beat into my head, has frequently been of use to me; and I often think of it, when I see pride mortified, and misfortunes brought upon people by their carrying their heads too high.

I long much to see again my native place; and once hoped to lay my bones there. I left it in 1723. I visited it in 1733, 1743, 1753, 1763; and in 1773 I was in England. In 1774, I had a sight of it, but could not enter, it being in possession of the enemy. I did hope to have been there in 1783, but could not obtain my dismission from this employment here; and now I fear I shall never have that happiness. My best wishes however attend my dear country, '*esto perpetua.*' It is now blessed with an excellent constitution: may it last for ever!

This powerful monarchy continues its friendship for the

United States. It is a friendship of the utmost importance to our security, and should be carefully cultivated. Britain has not yet well digested the loss of its dominion over us; and has still at times some flattering hopes of recovering it. Accidents may increase those hopes, and encourage dangerous attempts. A breach between us and France would infallibly bring the English again upon our backs; and yet we have some wild beasts among our countrymen, who are endeavoring to weaken that connexion.

Let us preserve our reputation, by performing our engagements; our credit, by fulfilling our contracts, and our friends, by gratitude and kindness: for we know not how soon we may again have occasion for all of them.

With great and sincere esteem,
I have the honor to be
Rev. Sir,
Your most obedient and
Most humble servant,
B. FRANKLIN.

Passy, May 12th, 1784

THE WHISTLE.

A True Story—Written to his Nephew.

WHEN I was a child, at seven years old, my friends, on a holiday, filled my pockets with coppers. I went directly to a shop where they sold toys for children; and, being charmed with the sound of a *whistle*, that I met by the way in the hands of another boy, I voluntarily offered him all my money for one. I then came home, and went whistling all over the house, much pleased with my *whistle*, but disturbing all the family. My brothers, and sisters, and cousins, understanding the bargain I had made, told me I had given four times as much for it as it was worth. This put me in mind what good things I might have bought with the rest of my money; and they laughed at me so much for my folly, that I cried with vexation, and the reflection gave me more chagrin than the *whistle* gave me pleasure.

This, however, was afterward of use to me, the impression continuing on my mind; so that often, when I was tempted to buy some unnecessary thing, I said to myself, *Don't give too much for the whistle;* and so I saved my money.

As I grew up, came into the world, and observed the actions of men, I thought I met with many, very many, who *gave too much for the whistle.*

When I saw any one too ambitious of court favors, sacrificing his time in attendance on levees, his repose, his liberty, his virtue, and perhaps his friends, to attain it, I have said to myself, *This man gives too much for his whistle.*

When I saw another fond of popularity, constantly employing himself in political bustles, neglecting his own affairs, and ruining them by that neglect; *He pays, indeed,* says I, *too much for his whistle.*

If I knew a miser, who gave up every kind of comfortable living, all the pleasure of doing good to others, all the esteem of his fellow-citizens, and the joys of benevolent friendship, for the sake of accumulating wealth; *Poor man,* says I, *you do indeed pay too much for your whistle.*

When I meet a man of pleasure, sacrificing every laudable improvement of the mind, or of his fortune, to mere corporeal sansations; *Mistaken man,* says I, *you are providing pain for yourself instead of pleasure; you give too much for your whistle.*

If I see one fond of fine clothes, fine furniture, fine equipages, all above his fortune, for which he contracts debts, and ends his career in prison; *Alas,* says I, *he has paid dear, very dear, for his whistle.*

When I see a beautiful, sweet-tempered girl, married to an ill-natured brute of a husband; *What a pity it is,* says I, *that she has paid so much for a whistle.*

In short, I conceived that great part of the miseries of mankind were brought upon them by the false estimates they had made of the value of things, and by their giving too much for their *whistles.*

A PETITION

To those who have the Superintendency of Education.

I ADDRESS myself to all the friends of youth, and conjure them to direct their compassionate regards to my unhappy fate, in order to remove the prejudices of which I am the victim. There are twin sisters of us: and the two eyes of man do not more resemble, nor are capable of being on better terms with each other than my sister and myself, were it not for the partiality of our parents, who made the most injurious distinctions between us. From my infancy, I have been led to consider my sister as a being of more elevated rank. I was suffered to grow up without the least instruction, while nothing was spared in her education. She had masters to teach her writing, drawing, music, and other accomplishments; but if by chance, I touched a pencil, a pen, or a needle, I was bitterly rebuked; and more than once I have been beaten for being awkward, and wanting a graceful manner. It is true, my sister associated me with her upon some occasions; but she always made a point of taking the lead, calling upon me only from necessity, or to figure by her side.

But conceive not, Sirs, that my complaints are instigated merely by vanity—No: my uneasiness is occasioned by an object much more serious. It is the practice in our family, that the whole business of providing for its subsistence falls upon my sister and myself. If any indisposition should attack my sister—and I mention it in confidence upon this occasion, that she is subject to the gout, the rheumatism, and cramp, without making mention of other accidents—what would be the fate of our poor family? Must not the regret of our parents be excessive, at having placed so great a difference between sisters who are so perfectly equal? Alas! we must perish from distress: for it would not be in my power even to scrawl a suppliant petition for relief, having been obliged to employ the hand of another in transcribing the request which I have now the honor to prefer to you.

Condescend, Sirs, to make my parents sensible of the injustice of an exclusive tenderness, and of the necessity of distributing their care and affection among all their children equally. I am, with profound respect,

Sirs, Your obedient servant,

THE LEFT HAND.

HANDSOME AND DEFORMED LEG.

THERE are two sorts of people in the world, who, with equal degrees of health and wealth, and the other comforts of life, become, the one happy, and the other miserable. This arises very much from the different views in which they consider things, persons, and events; and the effect of those different views upon their own minds. In whatever situation men can be placed, they may find conveniences and inconveniences; in whatever company, they may find persons and conversation more or less pleasing; at whatever table, they may meet with meats and drinks of better and worse taste, dishes better and worse dressed: in whatever climate, they will find good and bad weather; under whatever government, they will find good and bad laws, and good and bad administration of those laws: in whatever poem, or work of genius, they may see faults and beauties: in almost every face, and every person, they may diccover fine features and defects, good and bad qualities.

Under these circumstances, the two sorts of people above-mentioned fix their attention; those who are disposed to be happy, on the conveniences of things, the pleasant parts of conversation, the well-dressed dishes, the goodness of the wines, the fine weather, &c. and enjoy all with cheerfulness. Those who are to be unhappy, think and speak only of the contraries. Hence they are continually discontented themselves, and, by their remarks, sour the pleasures of society; offend personally many people, and make themselves everywhere disagreeable. If this turn of mind was founded in nature, such unhappy persons would be the more to be pitied. But as the disposition to criticise, and to be disgusted, is, perhaps, taken up originally by imitation, and is, unawares, grown into a habit, which, though at present strong, may nevertheless be cured when those who have it are convinced of its bad effect on their felicity; I hope this little admonition may be of service to them, and put them on changing a habit, which, though in the exercise it is chiefly an act of imagination, yet it has serious consequences in life, as it brings on real griefs and misfortunes. For as many are offended by, and nobody loves, this sort of people; no one shows them more than the most common civility and respect, and scarcely that; and this frequently puts them out of humor, and draws them into disputes and contentions. If they aim at obtaining some advantages in rank or fortune, nobody wishes them success, or will stir a step, or speak a word to favor their pretensions. If they incur public censure or disgrace, no one will defend or excuse, and many join to aggravate their misconduct, and render them completely odious. If these people will not change this bad habit, and condescend to be pleased with what is pleasing, without fretting themselves or others about the contraries, it is good for others to avoid an acquaintance with them, which is always disagreeable, and sometimes very inconvenient, especially when one finds one's self entangled in their quarrels.

An old philosophical friend of mine was grown from experience, very cautious in this particular, and carefully avoided any intimacy with such people. He had, like other philosophers, a thermometer to show him the heat of the weather; and a barometer to mark when it was likely to prove good or bad; but there being no instrument invented to discover, at first sight, this unpleasing disposition in a person, he, for that purpose, made use of his legs; one of which was remarkably handsome; the other, by some accident, crooked and deformed. If a stranger, at first interview, regarded his ugly leg more than his handsome one, he doubted him. If he spoke of it, and took no notice of the handsome leg, that was sufficient to determine my philosopher to have no further acquaintance with him. Every body has not this two-legged instrument; but every one, with a little attention, may observe signs of that carping, fault-finding disposition, and take the same resolution of avoiding the acquaintance of those infected with it. I therefore advise those critical, querulous, discontented, unhappy people, if they wish to be respected and beloved by others, and happy in themselves, they should *leave off looking at the ugly leg.*

CONVERSATION OF A COMPANY OF EPHEMERÆ.

With the Soliloquy of one advanced in Age.

TO MADAME BRILLIANT.

You may remember, my dear friend, that when we lately spent that happy day, in the delightful garden and sweet society of the *Moulin Joly*, I stopt a little in one of our walks, and staid some time behind the company. We had been shown numberless skeletons of a kind of little fly, called an Ephemeræ, whose successive generations, we were told, were bred and expired within the day. I happened to see a living company of them on a leaf, who appeared to be engaged in conversation. You know I understand all the inferior animal tongues; my too great application to the study of them is the best excuse I can give for the little progress I have made in your charming language. I listened through curiosity to the discourse of these little creatures; but as they, in their national vivacity, spoke three or four together, I could make but little of their conversation. I found, however, by some broken expressions that I heard now and then, they were disputing warmly on the merit of two foreign musicians, one a *cousin*, the other a *moscheto;* in which dispute they spent their time, seeming as regardless of the shortness of their life as if they had been sure of living a month. Happy people, thought I, you live certainly under a wise, just, and mild government, since you have no public grievances to complain of, nor any other subject of contention but the perfections or imperfections of foreign music. I turned my head from them to an old gray-headed one, who was single on another leaf, and talking to himself. Being amused with his soliloquy, I put it down in writing, in hopes it will likewise amuse her to whom I am so much indebted for the most pleasing of all amusements, her delicious company and heavenly harmony.

'It was,' says he, 'the opinion of learned philosophers of our race, who lived and flourished long before my time, that this vast world, the *Moulin Joly*, could not itself subsist more than eighteen hours: and I think there was some foundation for that opinion; since, by the apparent motion of the great luminary, that gives light to all nature, and which in my time has evidently declined considerably towards the ocean at the end of the earth, it must then finish its course, be extinguished in the waters that surround us, and leave the world in cold and darkness, necessarily producing universal death and destruction. I have lived seven of those hours: a great age, being no less than 420 minutes of time! How very few of us continue so long! I have seen generations born, flourish, and expire. My present friends are the children and grandchildren of the friends of my youth, who are now, alas, no more! and I must soon follow them; for, by the common course of nature, though still in health, I cannot expect to live above seven or eight minutes longer. What now avails all my toil and labor in amassing honey-dew on this leaf, which I cannot live to enjoy. What my political struggles I have been engaged in, for the good of my compatriot inhabitants of this bush, or my philosophical studies for the benefit of our race in general: (for in politics what can laws do without morals?) our present race of ephemeræ will in a course of minutes become corrupt, like those of other and older bushes, and consequently as wretched! And in philosophy how small our progress. Alas! art is long, and life is short! My friends would comfort me with the idea of a name, they say, I shall leave behind me; and they tell me I have lived long enough to nature and to glory. But what will fame be to an ephemeræ who no longer exists? and what will become of all history in the eighteenth hour, when the world itself, even the whole *Moulin Joly*, shall come to its end, and be buried in a universal ruin?'

To me, after all my eager pursuits, no solid pleasures now remain, but the reflection of a long life, spent in meaning well, the sensible conversation of a few good lady ephemeræ, and now and then a kind smile and a tune from the ever amiable Brilliant. B. FRANKLIN.

MORALS OF CHESS.

PLAYING at chess is the most ancient and universal game known among men; for its original is beyond the memory of history, and it has, for numberless ages, been the amusement of all the civilized nations of Asia, the Persians, the Indians, and the Chinese. Europe has had it above a thousand years, the Spaniards have spread it over their part of America, and it begins to make its appearance in these States. It is so interesting in itself, as not to need the view of gain to induce engaging in it; and thence it is never played for money. Those, therefore, who have leisure for such diversions, cannot find one that is more innocent; and the following piece, written with a view to correct (among a few young friends) some little improprieties in the practice of it, shows, at the same time, that it may, in its effects on the mind, be not merely innocent, but advantageous to the vanquished as well as the victor.

The game of chess is not merely an idle amusement. Several very valuable qualities of the mind, useful in the course of human life, are to be acquired or strengthened by it, so as to become habits, ready on all occasions. For life is a kind of chess, in which we have points to gain, and competitors or adversaries to contend with, and in which there is a vast variety of good and ill events, that are, in some degree, the effects of prudence or the want of it. By playing at chess then, we learn,

I. *Foresight*, which looks a little into futurity, considers the consequences that may attend an action; for it is continually occuring to the player. 'If I move this piece, what will be the advantage of my new situation? What use can my adversary make of it to annoy me? What other moves can I make to support it, and to defend myself from his attacks?'

II. *Circumspection*, which surveys the whole chess-board, or scene of action, the relations of the several pieces and situations, the dangers they are respectively exposed to, the several possibilities of their aiding each other, the probabilities that the adversary may make this or that move, and attack this or the other piece, and what different means can be used to avoid his stroke, or turn its consequences against him.

III. *Caution*, not to make our moves too hastily. This habit is best acquired by observing strictly the laws of the game, such as, 'If you touch a piece, you must move it somewhere; if you set it down, you must let it stand;' and it is therefore best that these rules should be observed: as the game more becomes the image of human life, and particularly of war; in which if you have incautiously put yourself into a bad and dangerous position, you cannot obtain your enemy's leave to withdraw your troops, and place them more securely, but you must abide all the consequences of your rashness.

And, lastly, we learn by chess the habit of *not being discouraged by present bad appearances in the state of our affairs*, the habit of *hoping for a favorable change*, and that of *persevering in the search of resources.* The game is so full of events there is such a variety of turns in it, the fortune of it is so subject to sudden vicissitudes, and one so frequently, after long contemplation, discovers the means of extricating one's self from a supposed insurmountable difficulty, that one is encouraged to continue the contest to the last, in hope of victory by our own skill, or at least of giving a stale mate, by the negligence of our adversary. And whoever considers, what in chess he often sees instances of, that particular pieces of success are apt to produce presumption, and its consequent inattention, by which the loss may be recovered, will learn not to be too much discouraged by the present success of his adversary, nor to despair of final good fortune, upon every little check he receives in the pursuit of it.

That we may, therefore, be induced more frequently to choose this beneficial amusement, in preference to others, which are not attended with the same advantages, every circumstance which may increase the pleasure of it should be regarded; and every action or word that is unfair, disrespectful, or that in any way may give uneasiness, should be avoided, as contrary to the immediate intention of both the players, which is to pass the time agreeably.

Therefore, first, If it is agreed to play according to the strict rules, then those rules are to be exactly observed by both parties, and should not be insisted on for one side, while deviated from by the other—for this is not equitable.

Secondly, If it is agreed not to observe the rules exactly, but one party demands indulgences, he should then be as willing to allow them to the other.

Thirdly, No false move should ever be made to extricate yourself out of a difficulty, or to gain an advantage. There can be no pleasure in playing with a person once detected in such unfair practices.

Fourthly, If your adversary is long in playing, you ought not to hurry him, or to express any uneasiness at his delay. You should not sing, nor whistle, nor look at your watch, nor take up a book to read, nor make a tapping with your feet on the floor, or with your fingers on the table, nor do any thing that may disturb his attention. For all these things displease; and they do not show your skill in playing, but your craftiness or your rudeness.

Fifthly, You ought not to endeavor to amuse and deceive your adversary, by pretending to have made bad moves, and saying that you have now lost the game, in order to make him secure and careless, and inattentive to your schemes, for this is fraud and deceit, not skill in the game.

Sixthly, You must not, when you have gained a victory, use any triumphing or insulting expression, nor show too much pleasure; but endeavor to console your adversary, and make him less dissatisfied with himself, by every kind of civil expression that may be used with truth: such as, 'You understand the game better than I, but you are a little inattentive; or, you play too fast: or, you had the best of the game, but something happened to divert your thoughts, and that turned it in my favor.'

Seventhly, If you are a spectator while others play, observe the most perfect silence. For if you give advice, you offend both parties; him against whom you gave it, because it may cause the loss of his game; and him in whose favor you gave it, because, though it be good, and he follows it, he loses the pleasure he might have had, if you had permitted him to think until it had occurred to himself. Even after a move, or moves, you must not, by replacing the pieces, show how it might have been placed better; for that displeases, and may occasion disputes and doubts about their true situation. All talking to the players lessens or diverts their attention, and is therefore unpleasing. Nor should you give the least hint to either party, by any kind of noise or motion. If you do, you are unworthy to be a spectator. If you have a mind to exercise or show your judgment, do it in playing your own game, when you have an opportunity, not in criticising, or meddling with, or counselling the play of others.

Lastly, If the game is not to be played rigorously, according to the rules above mentioned, then moderate your desire of victory over your adversary, and be pleased with one over yourself. Snatch not eagerly at every advantage offered by his unskilfulness or inattention; but point out to him kindly, that by such a move he places or leaves a piece in danger and unsupported; that by another he will put his king in a perilous situation, &c. By this generous civility (so opposite to the unfairness above forbidden) you may, indeed, happen to lose the game to your opponent, but you will win what is better, his esteem, his respect, and his affection; together with the silent approbation and good-will of impartial spectators.

THE ART OF PROCURING PLEASANT DREAMS.

Inscribed to Miss * * *,

BEING WRITTEN AT HER REQUEST.

As a great part of our life is spent in sleep, during which we have sometimes pleasing and sometimes painful dreams, it becomes of some consequence to obtain the one kind, and avoid the other; for whether real or imaginary, pain is pain, and pleasure is pleasure. If we can sleep without dreaming, it is well that painful dreams are avoided. If, while we sleep, we can have any pleasing dreams, it is, as the French say, *tant gagne*, so much added to the pleasure of life.

To this end it is, in the first place, necessary to be careful in preserving health, by due exercise and great temperance; for, in sickness, the imagination is disturbed; and disagreeable, sometimes terrible ideas, are apt to present themselves. Exercise should precede meals, not immediately follow them: the first promotes, the latter, unless moderate, obstructs digestion. If after exercise we feed sparingly, the digestion will be easy and good, the body lightsome, the temper cheerful, and all the animal functious performed agreeably. Sleep, when it follows, will be natural and undisturbed. While indolence, with full feeding, occasions nightmares and horrors inexpressible: we fall from precipices, are assaulted by wild beasts, murderers, and demons, and experience every variety of distress. Observe, however, that the quantities of food and exercise are relative things; those who move much may, and indeed ought, to eat more: those who use little exercise, should eat little. In general, mankind, since the improvement of cookery, eat about twice as much as nature requires. Suppers are not bad, if we have not dined; but restless nights naturally follow hearty suppers, after full dinners. Indeed, as there is a difference in constitutions, some rest well after these meals; it costs them only a frightful dream and an apoplexy, after which they sleep till doomsday. Nothing is more common in the newspapers, than instances of people, who, after eating a hearty supper, are found dead abed in the morning.

Another means of preserving health, to be attended to, is the having a constant supply of fresh air in your bed-chamber. It has been a great mistake, the sleeping in rooms exactly closed, and in beds surrounded by curtains. No outward air, that may come in to you, is so unwholesome as the unchanged air, often breathed, of a close chamber. As boiling water does not grow hotter by longer boiling, if the particles that receive greater heat can escape; so living bodies do not putrify, if the particles, as fast as they become putrid, can be thrown off. Nature expels them by the pores of the skin and lungs, and in a free open air, they are carried off; but, in a close room, we receive them again and again, though they become more and more corrupt. A number of persons crowded into a small room, thus spoil the air in a few minutes, and even render it mortal, as in the Black Hole at Calcutta. A single person is said only to spoil a gallon of air per minute, and therefore requires a longer time to spoil a chamberful; but it is done, however, in proportion, and many putrid disorders have hence their origin. It is recorded of Methusalem, who being the longest liver, may be supposed to have best preserved his health, that he slept always in the open air: for when he had lived five hundred years, an angel said to him, 'Arise, Methusalem, and build thee a house, for thou shalt live yet five hundred years longer.' But Methusalem answered and said; 'If I am to live but five hundred years longer, it is not worth while to build me a house—I will sleep in the open air as I have been used to do.' Physicians, after having for ages contended that the sick should not be indulged with fresh air, have at length discovered that it may do them good. It is therefore to be hoped, that they may in time discover likewise, that it is not hurtful to those who are in health, and that we may then be cured of the *aerophobia* that at present distresses weak minds, and makes them choose to be stifled and poisoned, rather than leave open the window of a bed-chamber, or put down the glass of a coach.

Confined air, when saturated with perspirable matter,* will

* What physicians call the perspirable matter, is that vapo. which passes off from our bodies, from the lungs, and through the pores of the skin. The quantity of this is said to be five eights of what we eat

not receive more; and that matter must remain in our bodies, and occasion diseases: but it gives some previous notice of its being about to be hurtful, by producing certain uneasiness, slight indeed at first, such as, with regard to the lungs, is a trifling sensation, and to the pores of the skin a kind of restlessness which is difficult to describe, and few that feel it know the cause of it. But we may recollect, that sometimes, on waking in the night, we have, if warmly covered, found it difficult to sleep again. We turn often, without finding repose in any position. This fidgettiness, to use a vulgar expression for want of a better, is occasioned wholly by an uneasiness in the skin, owing to the retention of the perspirable matter—the bed-clothes having received their quantity, and being saturated, refusing to take any more. To become sensible of this by an experiment, let a person keep his position in the bed, but throw off the bed-clothes, and suffer fresh air to approach the part uncovered of his body; he will then feel that part suddenly refreshed; for the air will immediately relieve the skin, by receiving, licking up, and carrying off, the load of perspirable matter that incommoded it. For every portion of cool air that approaches the warm skin, in receiving its part of that vapor, receives therewith a degree of heat that rarifies and renders it lighter, when it will be pushed away, with its burden, by cooler and therefore heavier fresh air; which, for a moment, supplies its place, and then, being likewise changed and warmed, gives way to a succeeding quantity. This is the order of nature, to prevent animals being infected by their own perspiration. He will now be sensible of the difference between the part exposed to the air, and that which, remaining sunk in the bed, denies the air access; for this part now manifests its uneasiness more distinctly by the comparison, and the seat of the uneasiness is more plainly perceived, than when the whole surface of the body was affected by it.

Here then is one great and general cause of unpleasing dreams. For when the body is uneasy, the mind will be disturbed by it, and disagreeable ideas of various kinds will, in sleep, be the natural consequences. The remedies, preventive and curative, follow:

1. By eating moderately (as before advised for health's sake) less perspirable matter is produced in a given time: hence the bed-clothes receive it longer before they are saturated; and we may, therefore, sleep longer, before we are made uneasy by their refusing to receive any more.

2. By using thinner and more porous bed-clothes, which

will suffer the perspirable matter more easily to pass through them, we are less incommoded, such being longer tolerable.

3. When you are awakened by this uneasiness, and find you cannot easily sleep again, get out of bed, beat up and turn your pillow, shake the bed-clothes well, with at least twenty shakes, then throw the bed open, and leave it to cool; in the meanwhile, continuing undrest, walk about your chamber, till your skin has had time to discharge its load, which it will do sooner as the air may be drier and colder. When you begin to feel the cold air unpleasant, then return to your bed; and you will soon fall asleep, and your sleep will be sweet and pleasant. All the scenes presented to your fancy will be of the pleasing kind. I am often as agreeably entertained with them, as by the scenery of an opera. If you happen to be too indolent to get out of bed, you may, instead of it lift up your bed-clothes with one arm and leg, so as to draw in a good deal of fresh air, and by letting them fall, force it out again; this, repeated twenty times, will so clear them of the perspirable matter they have imbibed, as to permit your sleeping well for some time afterward. But this latter method is not equal to the former.

Those who do not love trouble, and can afford to have two beds, will find great luxury in rising, when they wake in a hot bed, and going into the cool one. Such shifting of beds would also be of great service to persons ill of a fever, as it refreshes and frequently procures sleep. A very large bed, that will admit a removal so distant from the first situation as to be cool and sweet, may in a degree answer the same end.

One or two observations more will conclude this little piece. Care must be taken, when you lie down, to dispose your pillow so as to suit your manner of placing your head, and to be perfectly easy; then place your limbs so as not to bear inconveniently hard upon one another; as for instance, the joints of your ancles: for though a bad position may at first give but little pain, and be hardly noticed, yet a continuance will render it less tolerable, and the uneasiness may come on you while you are asleep, and disturb your imagination.

These are the rules of the art. But though they will generally prove effectual in producing the end intended, there is a case in which the most punctual observance of them will be totally fruitless. I do not mention the case to you, my dear friend: but my account of the art would be imperfect without it. The case is, when the person who desires to have the pleasant dreams, has not taken care to preserve, what is necessary above all things,

A GOOD CONSCIENCE.

ADVICE TO A YOUNG TRADESMAN.

Written anno 1748.

TO MY FRIEND, A. B.

"As you have desired it of me, I write the following hints, which have been of service to me, and may, if observed, be so to you.

REMEMBER that *time* is money. He that can earn ten shillings a day by his labor, and goes abroad, or sits idle one half of that day, though he spends but sixpence during his diversion or idleness, ought not to reckon *that* the only expense; he has really spent, or rather thrown away, five shillings besides.

Remember that *credit* is money. If a man lets his money lie in my hands after it is due, he gives me the interest, or so much as I can make of it during that time. This amounts to a considerable sum where a man has good and large credit, and makes good use of it.

Remember that money is of a prolific generating nature. Money can beget money, and its offspring can beget more, and so on. Five shillings turned is six; turned again it is seven and threepence: and so on till it becomes a hundred pounds. The more there is of it, the more it produces every turning, so that the profits rise quicker and quicker. He that kills a breeding sow, destroys all her offspring to the thousandth generation. He that murders a crown, destroys all that it might have produced, even scores of pounds.

Remember that six pounds a year is but a groat a day. For this little sum (which may be daily wasted either in time or expense, unperceived) a man of credit may, on his own security, have the constant possession and use of a hundred pounds. So much in stock, briskly turned by an industrious man, produces great advantage.

Remember this saying: 'The good paymaster is lord of another man's purse.' He that is known to pay punctually and exactly to the time he promises, may at any time, and on any occasion, raise all the money his friends can spare. This is sometimes of great use. After industry and frugality nothing contributes more to the raising of a young man in the world, than punctuality and justness in all his dealings: therefore never keep borrowed money an hour beyond the time you promised, lest a disappointment shut up your friend's purse for ever.

The most trifling actions that affect a man's credit are to be regarded. The sound of your hammer at five in the morning, or nine at night, heard by a creditor, makes him easy six months longer; but if he sees you at a billiard table, or hears your voice at a tavern, when you should be at work, he sends for his money the next day; demands it before he can receive it in a lump.

It shows, besides, that you are mindful of what you owe: it makes you appear a careful as well as an honest man, and that still increases your credit.

Beware of thinking all your own that you possess, and of living accordingly. It is a mistake that many people who have credit fall into. To prevent this, keep an exact account, for some time, both of your expenses and your income. If you take the pains at first to mention particulars, it will have this good effect; you will discover how wonderfully small trifling expenses mount up to large sums, and will discern what might have been, and may for the future be saved without occasioning any great inconvenience.

In short, the way to wealth, if you desire it, is as plain as the way to market. It depends chiefly on two words, *industry* and *frugality*; that is, waste neither *time* nor *money*, but make the best use of both. Without industry and frugality nothing will do, and with them every thing. He that gets all he can honestly, and saves all he gets (necessary expenses excepted,) will certainly become *rich*—if that Being, who governs the world, to whom all should look for a blessing on their honest endeavors, doth not in his wise providence otherwise determine.

An Old Tradesman.

NECESSARY HINTS TO THOSE THAT WOULD BE RICH.

Written anno 1736.

The use of money is all the advantage there is in having money.

For six pounds a year you may have the use of one hundred pounds, provided you are a man of known prudence and honesty.

He that spends a groat a day idly, spends idly above six pounds a year, which is the price for the use of one hundred pounds.

He that wastes idly a groat's worth of his time per day, one day with another, wastes the privilege of using one hundred pounds each day.

He that idly loses five shillings worth of time, loses five shillings, and might as prudently throw five shillings into the sea.

He that loses five shillings, not only loses that sum, but all the advantages that might be made by turning it in dealing, which, by the time that a young man becomes old, will amount to a considerable sum of money.

Again, he that sells upon credit, asks a price for what he sells equivalent to the principal and interest of his money for the time he is to be kept out of it; therefore, he that buys upon credit, pays interest for what he buys; and he that pays ready money, might let that money out to use: so that he that possesses any thing he has bought, pays interest for the use of it.

Yet, in buying goods, it is best to pay ready money, because, he that sells upon credit, expects to lose five per cent. by bad debts; therefore, he charges, on all he sells upon credit, an advance that shall make up that deficiency.

Those who pay for what they buy upon credit, pay their share of this advance.

He that pays ready money, escapes, or may escape that charge.

A penny sav'd is twopence clear;
A pin a day is a groat a year.

THE WAY TO MAKE MONEY PLENTY IN EVERY MAN'S POCKET.

At this time, when the general complaint is that—'money is scarce,' it will be an act of kindness to inform the moneyless now they may reinforce their pockets. I will acquaint them with the true secret of money-catching—the certain way to fill empty purses—and how to keep them always full. Two simple rules, well observed, will do the business.

First, Let honesty and industry be thy constant companions; and,

Secondly, Spend one penny less than thy clear gains.

Then shall thy hide-bound pocket soon begin to thrive, and will never again cry with the empty bellyache; neither will creditors insult thee, nor want oppress, nor hunger bite, nor nakedness freeze thee. The whole hemisphere will shine brighter, and pleasure spring up in every corner of thy heart. Now, therefore, embrace these rules and be happy. Banish the bleak winds of sorrow from thy mind, and live independent. Then shalt thou be a man, and not hide thy face at the approach of the rich, nor suffer the pain of feeling little when the sons of fortune walk at thy right hand; for independency, whether with little or much, is good fortune, and placeth thee on even ground with the proudest of the golden fleece. Oh, then, be wise, and let industry walk with thee in the morning, and attend thee until thou reachest the evening hour for rest. Let honesty be as the breath of thy soul, and never forget to have a penny, when all thy expenses are enumerated and paid: then shalt thou reach the point of happiness, and independence shall be thy shield and buckler, thy helmet and crown; then shall thy soul walk upright, nor stoop to the silken wretch because he hath riches, nor pocket an abuse because the hand which offers it wears a ring set with diamonds.

AN ECONOMICAL PROJECT.

A translation of this Letter appeared in one of the daily papers of Paris, about the year 1784. The following is the original piece, with some additions and corrections made by the Author.

To the Authors of the Journal.

MESSIEURS,

YOU often entertain us with accounts of new discoveries. Permit me to communicate to the public, through your paper, one that has lately been made by myself, and which I conceive may be of great utility.

I was the other evening in a grand company, where the new lamp of Messrs. Quinquet and Lange was introduced, and much admired for its splendor; but a general inquiry was made whether the oil it consumed was not in proportion to the light it afforded, in which case there would be no saving in the use of it. No one present could satisfy us on that point, which all agreed ought to be known, it being a very desirable thing to lessen, if possible, the expense of lighting our apartments, when every other article of family expense was so much augmented.

I was pleased to see this general concern for economy, for I love economy exceedingly.

I went home, and to bed, three or four hours after midnight, with my head full of the subject. An accidental sudden noise waked me about six in the morning, when I was surprised to find my room filled with light; and I imagined at first, that a number of those lamps had been brought into it; but, rubbing my eyes, I perceived the light came in at the windows. I got up and looked out to see what might be the occasion of it, when I saw the sun just rising above the horizon, from whence he poured his rays plentifully into my chamber, my domestic having negligently omitted the preceding evening to close the shutters.

I looked at my watch, which goes very well, and found that it was about six o'clock; and still thinking it something extraordinary that the sun should rise so early, I looked into the almanack, where I found it to be the hour given for his rising on that day. I looked forward, too, and found he was to rise still earlier every day till towards the end of June; and that at no time in the year he retarded his rising so long as till eight o'clock. Your readers, who with me have never seen any signs of sunshine before noon, and seldom regard the astronomical part of the almanack, will be as much astonished as I was, when they hear of his rising so early; and especially when I assure them, *that he gives light as soon as he rises.* I am convinced of this. I am certain of my fact. One cannot be more certain of any fact. I saw it with my own eyes. And having repeated this observation the three following mornings, I found always precisely the same result.

Yet it so happens, that when I speak of this discovery to others, I can easily perceive by their countenances, though they forbear expressing it in words, that they do not quite believe me. One, indeed, who is a learned natural philosopher, has assured me, that I must certainly be mistaken as to the circumstance of the light coming into my room; for it being well known, as he says, that there could be no light abroad at that hour, it follows that none could enter from without; and that of consequence, my windows being accidentally left open, instead of letting in the light, had only served to let out the darkness; and he used many ingenious arguments to show me how I might, by that means, have been deceived. I own that he puzzled me a little, but he did not satisfy me: and the subsequent observations I made as above mentioned, confirmed me in my first opinion.

This event has given rise, in my mind, to several serious and important reflections. I considered that, if I had not been awakened so early in the morning, I should have slept six hours longer by the light of the sun, and in exchange have lived six hours the following night by candle-light; and the latter being a much more expensive light than the former, my love of economy induced me to muster up what little arithmetic I was master of, and to make some calculations, which I shall give you, after observing, that utility is, in my opinion, the test of value in matters of invention, and that a discovery which can be applied to no use, or is not good for something, is good for nothing.

I took for the basis of my calculation the supposition, that there are 100,000 families in Paris, and that these families consume in the night half a pound of bougies, or candles, per hour. I think this is a moderate allowance, taking one family with another; for though I believe some consume less, I know that many consume a great deal more. Then estimating seven hours per day, as the medium quantity between the time of the sun's rising and ours, he rising during the six following months from six to eight hours before noon, and there being seven hours of course per night in which we burn candles, the account will stand thus:—

In the six months between the twentieth of March and the twentieth of September, there are Nights .	183
Hours of each night in which we burn candles .	7
Multiplication gives for the total number of hours	1,281
These 1,281 hours, multiplied by 100,000, the number of inhabitants given	128,100,000
One hundred and twenty-eight millions and one hundred thousand hours, spent at Paris by candle-light, which at half a pound of wax and tallow per hour, gives the weight of . . .	64,050,000
Sixty-four millions and fifty thousand pounds, which, estimating the whole at the medium price of thirty sols the pound, makes the sum of ninety-six millions and seventy-five thousand livres tournois	96,075,000

An immense sum! that the city of Paris might save every year, by the economy of using sunshine instead of candles.

If it should be said, that people are apt to be obstinately attached to old customs, and that it will be difficult to induce them to rise before noon, consequently my discovery can be of little use; I answer, *Nil desperandum.* I believe all who have common sense, as soon as they have learnt from this paper, that it is day-light when the sun rises, will contrive to rise with him: and to compel the rest, I would propose the following regulation:

First. Let a tax be laid of a louis per window, on every window that is provided with shutters to keep out the light of the sun.

Second. Let the same salutary operation of police be made use of to prevent our burning candles, that inclined us last winter to be more economical in burning wood; that is, let guards be placed in the shops of the wax and tallow-chandlers, and no family be permitted to be supplied with more than one pound of candles per week.

Third. Let guards also be posted to stop all the coaches, &c. that would pass the streets after sunset, except those of physicians, surgeons, and midwives.

Fourth. Every morning, as soon as the sun rises, let all the bells in every church be set a ringing: and if that is not sufficient, let cannon be fired in every street, to wake the sluggards effectually, and make them open their eyes to see their true interest.

All the difficulty will be in the first two or three days; after which the reformation will be as natural and easy as the present irregularity; for *ce n'est que le premier pas qui coute.* Oblige a man to rise at four in the morning, and it is more than probable he shall go willingly to bed at eight in the evening; and, having had eight hours' sleep, he will rise more willingly at four the following morning. But this sum of ninety-six millions and seventy-five thousand livres is not the whole of what may be saved by my economical project. You may observe that I have calculated upon only one-half of the year, and much may be saved in the other, though the days are shorter. Besides, the immense stock of wax and tallow left unconsumed during the summer, will probably make candles much cheaper for the ensuing winter, and continue cheaper as long as the proposed reformation shall be supported.

For the great benefit of this discovery, thus freely communicated and bestowed by me on the public, I demand neither place, pension, exclusive privilege, or any other reward whatever. I expect only to have the honor of it. And yet I know there are little envious minds who will, as usual, deny me this, and say, that my invention was known to the ancients, and perhaps they may bring passages out of the old books in proof of it. I will not dispute with these people that the ancients knew not the sun would rise at certain hours; they possibly had, as we have, almanacks that predicted it: but it does not follow from thence, that they knew *he gave light as soon as he rose.* This is what I claim as my discovery. If the ancients knew it, it must have been long since forgotten, for it certainly was unknown to the moderns, at least to the Parisians; which to prove, I need but use one plain simple argument. They are as well instructed, judicious, and prudent a people as exist any where in the world, all professing, like myself, to be lovers of economy; and, from the many heavy taxes required from them by the necessities of the state, have surely reason to be economical. I say, it is impossible that so sensible a people, under such circumstances, should have lived so long by the smoky, unwholesome, and enormously expensive light of candles, if they had really known that they might have had as much pure light of the sun for nothing. I am, &c.

AN ABONNE.

SKETCH OF AN ENGLISH SCHOOL.

For the Consideration of the Trustees of the Philadelphia Academy.

IT is expected that every scholar to be admitted into this school be at least able to pronounce and divide the syllables in reading, and to write a legible hand. None to be received that are under years of age.

FIRST, OR LOWEST CLASS.

Let the first class learn the English grammar rules, and at the same time let particular care be taken to improve them in orthography. Perhaps the latter is best done by pairing the scholars; two of those nearest equal in their spelling to be put together. Let these strive for victory; each propounding ten words every day to the other to be spelled. He that spells truly most of the other's words, is victor for that day; he that is victor most days in a month to obtain a prize, a pretty neat book of some kind, useful in their future studies. This method fixes the attention of children extremely to the orthography of words, and makes them good spellers very early. It is a shame for a man to be so ignorant of this little art, in his own language, as to be perpetually confounding words of like sound and different significations; the consciousness of which defect makes some men, otherwise of good learning and understanding, averse to writing even a common letter.

Let the pieces read by the scholars in this class be short; such as Croxal's fables and little stories. In giving the lesson, let it be read to them; let the meaning of the difficult words in it be explained to them; and let them con it over by themselves before they are called to read to the master or usher; who is to take particular care that they do not read too fast, and that they duly observe the stops and pauses. A vocabulary of the most usual difficult words might be formed for their ase, with explanations; and they might daily get a few of those words and explanations by heart, which would a little exercise their memories; or at least they might write a number of them in a small book for that purpose, which would help to fix the meaning of those words in their minds, and at the same time furnish every one with a little dictionary for his future use.

THE SECOND CLASS.

To be taught reading with attention, and with proper modulations of the voice, according to the sentiment and the subject.

Some short pieces, not exceeding the length of a Spectator, to be given this class for lessons, (and some of the easier Spectators would be very suitable for the purpose.) These lessons might be given every night as tasks; the scholars to study them against the morning. Let it then be required of them to give an account, first of the parts of speech, and construction of one or two sentences. This will oblige them to recur frequently to their grammar, and fix its principal rules in their memory. Next, of the intention of the writer, or the scope of the piece, the meaning of each sentence, and of every uncommon word. This would early acquaint them with the meaning and force of words, and give them that most necessary habit of reading with attention.

The master then to read the piece with the proper modulations of voice, due emphasis, and suitable action, where action is required; and put the youth on imitating his manner.

Where the author has used an expression not the best, let it be pointed out; and let his beauties be particularly remarked to the youth.

Let the lessons for reading be varied, that the youth may be made acquainted with good styles of all kinds in prose and verse, and the proper manner of reading each kind—sometimes a well-told story, a piece of a sermon, a general's speech to his soldiers, a speech in a tragedy, some part of a comedy, an ode, a satire, a letter, blank verse, Hudibrastic, heroic, &c. But let such lessons be chosen for reading, as contain some useful instruction, whereby the understanding or morals of the youth may at the same time be improved.

It is required that they should first study and understand the lessons, before they are put upon reading them properly to which end each boy should have an English Dictionary to help him over difficulties. When our boys read English to us, we are apt to imagine they understand what they read, because we do, and because it is their mother tongue. But they often read as parrots speak, knowing little or nothing of the meaning. And it is impossible a reader should give the due modulation to his voice, and pronounce properly, unless his understanding goes before his tongue, and makes him master of the sentiment. Accustoming boys to read aloud what they do not first understand, is the cause of those even set tones so common among readers, which, when they have once got a habit of using, they find so difficult to correct; by which means, among fifty readers we scarcely find a good one. For want of good reading, pieces published with a view to influence the minds of men, for their own or the public benefit, lose half their force. Were there but one good reader in a neighborhood, a public orator might be heard throughout a nation with the same advantages, and have the same effect upon his audience as if they stood within the reach of his voice.

THE THIRD CLASS.

To be taught speaking properly and gracefully, which is near akin to good reading, and naturally follows it in the studies of youth. Let the scholars of this class begin with learning the elements of rhetoric, from some short system, so as to be able to give an account of the most useful tropes and figures. Let all their bad habits of speaking, all offences against good grammar, all corrupt or foreign accents, and all improper phrases be pointed out to them. Short speeches from the Roman or other history, or from the parliamentary debates, might be got by heart, and delivered with the proper action, &c.—Speeches and scenes in our best tragedies and comedies, (avoiding every thing that could injure the morals of youth,) might likewise be got by rote, and the boys exercised in delivering or acting them; great care being taken to form their manner after the truest models.

For their farther improvement, and a little to vary their studies, let them now begin to read history, after having got by heart a short table of the principal epochs in chronology. They may begin with Rollin's Ancient and Roman Histories, and proceed at proper hours, as they go through the subsequent classes, with the best histories of our own nation and colonies. Let emulation be excited among the boys, by giving, weekly, little prizes, or other small encouragements to those who are able to give the best account of what they have read, as to times, places, names of persons, &c. This will make them read with attention, and imprint the history well in their memories. In remarking on the history, the master will have fine opportunities of instilling instruction of various kinds, and of improving the morals, as well as the understandings, of youth.

The natural and mechanic history, contained in the *Spectacle de la Nature*, might also be begun in this class, and continued through the subsequent classes, by other books of the same kind; for, next to the knowledge of duty, this kind of knowledge is certainly the most useful, as well as the most entertaining. The merchant may thereby be enabled better to understand many commodities in trade; the handicraftsman to improve his business by new instruments, mixtures, and materials, and frequently hints are given for new methods of improving land, that may be set on foot greatly to the advantage of a country.

THE FOURTH CLASS.

To be taught composition. Writing one's own language well, is the next necessary accomplishment after good speaking. It is the writing-master's business to take care that the boys make fair characters, and place them straight and even in the lines: but to form their style, and even to take care that the stops and capitals are properly disposed, is the part of the English master. The boys should be put on writing letters to each other on any common occurrences, and on various subjects, imaginary business, &c., containing little stories, accounts of their late reading, what parts of authors please them, and why; letters of congratulation, of compliment, of request, of thanks, of recommendation, of admonition, of consolation, of expostulation, excuse, &c. In these they should be taught to express themselves clearly, consisely, and naturally, without affected words or high-flown phrases. All their letters to pass through the master's hands, who is to point out the faults, advise the corrections, and commend what he finds right. Some of the best letters published in their own language, as Sir William Temple's, those of Pope and his friends, and some others, might be set before the youth as models, their beauties pointed out and explained by the master, the letters themselves transcribed by the scholar.

Dr. Johnson's *Ethices Elementa*, or First Principles of Morality, may now be read by the scholars, and explained by the master, to lay a solid foundation of virtue and piety in their minds. And as this class continues the reading of history, let them now, at proper hours, receive some farther instruction in chronology and in that part of geography (from the mathematical master) which is necessary to understand the maps and globes. They should also be acquainted with the modern names of the places they find mentioned in ancient writers. The exercises of good reading, and proper speaking, still continued at suitable times.

THE FIFTH CLASS.

To improve the youth in composition, they may now, besides continuing to write letters, begin to write little essays in prose, and sometimes in verse; not to make them poets, but for this reason, that nothing acquaints a lad so speedily with a variety of expression, as the necessity o finding such words and phrases, as will suit the measure, sound, and rhyme of verse, and at the same time well express the sentiment. These essays should all pass under the master's eye, who will point out their faults, and put the writer on correcting them. Where the judgment is not ripe enough for forming new essays, let the sentiments of a Spectator be given, and required to be clothed in the scholar's own words; or the circumstances of some good story: the scholar to find expression. Let them be put sometimes on abridging a paragraph of a diffuse author; sometimes on dilating or amplifying what is wrote more closely. And now let Dr. Johnson's *Noetica*, or First Principles of Human Knowledge, containing a logic, or art of reasoning, &c., be read by the youth, and the difficulties that may occur to them be explained by the master. The reading of history, and the exercise of good reading, and just speaking, still continued.

SIXTH CLASS.

In this class, besides continuing the studies of the preceding in history, rhetoric, logic, moral and natural philosophy, the best English authors may be read and explained; as Tillotson, Milton, Locke, Addison, Pope, Swift, the higher papers in the Spectator and Guardian, the best translations of Homer, Virgil, and Horace, of Telemachus, Travels of Cyrus, &c.

Once a year let there be public exercises in the hall; the trustees and citizens present. Then let fine gilt books be given as prizes to such boys as distinguish themselves, and excel the others in any branch of learning, making three degrees of comparison; giving the best prize to him that performs best. a less valuable one to him that comes up next to the best; and another to the third. Commendations, encouragement, and advice to the rest, keeping up their hopes, that by industry they may excel another time. The names of those that obtain the prize, to be yearly printed in a list.

The hours of each day are to be divided and disposed in such a manner as that some classes may be with the writing master, improving their hands, others with the mathematical master, learning arithmetic, accounts, geography, use of the globes, drawing, mechanics, &c.; while the rest are in the English school, under the English master's care.

Thus instructed, youth will come out of this school fitted for learning any business, calling, or profession, except in such wherein languages are required; and though unacquainted with any ancient or foreign tongue, they will be masters of their own, which is of more immediate and general use; and withal will have attained many other valuable accomplishments; the time usually spent in acquiring those languages, often without success, being here employed in laying such a foundation of knowledge and ability, as, properly improved, may qualify them to pass through and execute the several offices of civil life, with advantage and reputation to themselves and country.

ON MODERN INNOVATIONS IN THE ENGLISH LANGUAGE AND IN PRINTING.

TO NOAH WEBSTER, JUN. ESQ., AT HARTFORD.

DEAR SIR, *Philadelphia, Dec.* 26, 1789.

I RECEIVED sometime since your *Dissertation on the English Language.* It is an excellent work, and will be greatly useful in turning the thoughts of our countrymen to correct writing. Please to accept my thanks for it, as well as for the great hono you have done me in its dedication. I ought to have made this acknowledment sooner, but much indisposition prevented me.

I cannot but applaud your zeal for preserving the purity of our language both in its expression and pronunciation, and in correcting the popular errors several of our states are continually falling into with respect to both. Give me leave to mention some of them, though possibly they may have already occurred to you. I wish, however, that in some future publication of yours, you would set a discountenancing mark upon them. The first I remember, is the word *improved.* When I left New-England in the year 1723, this word had never been used among us, as far as I know, but in the sense of *ameliorated or made better*, except once in a very old book of Dr. Mather's, entitled '*Remarkable Providences.*' As that man wrote a very obscure hand, I remember that when I read that word in his book, used instead of the word *employed*, I conjectured that it was an error of the printer, who had mistaken a short *l* in the writing for an *r*, and a *y* with too short a tail for a *v*, whereby *employed* was converted into *improved*: but when I returned to Boston in 1733, I found this change had obtained favor, and was then become common; for I met with it often in perusing the newspapers, where it frequently made an appearance rather ridiculous. Such, for instance, as the advertisement of a country-house, which had been many years *improved* as a tavern; and in the character of a deceased country gentleman, that he had been, for more than thirty years, *improved* as a justice of peace. This use of the word *improve* is peculiar to New-England, and not to be met with among many other speakers of English, either on this or on the other side of the water.

During my late absence in France, I find that several other new words have been introduced into our parliamentary language. For example, I find a verb formed from the substantive *notice*. *I should not have* noticed *this, were it not that the gentleman*, &c. Also another verb from the substantive *advocate*: *The gentleman who* advocates, *or who has* advocated *that motion*, &c. Another from the substantive *progress*, the most awkward and abominable of the three: *The committee having* progressed, *resolved to adjourn*. The word *opposed*, though not a new word, I find used in a new manner, as, *The gentlemen who are opposed to this measure, to which I have also myself always been* opposed. If you should happen to be of my opinion, with respect to those innovations, you will use your authority in reprobating them.

The Latin language, long the vehicle used in distributing knowledge among the different nations of Europe, is daily more and more neglected; and one of the modern tongues, viz. French, seems, in point of universality, to have supplied its place. It is spoken in all the courts of Europe; and most of the literati, those even who do not speak it, have acquired a knowledge of it, to enable them easily to read the books that are written in it. This gives a considerable advantage to that nation. It enables its authors to inculcate and spread through other nations, such sentiments and opinions, on important points, as are most conducive to its interests, or which may contribute to its reputation, by promoting the common interests of mankind. It is, perhaps, owing to its being written in French, that Voltaire's Treatise on Toleration has had so sudden and so great an effect on the bigotry of Europe, as almost entirely to disarm it. The general use of the French language has likewise a very advantageous effect on the profits of the bookselling branch of commerce; it being well known, that the more copies can be sold that are struck off from one composition of types, the profits increase in a much greater proportion than they do in making a greater number of pieces in any other kind of manufacture. And at present there is no capital town in Europe without a French bookseller's shop corresponding with Paris. Our English bids fair to obtain the second place. The great body of excellent printed sermons in our language, and the freedom of our writings on political subjects, have induced a great number of divines, of different sects and nations, as well as gentlemen concerned in public affairs, to study it so far at least as to read it. And if we were to endeavor the facilitating its progress, the study of our tongue might become much more general. Those who have employed some part of their time in learning a new language, must have frequently observed, that while their acquaintance with it was imperfect, difficulties, small in themselves, have operated as great ones in obstructing their progress. A book, for example, ill printed, or a pronunciation in speaking not well articulated, would render a sentence unintelligible, which from a clear print or a distinct speaker, would have been immediately comprehended. If, therefore, we would have the benefit of seeing our language more generally known among mankind, we should endeavor to remove all the difficulties, however small, that discourage the learning of it. But I am sorry to observe that of late years, those difficulties, instead of being diminished, have been augmented.

In examining the English books that were printed between the Restoration and the accession of George the Second, we may observe, that all substantives were begun with a capital in which we imitated our mother tongue the German. This was more particularly useful to those who were not well acquainted with the English, there being such a prodigious number of our words that are both verbs and substantives, and spelt in the same manner, though often accented differently in pronunciation. This method has, by the fancy of printers, of late years been entirely laid aside; from an idea, that suppressing the capitals shows the character to greater advantage; those letters, prominent above the line, disturbing its even, regular appearance. The effect of this change is so considerable, that a learned man of France, who used to read our books, though not perfectly acquainted with our language, in conversation with me on the subject of our authors, attributed the greater obscurity he found in our modern books, compared with those of the period above mentioned, to a change of style for the worse in our writers; of which mistake I convinced him, by marking for him each substantive with a capital, in a paragraph, which he then easily understood, though before he could not comprehend it. This shows the inconvenience of that pretended improvement.

From the fondness for a uniform and even appearance of characters in a line, the printers have of late banished also the Italic types, in which words of importance to be attended to in the sense of the sentence, and words on which an emphasis should be put in reading, used to be printed. And lately another fancy has induced other printers to use the round *s* instead of the long one, which formerly served well to distinguish a word readily by its varied appearance. Certainly the omitting the prominent letter makes a line appear more even, but renders it less immediately legible, as the paring off all men's noses might smooth their features, but would render their physiognomies less distinguishable. Add to all these improvements backwards, another modern fancy that *gray* printing is more beautiful than black. Hence the English new books are printed in so dim a character as to be read with difficulty by old eyes, unless in a very strong light, and with good glasses. Whoever compares a volume of the Gentleman's Magazine printed between the years 1731 and 1740, with one of those printed in the last ten years, will be convinced of the much greater degree of perspicuity given by black than by the gray. Lord Chesterfield pleasantly remarked this difference to Faulkner, the printer of the Dublin Journal, who was vainly making encomiums on his own paper as the most complete of any in the world. 'But, Mr. Faulkner,' says my Lord, 'don't you think it might be still farther improved, by using paper and ink not quite so near of a color?' —For all these reasons I cannot but wish our American printers would, in their editions, avoid these fancied improvements, and thereby render their works more agreeable to foreigners in Europe, to the great advantage of our bookselling commerce.

Farther, to be more sensible of the advantage of clear and distinct printing, let us consider the assistance it affords in reading well aloud to an auditory. In so doing, the eye generally slides forward three or four words before the voice. If the sight clearly distinguishes what the coming words are, it gives time to order the modulation of the voice to express them properly. But if they are obscurely printed, or disguised by omitting the capitals or long ſ's, or otherwise, the reader is apt to modulate wrong; and, finding he has done so, he is obliged to go back and begin the sentence again; which lessons the pleasure of the hearers. This leads me to mention an old error in our mode of printing. We are sensible, that when a question is met with, in the reading, there is a proper variation to be used in the management of the voice: we have, therefore, a point called an interrogation, affixed to the question, to distinguish it. But this is absurdly placed at its end, so that the reader does not discover it till he finds that he was wrongly modulating his voice, and is therefore obliged to begin again the sentence. To prevent this, the Spanish printers, more sensibly, place an interrogation at the beginning as well as at the end of the question. We have another error of the same kind in printing plays, where something often occurs that is marked as spoken *aside*. But the word *aside* is placed at the end of the speech, when it ought to precede it, as a direction to the reader, that he may govern his voice accordingly. The practice of our ladies, in meeting five or six together, to form little busy parties, where each is employed in some useful work, while one reads to them, is so commendable in itself, that it deserves the attention of authors and printers to make it as pleasing as possible, both to the reader and hearers.

My best wishes attend you, being with sincere esteem,

Sir,

Your most obedient and

Very humble servant.

B. Franklin.

AN ACCOUNT OF THE HIGHEST COURT OF JUDICATURE IN PENNSYLVANIA.

THE COURT OF THE PRESS.

Power of this Court.

It may receive and promulgate accusations of all kinds, against all persons and characters among the citizens of the state, and against all inferior courts; and may judge, sentence, and condemn to infamy, not only private individuals but public bodies, &c. with or without inquiry or hearing, at the court's discretion.

Whose favor, or for whose emolument this court is established.

In favor of about one citizen in five hundred, who, by education, or practice in scribbling, has accquired a tolerable style as to grammar and construction, so as to bear printing; or who is possessed of a press and a few types. The five hundredth part of the citizens have the liberty of accusing and abusing the other four hundred and ninety-nine parts at their pleasure; or they may hire out their pens and press to others, for that purpose.

Practice of this court.

It is not governed by any of the rules of the common courts of law. The accused is allowed no grand jury to judge of the truth of the accusation before it is publicly made; nor is the name of the accuser made known to him, nor has he an opportunity of confronting the witnesses against him, for they are kept in the dark, as in the Spanish court of inquisition. Nor is there any petty jury of his peers sworn to try the truth of the charges. The proceedings are also sometimes so rapid, that an honest good citizen may find himself suddenly and unexpectedly accused, and in the same moment judged and condemned, and sentence pronounced against him that he is a rogue and a villain. Yet if an officer of this court receives the slightest check for misconduct in this his office, he claims immediately the rights of a free citizen by the constitution, and demands to know his accuser, to confront the witnesses, and have a fair trial by the jury of his peers.

The foundation of its authority.

It is said to be founded on an article in the state constitution, which establishes the liberty of the press—a liberty which every Pennsylvanian would fight and die for, though few of us, I believe, have distinct ideas of its nature and extent. It seems, indeed, somewhat like the liberty of the press, that felons have, by the common law of England, before conviction; that is, to be either pressed to death or hanged. If by the liberty of the press, we understood merely the liberty of discussing the propriety of public measures and political opinions, let us have as much of it as you please; but if it means the liberty of affronting, calumniating, and defaming one another, I, for my part, own myself willing to part with my share of it, whenever our legislators shall please to alter the law; and shall cheerfully consent to exchange my liberty of abusing others, for the privilege of not being abused myself.

By whom this court is commissioned or constituted.

It is not by any commission from the supreme executive council, who might previously judge of the abilities, integrity, knowledge, &c. of the persons to be appointed to this great trust, of deciding upon the characters and good fame of the citizens: for this court is above that council, and may accuse, judge, and condemn it at pleasure. Nor is it hereditary, as is the court of dernier resort in the peerage of England. But any man who can procure pen, ink, and paper, with a press, a few types, and a huge pair of blacking balls, may commissionate himself, and his court is immediately established in the plenary possession and exercise of its rights; for if you make the least complaint of the judge's conduct, he daubs his blacking balls in your face wherever he meets you: and besides tearing your private character to splinters, marks you out for the odium of the public, as an enemy to the liberty of the press.

Of the natural support of this court.

Its support is founded in the depravity of such minds as have not been mended by religion, nor improved by good education.

> There is a lust in man no charm can tame,
> Of loudly publishing his neighbor's shame.

Hence

> On eagle's wings immortal scandals fly,
> While virtuous actions are but born and die.—*Dryden.*

Whoever feels pain in hearing a good character of his neighbor, will feel a pleasure in the reverse. And of those who, despairing to rise in distinction by their virtues, are happy if others can be depressed to a level with themselves, there are a sufficient number in every great town to maintain one of these courts by subscription. A shrewd observer once said, that in walking the streets of a slippery morning, one might see where the good-natured people lived, by the ashes thrown on the ice before the doors: probably he would have formed a different conjecture of the temper of those whom he might find engaged in such subscriptions.

Of the checks proper to be established against the abuses of power in those courts.

Hitherto there are none. But since so much has been written and published on the federal constitution; and the necessity of checks in all parts of good government, has been so clearly and learnedly explained, I feel myself so far enlightened as to suspect some check may be proper in this part also; but I have been at a loss to imagine any that may not be construed an infringement of the sacred liberty of the press. At length, however, I think I have found one, that instead of diminishing general liberty, shall augment it; which is, by restoring to the people a species of liberty, of which they have been deprived by our laws—I mean the liberty of the cudgel! In the rude state of society prior to the existence of laws, if one man gave another ill language, the affronted person might return it by a box on the ear; and, if repeated, by a good drubbing; and this without offending against any law; but now the right of making such returns is denied, and they are punished as breaches of the peace, while the right of abusing seems to remain in full force; the laws made against it being rendered ineffectual by the liberty of the press.

My proposal then is, to leave the liberty of the press untouched, to be exercised in its full extent, force, and vigor, but to permit the liberty of the cudgel to go with it, *pari passu.* Thus, my fellow-citizens, if an impudent writer attacks your reputation—dearer perhaps to you than your life, and puts his name to the charge, you may go to him as openly, and break his head. If he conceals himself behind the printer, and you can nevertheless discover who he is, you may, in like manner, way-lay him in the night, attack him behind, and give him a good drubbing. If your adversary hires better writers than himself to abuse you more effectually, you may hire as many porters, stronger than yourself, to assist you in giving him a more effectual drubbing. Thus far goes my project as to *private* resentment and retribution. But if the public should ever happen to be affronted, as it ought to be, with the conduct of such writers, I would not advise proceeding immediately to these extremities, but that we should in moderation content ourselves with tarring and feathering, and tossing in a blanket.

If, however, it should be thought that this proposal of mine may disturb the public peace, I would then humbly recommend to our legislators to take up the consideration of both liberties, that of the press, and that of the cudgel; and by an explicit law mark their extent and limits: and at the same time that they secure the person of a citizen from assaults, they would likewise provide for the security of his reputation.

PAPER.

A POEM.

Some wit of old—such wits of old there were—
Whose hints show'd meaning, whose allusions care,
By one brave stroke to mark all human kind,
Call'd clear blank paper ev'ry infant mind;
When still, as opening sense her dictates wrote,
Fair virtue put a seal, or vice a blot.

The thought was happy, pertinent and true;
Methinks a genius might the plan pursue.
I, (can you pardon my presumption,) I—
No wit, no genius, yet for once will try.

Various the papers various wants produce,
The wants of fashion, elegance, and use.
Men are as various; and if right I scan,
Each sort of *paper* represents some *man*.

Pray note the fop—half powder and half lace—
Nice as a band-box were his dwelling-place:
He's the *gilt paper*, which apart you store,
And lock from vulgar hands in the 'scrutoire.

Mechanics, servants, farmers, and so forth,
Are *copy paper* of inferior worth;
Less priz'd, more useful, for your desk decreed,
Free to all pens, and prompt at ev'ry need.

The wretch, whom av'rice bids to pinch and spare,
Starve, cheat, and pilfer, to enrich an heir,
Is coarse *brown paper;* such as pedlers choose
To wrap up wares, which better men will use.

Take next the miser's contrast, who destroys
Health, fame, and fortune, in a round of joys.
Will any paper match him? Yes, throughout,
He's a true *sinking-paper*, past all doubt.

The retail politician's anxious thought
Deems *this* side always right, and *that* stark nought;
He foams with censure: with applause he raves—
A dupe to rumors, and a tool of knaves;
He'll want no type his weakness to proclaim,
While such a thing as *fools-cap* has a name.

The hasty gentleman, whose blood runs high
Who picks a quarrel, if you step awry,
Who can't a jest, or hint, or look endure:
What's he? What? *Touch-paper* to be sure.

What are our poets, take them as they fall,
Good, bad, rich, poor, much read, not read at all?
Them and their works in the same class you'll find;
They are the mere *waste-paper* of mankind.

Observe the maiden, innocently sweet,
She's fair *white-paper*, an unsullied sheet;
On which the happy man, whom fate ordains,
May write his *name*, and take her for his pains.

One instance more, and only one I'll bring;
'Tis the *great man* that scorns a little thing,
Whose thoughts, whose deeds, whose maxims are his own,
Form'd on the feelings of his heart alone:
True genuine *royal paper* is his breast;
Of all the kinds most precious, purest, best.

ON THE ART OF SWIMMING.

IN ANSWER TO SOME INQUIRIES OF M. DUBOURG ON THE SUBJECT.

I AM apprehensive that I shall not be able to find leisure for making all the disquisitions and experiments which would be desirable on this subject. I must therefore content myself with a few remarks.

The specific gravity of some human bodies, in comparison to that of water, has been examined by M. Robinson, in our Philosophical Transactions, volume 50, page 30, for the year 1757. He asserts, that fat persons with small bones float most easily upon water.

The diving bell is accurately described in our Transactions.

When I was a boy, I made two oval pallets, each about ten inches long, and six broad, with a hole for the thumb, in order to retain it fast in the palm of my hand. They much resemble a painter's pallet. In swimming, I pushed the edges of these forward, and I struck the water with their flat surfaces as I drew them back: I remember I swam faster by means of these pallets, but they fatigued my wrists. I also fitted to the soles of my feet a kind of sandals; but I was not satisfied with them, because I observed that the stroke is partly given by the inside of the feet and the ancles, not entirely with the soles of the feet.

We have here waistcoats for swimming, which are made of double sail-cloth, with small pieces of cork quilted in between them.

I know nothing of the *scaphandre* of M. de la Chapelle.

I know by experience, that it is a great comfort to a swimmer, who has a considerable distance to go, to turn himself sometimes on his back, and to vary in other respects the means of procuring a progessive motion.

When he is seized with the cramp in the leg, the method of driving it away is to give to the parts affected a sudden, vigorous, and violent shock; which he may do in the air, as he swims on his back.

During the great heats of summer, there is no danger in bathing, however warm we may be, in rivers which have been thoroughly warmed by the sun. But to throw one's self into cold spring water, when the body has been heated by exercise in the sun, is an imprudence which may prove fatal. I once knew an instance of four young men, who, having worked at harvests in the heat of the day, with a view of refreshing themselves, plunged into a spring of cold water: two died upon the spot, a third the next morning, and the fourth recovered with great difficulty. A copious draught of cold water, in similar circumstances, is frequently attended with the same effect in North America.

The exercise of swimming is one of the most healthy and agreeable in the world. After having swam for an hour or two in the evening, one sleeps coolly the whole night, even during the most ardent heat of summer. Perhaps the pores being cleansed, the insensible perspiration increases, and occasions this coolness. It is certain, that much swimming is the means of stopping a diarrhœa, and even of producing a constipation. With respect to those who do not know how to swim, or who are affected with a diarrhœa at a season which does not permit them to use that exercise, a warm bath, by cleansing and purifying the skin, is found very salutary, and often effects a radical cure. I speak from my own experience, frequently repeated, and that of others, to whom I have recommended this.

You will not be displeased if I conclude these hasty remarks by informing you, that as the ordinary method of swimming is reduced to the act of rowing with the arms and legs, and is consequently a laborious and fatiguing operation when the space of water to be crossed is considerable, there is a method in which a swimmer may pass to great distances with much facility, by means of a sail. This discovery I fortunately made by accident, and in the following manner:

When I was a boy, I amused myself one day with flying a paper kite; and approaching the bank of a pond, which was near a mile broad, I tied the string to a stake, and the kite ascended to a very considerable height above the pond, while I was swimming. In a little time, being desirous of amusing myself with my kite, and enjoying at the same time the pleasure of swimming, I returned, and loosing from the stake the string with the little stick which was fastened to it, went again into the water, where I found, that lying on my back, and holding the stick in my hands, I was drawn along the surface of the water in a very agreeable manner. Having then engaged another boy to carry my clothes round the pond, to a place which I pointed out to him, on the other side, I began to cross the pond with my kite, which carried me quite over without the least fatigue, and with the greatest pleasure imaginable. I was only obliged occasionally to halt a little in my course, and resist its progress, when it appeared that by following too quick, I lowered the kite too much; by doing which occasionally I made it rise again. I have never since that time practised this singular mode of swimming, though I think it not impossible to cross in this manner from Dover to Calais. The packet-boat, however, is still preferable.

NEW MODE OF BATHING.

EXTRACTS OF LETTERS TO M. DUBOURG.

London, July 28, 1768.

I GREATLY approve the epithet which you give, in your letter of the 8th of June, to the new method of treating the small-pox, which you call the *tonic* or bracing method; I will take occasion, from it, to mention a practice to which I have accustomed myself. You know the cold bath has long been in vogue here as a tonic: but the shock of the cold water hath always appeared to me, generally speaking, as too violent, and I have found it much more agreeable to my constitution to bathe in another element—I mean cold air. With this view I rise early almost every morning, and sit in my chamber without any clothes whatever, half an hour or an hour, according to the season, either reading or writing. This practice is not in the least painful, but, on the contrary, agreeable; and if I return to bed afterward, before I dress myself, as it sometimes happens, I make a supplement to my night's rest of one or two hours of the most pleasing sleep that can be imagined. I find no ill consequences whatever resulting from it, and that at least it does not injure my health, if it does not in fact contribute to its preservation. I shall therefore call it for the future a *bracing*, or *tonic* bath.

March 10, 1773.

I SHALL not attempt to explain why damp clothes occasion colds, rather than wet ones, because I doubt the fact; I imagine that neither the one nor the other contribute to this effect, and that the causes of colds are totally independent of wet and even of cold. I propose writing a short paper on this subject, the first moment of leisure I have at my disposal. In the meantime, I can only say, that having some suspicions that the common notion, which attributes to cold the property of stopping the pores and obstructing the perspiration was ill-founded, I engaged a young physician, who is making some experiments with Sanctorius's balance, to estimate the different proportions of his perspiration, when remaining one hour quite naked, and another warmly clothed. He pursued the experiment in this alternate manner for eight hours successively, and found his perspiration almost double during those hours in which he was naked.

OBSERVATIONS

ON THE GENERALLY PREVAILING DOCTRINES OF LIFE AND DEATH.

To the same.

YOUR observations on the causes of death, and the experiments which you propose for recalling to life those who appear to be killed by lightning, demonstate equally your sagacity and humanity. It appears that the doctrines of life and death, in general, are yet but little understood.

A toad buried in the sand will live, it is said, until the sand becomes petrified; and then, being enclosed in the stone, it may live for we know not how many ages. The facts which are cited in support of this opinion, are too numerous and too circumstantial not to deserve a certain degree of credit. As we are accustomed to see all the animals with which we are acquainted eat and drink, it appears to us difficult to conceive, how a toad can be supported in such a dungeon. But if we reflect that the necessity of nourishment which animals experience in their ordinary state, proceeds from the continual waste of their substance by perspiration; it will appear less incredible, that some animals, in a torpid state, perspiring less because they use no exercise, should have less need of aliment; and that others, which are covered with scales or shells, which stop perspiration, such as land and sea turtles, serpents, and some species of fish, should be able to subsist a considerable time without any nourishment whatever. A plant with its flowers, fades and dies immediately, if exposed to the air without having its roots immersed in a humid soil, from which it may draw a sufficient quantity of moisture to supply that which exhales from its substance, and is carrried off continually by the air. Perhaps, however, if it were buried in quicksilver, it might preserve, for a considerable space of time, its vegetable life, its smell and color. If this be the case, it might prove a commodious method of transporting from distant countries those delicate plants which are unable to sustain the inclemency of the weather at sea, and which require particular care and attention.

I have seen an instance of common flies preserved in a manner somewhat similar. They had been drowned in Madeira wine, apparently about the time it was bottled in Virginia, to be sent to London. At the opening of one of the bottles, at the house of a friend where I was, three drowned flies fell into the first glass that was filled. Having heard it remarked that drowned flies were capable of being revived by the rays of the sun, I proposed making the experiment upon these. They were therefore exposed to the sun, upon a sieve which had been employed to strain them out of the wine. In less than three hours, two of them by degress began to recover life. They commenced by some convulsive motions in the thighs, and at length they raised themselves upon their legs, wiped their eyes with their fore feet, beat and brushed their wings with their hind feet, and soon after began to fly, finding themselves in Old England, without knowing how they came thither. The third continued lifeless until sunset, when, losing all hopes of him, he was thrown away.

I wish it were possible, from this instance, to invent a method of embalming drowned persons in such a manner, that they may be recalled to life at any period, however distant: for, having a very ardent desire to see and observe the state of America a hundred years hence, I should prefer to an ordinary death, the being immersed in a cask of Madeira wine, with a few friends, until that time, then to be recalled to life by the solar warmth of my dear country! But since, in [illegible]obability, we live in an age too early, and too near the infancy of science, to see such an art brought in our time to its perfection, I must, for the present, content myself with the treat, which you are so kind as to promise me, of the resurrection of a fowl or a turkey-cock.

PRECAUTIONS

TO BE USED BY THOSE WHO ARE ABOUT TO UNDERTAKE A SEA VOYAGE.

When you intend to take a long voyage, nothing is better than to keep it a secret till the moment of your departure. Without this, you will be continually interrupted and tormented by visits from friends and acquaintances, who not only make you lose your valuable time, but make you forget a thousand things which you wish to remember; so that when you are embarked and fairly at sea, you recollect, with much uneasiness, affairs which you have not terminated, accounts that you have not settled, and a number of things which you proposed to carry with you, and which you find the want of every moment. Would it not be attended with the best consequences to reform such a custom, and to suffer a traveller, without deranging him, to make his preparations in quietness, to set apart a few days, when these are finished, to take leave of his friends, and to receive their good wishes for his happy return?

It is not always in one's power to choose a captain; though great part of the pleasure and happiness of the passage depends upon this choice, and though one must, for a time, be confined to his company, and be in some measure under his command. If he is a social, sensible man, obliging, and of a good disposition, you will be so much the happier. One sometimes meets with people of this description, but they are not common; however, if yours be not of this number, if he be a good seaman, attentive, careful, and active in the management of his vessel, you must dispense with the rest, for these are the most essential qualities.

Whatever right you may have, by your agreement with him to the provisions he has taken on board for the use of the passengers, it is always proper to have some private store which you may make use of occasionally. You ought, therefore, to provide good water, that of the ship being often bad; but you must put it into bottles, without which you cannot expect to preserve it sweet. You ought also to carry with you good tea, ground coffee, chocolate, wine of that sort which you like best, cider, dried raisins, almonds, sugar, capillaire, citrons, rum, eggs dipped in oil, portable soup, and bread twice baked. With regard to poultry, it is almost useless to carry any with you, unless you resolve to undertake the office of feeding and fattening them yourself. With the little care which is taken of them on board a ship, they are almost all sickly, and their flesh is as tough as leather.

All sailors entertain an opinion, which undoubtedly originated formerly from a want of water, and when it has been found necessary to be sparing of it, that poultry never know when they have drank enough, and that when water is given them at discretion, they generally kill themselves by drinking beyond measure. In consequence of this opinion, they give them water only once in two days, and even then in small quantities: but as they pour this water into troughs inclining on one side, which occasions it to run to the lower part, it thence happens that they are obliged to mount one upon the back of another in order to reach it; and there are some which cannot even dip their beaks in it. Thus continually tantalized and tormented by thirst, they are unable to digest their food, which is very dry, and they soon fall sick and die. Some of them are found thus every morning, and are thrown into the sea; while those which are killed for the table are scarcely fit to be eaten. To remedy this inconvenience, it will be necessary to divide their troughs into small compartments, in such a manner, that each of them may be capable of containing water; but this is seldom or never done. On this account, sheep and hogs are to be considered as the best fresh provisions that one can have at sea; mutton there being in general very good, and pork excellent.

It may happen that some of the provisions and stores, which I have recommended, may become almost useless, by the care which the captain has taken to lay in a proper stock: but in such a case you may dispose of it to relieve the poor passengers, who, paying less for their passage, are stowed among the common sailors, and have no right to the captain's provisons, except such part of them as is used for feeding the crew. These passengers are sometimes sick, melancholy, and dejected; and there are often women and children among them, neither of whom have an opportunity of procuring those things which I have mentioned, and of which perhaps they have the greatest need. By distributing amongst them a part of your superfluity, you may be of the greatest assistance to them. You may restore their health, save their lives and in short render them happy: which always affords the iveliest sensation to a feeling mind.

The most disagreeable thing at sea is the cookery; for there is not, properly speaking, any professed cook on board. The worst sailor is generally chosen for that purpose, who for the most part is equally dirty. Hence comes the proverb used among the English sailors, that *God sends meat, and the devil sends cooks.* Those, however, who have a better opinion of Providence, will think otherwise. Knowing that sea air, and the exercise or motion which they receive from the rolling of the ship, have a wonderful effect in whetting the appetite, they will say that Providence has given sailors bad cooks to prevent them from eating too much; or that, knowing they would have bad cooks, he has given them a good appetite to prevent them from dying with hunger. However, if you have no confidence in these succors of Providence, you may yourself, with a lamp and a boiler, by the help of a little spirits of wine, prepare some food, such as soup, hash, &c. A small oven made of tin-plate is not a bad piece of furniture; your servant may roast in it a piece of mutton or pork. If you are ever tempted to eat salt beef, which is often very good, you will find that cider is the best liquor to quench the thirst generally caused by salt meat or salt fish. Sea-biscuit, which is too hard for the teeth of some people, may be softened by steeping it; but bread double-baked is the best: for being made of good loaf-bread cut into slices, and baked a second time, it readily imbibes water, becomes soft, and is easily digested: it consequently forms excellent nourishment, much superior to that of biscuit, which has not been fermented.

I must here observe, that this double-baked bread was originally the real biscuit prepared to keep at sea; for the word *biscuit*, in French, signifies twice baked.* Peas often boil badly, and do not become soft; in such a case, by putting a two-pound shot into the kettle, the rolling of the vessel, by means of this bullet, will convert the peas into a porridge, like mustard.

Having often seen soup, when put upon the table at sea in broad flat dishes thrown out on every side by the rolling of the vessel, I have wished that our tin-men would make our soup-basins with divisions or compartments; forming small plates, proper for containing soup for one person only. By this disposition, the soup, in an extraordinary roll, would not

* It is derived from *bis* again, and *cuit* baked

be thrown out of the plate, and would not fall into the breasts of those who are at table, and scald them. Having entertained you with these things of little importance, permit me now to conclude with some general reflections upon navigation.

When navigation is employed only for transporting necessary provisions from one country, where they abound, to another where they are wanting: when by this it prevents famines, which were so frequent and so fatal before it was invented and became so common, we cannot help considering it as one of those arts which contribute most to the happiness of mankind. But when it is employed to transport things of no utility, or articles of luxury, it is then uncertain whether the advantages resulting from it are sufficient to counterbalance the misfortunes it occasions by exposing the lives of so many individuals upon the vast ocean. And when it is used to plunder vessels and transport slaves, it is evidently only the dreadful means of increasing those calamities which afflict human nature.

One is astonished to think on the number of vessels and men who are daily exposed in going to bring tea from China, coffee from Arabia, and sugar and tobacco from America all commodities which our ancestors lived very well without. The sugar trade employs nearly a thousand vessels; and that of tobacco almost the same number. With regard to the utility of tobacco, little can be said; and, with regard to sugar, how much more meritorious would it be to sacrifice the momentary pleasure which we receive from drinking it once or twice a day in our tea, than to encourage the numberless cruelties that are continually exercised in order to procure it for us?

A celebrated French moralist said, that, when he considered the wars which we foment in Africa to get negroes, the great number who of course perish in these wars; the multitude of these wretches who die in their passage, by disease, bad air, and bad provisions; and, lastly, how many perish by the cruel treatment they meet with in a state of slavery: when he saw a bit of sugar, he could not help imagining it to be covered with spots of human blood. But, had he added to these considerations the wars which we carry on against one another, to take and retake the islands that produce this commodity, he would not have seen the sugar simply spotted with blood, he would have beheld it entirely tinged with it.

These wars made the maritime powers of Europe, and the inhabitants of Paris and London, pay much dearer for their ugar than those of Vienna, though they are almost three hundred leagues distant from the sea. A pound of sugar, indeed, costs the former not only the price which they give for it, but also that which they pay in taxes, necessary to support the fleets and armies which serve to defend and protect the countries that produce it.

ON LUXURY, IDLENESS, AND INDUSTRY.

From a Letter to Benjamin Vaughan, Esq.† written in 1784.

It is wonderful how preposterously the affairs of this world are managed. Naturally one would imagine, that the interest of a few individuals should give way to general interest; but individuals manage their affairs with so much more application, industry, and address, than the public do theirs, that general interest most commonly gives way to particular. We assemble parliaments and councils, to have the benefit of their collected wisdom; but we necessarily have, at the same time, the inconvenience of their collected passions, prejudices, and private interests. By the help of these, artful men overpower their wisdom, and dupe its possessors; and if we may judge by the acts, arrests, and edicts, all the world over, for regulating commerce, an assembly of great men is the greatest fool upon earth.

I have not yet, indeed, thought of a remedy for luxury. I am not sure that in a great state it is capable of a remedy nor that the evil is in itself always so great as is represented. Suppose we include the definition of luxury all unnecessary expense, and then let us consider whether laws to prevent such expense are possible to be executed in a great country, and whether, if they could be executed, our people generally would be happier, or even richer. Is not the hope of being one day able to purchase and enjoy luxuries a great spur to labor and industry? May not luxury, therefore, produce more than it consumes, if, without such a spur, people would be, as they are naturally enough inclined to be, lazy and indolent. To this purpose I remember a circumstance. The skipper of a shallop, employed between Cape May and Philadelphia, had done us some small service, for which he refused to be paid. My wife, understanding that he had a daughter, sent her a present of a new-fashioned cap. Three years after, this skipper being at my house with an old far

---

† Member of parliament for the borough of Calne, in Wiltshire, between whom and our author there subsisted a very close friendship.

mer of Cape May, his passenger, he mentioned the cap, and how much his daughter had been pleased with it 'But (said he) it proved a dear cap with our congregation. 'How so?'—'When my daughter appeared with it at meeting, it was so much admired, that all the girls resolved to get such caps from Philadelphia; and my wife and I computed that the whole could not have cost less than a hundred pounds.' —'True (said the farmer), but you do not tell all the story. I think the cap was nevertheless an advantage to us; for it was the first thing that put our girls upon knitting worsted mittens for sale at Philadelphia, that they might have where-withal to buy caps and ribands there; and you know that that industry has continued, and is likely to continue and increase to a much greater value, and answer better purposes.'—Upon the whole, I was more reconciled to this little piece of luxury, since not only the girls were made happier by having fine caps, but the Philadelphians by the supply of warm mittens.

In our commercial towns upon the sea-coast, fortunes will occasionally be made. Some of those who grow rich, will be prudent, live within bounds, and preserve what they have gained for their posterity; others, fond of showing their wealth, will be extravagant and ruin themselves. Laws cannot prevent this; and perhaps it is not always an evil to the public. A shilling spent idly by a fool, may be picked up by a wiser person, who knows better what to do with it. It is therefore not lost. A vain, silly fellow builds a fine house, furnishes it richly, lives in it expensively, and in a few years ruins himself; but the masons, carpenters, smiths, and other honest tradesmen, have been by his employ assisted in maintaining and raising their families; the farmer has been paid for his labor, and encouraged, and the estate is now in better hands. In some cases, indeed, certain modes of luxury may be a public evil, in the same manner as it is a private one. If there be a nation, for instance, that exports its beef and linen, to pay for the importation of claret and porter, while a great part of its people live upon potatoes, and wear no shirts; wherein does it differ from the sot, who lets his family starve, and sells his clothes to buy drink? Our American commerce is, I confess, a little in this way. We sell our victuals to the islands for rum and sugar; the substantial necessaries of life for superfluities. But we have plenty, and live well nevertheless; though by being soberer, we might be richer.

The vast quantity of forest land we have yet to clear, and put in order for cultivation, will for a long time keep the body of our nation laborious and frugal. Forming an opinion of our people, and their manners, by what is seen among the inhabitants of the sea-ports, is judging from an improper sample. The people of the trading towns may be rich and luxurious, while the country possesses all the virtues that tend to promote happiness and public prosperity. Those towns are not much regarded by the country; they are hardly considered as an essential part of the States; and the experience of the last war has shown, that their being in the possession of the enemy did not necessarily draw on the subjection of the country; which bravely continued to maintain its freedom and independence notwithstanding.

It has been computed by some political arithmetician, that if every man and woman would work for four hours each day on something useful, that labor would produce sufficient to procure all the necessaries and comforts of life; want and misery would be banished out of the world, and the rest of the twenty-four hours might be leisure and pleasure.

What occasions then so much want and misery? It is the employment of men and women in works that produce neither the necessaries nor conveniences of life; who, with those who do nothing, consume necessaries raised by the laborious. To explain this:

The first elements of wealth are obtained by labor from the earth and waters. I have land, and raise corn. With this, if I feed a family that does nothing, my corn will be consumed, and at the end of the year I shall be no richer than I was at the beginning. But if, while I feed them, I employ them, some in spinning, others in making bricks, &c. for building, the value of my corn will be arrested and remain with me, and at the end of the year we may all be better clothed and better lodged. And if, instead of employing a man I feed in making bricks, I employ him in fiddling for me, the corn he eats is gone, and no part of his manufacture remains to augment the wealth and convenience of the family; I shall, therefore, be the poorer for this fiddling man, unless the rest of the family work more, or eat less, to make up the deficiency he occasions.

Look round the world, and see the millions employed in doing nothing, or in something that amounts to nothing, when the necessaries and conveniences of life are in question. What is the bulk of commerce, for which we fight and destroy each other, but the toil of millions for superfluities, to the great hazard and loss of many lives, by the constant dangers of the sea? How much labor is spent in building and fitting great ships, to go to China and Arabia for tea and coffee, to the West Indies for sugar, to America for tobacco? These things cannot be called the necessaries of life, for our ancestors lived very comfortable without them.

A question may be asked—Could all these people now employed in raising, making, or carrying superfluities, be subsisted by raising necessaries? I think they might. The world is large, and a great part of it still uncultivated. Many hundred millions of acres in Asia, Africa, and America, are still in a forest; and a great deal even in Europe. On a hundred acres of this forest, a man might become a substantial farmer; and a hundred thousand men employed in clearing each his hundred acres, would hardly brighten a spot large enough to be visible from the moon, unless with Herschel's telescope; so vast are the regions still in wood.

It is, however, some comfort to reflect that, upon the whole, the quantity of industry and prudence among mankind exceeds the quantity of idleness and folly. Hence the increase of good buildings, farms cultivated, and populous cities filled with wealth, all over Europe, which a few ages since were only to be found on the coast of the Mediterranean: and this notwithstanding the mad wars continually raging, by which are often destroyed, in one year, the works of many years' peace. So that we may hope, the luxury of a few merchants on the coast will not be the ruin of America.

One reflection more, and I will end this long rambling letter. Almost all the parts of our bodies require some expense. The feet demand shoes; the legs, stockings; the rest of the body, clothing; and the belly, a good deal of victuals. Our eyes, though exceeding useful, ask, when reasonable, only the cheap assistance of spectacles, which could not much impair our finances. But the eyes of other people are the eyes that ruin us. If all but myself were blind, I should want neither fine cloths, fine houses, nor fine furniture.

ON THE SLAVE TRADE.

Reading in newspapers the speech of Mr. Jackson in congress, against meddling with the affair of slavery, or attempting to mend the condition of slaves, it put me in mind of a similar speech, made about one hundred years since, by Sidi Mahomet Ibrahim, a member of the divan of Algiers, which may be seen in Martin's account of his consulship, 1687. It was against granting the petition of the sect called *Erika*, or *Purists*, who prayed for the abolition of piracy and slavery, as being unjust—Mr. Jackson does not quote it: perhaps he has not seen it. If, therefore, some of its reasonings are to be found in his eloquent speech, it may only shew that men's interests operate, and are operated on, with surprising similarity, in all countries and climates, whenever they are under similar circumstances. The African speech, as translated, is as follows:

'Alla Bismillah, &c. God is great, and Mahomet is his prophet.'

'Have these Erika considered the consequences of granting their petition? If we cease our cruises against the Christians, how shall we be furnished with the commodities their countries produce, and which are so necessary for us? If we forbear to make slaves of their people, who, in this hot climate, are to cultivate our lands? Who are to perform the common labors of our city, and of our families? Must we not be then our own slaves? And is there not more compassion and more favor due to us Mussulmen than to those Christian dogs?—We have now above fifty thousand slaves in and near Algiers. This number, if not kept up by fresh supplies, will soon diminish, and be gradually annihilated. If, then, we cease taking and plundering the infidels' ships, and making slaves of the seamen and passengers, our lands will become of no value, for want of cultivation; the rents of houses in the city will sink one half; and the revenues of government, arising from the share of prizes, must be totally destroyed.—And for what? To gratify the whim of a whimsical sect, who would have us not only forbear making more slaves, but even manumit those we have. But who is to indemnify their masters for the loss? Will the state do it? Is our treasury sufficient? Will the Erika do it? can they do it? Or would they, to do what they think justice to the slaves, do a greater injustice to the owners? And if we set our slaves free, what is to be done with them? few of them will return to their native countries; they know too well the greater hardships they must there be subject to. They will not embrace our holy religion: they will not adopt our manners: our people will not pollute themselves by intermarrying with them. Must we maintain them as beggars in our streets; or suffer our properties to be the prey of their pillage? for men accustomed to slavery will not work for a livelihood when not compelled.—And what is there so pitiable in their present condition? Were they not slaves in their own countries? Are not Spain, Portugal, France, and the Italian states, governed by despots, who hold all their subjects in slavery, without exception?

Even England treats her sailors as slaves; for they are, whenever the government pleases, seized and confined in ships of war, condemned not only to work, but to fight for small wages, or a mere subsistence, not better than our slaves are allowed by us. Is their condition then made worse by their falling into our hands? No: they have only exchanged one slavery for another; and I may say a better: for here they are brought into a land where the sun of Islamism gives forth its light, and shines in full splendor, and they have an opportunity of making themselves acquainted with the true doctrine, and thereby save their immortal souls. Those who remain at home have not that happiness. Sending the slaves home, then, would be sending them out of light into darkness.

'I repeat the question, what is to be done with them? I have heard it suggested, that they may be planted in the wilderness, where there is plenty of land for them to subsist on, and where they may flourish as a free state.—But they are, I doubt, too little disposed to labor without compulsion, as well as too ignorant to establish good government; and the wild Arabs would soon molest and destroy, or again enslave them. While serving us, we take care to provide them with every thing; and they are treated with humanity. The laborers in their own countries are, as I am informed, worse fed, lodged, and clothed. The condition of most of them is therefore already mended, and requires no farther improvement. Here their lives are in safety. They are not liable to be impressed for soldiers, and forced to cut one another's Christian throats, as in the wars of their own countries. If some of the religious mad bigots who now tease us with their silly petitions, have, in a fit of blind zeal, freed their slaves, it was not generosity, it was not humanity, that moved them to the action; it was from the conscious burden of a load of sins, and hope, from the supposed merits of so good a work, to be excused from damnation.—How grossly are they mistaken, in imagining slavery to be disavowed by the Alcoran! Are not the two precepts, to quote no more, 'Masters, treat your slaves with kindness—Slaves, serve your masters with cheerfulness and fidelity,' clear proofs to the contrary? Nor can the plundering of infidels be in that sacred book forbidden; since it is well known from it, that God has given the world, and all that it contains, to his faithful Mussulmen, who are to enjoy it, of right, as fast as they conquer it. Let us then hear no more of this detestable proposition, the manumission of Christian slaves; the adoption of which would, by depreciating our lands and houses, and thereby depriving so many good citizens of their properties, create universal discontent, and provoke insurrections, to the endangering of government, and producing general confusion. I have, therefore, no doubt, that this wise council will prefer the comfort and happiness of a whole nation of true believers, to the whim of a few Erika, and dismiss their petition.'

The result was, as Martin tells us, that the Divan came to this resolution: 'That the doctrine, that the plundering and enslaving the Christians is unjust, is at best problematical; but that it is the interest of this state to continue the practice, is clear; therefore, let the petition be rejected.'—And it was rejected accordingly.

And, since like motives are apt to produce, in the minds of men, like opinions and resolutions, may we not venture to predict, from this account, that the petitions to the parliament of England for abolishing the slave trade, to say nothing of other legislatures, and the debates upon them, will have a similar conclusion.

March 23, 1790. HISTORICUS.

OBSERVATIONS ON WAR.

By the original law of nations, war and extirpation were the punishment of injury. Humanizing by degrees, it admitted slavery instead of death: a farther step was, the exchange of prisoners instead of slavery: another, to respect more the property of private persons under conquest, and be content with acquired dominion. Why should not this law of nations go on improving? Ages have intervened between its several steps; but as knowledge of late increases rapidly, why should not those steps be quickened! Why should it not be agreed to, as the future law of nations, that in any war hereafter, the following description of men should be undisturbed, have the protection of both sides, and be permitted to follow their employments in security? viz.

1. Cultivators of the earth, because they labor for the subsistence of mankind.

2. Fishermen, for the same reason.

3. Merchants and traders in unarmed ships, who accommodate different nations by communicating and exchanging the necessaries and conveniences of life.

4. Artists and mechanics, inhabiting and working in open towns.

It is hardly necessary to add, that the hospitals of enemies should be unmolested—they ought to be assisted. It is for the interest of humanity in general, that the occasions of war, and the inducements to it, should be diminished. If rapine be abolished, one of the encouragements to war is taken away; and peace therefore more likely to continue and be lasting.

The practice of robbing merchants on the high seas—a remnant of the ancient piracy—though it may be accidentally beneficial to particular persons, is far from being profitable to all engaged in it, or to the nation that authorizes it. In the beginning of a war some rich ships are surprised and taken. This encourages the first adventurers to fit out more armed vessels: and many others to do the same. But the enemy at the same time become more careful, arm their merchant-ships better, and render them not so easy to be taken: they go also more under the protection of convoys. Thus, while the privateers to take them are multiplied, the vessels subjected to be taken, and the chances of profit, are diminished; so that many cruises are made wherein the expenses overgo the gains; and, as is the case in other lotteries, though particulars have got prizes, the mass of adventurers are losers; the whole expense of fitting out all the privateers during a war being much greater than the whole amount of goods taken.

Then there is the national loss of all the labor of so many men during the time they have been employed in robbing; who besides spend what they get in riot, drunkenness, and debauchery; lose their habits of industry; are rarely fit for any sober business after a peace, and serve only to increase the number of highwaymen and house-breakers. Even the undertakers, who have been fortunate, are by sudden wealth led into expensive living, the habit of which continues when the means of supporting it cease, and finally ruins them: a just punishment for their having wantonly and unfeelingly ruined many honest, innocent traders and their families, whose substance was employed in serving the common interest of mankind.

ON THE IMPRESS OF SEAMEN.

Notes copied from Dr. Franklin's writing in pencil in the margin of Judge Foster's celebrated argument in favor of the Impressing of Seamen (published in the folio edition of his works).

JUDGE FOSTER, p. 158. 'Every man.'—The conclusion here from the *whole to a part*, does not seem to be good logic. If the alphabet should say, Let us all fight for the defence of the whole; that is equal, and may, therefore, be just. But if they should say, Let A B C and D go out and fight for us, while we stay at home and sleep in whole skins; that is not equal, and therefore cannot be just.

Ib. 'Employ.'—If you please. The word signifies engaging a man to work for me, by offering him such wages as are sufficient to induce him to prefer my service. This is very different from compelling him to work on such terms as I think proper.

Ib. 'This service and employment,' &c.—These are false facts. His employment and service are not the same.—Under the merchant he goes in an unarmed vessel, not obliged to fight, but to transport merchandize. In the king's service he is obliged to fight, and to hazard all the dangers of battle. Sickness on board of king's ships is also more common and more mortal. The merchant's service, too, he can quit at the end of the voyage; not the king's. Also, the merchant's wages are much higher.

Ib. 'I am very sensible,' &c.—Here are two things put in comparison that are not comparable: viz. injury to seamen, and inconvenience to trade. Inconvenience to the whole trade of a nation will not justify injustice to a single seaman. It the trade would suffer without his service, it is able and ought to be willing to offer him such wages as may induce him to afford his service voluntarily.

Page 159. 'Private mischief must be borne with patience, for preventing a national calamity.' Where is this maxim in aw and good policy to be found? And how can that be a maxim which is not consistent with common sense? If the maxim had been, that private mischiefs, which prevent a national calamity, ought to be generously compensated by the nation, one might understand it: but that such private mischiefs are only to be borne with patience, is absurd!

Ib. 'The expedient,' &c. 'And,' &c. (Paragraphs 2 and 3).—Twenty ineffectual or inconvenient schemes will not justify one that is unjust.

Ib. 'Upon the foot of,' &c.—Your reasoning, indeed, like a lie, stands but upon one *foot;* truth upon two.

Page 160. 'Full wages.'—Probably the same they had in the merchant's service.

Page 174. 'I hardly admit,' &c.—(Paragraph 5).—When this author speaks of impressing, page 158, he diminishes the horror of the practice as much as possible, by presenting to the mind one sailor only suffering a '*hardship*' (as he tenderly calls it) in some '*particular cases*' only; and he places against this private mischief the inconvenience to the trade of the kingdom.—But if, as he supposes is often the case, the sailor who is pressed and obliged to serve for the defence of trade, at the rate of twenty-five shillings a month, could get three pounds fifteen shillings in the merchants' service, you take from him fifty shillings a month; and if you have 100,000 in your service, you rob this honest industrious part of society and their poor families of 250,000*l.* per month, or three millions a year, and at the same time oblige them to hazard their lives in fighting for the defence of your trade; to the defence of which all ought indeed to contribute (and sailors among the rest) in proportion to their profits by it: but this three millions is more than their share, if they do not pay with their persons; but when you force that, methinks you should excuse the other.

But, it may be said, to give the king's seamen merchants' wages would cost the nation too much, and call for more taxes. The question then will amount to this: whether it be just in a community, that the richer part should compel the poorer to fight in defence of them and their properties, for such wages as they think fit to allow, and punish them if they refuse? Our author tells us that it is '*legal.*' I have not law enough to dispute his authorities, but I cannot persuade myself that it is equitable. I will, however, own for the present, that it may be lawful when necessary; but then I contend that it may be used so as to produce the same good effects—*the public security*, without doing so much intolerable injustice as attends the impressing common seamen.—In order to be better understood, I would premise two things:—First, That voluntary seamen may be had for the service, if they were sufficiently paid. The proof is, that to serve in the same ship, and incur the same dangers, you have no occasion to impress captains, lieutenants, second lieutenants, midshipmen, pursers, nor many other officers. Why, but that the profits of their places, or the emoluments expected, are sufficient inducements? The business then is, to find money, by impressing, sufficient to make the sailors all volunteers, as well as their officers; and this without any fresh burden upon trade.—The second of my premises is, that twenty-five shillings a month, with his share of the salt beef, pork, and peas-pudding, being found sufficient for the subsistence of a hard-working seaman, it will certainly be so for a sedentary scholar or gentleman. I would then propose to form a treasury, out of which encouragements to seamen should be paid. To fill this treasury, I would impress a number of civil officers, who at present have great salaries, oblige them to serve in their respective offices for twenty-five shillings a month with their share of mess provisions, and throw the rest of their salaries into the seamen's treasury. If such a press-warrant were given me to execute, the first I would press should be a Recorder of Bristol, or a Mr. Justice Foster, because I might have need of his edifying example, to show how much impressing ought to be borne with; for he would certainly find, that though to be reduced to twenty-five shillings a month might be a '*private mischief*,' yet that, agreeably to his maxim of law and good policy, it '*ought to be borne with patience*,' for preventing a national calamity. Then I would press the rest of the judges; and, opening the red book, I would press every civil officer of government, from 50*l.* a year salary up to 50,000*l.* which would throw an immense sum into our treasury: and these gentlemen could not complain, since they would receive twenty-five shillings a month, and their rations; and this without being obliged to fight. Lastly, I think I would impress * * *

ON THE CRIMINAL LAWS AND THE PRACTICE OF PRIVATEERING.

Letter to Benjamin Vaughan, Esq.

MY DEAR FRIEND, *March*, 14, 1785

AMONG the pamphlets you lately sent me was one, entitled, *Thoughts on Executive Justice.* In return for that, I send you a French one on the same subject, *Observations concernant l'Exécution de l'Article II. de la Déclaration sur le Vol.* They are both addressed to the judges, but written, as you will see, in a very different spirit. The English author is for hanging *all* thieves. The Frenchman is for proportioning punishments to offences.

If we really believe, as we profess to believe, that the law of Moses was the law of God, the dictate of Divine wisdom, infinitely superior to human; on what principles do we ordain death as the punishment of an offence, which, according to that law, was only to be punished by a restitution of fourfold? To put a man to death for an offence which does not deserve death, is it not a murder? And, as the French writer says, *Doit-on punir un délit contre la société par un crime contre la nature?*

Superfluous property is the creature of society. Simple and mild laws were sufficient to guard the property that was merely necessary. The savage's bow, his hatchet, and his coat of skins, were sufficiently secured, without law, by the fear of personal resentment and retaliation. When, by virtue of the first laws, part of the society accumulated wealth and grew powerful, they enacted others more severe, and would protect their property at the expense of humanity. This was abusing their power, and commencing a tyranny. If a savage, before he entered into society, had been told—'Your neighbor, by this means, may become owner of a hundred deer; but if your brother, or your son, or yourself, having no deer of your own, and being hungry, should kill one, an infamous death must be the consequence,' he would probably have preferred his liberty, and his common right of killing any deer, to all the advantages of society that might be proposed to him.

That it is better a hundred guilty persons should escape, than that one innocent person should suffer, is a maxim that has been long and generally approved; never that I know of, controverted. Even the sanguinary author of the *Thoughts* agrees to it, adding well, 'that the very thought of *injured* innocence, and much more that of *suffering* innocence, must awaken all our tenderest and most compassionate feelings, and at the same time raise our highest indignation against the instruments of it. But,' he adds, 'there is no danger of *either*, from a strict adherence to the laws.—Really!—Is it then impossible to make an unjust law; and if the law itself be unjust, may it not be the very 'instrument' which ought 'to raise the author's and every body's indignation?' I see in the last newspapers from London, that a woman is capitally convicted at the Old Bailey, for privately stealing out of a shop some gauze, value fourteen shillings and threepence. Is there any proportion between the injury done by a theft, value fourteen shillings and threepence, and the punishment of a human creature, by death, on a gibbet? Might not that woman, by her labor, have made the reparation ordained by God in paying fourfold? Is not all punishment inflicted beyond the merit of the offence, so much punishment of innocence? In this light, how vast is the annual quantity, of not only *injured* but *suffering* innocence, in almost all the civilized states of Europe.

But it seems to have been thought, that this kind of innocence may be punished by way of *preventing* crimes. I have read, indeed, of a cruel Turk, in Barbary, who whenever he bought a new Christian slave, ordered him immediately to be hung up by the legs, and to receive a hundred blows of a cudgel on the soles of his feet, that the severe sense of the punishment, and fear of incurring it thereafter, might prevent the faults that should merit it. Our author himself would hardly approve entirely of this Turk's conduct in the government of slaves: and yet he appears to recommend something like it for the government of English subjects, when he applauds the reply of Judge Burnet to the convict horse-stealer; who, being asked what he had to say why judgment of death should not pass against him, and answering, that it was hard to hang a man for *only* stealing a horse, was told by the judge, 'Man, thou art not to be hanged *only* for stealing a horse, but that horses may not be stolen.' The man's answer, if candidly examined, will, I imagine, appear reasonable, as being founded on the eternal principle of justice and equity, that punishments should be proportioned to offences; and the judge's reply brutal and unreasonable, though the writer 'wishes all judges to carry it with them whenever they go the circuit, and to bear it, in their minds, as containing a wise reason for all the penal statutes which they are called upon to put in execution. It at once illustrates,' says he, 'the true grounds and reasons of all capital punishments whatsoever, namely, that every man's property, as well as his life, may be held sacred and inviolate.' Is there then no difference in value between property and life? If I think it right that the crime of murder should be punished with death, not only as an equal punishment of the crime, but to prevent other murders, does it follow that I must approve of inflicting the same punishment for a little invasion on my property by theft? If I am not myself so barbarous, so bloody-minded, and revengeful, as to kill a fellow-creature for stealing from me fourteen shillings and threepence, how can I approve of a law that does it? Montesquieu, who was himself a judge, endeavors to impress other maxims. He must have known what humane judges feel on such occasions, and what the effects of those feelings; and, so far from thinking that severe and excessive punishments prevents crimes, he asserts, as quoted by our French writer, that

'*L'atrocité des loix en empêche l'exécution.*

'*Lorsque la peine est sans mesure, on est souvent obligé de lui préférer l'impunité.*

'*La cause de tous les relâchemens vient de l'impunité des crimes, et non de la modération des peines.*'

It is said by those who know Europe generally, that there are more thefts committed and punished annually in England, than in all the other nations put together. If this be so, there must be a cause or causes for such a depravity in our common people. May not one be the deficiency of justice and morality in our national government, manifested in our oppressive conduct to subjects, and unjust wars on our neighbors? View the long-persisted in, unjust, monopolizing treatment of Ireland, at length acknowledged! View the plundering government exercised by our merchants in the Indies; the confiscating war made upon the American colonies; and, to say nothing of those upon France and Spain, view the late war upon Holland, which was seen by impartial Europe in no other light than that of a war of rapine and pillage; the hopes of an immense and easy prey being its only apparent, and probably its true and real, motive and encouragement. Justice is as strictly due between neighbor nations, as between neighbor citizens. A highwayman is as much a robber when he plunders in a gang, as when single; and a nation that makes an unjust war is only a great gang. After employing your people in robbing the Dutch, is it strange, that being put out of that employ by peace, they still continue robbing, and rob one another! *Piraterie*, as the French call it, or privateering, is the universal bent of the English nation, at home and abroad, wherever settled. No less than seven hundred privateers, were, it is said, commissioned in the last war! These were fitted out by merchants, to prey upon other merchants, who had never done them any injury. Is there probably any one of those privateering merchants of London, who were so ready to rob the merchants of Amsterdam, that would not as readily plunder another London merchant, of the next street, if he could do it with the same impunity? The avidity, the *alieni appetens* is the same; it is the fear alone of the gallows that makes the difference. How then can a nation, which among the honestest of its people has so many thieves by inclination, and whose government encouraged and commissioned no less than seven hundred gangs of robbers; how can such a nation have the face to condemn the crime in individuals, and hang up twenty of them in a morning! It naturally puts one in mind of a Newgate anecdote. One of the prisoners complained, that in the night somebody had taken his buckles out of his shoes. 'What the devil!' says another, 'have we then *thieves* amongst us! It must not be suffered. Let us search out the rogue, and pump him to death.'

There is, however, one late instance of an English merchant who will not profit by such ill-gotten gain. He was, it seems, part-owner of a ship, which the other owners thought fit to employ as a letter of marque, which took a number of French prizes. The booty being shared, he has now an agent here, inquiring, by an advertisement in the Gazette, for those who have suffered the loss, in order to make them, as far as in him lies, restitution. This conscientious man is a Quaker. The Scotch presbyterians were formerly as tender: for there is still extant an ordinance of the town-council of Edinburgh made soon after the Reformation, 'forbidding the purchase of prize goods, under pain of losing the freedom of the burgh for ever, with other punishment at the will of the magistrate the practice of making prizes being contrary to good conscience, and the rule of treating Christian brethren as we would wish to be treated; and such goods *are not to be sold by any godly man within this burgh.*' The race of these godly men in Scotland are probably extinct, or their principles abandoned, since, as far as that nation had a hand in promoting the war against the colonies, prizes and confiscations are believed to have been a considerable motive.

It has been for some time a generally-received opinion, that a military man is not to inquire whether a war be just or unjust? he is to execute his orders. All princes, who are disposed to become tyrants, most' probably approve of this opinion, and be willing to establish it: but is it not a dangerous one? since, on that principle, if the tyrant commands his army to attack and destroy not only an unoffending neighbor nation, but even his own subjects, the army is bound to obey. A negro slave, in our colonies, being commanded by his master to rob or murder a neighbor, or do any other immoral act, may refuse; and the magistrate will protect him in his refusal. The slavery then of a soldier is worse than that of a negro! A conscientious officer, if not restrained by the apprehension of its being imputed to another cause, may indeed resign, rather than be employed in an unjust war; but the private men are slaves for life: and they are, perhaps, incapaole of judging for themselves. We can only lament their fate, and still more that of a sailor, who is often dragged by force from his honest occupation, and compelled to imbrue his hands in perhaps innocent blood. But, methinks, it well behoves merchants (men more enlightened by their education, and perfectly free from any such force or obligation) to consider well of the justice of a war, before they voluntarily engage a gang of ruffians to attack their fellow-merchants of a neighboring nation, to plunder them of their property, and perhaps ruin them and their families, if they yield it; or to wound, maim, and murder them, if they endeavor to defend it. Yet these things are done by Christian merchants, whether a war be just or unjust; and it can hardly be just on both sides. They are done by English and American merchants, who nevertheless, complain of private theft, and hang by dozens the thieves they have taught by their own example.

It is high time, for the sake of humanity, that a stop were put to this enormity. The United States of America, though better situated than any European nature to make profit by privateering (most of the trade of Europe with the West Indies, passing before their doors), are, as far as in them lies, endeavoring to abolish the practice, by offering, in all their treaties with other powers, an article, engaging solemnly, that in case of future war, no privateer shall be commissioned on either side; and that unarmed merchant-ships, on both sides, shall pursue their voyages unmolested.* This will be a hap-

* This offer having been accepted by the late King of Prussia, a treaty of amity and commerce was concluded between that monarch and the United States, containing the following humane, philanthropic article; in the formation of which Dr. Franklin, as one of the American plenipotentiaries, was principally concerned, viz.

Art. XXIII. If war should arise between the two contracting parties, the merchants of either country, then residing in the other, shall be allowed to remain nine months to collect their debts and settle their affairs, and may depart freely, carrying off all their effects without molestation or hindrance; and all women and children, scholars of every faculty, cultivators of the earth, artisans, manufacturers, and fishermen, unarmed, and inhabiting unfortified towns, villages, and places, and, in general, all others whose occupations are for the common subsistence and benefit of mankind, shall be allowed to continue their respective employments, and shall not be molested in their persons, nor shall their houses or goods be burnt, or otherwise destroyed, nor their fields wasted the armed force of the enemy into whose power, by

py improvement of the law of nations. The humane and the just cannot but wish general success to the proposition.

With unchangeable esteem and affection,

I am, my dear friend,

Ever yours.

REMARKS CONCERNING THE SAVAGES OF NORTH AMERICA.

Savages we call them, because their manners differ from ours, which we think the perfection of civility; they think the same of theirs.

Perhaps if we could examine the manners of different nations with impartiality, we should find no people so rude as to be without any rules of politeness; nor any so polite as not to have some remains of rudeness.

The Indian men, when young, are hunters and warriors; when old, counsellors; for all their government is by the counsel or advice of the sages: there is no force, there are no prisons, no officers, to compel obedience, or inflict punishment. Hence they generally study oratory: the best speaker having the most influence. The Indian women till the ground, dress the food, nurse and bring up the children, and preserve and hand down to posterity the memory of public transactions. These employments of men and women are accounted natural and honorable. Having few artificial wants, they have abundance of leisure for improvement in conversation. Our laborious manner of life, compared with theirs, they esteem slavish and base; and the learning on which we value ourselves, they regard as frivolous and useless. An instance of this occurred at the treaty of Lancaster, in Pennsylvania, anno 1744, between the government of Virginia and the Six Nations. After the principal business was settled, the commissioners from Virginia acquainted the Indians by

---

the events of war, they may happen to fall; but if any thing is necessary to be taken from them for the use of such armed force, the same shall be paid for at a reasonable price. And all merchant and trading vessels employed in exchanging the products of different places, and thereby rendering the necessaries, conveniences, and comforts of human life more easy to be obtained and more general, shall be allowed to pass free and unmolested: and neither of the contracting powers shall grant or issue any commission to any private armed vessels, empowering them to take or destroy such trading vessels, or interrupt such commerce.

a speech, that there was at Williamsburg a college, with a fund for educating Indian youth; and if the chiefs of the Six Nations would send down half a dozen of their sons to that college, the government would take care that they should be well provided for, and instructed in all the learning of the white people. It is one of the Indian rules of politeness not to answer a public proposition the same day that it is made they think it would be treating it as a light matter, and that they show it respect by taking time to consider it, as of a matter important. They therefore deferred their answer till the day following: when their speaker began, by expressing their deep sense of the kindness of the Virginia government in making them that offer; 'for we know,' says he, 'that you highly esteem the kind of learning taught in those colleges, and that the maintenance of our young men, while with you, would be very expensive to you. We are convinced, therefore, that you mean to do us good by your proposal; and we thank you heartily. But you who are wise, must know, that different nations have different conceptions of things: and you will therefore not take it amiss, if our ideas of this kind of education happen not to be the same with yours. We have had some experience of it; several of our young people were formerly brought up at the colleges of the northern provinces; they were instructed in all your sciences; but when they came back to us, they were bad runners: ignorant of every means of living in the woods; unable to bear either cold or hunger; knew neither how to build a cabin, take a deer, or kill an enemy; spoke our language imperfectly; were therefore neither fit for hunters, warriors, or counsellors: they were totally good for nothing. We are however not the less obliged by your kind offer, though we decline accepting of it; and to show our grateful sense of it, if the gentlemen of Virginia will send us a dozen of their sons, we will take great care of their education, instruct them in all we know, and make men of them.'

Having frequent occasions to hold public councils, they have acquired great order and decency in conducting them. The old men sit in the foremost ranks, the warriors in the next, and the women and children hindmost. The business of the women is to take exact notice of what passes, imprint it in their memories, for they have no writing, and communicate it to the children. They are the records of the council, and they preserve tradition of the stipulations in treaties a hundred years back; which, when we compare with our writings, we always find exact. He that would speak, rises, The rest observe a profound silence. When he has finished, and sits down, they leave him five or six minutes to recollect, that, if he has omitted any thing he intended to say, or has any thing to add, he may rise again and deliver it. To interrupt another, even in common conversation, is reckoned highly indecent. How different this is from the conduct of a polite British House of Commons, where scarce a day passes without some confusion, that makes the speaker hoarse in calling *to order*; and how different from the mode of conversation, in many polite companies of Europe, where, if you do not deliver your sentences with great rapidity, you are cut off in the middle of it by the impatient loquacity of those you converse with, and never suffered to finish it!

The politeness of these savages in conversation is indeed carried to excess; since it does not permit them to contradict or deny the truth of what is asserted in their presence. By this means they, indeed, avoid disputes; but then it becomes difficult to know their minds, or what impression you make upon them. The missionaries, who have attempted to convert them to Christianity, all complain of this as one of the great difficulties of their mission. The Indians hear with patience the truths of the gospel explained to them, and give their usual tokens of assent and approbation: you would think they were convinced. No such matter—it is mere civility.

A Swedish minister having assembled the chiefs of the Susquehannah Indians, made a sermon to them, acquainting them with the principal historical facts on which our religion is founded: such as the fall of our first parents by eating an apple; the coming of Christ to repair the mischief; his miracles and sufferings, &c.—When he had finished, an Indian orator stood up to thank him. 'What you have told us,' says he, 'is all very good. It is indeed bad to eat apples. It is better to make them all into cider. We are much obliged by your kindness in coming so far to tell us those things which you have heard from your mothers. In return, I will tell you some of those which we have heard from ours.

'In the beginning, our fathers had only the flesh of animals to subsist on; and if their hunting was unsuccessful, they were starving. Two of our young hunters having killed a deer, made a fire in the woods to broil some parts of it. When they were about to satisfy their hunger, they beheld a beautiful young woman descend from the clouds, and seat herself on that hill which you see yonder among the blue mountains. They said to each other, it is a spirit that perhaps has smelt our broiled venison, and wishes to eat of it, let us offer some to her. They presented her with the tongue: she was pleased with the taste of it, and said, "Your kindness shall be rewarded. Come to this place after thirteen moons, and you shall find something that will be of great benefit in nourishing you and your children to the latest generations." They did so, and to their surprise, found plants they had never seen before; but which, from that ancient time, have been constantly cultivated among us, to our great advantage. Where her right hand had touched the ground, they found maize; where her left hand had touched it, they found kidney beans; and where her backside had sat on it, they found tobacco.' The good missionary, disgusted with this idle tale, said, 'What I delivered to you were sacred truths; but what you tell me is mere fable, fiction, and falsehood.' The Indian, offended, replied, 'My brother, it seems your friends have not done you justice in your education; they have not well instructed you in the rules of common civility. You saw that we, who understand and practise those rules, believed all your stories, why do you refuse to believe ours?'

When any of them come into our towns, our people are apt to crowd round them, gaze upon them, and incommode them where they desire to be private: this they esteem great rudeness, and the effect of the want of instruction in the rules of civility and good manners. 'We have,' said they, 'as much curiosity as you, and when you come into our towns, we wish for opportunities of looking at you; but for this purpose we hide ourselves behind bushes, where you are to pass, and never intrude ourselves into your company.'

Their manner of entering one another's villages has likewise its rules. It is reckoned uncivil in travelling strangers to enter a village abruptly, without giving notice of their approach. Therefore, as soon as they arrive within hearing, they stop and halloo, remaining there till invited to enter. Two old men usually come out to them and lead them in. There is in every village a vacant dwelling, called the stranger's house. Here they are placed, while the old men go round from hut to hut, acquainting the inhabitants that strangers are arrived, who are probably hungry and weary, and every one sends them what he can spare of victuals, and skins to repose on. When the strangers are refreshed, pipes and tobacco are brought: and then, but not before, conversation begins, with inquiries who they are, whither bound, what news, &c. and it usually ends with offers of service; if the strangers have occasion for guides, or any necessaries for continuing their journey; and nothing is exacted for the entertainment.

The same hospitality, esteemed among them as a principal virtue, is practised by private persons; of which *Conrad Weiser*, our interpreter, gave me the following instance. He had been naturalized among the Six Nations, and spoke well the Mohuck language. In going through the Indian country, to carry a message from our governor to the council at *Onondaga*, he called at the habitation of *Canassetego*, an old acquaintance, who embraced him, spread furs for him to sit on, placed before him some boiled beans and venison, and mixed some rum and water for his drink. When he was well refreshed, and had lit his pipe, Canassetego began to converse with him: asked him how he had fared the many years since they had seen each other, whence he then came, what occasioned the journey, &c. Conrad answered all his questions; and when the discourse began to flag, the Indian, to continue it, said, 'Conrad, you have lived long among the white people, and know something of their customs; I have been sometimes at Albany, and have observed, that once in seven days they shut up their shops, and assemble all in the great house; tell me what it is for? What do they do there?' 'They meet there,' says Conrad, 'to hear and learn *good things*.' 'I do not doubt,' says the Indian, 'that they tell you so, they have told me the same: but I doubt the truth of what they say, and I will tell you my reasons. I went lately to Albany, to sell my skins, and buy blankets, knives, powder, rum, &c. You know I used generally to deal with Hans Hanson; but I was a little inclined this time to try some other merchants. However, I called first upon Hans, and asked him what he would give for beaver. He said he could not give more than four shillings a pound: but, says he, I cannot talk on business now; this is the day when we meet together to learn *good things*, and I am going to the meeting. So I thought to myself, since I cannot do any business to-day, I may as well go to the meeting too, and I went with him. There stood up a man in black, and began to talk to the people very angrily. I did not understand what he said: but, perceiving that he looked much at me, and at Hanson, I imagined he was angry at seeing me there; so I went out, sat down near the house, struck fire, and lit my pipe, waiting till the meeting should break up. I thought too, that the man had mentioned something of beaver; I suspected it might be the subject of their meeting. So when they came out, I accosted my merchant, "Well, Hans," says I, "I hope you have agreed to give more than four shillings a pound." "No," says he, "I cannot give so much; I cannot give more than three shillings and sixpence." I then spoke to several other dealers, but they all sung the same song, three and sixpence, three and sixpence. This made it clear to me that my suspicion was right; and that, whatever they pretended of meeting to learn *good things*, the real purpose was to consult how to cheat Indians in the price of beaver. Consider but a little, Conrad, and you must be of my opinion. If they met so often to learn *good things*, they would certainly have learned some before this time. But they are still ignorant. You know our practice. If a white man, in travelling through our country, enters one of our cabins, we all treat him as I do you; we dry him if he is wet, we warm him if he is cold, and give him meat and drink, that he may allay his thirst and hunger; and we spread soft furs for him to rest and sleep on: we demand nothing in return.* But if I go into a white man's house at Albany, and ask for victuals and drink, they say, Where is your money? and if I have none, they say, Get out, you Indian dog. You see that they have not learned those little *good things* that we need no meetings to be instructed in, because our mothers taught them us when we were children; and therefore it is impossible their meetings should be, as they say, for any such purpose, or have any such effect; they are only to contrive *the cheating of Indians in the price of beaver.*'

* It is remarkable that, in all ages and countries, hospitality has been allowed as the virtue of those, whom the civilized were pleased to call barbarians; the Greeks celebrated the Scythians for it; the Saracens possessed it eminently; and it is to this day the reigning virtue of the wild Arabs. St. Paul, too, in the relation of his voyage and shipwreck, on the island of Melita, says, 'The barbarous people showed us no little kindness; for they kindled a fire, and received us every one, because of the present rain, and because of the cold.'—This note is taken from a small collection of Franklin's papers, printed for Dilly

TO MR. DUBOURG.

CONCERNING THE DISSENSIONS BETWEEN ENGLAND AND AMERICA.

London, October 2, 1770.

I SEE, with pleasure, that we think pretty much alike on the subject of English America. We of the colonies have never insisted that we ought to be exempt from contributing to the common expenses necessary to support the prosperity of the empire. We only assert, that having parliaments of our own, and not having representatives in that of Great Britain, our parliaments are the only judges of what we can and what we ought to contribute in this case; and that the English parliament has no right to take our money without our consent. In fact, the British empire is not a single state; it comprehends many; and though the parliament of Great Britain has arrogated to itself the power of taxing the colonies, it has no more right to do so, than it has to tax Hanover. We have the same king, but not the same legislatures.

The dispute between the two countries has already lost England many millions sterling, which it has lost in its commerce, and America has in this respect been a proportionable gainer, this commerce consisted principally of superfluities; objects of luxury and fashion, which we can well do without; and the resolution we have formed of importing no more till our grievances are redressed, has enabled many of our infant manufactures to take root; and it will not be easy to make our people abandon them, in future, even should a connexion more cordial than ever succeed the present troubles.—I have, indeed, no doubt, that the parliament of England will finally abandon its present pretensions, and leave us to the peaceable enjoyment of our rights and privileges.

B. FRANKLIN.

A comparison of the Conduct of the Ancient Jews, and of the Anti-federalists in the United States.

A ZEALOUS advocate for the proposed Federal Constitution in a certain public assembly said, that 'the repugnance of great part of mankind to good government was such, that he believed that if an angel from heaven was to bring down a constitution formed there for our use, it would nevertheless meet with violent opposition.'—He was reproved for the supposed extravagance of the sentiment; and he did not justify it.—Probably it might not have immediately occurred to him, that the experiment had been tried, and that the event was recorded in the most faithful of all histories, the Holy Bible; otherwise he might, as it seems to me, have supported his opinion by that unexceptionable authority.

The Supreme Being had been pleased to nourish up a single family, by continued acts of his attentive providence, until it became a great people: and having rescued them from bondage by many miracles performed by his servant Moses, he personally delivered to that chosen servant, in presence of the whole nation, a constitution and code of laws for their observance; accompanied and sanctioned with promises of great rewards, and threats of severe punishments, as the consequence of their obedience or disobedience.

This constitution, though the Deity himself was to be at its head (and it is therefore called by political writers, a theocracy), could not be carried into execution but by means of his ministers: Aaron and his sons were therefore commissioned to be, with Moses, the first established ministry of the new government.

One would have thought, that the appointment of men, who had distinguished themselves in procuring the liberty of their nation, and had hazarded their lives in openly opposing the will of a powerful monarch who would have retained that nation in slavery, might have been an appointment acceptable to a grateful people; and that a constitution framed for them by the Deity himself, might on that account have been secure of a universal welcome reception. Yet there was, in every one of the thirteen tribes, some discontented, restless spirits, who were continually exciting them to reject the proposed new government, and this from various motives.

Many still retained an affection for Egypt, the land of their nativity; and these, whenever they felt any inconvenience or hardship, through the natural and unavoidable effect of thei change of situation, exclaimed against their leaders as the authors of their trouble; and were not only for returning into Egypt, but for stoning their deliverers.* Those inclined to idolatry were displeased that their golden calf was destroyed. Many of the chiefs thought the new constitution might be injurious to their particular interests, that the profitable places would be *engrossed by the families and friends of Moses and*

* Numbers chap. xiv

Aaron, and others equally well born excluded.*—In Josephus, and the Talmud, we learn some particulars, not so fully narrated in the Scripture. We are there told, 'that Korah was ambitious of the priesthood; and offended that it was conferred on Aaron: and this, as he said, by the authority of Moses only, *without the consent of the people.* He accused Moses of having, by various artifices, fraudulently obtained the government, and deprived the people of their liberties; and of conspiring with Aaron to perpetuate the tyranny in their family. Thus, though Korah's real motive was the supplanting of Aaron, he persuaded the people that he meant only the public good; and they, moved by his insinuations, began to cry out—"Let us maintain the common liberty of our respective tribes; we have freed ourselves from the slavery imposed upon us by the Egyptians, and shall we suffer ourselves to be made slaves by Moses? If we must have a master, it were better to return to Pharaoh, who at least fed us with bread and onions, than to serve this new tyrant, who by his operations has brought us into danger of famine." Then they called into question the *reality of his conferences* with God: and objected to the privacy of the meeting, and the preventing any of the people from being present at the colloquies, or even approaching the place, as grounds of great suspicion. They accused Moses also of *peculation;* as embezzling part of the golden spoons and the silver chargers, that the princes had offered at the dedication of the altar,† and the offerings of gold by the common people,‡ as well as most of the poll-tax;§ and Aaron they accused of pocketing much of the gold, of which he pretended to have made a molten calf. Besides peculation, they charged Moses with ambition; to gratify which passion, he had, they said, deceived the people, by promising to bring them to a land flowing with milk and honey: instead of doing which, he had brought them from such a land; and that he thought light of all this mischief, provided he could make himself an absolute

---

* Numbers, chap. xvi. ver. 3. 'And they gathered themselves together against Moses and against Aaron, and said unto them, Ye take too much upon you, seeing all the congregation are holy, every one of them.—Wherefore then lift ye up yourselves above the congregation?'

† Numbers, chap. vii.

‡ Exodus, chap. xxxv. ver. 22.

§ Numbers, chap. iii. and Exodus, chap. xxx

prince.§ That, to support the new dignity with splendor in his family, the partial poll-tax already levied and given to Aaron|| was to be followed by a general one,¶ which would probably be augmented from time to time, if he were suffered to go on promulgating new laws, on pretence of new occasional revelations of the Divine will, till their whole fortunes were devoured by that aristocracy.

Moses denied the charge of peculation; and his accusers were destitute of proofs to support it; though *facts*, if real, are in their nature capable of proof. 'I have not,' said he (with holy confidence in the presence of God), 'I have not taken from this people the value of an ass, nor done them any other injury.' But his enemies had made the charge, and with some success among the populace; for no kind of accusation is so readily made, or easily believed, by knaves, as the accusation of knavery.

In fine, no less than two hundred and fifty of the principal men, 'famous in the congregation, men of renown,'** heading and exciting the mob, worked them up to such a pitch of frenzy, that they called out, Stone 'em, stone 'em, and thereby secure our liberties; and let us choose other captains, that they may lead us back into Egypt, in case we do not succeed in reducing the Canaanites.

On the whole, it appears that the Israelites were a people jealous of their new-acquired liberty, which jealousy was in itself no fault: but that, when they suffered it to be worked upon by artful men, pretending public good, with nothing really in view but private interest, they were led to oppose the establishment of the new constitution, whereby they brought upon themselves much inconvenience and misfortune. It farther appears from the same inestimable history, that when, after many ages, the constitution had become old and much abused, and an amendment of it was proposed, the populace, as they had accused Moses of the ambition of making himself a prince, and cried out, Stone him, stone him; so, excited by their high-priests and scribes, they exclaimed against the Messiah, that he aimed at becoming king of the Jews, and cried, Crucify him, crucify him. From

§ Numbers, chap. xvi. ver. 13. 'Is it a small thing that thou hast brought us up out of a land flowing with milk and honey, to kill us in this wilderness, except that thou make thyself altogether a prince over us?

|| Numbers, chap. iii

¶ Exodus, chap. xxx.

** Numbers, chap. xvi.

all which we may gather, that popular opposition to a public measure is no proof of its impropriety, even though the opposition be excited and headed by men of distinction.

To conclude, I beg I may not be understood to infer, that our general convention was divinely inspired when it formed the new federal constitution, merely because that constitution has been unreasonably and vehemently opposed; yet, I must own, I have so much faith in the general government of the world by Providence, that I can hardly conceive a transaction of such momentous importance to the welfare of millions now existing, and to exist in the posterity of a great nation, should be suffered to pass without being in some degree influenced, guided, and governed by that omnipotent, omnipresent, and beneficent Ruler, in whom all inferior spirits live, and move, and have their being.

NAUTICAL AFFAIRS.

Though Britain bestows more attention to trade than any other nation, and though it be the general opinion, that the safety of their state depends upon her navy alone; yet it seems not a little extraordinary, that most of the great improvements in ship-building have originated abroad. The best sailing-vessels in the royal navy have in general been French prizes. This, though it may admit of exceptions, cannot be upon the whole disputed.

Nor is Britain entirely inattentive to naval architecture; though it is no where scientifically taught, and those who devise improvements have seldom an opportunity of bringing them into practice. What a pity it is, that no contrivance should be adopted, for concentrating the knowledge that different individuals attain in this art, into one common focus, if the expression may be admitted. Our endeavors shall not be wanting, to collect together, in the best way we can, the scattered hints that shall occur under this head, not doubting but the public will receive with favor this humble attempt to waken the attention to a subject of such great national importance.

Dr. Franklin, among the other inquiries that had engaged his attention, during a long life spent in the uninterrupted pursuit of useful improvements, did not let this escape his notice; and many useful hints, tending to perfect the art of navigation, and to meliorate the condition of seafaring people, occur in his works. In France, the art of constructing ships has long been a favorite study, and many improvements in that branch have originated wtih them. Among the last of the Frenchmen, who have made any considerable improvement in this respect, is M. Le Roy, who has constructed a vessel well adapted to sail in rivers, where the depth of water is inconsiderable, and that yet was capable of being navigated at sea with great ease. This he effected in a great measure by the particular mode of rigging, which gave the mariners much greater power over the vessel than they could have when of the usual construction.

I do not hear that this improvement has in any case been adopted in Britain. But the advantages that would result from having a vessel of a small draught of water to sail with the same steadiness, and to lie equally near the wind, as one may do that is sharper built, are so obvious that many persons have been desirous of falling upon some way to effect it. About London, this has been attempted by means of *lee boards* (a contrivance now so generally known as not to require to be here particularly described), and not without effect. But these are subject to certain inconveniences, that render the use of them in many cases ineligible.

Others have attempted to effect the purpose by building vessels with more than one keel; and this contrivance, when adopted upon proper principles, promises to be attended with the happiest effects. But hitherto that seems to have been scarcely attended to. Time will be necessary to eradicate common notions of very old standing, before this can be effectually done.

Mr. W. Brodie, ship-master in Leith, has lately adopted a contrivance for this purpose, that seems to be at the same time very simple and extremely efficacious. Necessity, in this case, as in many others, was the mother of invention. He had a small, flat, ill-built boat, which was so ill constructed as sarcely to admit of carrying a bit of sail on any occasion, and which was at the same time so heavy to be rowed, that he found great difficulty in using it for his ordinary occasions. In reflecting on the means that might be adopted for giving this useless coble such a hold of the water as to admit of his employing a sail when he found it necessary, it readily occurred that a greater depth of keel would have this tendency. But a greater depth of keel, though it would have been useful for this purpose, he easily foresaw, would make his boat extremely inconvenient on many other occasions. To effect both purposes, he thought of adopting a movable keel, which would admit of being let down or taken up at pleasure. This idea he immediately carried into effect, by fixing a bar of iron of the depth he wanted, along each side of the keel, moving upon hinges that admitted of being moved in one direction, but which could not be bent back in the opposite direction. Thus, by means of a small chain fixed to each end, these movable keels could be easily lifted up at pleasure; so that when he was entering into a harbor, or shoal water, he had only to lift up his keels, and the boat was as capable of being managed there, as if he had wanted them entirely; and when he went out to sea, where there was depth enough, by letting them down, the lee keel took a firm hold of the water, (while the other floated loose) and gave such a steadiness to all its movements, as can scarcely be conceived by those who have not experienced it.

This gentleman one day carried me out with him in his boat to try it. We made two experiments. At first with a moderate breeze, when the movable keels were kept up, the boat, when laid as near the wind as it could go, made an angle with the wake of about 30 degrees; but when the keels were let down, the same angle did not exceed five or six degrees, being nearly parallel with the course.

At another time, the wind was right a-head, a brisk breeze. When we began to beat up against it, a trading sloop was very near us, steering the same course with us. The sloop went through the water a good deal faster than we could: but in the course of two hours beating to windward, we found that the sloop was left behind two feet in three; though it is certain, that if our false keels had not been let down, we could scarcely, in that situation, have advanced one foot for her three.

It is unnecessary to point out to seafaring men the benefits that may be derived from this contrivance in certain circumstances, as these will be very obvious to them.

NORTH-WEST PASSAGE.

Notwithstanding the many fruitless attempts that have been made to discover a north-west passage into the South Seas, it would seem that this important geographical question is not yet fully decided; for at a meeting of the Academy of Sciences, at Paris, held on the 13th of November last, M. Bauche, first geographer to the king, read a curious memoir concerning the north-west passage. M. de Mendoza, an intelligent captain of a vessel in the service of Spain, charged with the care of former establishments favorable to the marine has made a careful examination of the archives of several departments: there he has found the relation of a voyage made in the year 1598 by Lorenzo Herrero de Maldonada. There it appears, that at the entry into Davis's Straits, north lat. 60 degrees, and 28 of longitude, counting from the first meridian, he turned to the west, leaving Hudson's Bay on the south, and Baffin's Bay on the north. Arrived at lat. 65 and 297, he went toward the north by the straits of Labrador, till he reached 76 and 278; and finding himself in the Icy Sea, he turned south-west to lat. 60 and 235, where he found a strait, which separates Asia from America, by which he entered into the South Sea, which he called the Straits of Anian. This passage ought to be, according to M. Bauche, between William's Sound and Mount St. Elias. The Russians and Captain Cook have not observed it, because it is very narrow. But it is to be wished, that this important discovery should be verified, which has been overlooked for two centuries, in spite of the attempts which have been made on these coasts. M. Bauche calls this passage the Straits of Ferrer.

POSITIONS TO BE EXAMINED.

1. All food, or subsistence for mankind, arises from the earth or waters.

2. Necessaries of life that are not foods, and all other convemences, have their value estimated in the proportion of food consumed while we are employed in procuring them.

3. A small people with a large territory, may subsist on the productions of nature, with no other labor than that of gathering the vegetables and catching the animals.

4. A large people with a small territory, find these insufficient; and, to subsist, must labor the earth, to make it produce greater quantities of vegetable food, suitable to the nourishment of men, and of the animals they intend to eat.

5. From this labor arises a great increase of vegetable and animal food, and of materials for clothing; as flax, wool silk, &c. The superfluity of these is wealth. With this wealth we pay for the labor employed in building our houses, cities, &c. which are therefore only subsistence thus metamorphosed.

6. Manufactures are only another shape into which so much provisions and subsistence are turned, as were in value equal to the manufactures produced. This appears from hence, that the manufacturer does not, in fact, obtain from the employer, for his labor, more than a mere subsistence, including raiment, fuel, and shelter; all which derive their value from the provisions consumed in procuring them.

7. The produce of the earth, thus converted into manufactures, may be more easily carried into distant markets, than before such conversion.

8. Fair commerce is where equal values are exchanged for equal, the expense of transport included. Thus, if it costs A in England, as much labor and charge to raise a bushel of wheat, as it costs B in France to produce four gallons of wine, then are four gallons of wine the fair exchange for a bushel of wheat, A and B meeting at half distance with their commodities to make the exchange. The advantage of this fair commerce is, that each party increases the number of his enjoyments, having, instead of wheat alone, or wine alone, the use of both wheat and wine.

9. Where the labor and expense of producing both commodities are known to both parties, bargains will generally be fair and equal. Where they are known to one party only, bargains will often be unequal, knowledge taking its advantage of ignorance.

10. Thus he that carries a thousand bushels of wheat abroad to sell, may not probably obtain so great a profit thereon, as if he had first turned the wheat into manufactures, by subsisting therewith the workmen while producing those manufactures, since there are many expediting and facilitating methods of working, not generally known ; and strangers to the manufactures, though they know pretty well the expense of raising wheat, are unacquainted with those short methods of working ; and thence, being apt to suppose more labor employed in the manufacture than there really is, are more easily imposed on in their value, and induced to allow more for them than they are honestly worth.

11. Thus the advantage of having manufactures in a country does not consist, as is commonly supposed, in their highly advancing the value of rough materials, of which they are formed ; since, though sixpennyworth of flax may be worth twenty shillings when worked into lace, yet the very cause of its being worth twenty shillings is that, besides the flax, it has cost nineteen shillings and sixpence in subsistence to the manufacturer. But the advantage of manufactures is, that, under that shape, provisions may be more easily carried to a foreign market ; and by their means our traders may more easily cheat strangers. Few, where it is not made, are judges of the value of lace The importer may demand forty, and perhaps get thirty shillings for that which cost him but twenty.

12. Finally, there seems to be but three ways for a nation to acquire wealth. The first is by war, as the Romans did, in plundering their conquered neighbors; this is robbery.—The second by commerce, which is generally cheating.—The third by agriculture, the only honest way wherein man receives a real increase of the seed thrown into the ground, in a kind of continual miracle, wrought by the hand of God in his favor, as a reward for his innocent life and his virtuous industry. B. FRANKLIN.

PRELIMINARY ADDRESS TO THE PENNSYLVANIA ALMANACK, ENTITULED, 'POOR RICHARD'S ALMANACK, FOR THE YEAR 1758.'

Written by Dr. Franklin.

I HAVE heard, that nothing gives an author so great pleasure as to find his works respectfully quoted by other learned authors. This pleasure I have seldom enjoyed; for though I have been, if I may say it without vanity, an eminent author (of Almanacks) annually now a full quarter of a century, my brother authors in the same way (for what reason I know not) have ever been very sparing in their applauses; and no other author has taken the least notice of me: so that, did not my writings produce me some solid pudding, the great deficiency of praise would have quite discouraged me.

I concluded, at length, that the people were the best judges of my merit, for they buy my works; and, besides, in my rambles, where I am not personally known, I have frequently heard one or other of my adages repeated, with 'As poor Richard says,' at the end on't. This gave me some satisfaction, as it showed not only that my instructions were regarded, but discovered likewise some respect for my authority; and I own, that to encourage the practice of remembering and reading those wise sentences, I have sometimes quoted myself with great gravity.

Judge then how much I have been gratified by an incident which I am going to relate to you. I stopped my horse lately where a great number of people were collected at an auction of merchant's goods. The hour of sale not being come, they were conversing on the badness of the times; and one of the company called to a plain, clean, old man, with white locks, 'Pray, father Abraham, what think you of the times? Won't these heavy taxes quite ruin the country? How shall we be ever able to pay them? What would you advise us to?' Father Abraham stood up, and replied,—'If you'd have my advice, I'll give it to you in short; "for a word to the wise is enough; and many words won't fill a bushel," as poor Richard says.' They joined in desiring him to speak his mind; and, gathering round him, he proceeded as follows:

'Friends (says he) and neighbors, the taxes are indeed very heavy; and if those laid on by the government were the only ones we had to pay, we might more easily discharge them; but we have many others, and much more grievous to some of us. We are taxed twice as much by our idleness, three times as much by our pride, and four times as much by our folly; and from these taxes the commissioners cannot ease or deliver us, by allowing an abatement. However, let us hearken to good advice, and something may be done for us; "God helps them that help themselves," as poor Richard says in his Almanack.

'It would be thought a hard government that should tax its people one-tenth part of their time, to be employed in its service; but idleness taxes many of us much more, if we reckon all that is spent in absolute sloth, or doing of nothing, with that which is spent in idle employments, or amusements that amount to nothing. Sloth, by bringing on diseases, absolutely shortens life. "Sloth, like rust, consumes faster than labor wears, while the key, often used, is always bright," as poor Richard says. "But dost thou love life? then do not squander time, for that's the stuff life is made of," as poor Richard says. How much more than is necessary do we spend in sleep! forgetting, that "the sleeping fox catches no poultry and that there will be sleeping enough in the grave," as poor Richard says. "If time be of all things the most precious, wasting time must be (as poor Richard says) the greatest prodigality;" since, as he elsewhere tells us, "Lost time is never found again; and what we call time enough always proves little enough." Let us then up and be doing, and doing to the purpose: so by diligence shall we do more with less perplexity. "Sloth makes all things difficult, but industry all easy," as poor Richard says; and, "he that riseth late must trot all day, and shall scarce overtake his business at night; while laziness travels so slowly, that poverty soon overtakes him," as we read in poor Richard; who adds, "Drive thy business, let not that drive thee;" and, "early to bed, and early to rise, makes a man healthy, wealthy, and wise."

'So what signifies wishing and hoping for better times? We make these times better if we bestir ourselves. "Industry needs not wish," as poor Richard says; and, "He that lives upon hope will die fasting." "There are no gains without pains; then help hands, for I have no lands; or if I have, they are smartly taxed;" and (as poor Richard likewise observes), "He that hath a trade hath an estate, and he that hath a calling hath an office of profit and honor;" but then the trade must be worked at, and the calling well followed, or neither the estate nor the office will enable us to pay our taxes If we are industrious we shall never starve; for, as poor Richard says, "At the working man's house hunger looks in, but dares not enter." Nor will the bailiff or the constable enter for "Industry pays debts, but despair increaseth them," says poor Richard. What though you have found no treasure, nor has any rich relation left you a legacy? "Diligence is the mother of good luck," as poor Richard says; and "God gives all things to industry; then plough deep while sluggards sleep and you will have corn to sell and to keep," says poor Dick Work while it is called to-day; for you know not how much you may be hindered to-morrow; which makes poor Richard say, "One to-day is worth two to-morrows," and farther, "Have you somewhat to do to-morrow, do it to-day." "If you were a servant, would you not be ashamed that a good master should catch you idle? Are you then your own master, be ashamed to catch yourself idle," as poor Dick says. When there is so much to be done for yourself, your family, and your gracious king, be up by peep of day; "Let not the sun look down, and say, Inglorious here he lies!" Handle your tools without mittens; remember, "that the cat in gloves catches no mice," as poor Richard says. It is true, there is much to be done, and perhaps you are weak-handed; but stick to it steadily, and you will see great effects; for, "continual dropping wears away stones, and by diligence and patience the mouse ate into the cable; and light strokes fell great oaks," as poor Richard says in his Almanack, the year I cannot just now remember.

'Methinks I hear some of you say, "Must a man afford himself no leisure?"—I will tell thee, my friend, what poor Richard says: "Employ thy time well, if thou meanest to gain leisure; and since thou art not sure of a minute, throw not away an hour." Leisure is time for doing something useful: this leisure the diligent man will obtain, but the lazy man never; so that, as poor Richard says, "A life of leisure and a life of laziness are two things." Do you imagine that sloth will afford you more comfort than labor? No; for, as poor Richard says, "Troubles spring from idleness, and grievous toils from needless ease: many without labor would live by their own wits only; but they break for want of stock.

Whereas industry gives comfort, and plenty and respect. Fly pleasures, and they'll follow you; the diligent spinner has a large shift; and, now I have a sheep and a cow, every body bids me good morrow;" all which is well said by poor Richard.

'But with our industry, we must likewise be steady, and settled, and careful, and oversee our own affairs with our own eyes, and not trust too much to others; for, as poor Richard says,

"I never saw an oft-removed tree,
Nor yet an oft-removed family,
That throve so well as one that settled be."

'And again, "Three removes are as bad as a fire;" and again, "Keep thy shop, and thy shop will keep thee;" and again, "If you would have your business done, go; if not, send." And again,

"He that by the plough would thrive,
Himself must either hold or drive."

And again, "The eye of the master will do more work than both his hands;" and again, "Want of care does us more damage than want of knowledge;" and again, "Not to oversee workmen is to leave them your purse open." Trusting too much to other's care is the ruin of many: for, as the Almanack says, "In the affairs of the world, men are saved not by faith, but by the want of it;" but a man's own care is profitable; for, saith poor Dick, "Learning is to the studious, and riches to the careful, as well as power to the bold, and heaven to the virtuous." And, farther, "If you would have a fruitful servant, and one that you like, serve yourself." And again, he adviseth to circumspection and care, even in the smallest matters, because sometimes, "A little neglect may breed great mischief;" adding, "For want of a nail the shoe was lost; for want of a shoe the horse was lost; and for want of a horse the rider was lost;" being overtaken and slain by the enemy, all for want of care about a horse-shoe nail.

'So much for industry, my friends, and attention to one's own business; but to these we must add frugality, if we would make our industry more certainly successful. A man may, if he knows not how to save as he gets, "keep his nose all his life to the grindstone, and die not worth a groat at last." "A fat kitchen makes a lean will," as poor Richard says; and,

"Many estates are spent in the getting;
Since women for tea forsook spinning and knitting,
And men for punch forsook hewing and splitting."

13

"If you would be wealthy (says he, in another Almanack), think of saving as well as of getting: the Indians have not made Spain rich, because her out-goes are greater than her incomes."

'Away then with your expensive follies, and you will not have much cause to complain of hard times, heavy taxes, and chargeable families; for, as poor Dick says,

"Women and wine, game and deceit,
Make the wealth small, and the want great."

'And, farther, "What maintains one vice, would bring up two children." You may think, perhaps, that a little tea, or a little punch now and then, diet a little more costly, clothes a little finer, and a little entertainment now and then, can be no great matter; but remember what poor Richard says, "Many a little makes a meikle;" and farther, "Beware of little expenses; a small leak will sink a great ship;" and again, "Who dainties love, shall beggars prove;" and, moreover, 'Fools make feasts, and wise men eat them."

'Here you are all got together at this sale of fineries and nicknacks. You call them *goods;* but if you do not take care, they will prove *evils* to some of you. You expect they will be sold cheap, and perhaps they may for less than they cost: but if you have no occasion for them, they must be dear to you. Remember what poor Richard says, "Buy what thou hast no need of, and ere long thou shalt sell thy necessaries." And again, "At a great pennyworth pause a while." He means, that perhaps the cheapness is apparent only, or not real; or the bargain, by straitening thee in thy business, may do thee more harm than good. For in another place he says, "Many have been ruined by buying good pennyworths." Again, as poor Richard says, "It is foolish to lay out money in a purchase of repentance;" and yet this folly is practised every day at auctions, for want of minding the Almanack. "Wise men (as poor Dick says) learn by others' harms, fools scarcely by their own; but *Felix quem faciunt aliena pericula cautum.*" Many a one, for the sake of finery on the back, have gone with a hungry belly, and half starved their families: "Silk and satins, scarlet and velvets (as poor Richard says), put out the kitchen fire." These are not the necessaries of life, they can scarcely be called the conveniences; and yet only because they look pretty, how many want to have them? The artificial wants of mankind thus become more numerous than the natural; and, as poor Dick says, "For one poor person there are a hundred indigent." By these and other extravagances, the genteel are reduced to poverty, and forced to borrow of those whom they formerly despised, but who, through industry and frugality, have maintained their standing; in which case, it appears plainly, "A ploughman on his legs is higher than a gentleman on his knees," as poor Richard says. Perhaps they have had a small estate left them, which they knew not the getting of: they think, "It is day, and will never be night:" that a little to be spent out of so much is not worth minding: "A child and a fool (as poor Richard says) imagine twenty shillings and twenty years can never be spent; but always by taking out of the meal-tub, and never putting in, soon comes to the bottom;" then, as poor Dick says, "When the well is dry they know the worth of water." But this they might have known before, if they had taken his advice: "If you would know the value of money, go and try to borrow some; for he that goes a borrowing goes a sorrowing; and, indeed, so does he that lends to such people, when he goes to get it again." Poor Dick farther advises, and says,

"Fond pride of dress is sure a very curse;
Ere fancy you consult, consult your purse."

And again, "Pride is as loud a beggar as Want, and a great deal more saucy." When you have bought one fine thing, you must buy ten more, that your appearance may be all of a piece; but poor Dick says, "It is easier to suppress the first desire, than to satisfy all that follow it." And it is as truly folly for the poor to ape the rich, as the frog to swell in order to equal the ox.

"Vessels large may venture more,
But little boats should keep near shore."

'Tis, however, a folly soon punished; for, "Pride that dines on vanity, sups on contempt," as poor Richard says. And, in another place, "Pride breakfasted with Plenty, dined with Poverty, and supped with Infamy." And, after all, of what use is this pride of appearance, for which so much is risked, so much is suffered? It cannot promote health, or ease pain, it makes no increase of merit in the person; it creates envy; it hastens misfortunes.

"What is a butterfly? at best,
He's but a caterpillar drest,
The gaudy fop's his picture just,"

as poor Richard says.

'But what madness must it be to run in debt for these superfluities! We are offered by the terms of this sale six months' credit; and that perhaps has induced some of us to attend it, because we cannot spare the ready money, and hope now to be fine without it. But, ah! think what you do when you run in debt. You give to another power over your liberty. If you cannot pay at the time, you will be ashamed to see your creditor: you will be in fear when you speak to him; you will make poor, pitiful, sneaking excuses, and by degrees come to lose your veracity, and sink into base downright lying; for, as poor Richard says, "the second vice is lying · the first is running in debt." And again, to the same purpose, "Lying rides upon debt's back;" whereas a free-born Englishman ought not to be ashamed nor afraid to speak to any man living. But poverty often deprives a man of all spirit and virtue: "It is hard for an empty bag to stand upright," as poor Richard truly says. What would you think of that prince, or that government, who would issue an edict, forbidding you to dress like a gentleman or a gentlewoman, on pain of imprisonment or servitude? Would you not say, that you were free, have a right to dress as you please, and that such an edict would be a breach of your privileges, and such a government tyrannical? And yet you are about to put yourself under that tyranny when you run in debt for such dress! Your creditor has authority, at his pleasure, to deprive you of your liberty, by confining you in jail for life, or by selling you for a servant, if you should not be able to pay him. When you have got your bargain, you may, perhaps, think little of payment; but "Creditors (poor Richard tells us) have better memories than debtors;" and in another place he says, "Creditors are a superstitious sect, great observers of set days and times." The day comes round before you are aware, and the demand is made before you are prepared to satisfy it. Or if you bear your debt in mind, the term which at first seemed so long, will, as it lessens, appear extremely short. Time will seem to have added wings to his heels as well as at his shoulders. "Those have a short Lent (saith poor Richard) who owe money to be paid at Easter." Then since, as he says, "The borrower is a slave to the lender and the debtor to the creditor;" disdain the chain, preserve your freedom, and maintain your independency: be industrious and free; be frugal and free. At present, perhaps you may think yourselves in thriving circumstances, and that you can bear a little extravagance without injury; but

"For age and want save while you may,
No morning sun lasts a whole day,"

as poor Richard says. Gain may be temporary and uncertain; but ever, while you live, expense is constant and certain: and "it is easier to build two chimneys, than to keep one in fuel," as poor Richard says. So "Rather go to bed supperless than rise in debt."

"Get what you can, and what you get hold,
'Tis the stone that will turn all your lead into gold,"

as poor Richard says. And when you have got the philosopher's stone, sure you will no longer complain of bad times, on the difficulty of paying taxes.

'This doctrine, my friends, is reason and wisdom; but, after all, do not depend too much upon your own industry, and frugality, and prudence, though excellent things; for they may be blasted without the blessing of Heaven: and therefore ask that blessing humbly, and be not uncharitable to those that at present seem to want it, but comfort and help them. Remember Job suffered, and was afterward prosperous.

'And now, to conclude, "Experience keeps a dear school, but fools will learn in no other, and scarce in that; for it is true, we may give advice, but we cannot give conduct," as poor Richard says. However, remember this, "They that will not be counselled, cannot be helped," as poor Richard says; and, farther, that "If you will not hear Reason, she will surely rap your knuckles."

Thus the old gentleman ended his harangue. The people heard it, and approved the doctrine, and immediately practised the contrary, just as if it had been a common sermon; for the auction opened, and they began to buy extravagantly, notwithstanding all his cautions, and their own fear of taxes. I found the good man had thoroughly studied my Almanacks, and digested all I had dropped on those topics, during the course of twenty-five years. The frequent mention he made of me, must have tired every one else: but my vanity was wonderfully delighted with it, though I was conscious that not a tenth part of the wisdom was my own, which he ascribed to me, but rather the gleanings that I had made of the sense of all ages and nations. However, I resolved to be the better for the echo of it; and though I had first determined to buy stuff for a new coat, I went away, resolved to wear my old one a little longer. Reader, if thou wilt do the same, thy profit will be as great as mine.

I am, as ever, thine to serve thee,

RICHARD SAUNDERS.

THE INTERNAL STATE OF AMERICA.

Being a true Description of the Interest and Policy of that vast Continent.

THERE is a tradition, that, in the planting of New England the first settlers met with many difficulties and hardships: as is generally the case when a civilized people attempt establishing themselves in a wilderness country. Being piously disposed, they sought relief from Heaven, by laying their wants and distresses before the Lord, in frequent set days of fasting and prayer. Constant meditation and discourse on these subjects kept their minds gloomy and discontented; and, like the children of Israel, there were many disposed to return to that Egypt which persecution had induced them to abandon. At length, when it was proposed in the Assembly to proclaim another fast, a farmer of plain sense rose and remarked, that the inconveniences they suffered, and concerning which they had so often wearied Heaven with their complaints, were not so great as they might have expected, and were diminishing every day as the colony strengthened; that the earth began to reward their labor, and to furnish liberally for their subsistence; that the seas and rivers were found full of fish, the air sweet, the climate healthy; and, above all, that they were there, in the full enjoyment of liberty, civil and religious: he therefore thought, that reflecting and conversing on these subjects would be more comfortable, as tending more to make them contented with their situation; and that it would be more becoming the gratitude they owed to the Divine Being, if instead of a fast, they should proclaim a thanksgiving. His advice was taken; and from that day to this they have, in every year, observed circumstances of public felicity sufficient to furnish employment for a thanksgiving day; which is therefore constantly ordered and religiously observed.

I see in the public newspapers of different States frequen complaints of *hard times, deadness of trade, scarcity of money* &c. &c. It is not my intention to assert or maintain that these complaints are entirely without foundation. There can be no country or nation existing, in which there will not be some people so circumstanced as to find it hard to gain a livelihood; people, who are not in the way of any profitable trade, with whom money is scarce, because they have nothing to give in exchange for it; and it is always in the power of a small number to make a great clamor. But let us take a cool view of the general state of our affairs, and perhaps the prospect will appear less gloomy than has been imagined.

The great business of the continent is agriculture. For one artizan, or merchant, I suppose we have at least one hundred farmers, by far the greatest part cultivators of their own fertile lands, from whence many of them draw not only food necessary for their subsistence, but the materials of their clothing, so as to need very few foreign supplies: while they have a surplus of productions to dispose of, whereby wealth is gradually accumulated. Such has been the goodness of Divine Providence to these regions, and so favorable the climate, that, since the three or four years of hardship in the first settlement of our fathers here, a famine or scarcity has never been heard of amongst us; on the contrary, though some years may have been more, and others less plentiful, there has always been provision enough for ourselves, and a quantity to spare for exportation. And although the crops of last year were generally good, never was the farmer better paid for the part he can spare commerce, as the published price-currents abundantly testify. The lands he possesses are also continually rising in value with the increase of population; and, on the whole, he is enabled to give such good wages to those who work for him, that all who are acquainted with the old world must agree, that in no part of it are the laboring poor so generally well fed, well clothed, well lodged, and well paid, as in the United States of America.

If we enter the cities, we find that since the Revolution, the owners of houses and lots of ground have had their interest vastly augmented in value; rents have risen to an astonishing height, and thence encouragement to increase building, which gives employment to an abundance of workmen, as does also the increased luxury and splendor of living of the inhabitants thus made richer. These workmen all demand and obtain much higher wages than any other part of the world would afford them, and are paid in ready money. This rank of people therefore do not, or ought not, to complain of hard times; and they make a very considerable part of the city inhabitants.

At the distance I live from our American fisheries, I can not speak of them with any degree of certainty; but I have not heard that the labor of the valuable race of men employed in them is worse paid, or that they meet with less success, than before the Revolution. The whalemen indeed have been deprived of one market for their oil, but another, I hear, is opening for them, which it is hoped may be equally advantageous; and the demand is constantly increasing for their spermaceti candles, which therefore bear a much higher price than formerly.

There remain the merchants and shop-keepers. Of these though they make but a small part of the whole nation, the number is considerable, too great indeed for the business they are employed in; for the consumption of goods in every country has its limits; the faculties of the people, that is, their ability to buy and pay, are equal to a certain quantity of merchandise. If merchants calculate amiss on this proportion and import too much, they will of course find the sale dull for the overplus, and some of them will say that trade languishes. They should, and doubtless will, grow wiser by experience, and import less.

If too many artificers in town, and farmers from the country, flattering themselves with the idea of leading easier lives, turn shopkeepers, the whole natural quantity of that business divided among them all may afford too small a share for each, and occasion complaints that trading is dead; these may also suppose that it is owing to scarcity of money, while in fact, it is not so much from the fewness of buyers, as from the excessive number of sellers, that the mischief arises; and, if every shopkeeping farmer and mechanic would return to the use of his plough and working tools, there would remain of widows, and other women, shopkeepers sufficient for the business, which might then afford them a comfortable maintenance.

Whoever has travelled through the various parts of Europe, and observed how small is the proportion of people in affluence or easy circumstances there, compared with those in poverty and misery; the few rich and haughty landlords, the multitude of poor, abject, rack-rented, tithe-paying tenants, and half-paid and half-starved ragged laborers; and views here the happy mediocrity that so generally prevails throughout these States, where the cultivator works for himself, and supports his family in decent plenty; will, methinks, see abundant reason to bless Divine Providence for the evident and great difference in our favor, and be convinced that no nation known to us enjoys a greater share of human felicity.

It is true, that in some of the States there are parties and discords; but let us look back, and ask if we were ever without them? Such will exist wherever there is liberty; and perhaps they help to preserve it. By the collision of different sentiments, sparks of truth are struck out, and political light is obtained. The different factions, which at present divide us, aim all at the public good; the differences are only about the various modes of promoting it. Things, actions, measures, and objects of all kinds, present themselves to the minds of men in such a variety of lights, that it is not possible we should all think alike at the same time on every subject, when hardly the same man retains at all times the same ideas of it. Parties are therefore the common lot of humanity; and ours are by no means more mischievous or less beneficial than those of other countries, nations, and ages, enjoying in the same degree the same blessing of political liberty.

Some indeed among us are not so much grieved for the present state of our affairs, as apprehensive for the future. The growth of luxury alarms them, and they think we are from that alone in the high road to ruin. They observe, that no revenue is sufficient without economy, and that the most plentiful income of a whole people from the natural productions of their country may be dissipated in vain and needless expenses; and poverty be introduced in the place of affluence.—This may be possible. It however rarely happens; for there seems to be in every nation a greater proportion of industry and frugality, which tend to enrich, than of idleness and prodigality, which occasion poverty; so that upon the whole there is a continual accumulation. Reflect what Spain, Gaul, Germany, and Britain were in the time of the Romans, inhabited by people little richer than our savages, and consider the wealth that they at present possess, in numerous well-built cities, improved farms, rich movables, magazines stocked with valuable manufactories, to say nothing of plate, jewels, and coined money; and all this, notwithstanding their bad, wasteful, plundering governments, and their mad destructive wars; and yet luxury and extravagant living has never suffered much restraint in those countries. Then consider the great proportion of industrious frugal farmers, inhabiting the interior parts of these American States, and of whom the body of our nation consists, and judge whether it is possible that the luxury of our sea-ports can be sufficient to ruin such a country.—If the importation of foreign luxuries could ruin a people, we should probably have been ruined long ago; for the British nation claimed a right, and practised it, of importing among us, not only the superfluities of their own production, but those of every nation under heaven; we bought and consumed them, and yet we flourished and grew rich. At present our independent governments may do what we could not then do, discourage by heavy duties, or prevent by heavy prohibitions, such importations, and thereby grow richer;—if indeed, which may admit of dispute, the desire of adorning ourselves with fine clothes, possessing fine furniture, with elegant houses, &c. is not, by strongly inciting to labor and industry, the occasion of producing a greater value than is consumed in the gratification of that desire.

The agriculture and fisheries of the United States are the great sources of our increasing wealth. He that puts a seed into the earth is recompensed, perhaps, by receiving forty out of it, and he who draws a fish out of our water draws up a piece of silver.

Let us (and there is no doubt but we shall) be attentive to these, and then the power of rivals, with all their restraining and prohibiting acts, cannot much hurt us. We are sons of the earth and seas, and, like Antæus in the fable, if in wrestling with a Hercules, we now and then receive a fall, the touch of our parents will communicate to us fresh strength and vigor to renew the contest.

INFORMATION TO THOSE WHO WOULD REMOVE TO AMERICA.

Many persons in Europe have directly, or by letter, expressed to the writer of this, who is well acquainted with North America, their desire of transporting and establishing themselves in that country, but who appear to have formed, through ignorance, mistaken ideas and expectations of what is to be obtained there; he thinks it may be useful, and prevent inconvenient, expensive, and fruitless removals and voyages of improper persons, if he gives some clearer and truer notions of that part of the world than appear to have hitherto prevailed.

He finds it is imagined by numbers, that the inhabitants of North America are rich, capable of rewarding, and disposed to reward, all sorts of ingenuity: that they are at the same time ignorant of all the sciences, and consequently that strangers, possessing talents in the belles lettres, fine arts, &c. must be highly esteemed, and so well paid as to become easily rich themselves; that there are also abundance of profitable offices to be disposed of which the natives are not qualified to fill; and that having few persons of family among them, strangers of birth must be greatly respected, and of course easily obtain the best of those offices, which will make all their fortunes: that the governments too, to encourage emigrations from Europe, not only pay the expense of personal transportation, but give lands gratis to strangers, with negroes to work for them, utensils for husbandry, and stocks of cattle. These are all wild imaginations; and those who go to America with expectations founded upon them, will surely find themselves disappointed.

The truth is, that though there are in that country few people so miserable as the poor of Europe, there are also very few that in Europe would be called rich; it is rather a general happy mediocrity that prevails. There are few great proprietors of the soil, and few tenants; most people cultivate their own lands, or follow some handicraft or merchandise; very few rich enough to live idly upon their rents or incomes, or to pay the high prices given in Europe for painting, statues, architecture, and the other works of art that are more curious than useful. Hence the natural geniuses that have arisen in America, with such talents, have uniformly quitted that country for Europe, where they can be more suitably rewarded. It is true that letters and mathematical knowledge are in esteem there, but they are at the same time more common than is apprehended; there being already existing nine colleges, or universities, viz. four in New England, and one in each of the provinces of New-York, New Jersey, Pennsylvania, Maryland, and Virginia—all furnished with learned professors; besides a number of smaller academies; these educate many of their youth in the languages, and those sciences that qualify men for the professions of divinity, law, or physic. Strangers, indeed, are by no means excluded from exercising those professions; and the quick increase of inhabitants every where gives them a chance of employ, which they have in common with the natives. Of civil offices or employments, there are few; no superfluous ones, as in Europe; and it is a rule established in some of the States that no office should be so profitable as to make it desirable. The 36th article of the constitution of Pennsylvania runs expressly in these words: 'As every freeman, to preserve his independence (if he has not a sufficient estate), ought to have some profession, calling, trade, or farm, whereby he may honestly subsist, there can be no necessity for, nor use in establishing, offices of profit; the usual effects of which are dependence and servility unbecoming freemen, in the possessors and expectants; faction, contention, corruption, and disorder among the people. Wherefore, whenever an office through increase of fees or otherwise. becomes so profitable as to occasion many to apply for it, the profits ought to be lessened by the legislature.

These ideas prevailing more or less in the United States, it cannot be worth any man's while, who has a means of living at home, to expatriate himself in hopes of obtaining a profitable civil office in America; and as to military offices, they are at an end with the war, the armies being disbanded. Much less is it advisable for a person to go thither, who has no other quality to recommend him than his birth. In Europe it has indeed its value; but it is a commodity that cannot be carried to a worse market than to that of America, where people do not inquire concerning a stranger, *What is he?* but *What can he do?* If he has any useful art, he is welcome; and if he exercises it, and behaves well, he will be respected by all that know him; but a mere man of quality, who on that account wants to live upon the public by some office or salary, will be despised and disregarded. The husbandman is in honor there, and even the mechanic, because their employments are useful. The people have a saying, that God Almighty is himself a mechanic, the greatest in the universe; and he is respected and admired more for the variety, ingenuity, and utility of his handicraft works, than for the antiquity of his family. They are pleased with the observation of a negro, and frequently mention it, that Boccarorra (meaning the white man) make de black man workee, make de horse workee, make de ox workee, make ebery ting workee, only de hog. He, de hog, no workee; he eat, he drink, he walk about, he go to sleep when he please, he libb like a gentleman. According to these opinions of the Americans, one of them would think himself more obliged to a genealogist, who could prove to him that his ancestors and relations for ten generations had been ploughmen, smiths, carpenters, turners, weavers, tanners, or even shoemakers, and consequently that they were useful members of society; than if he could only prove that they were gentlemen, doing nothing of value, but living idly on the labors of others, mere *fruges consumere nati*,* and otherwise *good* for *nothing*, till by their death their estates, like the carcass of the negro's gentleman-hog, come to be *cut up*.

With regard to encouragements for strangers from government, they are really only what are derived from good laws and liberty. Strangers are welcome, because there is room enough for them all, and therefore the old inhabitants

---

* . . . . born
Merely to eat up the corn.—*Watts*

are not jealous of them; the laws protect them sufficiently, so that they have no need of the patronage of great men; and every one will enjoy securely the profits of his industry. But if he does not bring a fortune with him, he must work and be industrious to live. One or two years' residence give him all the rights of a citizen; but the government does not at present, whatever it may have done in former times, hire people to become settlers, by paying their passage, giving land, negroes, utensils, stock, or any other kind of emolument whatsoever. In short, America is the land of labor; and by no means what the English call *Lubberland*, and the French *Pays de Cocagne*, where the streets are said to be paved with half-peck loaves, the houses tiled with pan-cakes, and where the fowls fly about ready roasted, crying, *Come eat me!*

Who then are the kind of persons to whom an emigration to America may be advantageous? And what are the advantages they may reasonably expect?

Land being cheap in that country, from the vast forests still void of inhabitants, and not likely to be occupied in an age to come, insomuch that the property of a hundred acres of fertile soil, full of wood, may be obtained near the frontiers, in many places, for eight or ten guineas, hearty young laboring men, who understand the husbandry of corn and cattle, which is nearly the same in that country as in Europe, may easily establish themselves there. A little money, saved of the good wages they receive there while they work for others, enables them to buy the land and begin their plantation, in which they are assisted by the good-will of their neighbors, and some credit. Multitudes of poor people from England, Ireland, Scotland, and Germany, have by this means in a few years become wealthy farmers, who in their own countries, where all the lands are fully occupied, and the wages of labor low, could never have emerged from the mean condition wherein they were born.

From the salubrity of the air, the healthiness of the climate, the plenty of good provisions, and the encouragement to early marriages, by the certainty of subsistence in cultivating the earth, the increase of inhabitants by natural generation is very rapid in America, and becomes still more so by the accession of strangers: hence there is a continual demand for more artisans of all the necessary and useful kinds, to supply those cultivators of the earth with houses, and with furniture and utensils of the grosser sorts, which cannot so well be brought from Europe. Tolerably good workmen in any of those mechanic arts, are sure to find employ, and to be well paid for their work, there being no restraints preventing strangers from exercising any art they understand, nor any permission necessary. If they are poor, they begin first as servants or journeymen; and if they are sober, industrious, and frugal, they soon become masters, establish themselves in business, marry, raise families, and become respectable citizens.

Also, persons of moderate families and capitals, who, having a number of children to provide for, are desirous of bringing them up to industry, and to secure estates to their posterity, have opportunities of doing it in America, which Europe does not afford. There they may be taught and practise profitable mechanic arts, without incurring disgrace on that account: but, on the contrary, acquiring respect to such abilities. There small capitals laid out in lands, which daily become more valuable by the increase of people, afford a solid prospect of ample fortunes thereafter for those children. The writer of this has known several instances of large tracts of land bought on what was then the frontiers of Pennsylvania, for ten pounds per hundred acres, which, after twenty years, when the settlements had been extended far beyond them, sold readily, without any improvement made upon them, for three pounds per acre. The acre in America is the same with the English acre, or the acre of Normandy.

Those who desire to understand the state of government in America, would do well to read the constitutions of the several States, and the articles of confederation which bind the whole together for general purposes, under the direction of one Assembly, called the Congress. Those constitutions have been printed, by order of Congress, in America; two editions of them have been printed in London; and a good translation of them in French, has lately been published at Paris.

Several of the princes of Europe having of late, from an opinion of advantage to arise by producing all commodities and manufactures within their own dominions, so as to diminish or render useless their importations, have endeavored to entice workmen from other countries, by high salaries, privileges, &c. Many persons pretending to be skilled in various great manufactures, imagining that America must be in want of them, and that the Congress would probably be disposed to imitate the princes above-mentioned, have proposed to go over on condition of having their passages paid, lands given, salaries appointed, exclusive privileges for terms of years, &c. Such persons, on reading the articles of confederation, will find that the Congress have no power committed to them, or money put into their hands, for such purposes; and that, if any such encouragement is given, it must be by the government of some separate State. This, however, has rarely been done in America; and when it has been done, it has rarely succeeded, so as to establish a manufacture, which the country was not yet so ripe for as to encourage private persons to set it up; labor being generally too dear, and hands difficult to be kept together, every one desiring to be a master, and the cheapness of land inclining many to leave trades for agriculture. Some indeed have met with success, and are carried on to advantage; but they are generally such as require only a few hands, or wherein great part of the work is performed by machines. Goods that are bulky, and of so small a value as not well to bear the expense of freight, may often be made cheaper in the country than they can be imported; and the manufacture of such goods will be profitable wherever there is a sufficient demand. The farmers in America produce indeed a good deal of wool and flax, and none is exported—it is all worked up; but it is in the way of domestic manufacture, for the use of the family. The buying up quantities of wool and flax, with the design to employ spinners, weavers, &c. and form great establishments, producing quantities of linen and woollen goods for sale, has been several times attempted in different provinces; but those projects have generally failed, goods of equal value being imported cheaper. And when the governments have been solicited to support such schemes by encouragements, in money, or by imposing duties on importation of such goods, it has been generally refused, on this principle, that if the country is ripe for the manufacture, it may be carried on by private persons to advantage; and, if not, it is folly to think of forcing nature. Great establishments of manufacture, require great numbers of poor to do the work for small wages; those poor are to be found in Europe, but will not be found in America, till the lands are all taken up and cultivated, and the excess of people who cannot get land want employment. The manufacture of silk, they say, is natural in France, as that of cloth in England, because each country produces in plenty the first material; but if England will have a manufacture of silk as well as that of cloth, and France of cloth as well as that of silk, these unnatural operations must be supported by mutual prohibitions, or high duties on the importation of each other's goods; by which means the workmen are enabled to tax the home consumer by greater prices, while the higher wages they receive makes them neither happier nor richer, since they only drink more and work less. Therefore the governments in America do nothing to encourage such projects. The people by this means are not imposed on either by the merchant or mechanic: if the merchant demands too much profit on imported shoes, they buy of the shoemaker; and if he asks too high a price, they take them of the merchant; thus the two professions are checks on each other. The shoemaker, however, has, on the whole, a considerable profit upon his labor in America, beyond what he had in Europe, as he can add to his price a sum nearly equal to all the expenses of freight and commission, risk or assurance, &c. necessarily charged by the merchant. And the case is the same with the workman in every other mechanic art. Hence it is, that the artisans generally live better and more easily in America than in Europe; and such as are good economists make a comfortable provision for age, and for their children. Such may, therefore, remove with advantage to America.

In the old long-settled countries of Europe, all arts, trades, professions, farms, &c. are so full, that it is difficult for a poor man who has children to place them where they may gain, or learn to gain, a decent livelihood. The artisans, who fear creating future rivals in business, refuse to take apprentices, but upon conditions of money, maintenance, or the like, which the parents are unable to comply with. Hence the youth are dragged up in ignorance of every gainful art and obliged to become soldiers, or servants, or thieves, for a subsistence. In America, the rapid increase of inhabitants takes away that fear of rivalship, and artisans willingly receive apprentices from the hope of profit by their labor, during the remainder of the time stipulated, after they shall be instructed. Hence it is easy for poor families to get their children instructed; for the artisans are so desirous of apprentices, that many of them will even give money to the parents, to have boys from ten to fifteen years of age bound apprentices to them, till the age of twenty-one; and many poor parents have, by that means, on their arrival in the country, raised money enough to buy land sufficient to establish themselves, and to subsist the rest of the family by agriculture. These contracts for apprentices are made before a magistrate, who regulates the agreement according to reason and justice;

and, having in view the formation of a future useful citizen, obliges the master to engage by a written indenture, not only that, during the time of service stipulated, the apprentice shall be duly provided with meat, drink, apparel, washing, and lodging, and at its expiration with a complete new suit of clothes, but also, that he shall be taught to read, write, and cast accounts; and that he shall be well instructed in the art or profession of his master, or some other, by which he may afterward gain a livelihood, and be able in his turn to raise a family. A copy of this indenture is given to the apprentice or his friends, and the magistrate keeps a record of it, to which recourse may be had, in case of failure by the master in any point of performance. This desire among the masters to have more hands employed in working for them, induces them to pay the passage of young persons of both sexes, who, on their arrival, agree to serve them one, two, three, or four years; those who have already learned a trade, agreeing for a shorter term, in proportion to their skill, and the consequent immediate value of their service: and those who have none, agreeing for a longer term, in consideration of being taught an art their poverty would not permit them to acquire in their own country.

The almost general mediocrity of fortune that prevails in America, obliging its people to follow some business for subsistence, those vices that arise usually from idleness, are in a great measure prevented. Industry and constant employment are great preservatives of the morals and virtue of a nation. Hence bad examples to youth are more rare in America, which must be a comfortable consideration to parents. To this may be truly added, that serious religion, under its various denominations, is not only tolerated, but respected and practised. Atheism is unknown there; and infidelity rare and secret; so that persons may live to a great age in that country without having their piety shocked by meeting with either an atheist or an infidel. And the Divine Being seems to have manifested his approbation of the mutual forbearance and kindness with which the different sects treat each other, by the remarkable prosperity with which he has been pleased to favor the whole country.

THOUCHTS ON COMMERCIAL SUBJECTS.

Of Embargoes upon Corn, and of the Poor.

In inland high countries, remote from the sea, and whose rivers are small, running *from* the country, and not to it, as is the case with Switzerland; great distress may arise from a course of bad harvests, if public granaries are not provided and kept well stored. Anciently, too, before navigation was so general, ships so plenty, and commercial transactions so well established; even maritime countries might be occasionally distressed by bad crops. But such is now the facility of communication between those countries, that an unrestrained commerce can scarce ever fail of procuring a sufficiency for any of them. If indeed any government is so imprudent as to lay its hands on imported corn, forbid its exportation, or compel its sale at limited prices, there the people may suffer some famine from merchants avoiding their ports. But wherever commerce is known to be always free, and the merchant absolute master of his commodity, as in Holland, there will always be a reasonable supply.

When an exportation of corn takes place, occasioned by a higher price in some foreign countries, it is common to raise a clamor, on the supposition that we shall thereby produce a domestic famine. Then follows a prohibition, founded on the imaginary distresses of the poor. The poor, to be sure, if in distress, should be relieved; but if the farmer could have a high price for his corn from the foreign demand, must he by a prohibition of exportation be compelled to take a low price, not of the poor only, but of every one that eats bread, even the richest? The duty of relieving the poor is incumbent on the rich; but by this operation the whole burden of it is laid on the farmer, who is to relieve the rich at the same time. Of the poor, too, those who are maintained by the parishes have no right to claim this sacrifice of the farmer; as while they have their allowance, it makes no difference to them, whether bread be cheap or dear. Those working poor, who now mind business only *five* or *four* days in the week, if bread should be so dear as to oblige them to work the whole *six* required by the commandment, do not seem to be aggrieved, so as to have a right to public redress. There will then remain, comparatively, only a few families in every district, who, from sickness or a great number of children, will be so distressed by a high price of corn, as to need relief; and these should be taken care of by particular benefactions, without restraining the farmer's profit.

Those who fear that exportation may so far drain the country of corn, as to starve ourselves, fear what never did, nor never can happen. They may as well, when they view the tide ebbing towards the sea, fear that all the water will leave the river. The price of corn, like water, will find its own level. The more we export, the dearer it becomes at home; the more is received abroad, the cheaper it becomes there; and, as soon as these prices are equal, the exportation stops of course. As the seasons vary in different countries, the calamity of a bad harvest is never universal. If, then, all ports were always open, and all commerce free, every maritime country would generally eat bread at the medium price, or average of all the harvests; which would probably be more equal than we can make it by our artificial regulations, and therefore a more steady encouragement to agriculture. The nation would all have bread at this middle price: and that nation, which at any time inhumanly refuses to relieve the distresses of another nation, deserves no compassion when in distress itself.

Of the Effects of Dearness of Provisions upon Working, and upon Manufactures.

The common people do not work for pleasure generally, but from necessity. Cheapness of provisions makes them more idle; less work is then done, it is then more in demand proportionally, and of course the price rises. Dearness of provisions obliges the manufacturer to work more days and more hours: thus more work is done than equals the usual demand: of course it becomes cheaper, and the manufactures in consequence.

Of an open Trade.

Perhaps, in general, it would be better if government meddled no farther with trade, than to protect it, and let it take its course. Most of the statutes or acts, edicts, or arrests, and placarts of parliaments, princes, and states, for regulating, directing, or restraining of trade, have, we think, been either political blunders, or jobs obtained by artful men for private advantage under pretence of public good. When Colbert assembled some of the wise old merchants of France, and desired their advice and opinion how he could best serve and promote commerce; their answer, after consultation, was in three words only, *Laissez nous faire*; 'Let us alone.'—It is said by a very solid writer of the same nation, that he is well advanced in the science of politics, who knows the full force of that maxim, *Pas trop gouverner*, 'not to govern too much;' which, perhaps, would be of more use when applied to trade, than in any other public concern. It were therefore to be wished, that commerce were as free between all the nations of the world as it is between the several counties of England; so would all, by mutual communications, obtain more enjoyments. Those counties do not ruin each other by trade, neither would the nations. No nation was ever ruined by trade, even, seemingly the most disadvantageous..

Whenever desirable superfluities are imported, industry is excited, and thereby plenty is produced. Were only necessaries permitted to be purchased, men would work no more than was necessary for that purpose.

Of Prohibitions with respect to the Exportation of Gold and Silver.

Could Spain and Portugal have succeeded in executing their foolish laws for *hedging in the cuckoo*, as Locke calls it, and have kept at home all the gold and silver, those metals would by this time have been of little more value than so much lead or iron. Their plenty would have lessened their value. We see the folly of these edicts; but are not our own prohibitory and restrictive laws, that are professedly made with intention to bring a balance in our favor from our trade with foreign nations to be paid in money, and laws to prevent the necessity of exporting that money, which if they could be thoroughly executed, would make money as plenty, and of as little value; I say, are not such laws akin to those Spanish edicts; follies of the same family?

Of the Returns for Foreign Articles.

In fact, the *produce of other countries* can hardly be obtained, unless by fraud and rapine, without giving the *produce of our land or our industry* in exchange for them. If we have mines of gold and silver, gold and silver may then be called the produce of our land; if we have not, we can only fairly obtain those metals by giving for them the produce of our land or industry. When we have them, they are then only that produce or industry in another shape; which we may give, if the trade requires it, and our other produce will not suit, in exchange for the produce of some other country that furnishes what we have more occasion for or more desire. When we have to an inconvenient degree, parted with our gold and silver, our industry is stimulated afresh to procure more; that by its means we may contrive to procure the same advantages.

Of Restraints upon Commerce in Time of War.

When princes make war by prohibiting commerce, each may hurt himself as much as his enemy. Traders, who by their business are promoting the common good of mankind, as well as farmers and fishermen, who labor for the subsistence of all, should never be interrupted or molested in their business, but enjoy the protection of all in the time of war, as well as in the time of peace.

This policy, those we are pleased to call barbarians have, in a great measure, adopted: for the trading subjects of any power, with whom the emperor of Morocco may be at war, are not liable to capture when within sight of his land, going or coming; and have otherwise free liberty to trade and reside in his dominions.

As a maritime power, we presume it is not thought right that *Great Britain* should grant such freedom, except partially, as in the case of war with France, when tobacco is allowed to be sent thither under the sanction of passports.

Exchanges in Trade may be gainful to each Party.

In transactions of trade it is not to be supposed that, like gaming, what one party *gains* the other must necessarily *lose*. The gain to each may be equal. If A has more corn than he can consume, but wants cattle, and B has more cattle, but wants corn, exchange is gain to each: hereby the common stock of comforts in life is increased.

Of Paper Credit.

It is impossible for government to circumscribe or fix the extent of paper credit, which must of course fluctuate. Government may as well pretend to lay down rules for the operations, or the confidence of every individual in the course of his trade. Any seeming temporary evil arising must naturally work its own cure.

HUMOROUS ACCOUNT OF A CUSTOM AMONG THE AMERICANS, ENTITLED WHITE-WASHING.

Attributed to the Pen of Dr. Franklin.

Although the following article has not yet appeared in any collection of the works of this great philosopher, we are inclined to receive the general opinion (from the plainness of the style, and the humor which characterizes it), to be the performance of Dr. Franklin:—

My wish is to give you some account of the people of these new States, but I am far from being qualified for the purpose, having as yet seen little more than the cities of New York and Philadelphia. I have discovered but few national singularities among them. Their customs and manners are nearly the same with those of England, which they have long been used to copy. For, previous to the Revolution, the Americans were from their infancy taught to look up to the English as patterns of perfection in all things. I have observed, however, one custom, which, for aught I know, is peculiar to this country; an account of it will serve to fill up the remainder of this sheet, and may afford you some amusement.

When a young couple are about to enter into the matrimonial state, a never-failing article in the marriage-treaty is, that the lady shall have and enjoy the free and unmolested exercise of the rights of *white-washing*, with all its ceremonials, privileges, and appurtenances. A young woman would forego the most advantageous connexion, and even disappoint the warmest wish of her heart, rather than resign the invaluable right. You would wonder what this privilege of *white-washing* is: I will endeavor to give you some idea of the ceremony, as I have seen it performed.

There is no season of the year in which the lady may not claim her privilege, if she pleases; but the latter end of May is most generally fixed upon for the purpose. The attentive husband may judge by certain prognostics when the storm is nigh at hand. When the lady is unusually fretful, finds fault with the servants, is discontented with the children, and complains much of the filthiness of every thing about her—these are signs which ought not to be neglected; yet they are not decisive, as they sometimes come on and go off again, without producing any farther effect. But if, when the husband rises in the morning, he should observe in the yard a wheelbarrow with a quantity of lime in it, or should see certain buckets with lime dissolved in water, there is then no time to be lost; he immediately locks up the apartment or closet where his papers or his private property is kept, and putting the key in his pocket, betakes himself to flight: for a husband, however beloved, becomes a perfect nuisance during this season of female rage, his authority is superseded, his commission is suspended, and the very scullion, who cleans the brasses in the kitchen, becomes of more consideration and importance than him. He has nothing for it, but to abdicate, and run from an evil which he can neither prevent nor mollify.

The husband gone, the ceremony begins. The walls are in a few minutes stripped of their furniture; paintings, prints, and looking-glasses, lie in a huddled heap about the floors; the curtains are drawn from the testers, the beds crammed into the windows; chairs and tables, bedsteads and cradles, crowd the yard; and the garden fence bends beneath the weight of carpets, blankets, cloth cloaks, old coats, and ragged breeches. *Here* may be seen the lumber of the kitchen, forming a dark and confused mass: for the fore-ground of the picture, gridirons and frying-pans, rusty shovels and broken tongs, spits and pots, and the fractured remains of rush-bottomed chairs. *There* a closet has disgorged its bowels, cracked tumblers, broken wine glasses, phials of forgotten physic, papers of unknown powders, seeds and dried herbs, handfuls of old corks, tops of tea-pots, and stoppers of departed decanters;—from the rag-hole in the garret to the rat-hole in the cellar, no place escapes unrummaged. It would seem as if the day of general doom was come, and the utensils of the house were dragged forth to judgment. In this tempest, the words of Lear naturally present themselves, and might, with some alteration, be made strictly applicable:

——Let the great gods,
That keep this dreadful pudder o'er our heads,
Find out their en'mies now. Tremble, thou wretch,
That hast within thee, undivulged crimes,
Unwhipt of justice!—
——Close pent-up guilt,
Raise your concealing continents, and ask
These dreadful summoners grace!

This ceremony completed, and the house thoroughly evacuated, the next operation is to smear the walls and ceilings of every room and closet with brushes dipped in a solution of lime, called *white-wash;* to pour buckets of water over every floor, and scratch all the partitions and wainscots with rough brushes wet with soap-suds, and dipped in stone-cutter's sand. The windows by no means escape the general deluge. A servant scrambles out upon the pent-house, at the risk of her neck, and with a mug in her hand, and a bucket within reach, she dashes away innumerable gallons of water against the glass panes; to the great annoyance of the passengers in the street.

I have been told that an action at law was once brought against one of these water-nymphs, by a person who had a new suit of clothes spoiled by this operation; but, after long argument, it was determined by the whole court, that the action would not lie, inasmuch as the defendant was in the exercise of a legal right, and not answerable for the consequences; and so the poor gentleman was doubly nonsuited; for he lost not only his suit of clothes, but his suit at law.

These smearings and scratchings, washings and dashings, being duly performed, the next ceremony is to cleanse and replace the distracted furniture. You may have seen a house raising, or a ship-launch, when all the hands within reach are collected together: recollect if you can the hurry, bustle, confusion, and noise of such a scene, and you will have some idea of this cleaning match. The misfortune is, that the sole object is to make things clean; it matters not how many useful, ornamental, or valuable articles are mutilated, or suffer death, under the operation: a mahogany chair and carved frame undergo the same discipline; they are to be made *clean* at all events; but their preservation is not worthy of attention. For instance, a fine large engraving is laid flat upon the floor; smaller prints are piled upon it, and the superincumbent weight cracks the glasses of the lower tier; but this is of no consequence. A valuable picture is placed leaning against the sharp corner of a table; others are made to lean against that, until the pressure of the whole forces the corner of the table through the canvass of the first. The frame and glass of a fine print are to be *cleaned;* the spirit and oil used on this occasion are suffered to leak through and spoil the engraving; no matter. if the glass is clean, and the frame shine, it is sufficient, the rest is not worthy of consideration. An able arithmetician has made an accurate calculation, founded on long experience and has discovered, that the losses and destructions incident to two white-washings are equal to one removal, and three removals equal to one fire.

The cleaning frolic over, matters begin to resume their pristine appearance. The storm abates, and all would be well again, but it is impossible that so great a convulsion, in so small a communion, should not produce some farther effects. For two or three weeks after the operation the family are usually afflicted with sore throats or sore eyes, occasioned by the caustic quality of the lime, or with severe colds from the exhalations of wet floors or damp walls.

I know a gentleman, who was fond of accounting for every thing in a philosophical way. He considers this, which I have called a custom, as a real periodical disease, peculiar to the climate. His train of reasoning is ingenious and whimsical, but I am not at leisure to give you a detail. The result was, that he found the distemper to be incurable; but after much study he conceived he had discovered a method to divert the evil he could not subdue. For this purpose he caused a small building, about twelve feet square, to be erected in his garden, and furnished with some ordinary chairs and tables; and a few prints of the cheapest sort were hung against the walls. His hope was, that when the white-washing frenzy seized the females of his family, they might repair to this apartment, and scrub, and smear, and scour, to their heart's content; and so spend the violence of the disease in this out-post, while he enjoyed himself in quiet at head-quarters. But the experiment did not answer his expectation; it was impossible it should, since a principal part of the gratification consists in the lady's having an uncontrolled right to torment her husband at least once a year, and to turn him out of doors, and take the reins of government into her own hands.

There is a much better contrivance than this of the philosopher's; which is, to cover the walls of the house with paper; this is generally done; and though it cannot abolish, it at least shortens the period of female dominion. The paper is decorated with flowers of various fancies, and made so ornamental, that the women have admitted the fashion without perceiving the design.

There is also another alleviation of the husband's distress; he generally has the privilege of a small room or closet for his books and papers, the key of which he is allowed to keep. This is considered as a privileged place, and stands like the land of Goshen amid the plagues of Egypt. But then he must be extremely cautious, and ever on his guard; for should he inadvertently go abroad and leave the key in his door, the housemaid, who is always on the watch for such an opportunity, immediately enters in triumph with buckets, brooms, and brushes; takes possession of the premises, and forthwith puts all his books and papers *to rights*—to his utter confusion, and sometimes serious detriment. For instance:

A gentleman was sued by the executors of a tradesman, on a charge found against him in the deceased's books, to the amount of 30*l*. The defendant was strongly impressed with an idea that he had discharged the debt and taken a receipt but as the transaction was of long standing, he knew not where to find the receipt. The suit went on in course, and the time approached when judgment would be obtained against him. He then sat seriously down to examine a large bundle of old papers, which he had untied and displayed on a table for that purpose. In the midst of his search, he was suddenly called away on business of importance; he forgot to lock the door of his room. The housemaid, who had been long looking out for such an opportunity, immediately entered with the usual implements, and with great alacrity fell to cleaning the room and putting things *to rights*. The first object that struck her eye was the confused situation of the papers on the table; these were without delay bundled together like so many dirty knives and forks; but in the action a small piece of paper fell unnoticed on the floor, which happened to be the very receipt in question: as it had no very respectable appearance, it was soon after swept out with the common dirt of the room, and carried in a rubbish pan into the yard. The tradesman had neglected to enter the credit in his book; the defendant could find nothing to obviate the charge, and so judgment went against him for the debt and costs. A fortnight after the whole was settled, and the money paid, one of the children found the receipt among the rubbish in the yard.

There is also another custom peculiar to the city of Philadelphia, and nearly allied to the former. I mean that of washing the pavement before the doors every Saturday evening. I at first took this to be a regulation of the police; but, on farther inquiry, find it is a religious rite, preparatory to the Sabbath; and is, I believe, the only religious rite in which the numerous sectaries of this city perfectly agree. The ceremony begins about sunset, and continues till about ten or eleven at night. It is very difficult for a stranger to walk the streets on those evenings; he runs a continual risk of having a bucket of dirty water thrown against his legs; but a Philadelphian born, is so much accustomed to the danger, that he avoids it with surprising dexterity. It is from this circumstance that a Philadelphian may be known any where by his gait. The streets of New-York are paved with rough stones; these indeed are not washed, but the dirt is so thoroughly swept from before the doors, that the stones stand up sharp and prominent, to the great inconvenience of those who are not accustomed to so rough a path. But habit reconciles every thing. It is diverting enough to see a Philadelphian at New-York; he walks the streets with as much most painful caution, as if his toes were covered with corns, or his feet lamed with the gout; while a New-Yorker, as little approving the plain masonry of Philadelphia, shuffles along the pavement like a parrot on a mahogany table.

It must be acknowledged, that the ablutions I have mentioned are attended with no small inconvenience; but the women would not be induced, from any consideration, to resign their privilege. Notwithstanding this, I can give you the strongest assurances, that the women of America make the most faithful wives and the most attentive mothers in the world; and I am sure you will join me in opinion, that if a married man is made miserable only *one* week in a whole year, he will have no great cause to complain of the matrimonial bond.

I am, &c.

ANSWER TO THE ABOVE.

IN THE CHARACTER OF A LADY; BUT REALLY BY THE SAME HAND.

SIR,

I HAVE lately seen a letter upon the subject of *white-washing*, in which that necessary duty of a good housewife is treated with unmerited ridicule. I should probably have forgot the foolish thing by this time: but the season coming on which most women think suitable for cleansing their apartments from the smoke and dirt of the winter, I find this saucy author dished up in every family, and his flippant performance quoted wherever a wife attempts to exercise her reasonable prerogative, or execute the duties of her station. Women generally employ their time to better purpose than scribbling. The cares and comforts of a family rest principally upon their shoulders; hence it is that there are but few female authors; and the men, knowing how necessary our attentions are to their happiness, take every opportunity of discouraging literary accomplishments in the fair sex. You hear it echoed from every quarter,—'My wife cannot make verses, it is true; but she makes an excellent pudding: she can't correct the press, but she can correct her children, and scold her servants with admirable discretion: she can't unravel the intricacies of political economy and federal government; but she can knit charming stockings.' And this they call praising a wife, and doing justice to her character, with much nonsense of the like kind.

I say, women generally employ their time to much better purpose than scribbling; otherwise this facetious writer had not gone so long unanswered. We have ladies who sometimes lay down the needle, and take up the pen; I wonder none of them have attempted some reply. For my part, I do not pretend to be an author. I never appeared in print in my life, but I can no longer forbear saying something in answer to such impertinence, circulate how it may. Only, sir, consider our situation. Men are naturally inattentive to the decencies of life; but why should I be so complaisant? I say, they are naturally filthy creatures. If it were not that their connexion with the refined sex polished their manners, and had a happy influence on the general economy of life, these lords of the creation would wallow in filth, and populous cities would infect the atmosphere with their noxious vapors. It is the attention and assiduity of the women that prevent men from degenerating into mere swine. How important then are the services we render; and yet for these very services we are made the subject of ridicule and fun. Base ingratitude! Nauseous creatures! Perhaps you may think I am in a passion. No, sir, I do assure you I never was more composed in my life, and yet it is enough to provoke a saint to see how unreasonably we are treated by the men. Why now, there's my husband—a good-enough sort of a man in the main—but I will give you a sample of him. He comes into the parlor the other day, where, to be sure, I was cutting up a piece of linen. 'Lord!' says he, 'what a flutter here is! I can't bear to see the parlor look like a tailor's shop: besides, I am going to make some important philosophical experiments, and must have sufficient room.' You must know my husband is one of your would-be philosophers. Well, I bundled up my linen as quick as I could, and began to darn a pair of ruffles, which took no room, and could give no offence. I thought, however, I would watch my lord and master's important business. In about half an hour the tables were covered with all manner of trumpery, bottles of water, phials of drugs, pasteboard, paper and cards, glue, paste, and gum-arabic; files, knives, scissors, needles, rosin, wax, silk, thread, rags, jags, tags, books, pamphlets, and papers. Lord bless me! I am almost out of breath, and yet I have not enumerated half the articles.

Well, to work he went, and although I did not understand the object of his manœuvres, yet I could sufficiently discover that he did not succeed in any one operation. I was glad of that, I confess, and with good reason too: for, after he had fatigued himself with mischief, like a monkey in a china-shop, and had called the servants to clear every thing away, I took a view of the scene my parlor exhibited. I shall not even attempt a minute description; suffice it to say, that he had overset his ink-stand, and stained my best mahogany table with ink; he had spilt a quantity of vitriol, and burnt a large hole in my carpet: my marble hearth was all over spotted with melted rosin: beside this, he had broken three china cups, four wine-glasses, two tumblers, and one of my handsomest decanters. And, after all, as I said before, I perceived that he had not succeeded in any one operation. By the bye, tell your friend, the white-wash scribbler, that this is one means by which our closets become furnished with halves of china bowls, cracked tumblers, broken wine-glasses, tops of tea-pots, and stoppers of departed decanters. I say, I took a view of the dirt and devastation my philosophic husband had occasioned; and there I sat, like Patience on a monument, smiling at grief; but it worked inwardly. I would almost as soon the melted rosin and vitriol had been in his throat, as on my dear marble hearth, and my beautiful carpet. It is not true that women have no power over their own feelings; for notwithstanding this provocation, I said nothing, or next to nothing: for I only observed, very pleasantly, what a lady of my acquaintance had told me, that the reason why philosophers are called *literary* men, is because they make a great *litter:* not a word more: however, the servant cleared away, and down sat the philosopher. A friend dropt in soon after—'Your servant, sir, how do you do?' 'O Lord, I am almost fatigued to death; I have been all the morning making philosophical experiments.' I was now more hardly put to it to smother a laugh, than I had been just before to contain my rage; my *precious* went out soon after, and I, as you may suppose, mustered all my forces: brushes, buckets, soap, sand, limeskins, and cocoa-nut shells, with all the powers of housewifery were immediately employed. I was certainly the best philosopher of the two: for my experiments succeeded, and his did not. All was well again, except my poor carpet—my vitriolized carpet, which still continued a mournful memento of philosophic fury, or rather philosophic folly. The operation was scarce over, when in came my experimental philosopher, and told me, with all the indifference in the world, that he had invited six gentlemen to dine with him at three o'clock. It was then past one. I complained of the short notice; 'Poh! poh!' said he, 'you can get a leg of mutton, and a loin of veal, and a few potatoes, which will do well enough.' Heavens! what a chaos must the head of a philosopher be! a leg of mutton, a loin of veal, and potatoes! I was at a loss whether I should laugh or be angry; but there was no time for determining: I had but an hour and a half to do a world of business in. My carpet, which had suffered in the cause of experimental philosophy in the morning, was destined to be most shamefully dishonored in the afternoon by a deluge of nasty tobacco juice. Gentlemen smokers love segars better than carpets. Think, sir, what a woman must endure under such circumstances; and then, after all, to be reproached will her cleanliness, and to have her white-washings, her scourings, and scrubbings made the subject of ridicule, it is more than patience can put up with. What I have now exhibited is but a small specimen of the injuries we sustain from the boasted superiority of men. But we will not be laughed out of our cleanliness. A woman would rather be called any thing than a *slut*, as a man would rather be thought a knave than a fool. I had a great deal more to say, but am called away; we are just preparing to white-wash, and of course I have a great deal of business on my hands. The white-wash buckets are paraded, the brushes are ready, my husband is gone off—so much the better; when we are upon a thorough cleaning, the first dirty thing to be removed is one's husband. I am called for again. Adieu.

FINAL SPEECH OF DR. FRANKLIN IN THE LATE FEDERAL CONVENTION.*

MR. PRESIDENT,

I CONFESS that I do not entirely approve of this constitution at present; but, Sir, I am not sure I shall never approve it; for having lived long, I have experienced many instances of being obliged, by better information, or fuller consideration, to change opinions even on important subjects, which I once thought right, but found to be otherwise. It is, therefore, that the older I grow, the more apt I am to

---

* Our reasons for ascribing this speech to Dr. Franklin, are its internal evidence, and its having appeared with his name, during his life-time uncontradicted in an American periodical publication

doubt my own judgment, and to pay more respect to the judgment of others. Most men, indeed, as well as most sects in religion, think themselves in possession of all truth, and that whenever others differ from them, it is so far error. Steel, a protestant, in a dedication, tells the Pope, that, 'the only difference between our two churches, in their opinions of the certainty of their doctrine is, the Roman church is infallible, and the church of England never in the wrong.' But, though many private persons think almost as highly of their own infallibility as that of their sect, few express it so naturally as a certain French lady, who, in a little dispute with her sister, said, 'I don't know how it happens, sister, but I meet with nobody but myself that is always in the right.' *Il n'y a que moi qui a toujours raison.* In these sentiments, Sir, I agree to this constitution, with all its faults, if they are such; because I think a general government necessary for us, and there is no form of government but what may be a blessing, if well administered; and I believe, farther, that this is likely to be well administered for a course of years, and can only end in despotism, as other forms have done before it, when the people shall become so corrupted as to need despotic government, being incapable of any other. I doubt, too, whether any other convention we can obtain, may be able to make a better constitution: for when you assemble a number of men, to have the advantage of their joint wisdom, you inevitably assemble with those men all their prejudices, their passions, their errors of opinion, their local interests, and their selfish views. From such an assembly can a perfect production be expected? It therefore astonishes me, Sir, to find this system approaching so near to perfection as it does; and I think it will astonish our enemies, who are waiting with confidence, to hear that our councils are confounded, like those of the builders of Babel, and that our States are on the point of separation, only to meet hereafter for the purpose of cutting each other's throats.

Thus I consent, Sir, to this constitution, because I expect no better, and because I am not sure that this is not the best. The opinions I have had of its errors I sacrifice to the public good. I have never whispered a syllable of them abroad. Within these walls they were born, and here they shall die. If every one of us, in returning to our constituents, were to report the objections he has had to it, and endeavor to gain partisans in support of them, we might prevent its being generally received, and thereby lose all the salutary effects and great advantages resulting naturally in our favor among foreign nations, as well as among ourselves, from our real or apparent unanimity. Much of the strength and efficiency of any government, in procuring and securing happiness to the people, depends on opinion; on the general opinion of the goodness of that government, as well as of the wisdom and integrity of its govenors.

I hope, therefore, that for our own sakes, as a part of the people, and for the sake of our posterity, we shall act heartily and unanimously in recommending this constitution, wherever our influence may extend, and turn our future thoughts and endeavors to the means of having it well administered.

On the whole, Sir, I cannot help expressing a wish, that every member of the Convention, who may still have objections, would with me, on this occasion, doubt a little of his own infallibility, and, to make manifest our unanimity, put his name to this instrument.

[The motion was then made for adding the last formula, viz.

Done in Convention, by the unanimous consent, &c. which was agreed to, and added accordingly.]

PREFERENCE OF BOWS AND ARROWS IN WAR TO FIRE-ARMS.

TO MAJOR-GENERAL LEE.

DEAR SIR, Philadelphia, Feb. 11, 1736.

THE bearer, Mons. Arundel, is directed by the Congress to repair to General Schuyler, in order to be employed by him in the artillery service. He proposes to wait on you in his way, and has requested me to introduce him by a line to you. He has been an officer in the French service, as you will see by his commissions; and, professing a good will to our cause, I hope he may be useful in instructing our gunners and matrosses: perhaps he may advise in opening the nailed cannon.

I received the enclosed the other day from an officer, Mr Newland, who served in the two last wars, and was known by General Gates, who spoke well of him to me when I was at Cambridge. He is desirous now of entering into your service. I have advised him to wait upon you at New-York.

They still talk big in England, and threaten hard; but their language is somewhat civiller. at least not quite so disrespectful to us. By degrees they come to their senses; but too late, I fancy, for their interest.

We have got a large quantity of saltpetre, one hundred and twenty tons, and thirty more expected. Powder mills are now wanting; I believe we must set to work and make it by hand. But I still wish, with you, that pikes could be introduced, and I would add bows and arrows: these were good weapons, and not wisely laid aside.

1. Because a man may shoot as truly with a bow as with a common musket.

2. He can discharge four arrows in the time of charging and discharging one bullet.

3. His object is not taken from his view by the smoke of his own side.

4. A flight of arrows seen coming upon them terrifies and disturbs the enemy's attention to his business.

5. An arrow sticking in any part of a man, puts him *hors du combat* till it is extracted.

6. Bows and arrows are more easily provided every where than muskets and ammunition.

Polydore Virgil, speaking of one of our battles against the French in Edward the Third's reign, mentions the great confusion the enemy was thrown into, *sagittarum nube*, from the English; and concludes, *Est res profecto dictu mirabilis ut tantus ac potens exercitus a solis ferè Anglicis sagittariis victus fuerit; adeo Anglus est sagittipotens, et id genus armorum valet.* If so much execution was done by arrows when men wore some defensive armor, how much more might be done now that it is out of use!

I am glad you are come to New-York, but I also wish you could be in Canada. There is a kind of suspense in men's minds here at present, waiting to see what terms will be offered from England. I expect none that we can accept; and when that is generally seen, we shall be more unanimous and more decisive: then your proposed solemn league and convenant will go better down, and perhaps most of our other strong measures be adopted.

I am always glad to hear from you, but I do not deserve your favors, being so bad a correspondent. My eyes will now hardly serve me to write by night, and these short days have been all taken up by such variety of business that I seldom can sit down ten minutes without interruption—God give you success!

I am, with the greatest esteem,

Yours affectionately,

15 B. FRANKLIN.

ON THE THEORY OF THE EARTH

TO ABBE SOULIAVE.

SIR, *Passy, September* 22, 1782.

I RETURN the papers with some corrections. I did not find coal-mines under the calcareous rock in Derbyshire. I only remarked, that at the lowest part of that rocky mountain which was in sight, there were oyster shells mixed with the stone; and part of the high country of Derby being probably as much above the level of the sea as the coal-mines of Whitehaven were below, it seemed a proof that there had been a great bouleversement in the surface of that island, some part of it having been depressed under the sea, and other parts, which had been under it, being raised above it. Such changes in the superficial parts of the globe seemed to me unlikely to happen if the earth were solid at the centre. I therefore imagined that the internal parts might be a fluid more dense, and of greater specific gravity than any of the solids we are acquainted with; which therefore might swim in or upon that fluid. Thus the surface of the globe would be a shell, capable of being broken and disordered by the violent movements of the fluid on which it rested. And as air has been compressed by art so as to be twice as dense as water, in which case, if such air and water could be contained in a strong glass vessel, the air would be seen to take the lowest place, and the water to float above and upon it; and, as we know not yet the degree of density to which air may be compressed, and M. Amontons calculated, that its density increasing as it approached the centre in the same proportion as above the surface, it would, at the depth of leagues, be heavier than gold, possibly the dense fluid occupying the internal parts of the globe might be air compressed. And as the force of expansion in dense air when heated, is in proportion to its density; this central air might afford another agent to move the surface, as well as be of use in keeping alive the central fires; though, as you observe, the sudden rarefaction of water, coming into contact with those fires, may be an agent sufficiently strong for that purpose, when acting between the incumbent earth, and the fluid on which it rests.

If one might indulge imagination in supposing how such a globe was formed, I should conceive, that all the elements in separate particles, being originally mixed in confusion, and occupying a great space, they would (as soon as the Almighty fiat ordained gravity, or the mutual attraction of certain parts, and the mutual repulsion of other parts, to exist) all move towards their common centre; that the air being a fluid whose parts repel each other, though drawn to the common centre by their gravity, would be densest towards the centre, and rarer as more remote; consequently, all bodies, lighter than the central parts of that air, and immersed in it, would recede from the centre and rise till they arrive at that region of the air which was of the same specific gravity with themselves, where they would rest; while other matter mixed with the lighter air, would descend, and the two, meeting, would form the shell of the first earth, leaving the upper atmosphere nearly clear. The original movement of the parts towards their common centre would form a whirl there: which would continue in the turning of the new formed globe upon its axis, and the greatest diameter of the shell would be in its equator. If by any accident afterward the axis should be changed, the dense internal fluid, by altering its form, must burst the shell, and throw all its substance into the confusion in which we find it. I will not trouble you at present with my fancies concerning the manner of forming the rest of our system. Superior beings smile on our Theories, and at our presumption in making them. I will just mention that your observation of the ferruginous nature of the lava, which is thrown out from the depths of our volcanoes gave me great pleasure. It has long been a supposition of mine, that the iron contained in the substance of the globe has made it capable of becoming, as it is, a great magnet; that the fluid of magnetism exists perhaps in all space; so that there is a magnetical North and South of the universe, as well as of this globe; and that if it were possible for a man to fly from star to star, he might govern his course by the compass: that it was by the power of this general magnetism this globe became a particular magnet. In soft or hot iron the fluid of magnetism is naturally diffused equally; when within the influence of a magnet, it is drawn to one end of the iron, made denser there and rarer at the other. While the iron continues soft and hot, it is only a temporary magnet; if it cools or grows hard in that situation, it becomes a permanent one, the magnetic fluid not easily resuming its equilibrium. Perhaps it may be owing to the permanent magnetism of this globe, which it had not at first, that its axis is at present kept parallel to itself, and not liable to the changes it formerly suffered, which occasioned the rupture of its shell, the submersions and emersions of its lands, and the confusion of its seasons. The present polar and equatorial diameters differing from each other near ten leagues, it is easy to conceive, in case some power should shift the axis gradually, and place it in the present equator, and make the new equator pass through the present poles, what a sinking of waters would happen in the present equatorial regions and what a rising in the present polar regions; so tha vast tracts would be discovered that now are under water, and others covered that now are dry, the water rising and sinking in the different extremes near five leagues! Such an operation as this possibly occasioned much of Europe, and, among the rest, of this mountain of Passy, on which I live, and which is composed of limestone, rock, and sea-shells, to be abandoned by the sea, and to change its ancient climate, which seems to have been a hot one. The globe being now become a perfect magnet, we are perhaps safe from any future change of its axis. But we are still subject to the accidents on the surface, which are occasioned by a wave in the internal ponderous fluid: and such a wave is produced by the sudden violent explosion you mention, happening from the junction of water and fire under the earth, which not only lifts the incumbent earth that is over the explosion, but impressing with the same force the fluid under it, creates a wave that may run a thousand leagues, lifting, and thereby shaking successively, all the countries under which it passes. I know not whether I have expressed myself so clearly, as not to get out of your sight in these reveries. If they occasion any new inquiries, and produce a better hypothesis, they will not be quite useless. You see I have given a loose to imagination, but I approve much more your method of philosophizing, which proceeds upon actual observation, makes a collection of facts, and concludes no farther than those facts will warrant. In my present circumstances, that mode of studying the nature of the globe is out of my power, and therefore I have permitted myself to wander a little in the wilds of fancy. With great esteem, I have the honor to be, Sir, &c.

B. Franklin.

P. S. I have heard that chemists can by their art decompose stone and wood, extracting a considerable quantity of water from the one, and air from the other. It seems natural to conclude from this, that water and air were ingredients in their original composition; for men cannot make new matter of any kind. In the same manner do we not suppose, that when we consume combustibles of all kinds, and produce heat or light, we do not create that heat or light, we only decompose a substance which received it originally as a part of its composition? Heat may thus be considered as originally in a fluid state; but, attracted by organized bodies in their growth, becomes a part of the solid. Besides this, I can conceive that, in the first assemblage of the particles of which this earth is composed, each brought its portion of the loose heat that had been connected with it, and the whole, when pressed together, produced the internal fire which still subsists.

LOOSE THOUGHTS

ON THE UNIVERSAL FLUID, &c.

Passy, June 25, 1784.

Universal space, as far as we know of it, seems to be filled with subtle fluid, whose motion, or vibration, is called light.

This fluid may possibly be the same with that which, being attracted by and entering into other more solid matter, dilates the substance, by separating the constituent particles, and so rendering some solids fluid, and maintaining the fluidity of others: of which fluid when our bodies are totally deprived, they are said to be frozen; when they have a proper quantity they are in health, and fit to perform all their functions; it is then called natural heat: when too much, it is called fever; and when forced into the body in too great a quantity from without, it gives pain by separating and destroying the flesh, and is then called burning; and the fluid so entering and acting is called fire.

While organized bodies, animal or vegetable, are augmenting in growth, or are supplying their continual waste, is not this done by attracting and consolidating this fluid called fire, so as to form of it a part of their substance? and is it not a separation of the parts of such substance, which, dissolving its solid state, sets that subtle fluid at liberty, when it again makes its appearance as fire?

For the power of man relative to matter seems limited to the dividing it, or mixing the various kinds of it, or changing its form and appearance by different compositions of it; but does not extend to the making or creating of new matter, or annihilating the old: thus, if fire be an original element, or kind of matter, its quantity is fixed and permanent in the world. We cannot destroy any part of it, or make addition to it; we can only separate it from that which confines it, and set it at liberty, as when we put wood in a situation to be burnt; or transfer it from one solid to another, as when we make lime by burning stone, a part of the fire dislodged from the wood being left in the stone. May not this fluid when at liberty be capable of penetrating and entering into all bodies, organized or not; quitting easily in totality those not organized; and quitting easily in part those which are; the part assumed and fixed remaining till the body is dissolved?

It is not this fluid which keeps asunder the particles of air, permitting them to approach, or separating them more, in proportion as its quantity is diminished or argumented. Is it not the greater gravity of the particles of air, which forces the particles of this fluid to mount with the matters to which it is attached, as smoke or vapour?

Does it not seem to have a great affinity with water, since it will quit a solid to unite with that fluid, and go off with it in vapor, leaving the solid cold to the touch, and the degree measurable by the thermometer?

The vapor rises attached to this fluid; but at a certain height they separate, and the vapor descends in rain, retaining but little of it, in snow or hail less. What becomes of that fluid? Does it rise above our atmosphere, and mix equally with the universal mass of the same kind? Or does a spherical stratum of it, denser, or less mixed with air, attracted by this globe, and repelled or pushed up only to a certain height from its surface, by the greater weight of air, remain there surrounding the globe, and proceeding with it round the sun?

In such case, as there may be a continuity or communication of this fluid through the air quite down to the earth, is it not by the vibrations given to it by the sun that light appears to us; and may it not be, that every one of the infinitely small vibrations, striking common matter with a certain force, enter its substance, are held there by attraction, and augmented by succeeding vibrations, till the matter has received as much as their force can drive into it?

Is it not thus that the surface of this globe is continually heated by such repeated vibrations in the day, and cooled by the escape of the heat when those vibrations are discontinued in the night, or intercepted and reflected by clouds?

Is it not thus that fire is amassed, and makes the greatest part of the substance of combustible bodies?

Perhaps when this globe was first formed, and its original particles took their place at certain distances from the centre, in proportion to their greater or less gravity, the fluid fire, attracted towards that centre, might in great part be obliged, as lightest, to take place above the rest, and thus form the sphere of fire above supposed, which would afterward be continually diminishing by the substance it afforded to organized bodies; and the quantity restored to it again by the burning or other separating of the parts of those bodies.

Is not the natural heat of animals thus produced, by separating in digestion the parts of food, and setting their fire at liberty?

Is it not this sphere of fire which kindles the wandering globes that sometimes pass through it in our course round the sun, have their surface kindled by it and burst when their included air is greatly rarified by the heat on their burning surfaces?

THE END.

www.ingramcontent.com/pod-product-compliance
Lightning Source LLC
Chambersburg PA
CBHW030815020726
47499CB00006B/1918

* 9 7 8 3 3 3 7 0 3 0 1 8 6 *